DETOUR

Also by James Siegel

Epitaph
Derailed

DETOUR

JAMES SIEGEL

timewarner
books

First published in the United States of America in March 2005 by Warner Books
First published in Great Britain in March 2005 by Time Warner Books

A CIP catalogue record for this book is available from the British Library.

Hardback ISBN 0 316 72746 6
C-format ISBN 0 316 72747 4

Printed and bound in Great Britain by Clays Ltd, St Ives plc

Time Warner Books
An imprint of
Time Warner Book Group UK
Brettenham House
Lancaster Place
London WC2E 7EN

www.twbg.co.uk

To Sara Anne Freed, a remarkable editor and an even better human being, who took a chance on me, for which I'll be eternally grateful.

I'd like to thank Richard Pine, a remarkable agent, Rick Horgan for his editorial wisdom, and Larry Kirshbaum for getting into the trenches with me. Also, all my Colombian friends who took the time to tell me where I screwed up.

DETOUR

PROLOGUE

It's an old saying. An adage. A reassuring word to the wise. Or actually, to the scared. It's meant to mollify, to calm, to show one the utter silliness of their thinking.

You say it when someone's frightened to do something.

To travel, for instance.

To ride the rails. Hop a plane. Charter a boat.

To scuba dive. Jet-ski. Rollerblade. Balloon.

They're frightened a terrible *something* will befall them, that they'll set out to experience an enjoyable afternoon, a day, a vacation, a life, but instead, they'll end up dead.

And what do you say to them?

There's more chance you'll get hit by a bus while crossing the street.

Because how often does *that* happen, huh?

He kept a secret file in his bottom drawer, buried beneath his myriad charts, pulled out and dusted off for special occasions, as a kind of reminder.

J. Boksi, thirty-eight, about to be engaged. He was walking out of the jewelers, admiring the sparkling oval-cut two-carat ring set in filigreed white gold.

1

S. Lewes, twenty-two, newly earned MBA in business administration from Bucknell University. She was coming from her first job interview and staring up at the grandest buildings she'd ever seen.

T. Noonan, seventy, doting grandfather. He was taking a walk with his four-year-old grandson and explaining why Batman could not beat Superman in a fair fight, never ever, not on your life.

E. Riskin, sixty.

C. Meismer, seventy-eight.

R. Vaz, thirty-three.

L. Parkins, eleven.

J. Barbagallo, thirty-five.

R. and S. Parks, eighteen-year-old twins.

They'd all been hit by a bus while crossing the street.
Every single one of them.
They were all dead.
It reminded him that despite what you think, it can happen.
It can.
It can even happen to you.

The Insurance Actuary calculates the tipping point between risk and probability, thereby hoping to reduce the likelihood of undesirable events.

— *The Actuary Handbook*

Chances are, your chances are, pretty good.

— Johnny Mathis

ONE

*B*uenas tardes.

When they got to Bogotá, the first thing Paul and Joanna saw was a man with no head.

A picture of the man in question, apparently once the deputy mayor of Medellín, was plastered across various table-sized posters stuck to the walls in El Dorado Airport, all of them advertising different Bogotá newspapers. The man was carelessly sprawled in the middle of the street, as if he were just taking a much-needed rest. Except his shirt was stained with dried blood, and he was clearly missing something important. It had been blown off by a car bomb, which had been set by either the leftist FARC or the rightest USDF – depending on which theory you chose to believe.

Paul thought it was a hell of a welcome. But all in all, he still felt like saying *thanks*.

Glad to be here.

That's because flight 31 from JFK to Colombia had lasted eighteen hours, which was eleven hours longer than it was supposed to. There'd been a five-hour delay in Kennedy and an unscheduled stop in Washington, D.C., to pick up baggage belonging to a Colombian diplomat who'd remained nameless.

They'd sat on a broiling Washington tarmac for hours – with no Bloody Marys or gin and tonics to cut the boredom or beat the heat. Serving alcohol during ground delays was apparently an FAA no-no. That was probably a good idea. The general disposition on board had grown angry and mutinous – with the possible exception of Joanna and the passenger to Paul's right, who calmly stared straight ahead into the seat back in front of him.

He was an amateur ornithologist, he volunteered.

He was used to waiting. He was off to the jungles of northern Colombia to hunt for the yellow-breasted toucan.

Paul kept looking at his wristwatch and wondering why it wasn't moving.

Joanna, mostly a bastion of calm, had reminded him that they'd waited five years. Ten hours, more or less, wouldn't kill them.

She was right, of course.

The New York delay, the eight-hour Washington layover, the increasingly fetid cabin, *wouldn't* kill him. He knew what would kill people and what wouldn't. After all, he was an actuary for a major insurance company, whose logo – a pair of paternal cradling hands – appeared regularly on sickly-sweet commercials twenty times a day. He could spin the risk ratios on all sorts of everyday activities, recite the percentages of accident and death chapter and verse.

He knew that the odds of dying in a plane, for example, were exactly 1 in 354,319 – even with the recent small bump due to men whose first name was *Al* and last name was *Qaeda*. A delay in take-off would be in actuary-speak: *statistically insignificant.*

Plane delays couldn't kill you.

Car bombs could.

Speaking of which.

The sight of the headless man admittedly threw them just a little. As they walked from the gate in the general direction of baggage claim, Joanna noticed the first gruesome poster and immediately turned away, while Paul felt the first vague prickling of fear.

Worming their way through customs under the sullen eyes of

soldiers with shouldered AK-47s didn't exactly help. When they finally made it through baggage, they were approached by a stooped white-haired man holding a crude hand-lettered sign over his head.

Breidbard, Paul, it said. Their last name was misspelled.

'I guess I'm considered luggage,' Joanna whispered to him.

The old man introduced himself as *Pablo* and timidly shook Paul's hand. He picked up all three of their suitcases in one swift motion. When Paul tried to wrest at least one bag back from this man who, after all, had to be thirty years older than *he* was, Pablo politely refused.

'Is fine,' he said, smiling. 'Please follow . . .'

Pablo had been hired through the local Santa Regina Orphanage. He would be their man in Bogotá, he explained. He'd drive for them, shop for them, and help guide them through the entire process. He'd accompany them everywhere, he told them.

It was reassuring to hear.

Pablo led them through the unruly and suffocating crowd. All airports were experiments in barely managed chaos, but El Dorado was worse. The crowd seemed like soccer fans who'd lost – loud, milling, and dangerous. Paul, who'd done a little boning up on his Spanish, forgot the word for *excuse me* and had to resort to a primitive form of sign language in an effort to get people to move out of the way. Most simply ignored him, or looked at him as if he were touched in the head. He eventually relied on out-and-out shoving to navigate their way out.

Getting through the crowd was just one of their problems.

The other was keeping up with Speedy Gonzalez, a.k.a. Pablo.

He seemed remarkably spry for a man who had to be pushing seventy. Even while carrying three bulging suitcases.

'Think he's chewing coca or something?' Joanna asked. Joanna ran three mornings a week and could do a good hour and a half on the StairMaster, but even she was having trouble keeping pace.

'Pablo!' Paul had to shout his name once, twice, three times, before Pablo finally turned around and noticed that the two people whom he was supposed to stick to like glue were out of breath and falling dangerously behind.

'Sorry,' he said almost sheepishly. 'I'm used to . . . how you say . . . *giddyap.*' He smiled.

'That's okay,' Paul said. 'We just don't want to lose you.'

They'd made it through the sliding front doors and were on the outskirts of a vast parking lot directly adjacent to the terminal. A sea of cars, dotted with small eddies of slowly strolling passengers, seemed to stretch endlessly in all directions.

'What's that odor?' Joanna asked.

Paul sniffed the air; *motor oil and diesel fuel,* he was about to say. But Joanna possessed an uncannily accurate sense of smell, more an olfactory intuition, so he kept quiet.

'Ahh . . . ,' Pablo said. 'Wait.' He gently placed the suitcases on the cracked pavement, then walked a good twenty feet to what appeared, at least at this distance, to be some kind of ticket booth.

It wasn't. He returned holding two tightly wrapped packages trailing tiny plumes of steam.

'Empanadas,' he said, handing them to Paul and Joanna. *'Pollo.'*

'Chicken,' Paul whispered in Joanna's ear.

'Thanks,' Joanna whispered back, 'I've eaten at Taco Bell too.' Then she asked Pablo, 'How much do we owe you?'

Pablo shook his head. *'Nada.'*

'Thank you, Pablo – that's very generous of you.' Joanna took a bite of her empanada, then was forced to lick a dollop of red sauce which had trickled down past her lower lip. 'Mmmmm – it's *really* good.'

Pablo grinned. Paul thought that his face looked tender and tough at the same time – or, at the least, weathered.

'Wait here, I go for the car,' Pablo said out of deference to their obviously inferior constitutions.

'He's sweet, isn't he?' Joanna said after Pablo had disappeared into a row of Volkswagens, Renaults, and Mini Coopers.

8

'Yes, maybe we should adopt *him*,' Paul answered. He took her free hand and squeezed – it was sticky with perspiration. 'Excited?'

She nodded. 'Oh yeah.'

'On a scale of one to ten?'

'Six hundred and eleven.'

'That's all, huh?'

Two minutes later Pablo reappeared behind the wheel of a vintage blue Peugeot.

TWO

Their lawyer had booked them into a hotel with a French name, an American-style ambience, and an upscale Bogotá location. The area was called Calle 93, crammed with fashionable boutiques, high-rise hotels, and hip-looking restaurants with blue-tinted windows.

Their hotel was L'Esplanade, a name reeking of French chic, but its lobby coffee shop had Texas steerburgers and Philly fries on the menu.

Their tenth-floor suite had an unimpeded view of the surrounding green mountains. When Joanna pulled up the shades and made Paul look at them, he couldn't help wondering if armed insurgents were looking back. He decided not to share those feelings with his wife.

They'd been dutifully warned about coming to Colombia, of course.

Their original lawyer had urged them to try somewhere else. Anywhere else.

Korea, he'd suggested. Hungary. *How do you feel about China?* Colombia, he'd insisted, was too volatile. The sale of bulletproof glass was *a national growth industry,* he'd added.

But Korea or Hungary or China could take up to four years.

In Colombia it was two months. Max.

After waiting five long and agonizing years to become parents, four more years had seemed intolerable. Desperation arm-wrestled prudence and won hands down.

They were promptly steered to another lawyer, who specialized in Latin America.

His name was Miles Goldstein, and what he actually seemed to specialize in was enthusiasm. He was warmly effusive, seemingly indefatigable, and unabashedly committed. In this particular case, to bringing two dispossessed and suffering factions together. There were babies out there who needed homes; there were couples out there who needed babies. His mission was to make both parties happy. A handwoven sampler hung on the wall directly above his desk.

He who saves one child saves the world.

It was hard not to like a lawyer who subscribed to that kind of thinking.

Miles assured them that while Colombia wasn't an oasis of peace, the capital city was pretty much no problem. The struggle between leftists and rightists had been going on for thirty years – it had become just another feature of the landscape. But that landscape was mostly north, mountainous, and far away from Bogotá. In fact, according to a recent survey in *Destinations* magazine, a photocopy of which Miles produced from his desk drawer and handed to them, Bogotá was safer than Switzerland.

You've really got to watch your back in Zurich, Miles said.

PABLO HAD BEEN TRUE TO HIS WORD.

He'd driven them up to the doorstep, then flew inside with their luggage, forgoing the proffered help from an obviously pissed-off bellboy. When Paul and Joanna followed Pablo into the loud Art Deco lobby, a fawning concierge with dyed-blond hair and a slight lisp was waiting to show them to their room.

11

Pablo promised to return in three hours to take them to the orphanage.

After he had left, Paul laid himself out on the generously sized bed and said, 'I wish I could fall asleep, but I can't.'

Two hours later he woke up and said, 'What time is it?'

Joanna was over by the window reading the latest issue of *Mother & Baby* magazine. Paul couldn't help remembering that she'd begun her subscription over four years ago.

'Sorry you couldn't sleep, honey,' she said.

'I guess it caught up with me.'

'I guess.'

'Did you nap?'

'Uh-uh. Too jazzed.'

'What time is it?'

'One hour till Pablo comes back.'

'One hour. Well . . .'

Joanna put the magazine facedown and smiled at him. The cover was a startling close-up of a newborn's eyes: baby blue. 'It's surreal, isn't it?' Joanna said.

'*Surreal*'s a good word.'

'I mean, in one hour we're going to meet her.'

'Yeah. Shouldn't I be pacing or something?'

'Or something.'

'Well, I would pace. But there's not enough room. Consider me mentally pacing.'

'Paul?'

'Yeah?'

'I'm so happy. I think.'

'Why just *think*?'

'Because I'm so scared.'

It wasn't like Joanna to be scared of anything – that was *his* department. It was enough to get him off the bed and over to her chair, where he shook off the pins and needles in his legs and leaned down to hug her. She put her head back on his shoulder and he

12

smelled equal parts shampoo, Chanel No. 5, and, yes, the slightly acrid odor of fear.

'You're going to be great,' Paul said. 'Wonderful.'

'How do you know?'

'Because you've been babying me for ten years, and *I* don't have any complaints. Because I say so.'

'Oh well, if you say so . . .'

She lifted her head and he kissed her full on the lips. Nice lips, he thought. Beautiful lips. She was one of those women who look good falling out of bed – maybe better, since makeup seemed to cover up her features rather than do anything to enhance them. Pale, lightly freckled skin, with powder-blue eyes – the kind they hand-paint on delicate porcelain dolls. Delicate, however, wouldn't necessarily be one of the adjectives he'd use to describe Joanna. Strong, smart, *focused,* was more like it. On certain occasions he'd been known to refer to her as *Xena, warrior princess* – always affectionately, of course, and usually under his breath. She'd be thirty-seven in less than two weeks, but she still looked, well, *twenty*-seven. From time to time he wondered if she'd always look that way to him, if generally happy couples tend to see each other the way they were back when, till they suddenly wake up around sixty or so and wonder who that middle-aged person is sleeping next to them.

'What if I'm completely incompetent?' she said. 'I don't have a degree in this.'

'I'm told it comes naturally.'

'You evidently haven't read *Mother & Baby.*'

'That's okay. You have,' he said.

'Fine. I'll stop panicking.'

'Great. Next time I panic and you reassure.'

'Deal.'

'I'm going to take a shower. I feel like I've been on a plane for two days.'

'You have been on a plane for two days.'

'See, I knew there was a reason.'

PABLO CAME TWENTY MINUTES EARLY. APPARENTLY, THAT WHOLE *mañana* thing was an ethnic stereotype without merit.

He knocked on their door, then politely waited outside, even after Joanna had virtually begged him to come inside and sit down.

Paul, who was only half dressed, had to hastily scramble into the rest of his clothes. Black linen pants and a slightly rumpled white shirt he'd neglected to take out of his suitcase. He took quick stock of himself in the mirror and saw pretty much what he expected: a face stuck somewhere between boyishness and creeping middle age, someone who was clearly the sum of his parts, none of which would've stood out in a crowd. Well, clothes make the man. He topped off his outfit with his red-striped *power* tie. After all, he was preparing for the most important meeting of his life.

The Peugeot was softly idling in front of the hotel.

Paul noticed the hotel doorman whisper something in Pablo's ear as he bent over to usher them into the backseat. A kind of rumba was playing on the radio.

'What did he say?' Paul asked Pablo after he had pulled away from the curb.

'He wished you *Many Blessings.*'

'Oh. You told him where we're going?'

'Yes.'

'Do you do this a lot, Pablo?' Joanna asked. 'With many couples?'

Pablo nodded. '*Happy* job, no?'

'Sure,' Joanna said. 'I think so.'

They passed a convoy of soldiers hunched together in an open made-in-Detroit Jeep. Paul couldn't help remembering the phalanx of armed sentries at the airport.

'Lots of soldiers around, huh?' Paul said.

'Soldiers? *Sí.*'

'How have things been?' Paul asked, a little hesitant to ask a question he might not like the answer to.

14

'*Things?*'

'The rebels? FARC?' It sounded like a curse, Paul thought. He imagined that to the vast majority of Colombians, it was. *The Revolutionary Armed Forces of Colombia.* The leftist guerrillas already holding much of the north, and most likely the group responsible for blowing the deputy mayor of Medellín to kingdom come.

Of course, there was always the chance the car bomb had been perpetrated by the right. FARC was embroiled in a long dirty war against the *United Self-Defense Forces,* or USDF, a rightist paramilitary organization of singular brutality.

On the way out of the airport, they'd passed a wall covered in red graffiti, which looked uncomfortably like fresh arterial spray, as if it had been written in blood.

Libre Manuel Riojas. Manuel Riojas was the reputed USDF commander, currently residing in an American prison for drug transgressions.

Pablo shook his head. 'I don't listen . . . No politics.'

'Yes. That's probably wise.'

'*Sí.*'

'Still, it must be scary sometimes?'

'Scary.' Pablo derisively waved a hand. 'I mind my business. Don't read the papers. It's all bad.'

Before departing, Paul had sent away for a video titled *The Colombian Way of Life.* After he'd watched the first five minutes, it was painfully obvious it had been created for schoolkids under the age of twelve. The video followed two teenagers, Mauricio and Paula, walking around sunny Bogotá, their intent being to show that *there's more to this modern South American city than coffee, cocaine, and guerrilla violence* – or so stated the back blurb.

Pablo was driving them past a street of sprawling mansions. At least Paul assumed there were mansions back there somewhere – you couldn't actually see them. An unbroken ten-foot-high stucco wall was in the way. Electronic gates periodically announced the

15

demarcation of each new property, their names spelled out in tile mosaics embedded into the wall.

Casa de Flora.

Casa de Playa.

They passed a spotted dog with its ribs showing, urinating against the burnt-orange wall of the Casa de Fuego.

Something was unnerving about the scene. It took Paul a while to understand what it was.

Yes. The lack of people.

Except for several beggars, emaciated-looking women listlessly cradling babies in their laps, there was absolutely no one in view. Not in this neighborhood. They were all tucked out of sight, hidden behind a modern wall of Jericho.

La Calera, Pablo told them when Paul asked what the neighborhood was called.

Then, thankfully, their surroundings began to change.

Some scattered electronic and appliance stores, then small *cafeterías* advertising empanadas, *patatas,* and *huevos,* followed by a glut of news vendors, *lotería* shops, *supermercados,* various bustling places of commerce – the whole enchilada. A cacophony of smells wafted in through the half-cracked windows: bus exhaust, flowers, raw fish, newsprint – Paul was tempted to ask Joanna for a full rundown. They were clearly in the midst of the completely normal life of a capital city, just as Miles had promised. And Paul wondered if there was a kind of conscious denial at work here – if there *had* to be an ostrichlike mentality in a country where deputy mayors had their heads blown off on a regular basis. If Colombians were able to wall off pieces of their conscious mind from the ongoing war, much as they carefully walled off poverty from the upper classes in the La Calera district.

He stopped musing; there was a sign just ahead tucked into a small grove of trees.

Santa Regina Orfanato.

'Here,' Pablo whispered. He pulled into a hidden driveway and stopped the car. A locked gate; a black buzzer set in brass.

Pablo turned off the ignition, got out, and pushed the button. *'Pablo,'* he said, *'Señor y Señora Breidbart.'*

The gate swung open ten seconds later. Pablo got back in and methodically started up the car. He drove into an inner courtyard shaded by tall, spindly pines.

'Come on,' Señor Breidbart said when the car stopped again. 'Let's go meet our daughter.'

THREE

Paul couldn't actually feel his legs.

He knew he had them – he was clearly and unmistakably *standing* on them, but they felt missing in action. Gone.

A second ago a short mestiza nurse in starched white had shuffled into the room hugging a pink baby blanket to her chest.

Inside this baby blanket, Paul knew, was a baby.

Not just a baby.

His baby.

WHEN THEY'D ENTERED THE STERILE ANTEROOM, THEY WAITED A good twenty minutes for Santa Regina's director, María Consuelo, to come greet them. It felt longer than the plane flight. Paul stood up, sat down, walked around, looked out the window, sat down, stood up again. He counted the black tiles in the floor pattern, finding a familiar solace in numbers – there were twenty-eight of them. Occasionally, he squeezed Joanna's hand and offered her wan smiles of encouragement. Finally, María entered the room, a petite earnest-looking woman with jet-black hair wrapped tightly in a bun. She was followed by a small bustling entourage.

She greeted Paul and Joanna by their first names, as if they were old friends who'd come visiting, instead of prospective parents come begging. Then she dutifully introduced the members of her staff – the head nurse, two teachers, and her personal assistant – all of whom shook hands with them before departing in turn. María led them into her office, where they arranged themselves around a small table covered in neatly stacked piles of magazines, and then spent *another* twenty minutes sipping bitter coffee – brought in by a somber teenage girl – and making generally awkward small talk.

Maybe it wasn't small talk.

Paul felt increasingly as if it were the *oral exam,* the written part of the test having already been aced: employment checks, bank statements, stock certificates, mortgage slips, various recommendations from family and friends attesting to their good character and all-around worthiness. And the heartfelt letter it had taken Paul a solid week to compose, rip up, rewrite, painstakingly edit, and finally send off.

My wife and I are writing this letter to tell you who we are. And who we want to be. Parents.

María began by thanking them for the care package they'd sent the orphanage – diapers, bottles, formula, toys – a kind of authorized bribe Miles assured them was pro forma when adopting in Latin America.

Then she got down to business.

She asked Paul about his job – *an insurance man, isn't that so, Paul?* Well, yes – though he didn't tell her that in his case, being an insurance man meant locking himself away in a small room and compiling the stats that set the rates real insurance men went and charged you. That his life's work consisted of calculating the risk in every known human activity, swimming through streams of raw data in an effort to reduce life to a semimanageable minefield. The definition of an actuary: *someone who wants to be an accountant but doesn't have the personality.*

'How long have you been employed there?' she asked.

19

'Eleven years,' he answered, wondering if that categorized him as a solid breadwinner or a working transient. Regardless, he knew she already had this information. Maybe she was simply testing his truthfulness.

Then things got a little stickier.

She asked Joanna about *her* job.

Human resources executive for a pharmaceutical firm. Only it became clear that María wasn't really inquiring about the nature of Joanna's job, as much as asking her whether or not she was intending to *give it up,* now that she had an infant daughter to take care of.

Good question.

One that Paul and Joanna had spent more than a few weekends debating themselves, without ever quite reaching a definitive answer. Paul could tell from María's tone of voice that she thought Joanna giving up her job would probably be a good idea.

For a moment Joanna said nothing, and all Paul could hear was the sound of the sputtering room fan, the electrical hum of the fluorescent lighting, and his own inner voice, which was screaming at Joanna to *lie.*

Just this once.

The problem was, lying wasn't really part of her M.O. She was awfully good at spotting them – lies, half-truths, gross misstatements of fact – but just about incapable of letting one pass her lips.

'I'm taking a leave of absence,' Joanna said.

Well, okay, Paul thought, true enough.

'How *long*?' María asked.

Paul found himself staring at the picture gallery that took up half the wall of María's office – multishaded adolescent faces peering out from backyard decks, swimming pools, playrooms, Little League fields, from under cocked college graduation caps – and wondering whether his daughter's picture would be gracing that wall.

'I'm not sure,' Joanna said.

Paul looked back at María and smiled. He must've looked like an overgrown child hoping for candy.

'I know I'll end up doing what's best for the baby and best for me,' Joanna said. 'I'll be a good mother.'

María sighed. She reached for Joanna's hand. It was a gesture Paul had seen doctors and priests make when they were about to impart bad news – one priest in particular, when Paul was eleven years old and it was his hand being reached for, patted, and held tight. The day his mom died.

'Joanna,' María said, 'I, too, am sure you'll be a good mother.' She smiled.

It took Paul a minute to understand that they'd passed.

Test over.

He felt a reservoir of pent-up anxiety flooding out of him. But only for a moment.

Because María said, 'I think it's time you met your daughter.'

María kept talking, but Paul pretty much stopped listening.

Her voice was being drowned out by the sound of his own heartbeat, which seemed raucous and dangerously irregular. And another sound too – heavy footsteps that were slowly but steadily advancing down the hall. Paul became preternaturally aware of the rivers of sweat virtually flowing down both arms.

Was that *her*?

The footsteps passed by and faded into silence.

Then, after a minute or two during which Paul found it difficult to breathe, a new set of footsteps appeared on his radar screen, grew in volume and texture and clarity, and seemed to stop just outside the door.

María said, 'I know you're anxious to meet her. She's *beautiful*.'

They'd received a tiny black-and-white photograph, that's all – passport-sized, dark, and maddeningly blurred.

The door slowly opened. The overhead fan was clearly spinning. Paul could swear the air turned stock-still.

The dark-skinned nurse walked into the room hugging a fuzzy

baby blanket to her chest. Paul and Joanna shot up as Paul's legs lost all sensation, as if he were balancing on stilts.

Slowly, the nurse peeled back the top section of blanket, revealing spiky dark hair and two bottomless black eyes. The effect was a kind of infant *punk,* a beguiling mixture of innocence and attitude.

Paul fell immediately and terminally in love.

He was reminded of the first time he saw Joanna, across an airport waiting lounge filled with tired and frustrated people, wearily looking up to witness this pale-skinned and blue-eyed vision of loveliness haranguing an unforthcoming airline employee for information. Femininity and fearlessness seemed to meet in equal proportion, and he'd experienced something akin to a cocaine-induced rush, something he'd tried a few times in his frat days. That joyous but dangerous burst of pure exultation, which threatened to race your heart to heights of ecstasy, or break it in two.

Possibly both.

The nurse held their daughter out to them, and somehow Paul reached out for her first. The instant he pressed her to his chest, she felt as if she belonged there.

Joanna leaned in and softly brushed the baby's forehead with one perfectly manicured finger. The baby opened her tiny mouth.

'Look,' Paul said to no one in particular, 'she's *smiling* at us.'

María laughed. 'It's gas, I think. She's a beauty, though, no?'

'Oh yes,' Paul said, 'she's a beauty.' His daughter's skin was the palest shade of olive. Her nocturnal eyes seemed to express an intimate kind of understanding. That she'd finally come home.

Paul looked up at Joanna. Tears had reduced her eyes to two pale blue lakes.

María Consuelo beamed at them.

'I knew this child was meant for you,' she said. 'I *always* know. Have you chosen a name yet?'

'Yes,' Paul said. 'Joelle.' It was an amalgam of *Joseph,* Joanna's paternal grandfather, and *Ellen,* his mom. Both deceased. Both sorely missed, especially now.

'Joelle.' María sounded it out, then shook her head affirmatively. It had passed muster.

'Can I, honey?' Joanna put her arms out and Paul tentatively handed the baby over. She was so unbearably light, so ridiculously tiny, he was afraid that she might disappear at any second.

But no.

Joanna gathered her up in her arms and cooed.

'Ooooh . . . yes, Joelle . . . Gooood girl . . . Mommy's here . . .' She placed her pinkie into Joelle's tiny hand and Joelle fastened onto it.

A kind of circle had been formed, Paul thought: Joanna, Joelle, and himself. A circle is self-contained and self-sufficient.

It has no beginning and no end, forever.

FOUR

On the way back from Santa Regina, they passed a field of human heads.

Maybe they should've taken that as a sign, an omen signaling what was to come. But that's the *problem* with omens – they only become omens based on later events.

There was Joanna pressing a very sleepy Joelle to her chest.

There was Paul mentally traversing the newly discovered terrain of fatherhood.

There were twenty heads sticking up out of the ground.

Heads that were clearly and emphatically, well, *alive*. They were blinking their eyes, opening their mouths, slowly looking up and down, left and right.

'*Hambre,*' Pablo said, sighing.

'What?' Paul said. *Hambre* meant what? *Hunger.*

Joanna had seen them too. She'd instinctively brought Joelle closer to her chest as if to protect her, her maternal instinct suddenly pressed into action.

Pablo said, 'They are *protesta.*'

Hunger strike.

They'd buried themselves up to their necks in a section of un-

24

paved road. Twenty or thirty of them, mostly young men and women. They looked like something out of Hieronymus Bosch, Paul thought, doomed penitents trapped in the third circle of hell.

'What are they protesting?' Joanna asked.

Pablo shrugged. 'Conditions,' he said.

'How long have they – ?'

'Long time,' Pablo said. 'Four, five weeks.'

Maybe not much longer.

The first thing Paul heard was the siren.

An ambulance, he guessed – because he saw a station wagon with *Ambulancia* painted on its side suddenly pulling up onto the sidewalk. Its roof light was conspicuously inert. No, the siren was coming from somewhere else.

Two police cars. *Urbano guardia.* One of them cutting right in front of them, causing Pablo to jam the brakes and veer suddenly to the left, where their car came to rest with its front bumper virtually touching a brick wall.

Joelle began crying.

She wasn't the only one.

The policemen used long black nightsticks.

It looked like that bar game where little plastic groundhogs pop their heads up in random order and you score points by bopping them on the head. Only in the bar game they can pop back down. They can lie low and hide.

Not here.

In mere minutes, minutes in which Joelle grew increasingly agitated and Pablo attempted to turn the car around, the ground turned scarlet.

Which is why the ambulance was there – the result of good civic planning.

Pablo finally managed to get the car in the opposite direction and take off down a ridiculously narrow side street, barely avoiding sudden streams of people running from all directions to watch.

25

The field of bloodied heads receded into the distance. It was harder for Paul to get the sight out of his head.

Joanna was shaking – or was that him? When he put his arm around her and hugged, it was hard to tell. He'd been here a day, he thought, *less* than a day, but he was increasingly convinced that Bogotá wasn't third world as much as fourth dimension.

Locombia, he'd overheard someone on the plane refer to Colombia: the mad country.

He had a pretty good idea now what they were talking about.

He was ecstatic that they were taking Joelle from here. They might've come to Colombia to rescue themselves – from loneliness, the doldrums, a life without kids – but they were rescuing her too. From *this*. Joelle would grow up in a place of relative safety and calm. Where she'd never see people buried up to their necks in a city street, and even if she did, policemen wouldn't be bludgeoning them half to death.

Pablo asked if they were all right.

'Yes,' Paul answered, aware that Pablo seemed remarkably undisturbed by the incident. Maybe when you lived in Colombia, it was just another day at the office.

When they entered the hotel elevator, Paul smiled at the middle-aged Colombian couple who walked in seconds later, expecting the smile *back* that seemed to be the right of new parents everywhere. No dice. He was greeted with cool and unmistakable hostility.

For a moment he wondered if it was simply their nationality. Weren't Americans targets of *everyone's* anger these days? But the man whispered something to his wife in Spanish, and among the Spanish words was a word Paul recalled from his high school foreign-language labors. *Niña.*

It wasn't because of who they were. It was what they were *doing*. Adopting a baby.

A *Colombian* baby.

They were just two more Americans doing what Americans had always done in countries not their own. Depriving it of its natural resources. First gold and oil and coal and gas. Now babies. Paul hadn't considered that point of view before. Now that he found himself in an uncomfortably frigid elevator, he did. It made him feel a little less like a rescuer and more like a pillager.

Luckily, their floor came first. He ushered Joanna out of the elevator and down the hall.

'Did you see that?' he asked Joanna.

'What?'

'Those people. In the elevator.' He slipped his key into the lock and opened the door.

'Talk low,' Joanna said. 'Joelle's sleeping.'

'That couple,' Paul whispered. 'They looked like they wanted to have us deported. Or shot.'

'*What?*'

Maybe Joanna had been trying to forget what she'd just seen on that street. She hadn't noticed.

'They *hated* us, Joanna.'

'You can't be serious. They don't even know us.' Joanna slowly settled into an armchair, where she looked close to collapse.

'They don't have to know us. They don't approve of us. We're taking their children from them.'

'*Their* children? What are you talking about?'

'Their country's children. Colombia's children. I'm telling you, they looked like I should be handing her back.'

'It doesn't matter. That's them. Everyone else has been perfectly nice to us.'

'Everyone else is taking our money. That might color things a little.'

Joanna wasn't listening anymore.

She was staring down at her child, busy doing what mothers do, he supposed – basking in that part of the unbroken circle where even fathers don't dare to tread.

FIVE

This is how they met Galina.

They'd fallen into a half-stupor by the armchair and awakened to a shrill, deafening alarm that turned out to be their daughter. They immediately knew they were in trouble.

They'd forgotten to sterilize the bottles they'd brought with them from New York.

They'd forgotten to sterilize the nipples.

All the things the nurse at Fana had gone over with them ad nauseam.

There was a kitchenette just off the sitting room. Paul threw a pot of water on the stove, then began frantically looking for something to open up the cans of baby formula. Joelle's screams reached heretofore unknown decibel levels.

Paul dropped two bottles and nipples into barely boiling water, but there wasn't a can opener to be found. Both kitchen drawers were starkly empty.

Joanna rocked Joelle while walking back and forth from the kitchenette to the bed, which only seemed to cause Joelle to scream louder, if that were humanly possible. Joanna, fearless, indomitable, a four-year subscriber to *Mother & Baby* magazine, looked scared out of her mind.

There was a knock on the door.

Paul began rehearsing his apologies on the way to open it. *New baby, hungry, sorry for any—*

It was Pablo. And a woman.

'Galina,' he said, evidently the woman's name. 'She's your nurse.'

PABLO'S JOB DESCRIPTION PROVED TO BE A MODEST ONE. Technically, Galina might've been a nurse, but she was really a miracle worker.

Joanna, who still maintained at least a tenuous connection to the Catholic Church of her youth, was ready to nominate her for sainthood.

'Do you see this?' Joanna whispered to him.

Galina had managed to calm Joelle, retrieve the sterilized bottles and nipples, and locate a can opener for the formula, all in less than two minutes. At the moment, she was providing a startling display of ambidexterity, feeding Joelle in the crook of her left arm while arranging an impromptu changing table with her right.

Paul thought she looked pretty much like what a baby nurse should look like – anywhere from her mid-fifties to her mid-seventies, with a gentle face highlighted by pronounced laugh lines and soft gray eyes that seemed to resonate with the patience of, well . . . a saint.

'Can *I* do that?' Joanna asked her, but she was gently waved away.

'Plenty times to do this when you take your baby home,' Galina said. Her English was excellent. 'You watch me now.'

So Joanna did. Paul too, who'd vowed to be the kind of hands-on father that actually pitched in.

Galina finished feeding Joelle, then proceeded to demonstrate her burping technique, which was, of course, perfect. One firm pat on the back and Joelle made a noise that sounded like a bottle of sparkling Evian being opened. Galina gently placed Joelle down on the kitchen-counter-turned-changing-table and relieved her of her soiled diaper, with Paul acting as number one helper.

He was happy to note that the unpleasantness of changing a baby's diapers was mitigated by the baby in question being *yours*.

The hotel had placed a small white crib in the corner of their bedroom. Galina put Joelle facedown on the freshly laundered sheets and pulled a pink coverlet up to her neck.

'Um . . .' Joanna looked plainly uncomfortable about something.

'Yes, Mrs Breidbart?' Galina said.

'Call me Joanna, please.'

'Joanna?'

'Isn't . . . I thought a baby needs to be put on her *back*. When she sleeps. So she doesn't choke or get SIDS.'

'SIDS?' Galina smiled and shook her head. 'The stomach is fine,' she said.

'Well, yes, but . . . I read something, there were some studies done five years ago and they said –'

'Stomach is *fine*, Joanna,' she repeated, and patted her on the shoulder.

Now Joanna didn't look so happy at being called by her first name.

An uncomfortable silence suddenly permeated the room.

Paul thought that a kind of trespass had been committed, only he wasn't sure who'd trespassed upon whom. Joanna was Joelle's mother, true. Galina was her nurse. Her highly experienced and, by all evidence, *highly competent* nurse. A jury might have a tough time with this one.

Galina broke the silence first.

'If it makes you more comfortable, Joanna,' she said, and reached into the crib, gently turning Joelle over onto her back.

In the battle of wills the other guy had apparently blinked.

SIX

You didn't say anything,' Joanna said.

Joanna wasn't sleeping. Paul wasn't either, but only because she'd just woken him.

Said anything *when*? He'd been in the middle of a dream involving a college girlfriend and a torpid tropical beach, and for a moment he was shocked to be on a bed in what was obviously a hotel room.

In Bogotá. Yes.

Consciousness continued to fill in like a Polaroid being furiously waved in the air. He was in a hotel room in Bogotá. With his wife.

And his new baby daughter.

Not with Galina, though. She'd departed for home after allowing them to go downstairs for dinner, where they couldn't find a single Colombian dish on the menu.

Galina was what Joanna was talking about. He hadn't said anything when Joanna accused Galina of putting Joelle to sleep the wrong way.

'I thought discretion was the better part of valor,' Paul said.

'I see. I read babies are supposed to sleep on their backs, Paul.'

'Maybe she hadn't read the same articles.'

31

'Books.'

'Right, books. She probably hadn't read those either.'

'You should've taken my side.'

Paul considered that one. That maybe he should've taken her side. He was tempted to point out that they were novices here, and that all things considered, he was inclined to go with empirical knowledge over self-help books and *Mother & Baby* magazine. On the other hand, if he agreed with her, he had a reasonable chance of being able to turn over and go back to sleep.

'Yes, sorry,' Paul said. 'I should've, I guess.'

'You *guess*? We're her parents now. We have to support each other.'

'You mean we didn't have to support each other before?'

Joanna sighed and rolled away from him. 'Forget it.'

It was clear that Joanna didn't actually *mean* he should forget it.

'Look,' Paul said. 'I didn't know who was right. Suddenly, this baby is ours. We're . . . *responsible* for her. Galina seemed to know what she's doing. I mean, it's her *job*.'

It occurred to Paul that the process of becoming a circle might involve some growing pains. God knows, they'd had enough of them trying to *have* a baby.

Take sex, for instance.

You could pretty much mark its decline from the moment they'd decided to start a family.

As Paul remembered it, they'd been lying on a nice four-poster bed in Amagansett, Long Island, sloshed on California cabernet. When Joanna said *I don't have my diaphragm in,* he didn't say *okay, I'll wait,* and she didn't get up and get it.

They'd been married six years. They were thirty-two years old. They were drunk and horny and certifiably in love.

It would turn out to be the last spontaneous moment they'd have involving the act of conception.

When her period came a month later, they immediately decided to have another go at it.

This time there was no California cabernet and no Amagansett surf. The results were pretty much the same.

Her *friend* came right on schedule. Again. Only it wasn't a friend anymore, as much as an embarrassing if intimate relation she thought she'd booted out of the house, only to discover sitting back out on her front stoop.

In the Breidbart household, menstrual tension became decidedly *post.*

They soon began the exhausting roundelay of doctors in search of ever-elusive answers, as sex continued its slow and painful evolution from lovemaking to *baby*-making.

At one point he'd needed to shoot her with fertility drugs exactly one half hour before they performed sex. And it *was* a kind of performance – increasingly a *command* performance, summoned to do his duty at various times of the day and night. These times predicated on all sorts of physical factors, none of which had anything to do with actual lust.

A subtle kind of blame game ensued. When a thorough testing of Paul's sperm revealed that he had a below-average and barely serviceable sperm count, he'd sensed a slight shift in the air. The word *you* seemed to enter Joanna's conversation with greater frequency and with what he perceived as an accusatory intonation.

When a thorough testing of Joanna's ovaries revealed a slight abnormality that could, in some cases, inhibit proper fertilization, Paul had returned the favor. It was cruel and unforgiving.

It was also impossible to stop.

For both of them.

And it wasn't just each other who began getting on their nerves. Other people too. Lifelong friends of Joanna's, for instance, whose only crime was their apparently unlimited aptitude for getting pregnant. Including her best friend, Lisa, with two towheaded toddlers, right across the hall. Complete strangers began bugging them as well. Three seconds into meeting them, they'd invariably ask the k-question. *Have any kids?* Paul wondered why that wasn't considered unconscionably rude. Did *they* go around asking strange couples if they owned a car, or a decent bank account, or an in-ground swimming pool?

Eventually, their long road of futility inexorably led them to the new great hope of infertile couples everywhere. In vitro fertilization, otherwise known as *your last chance*. It was a kind of roulette wheel for high-stakes gamblers. After all, it was ten thousand dollars a spin. And Paul could've recited an entire actuarial table on its success rate – 28.5 percent, with the odds getting lower with each attempt.

They took Paul's sperm. They took Joanna's eggs. They formally introduced them. They sat back and hoped the romance would take.

It didn't.

They tried once.

They tried twice.

They tried three times.

They were up to forty thousand and counting when a remarkable thing happened.

It came the morning after a particularly bad night.

All their thinly nuanced charges had finally turned the air poisonous and explosive. Perhaps that wasn't surprising given that all exhalations are made of carbon dioxide; it had just been waiting for a match. In this case, a *shouting* match where they both said – okay, *screamed* – things better left unmentioned. Joanna had dissolved into tears, and Paul had sullenly disappeared into the den to watch some b-ball, which, given the general state of the New York Knicks, hadn't improved his mood any.

They were walking it off the next morning in Central Park, neither one saying much to the other, when they passed the playground off 66th Street. The sound of laughing children was particularly hurtful that morning, a lacerating reminder of what they couldn't have.

Paul was about to execute a detour when a small girl wandered past them in the futile process of capturing a runaway pink balloon. She was dark, Latin, and impossibly cute.

'Where's your mother?' Joanna had asked her.

But the more interesting question would have been, *who's* your mother? The woman who came breathlessly running up to them just a few seconds later, gently admonishing her daughter for running away. This woman was blonde, pale, and about their age. She picked up her giggling daughter, nuzzled her neck, smiled at Paul and Joanna, and retreated back to the seesaws.

Up to that moment they hadn't thought about it.

Adopting.

Maybe they'd just needed to see it in the flesh.

That afternoon when they got back to the apartment, Joanna asked Paul to take out the garbage. Surprisingly, this garbage consisted of syringes, thermometers, various fertility drugs, dutifully recorded journals, and everything else they'd accumulated in an effort to have a baby. Paul gladly dumped it all into the incinerator room.

When he got back inside, they'd ended up making love the way they used to – which, all things considered, was pretty terrific.

They went to a lawyer the very next day.

Now Paul could hear Joanna next to him in the dark. And the soft, soothing sound of Joelle's breathing. He rolled over and kissed his wife on the mouth.

'Next time I'll support you. Okay?'

He could sense her smile in the dark.

All systems were go for reentry into the land of Nod.

Except Joelle woke up.

And screamed.

SEVEN

It began the next afternoon.

Galina put Joelle in for her afternoon nap. She hummed a plaintive lullaby over the crib. Paul cocked his head from the bathroom, listening to Galina's lilting voice. When he came out, freshly shaven and only slightly sleep-deprived, Galina suggested that he and Joanna get some fresh air. The baby was asleep. Galina would be there for another few hours.

It was technically winter in Colombia, but even mountain-bound Bogotá was close enough to the equator to retain a dreamy warmth. Joelle *was* sleeping – a walk seemed like just what the doctor ordered.

They turned right out the hotel lobby and soon passed the kind of stores only tourists and one percent of the Colombian population could afford to walk into.

Hermès.

Louis Vuitton.

Oscar de la Renta.

They walked hand in hand, and Paul congratulated himself on his tactical maneuver last night in bed. Things were clearly fine between them.

Joanna had fed Joelle this morning, while he'd pulled diaper duty. They'd taken turns babbling nonstop baby talk at her. That is, when they weren't telling each other how remarkably gorgeous she was. How unbelievably expressive her face seemed. What an unusually sweet disposition she had. Obviously, some natural law was at work here, able to turn two reasonably intelligent people into love-struck idiots.

Paul, though, was kind of enjoying idiothood.

Now he squeezed Joanna's hand as they waited at a curb. He kissed her neck when they stopped and lingered before an art gallery window. A Botero exhibition, the Latin American painter who portrayed everyone as grossly distended, fat, and swollen, like Thanksgiving parade balloons.

After they had strolled a few more blocks, he found he missed his daughter. This was a new experience – going somewhere and leaving a piece of yourself behind. He felt . . . *incomplete*. The circle needed to be closed again.

'Want to go back?' he asked Joanna.

'I was about to say the same thing.'

'I think I'm going to call her Jo,' Paul said after they had crossed the street and turned back toward L'Esplanade. Two couples on mopeds gunned their engines and surged past them, spitting out a thin cloud of blue exhaust.

'Ugh,' Joanna said; evidently, she wasn't referring to the noxious fumes.

'Something wrong with *Jo*?'

'When you tried to call me Jo, I threatened you with bodily harm. I think I *did* you bodily harm.'

'Yeah. Why was that again?'

'I dated a Joe, remember? He was unemployed and psychotic – not in that order. So all things being equal,' Joanna said, 'I'd prefer that you not call her Jo.'

'Fine. What about *Joey*?'

'Like in Buttafuoco?'

'Like in Breidbart.'

'How about we *start* with *Joelle*? Just so the poor kid learns her name.'

They were passing a toy store, its window stocked floor-to-ceiling with dolls, trucks, video games, stuffed animals, soccer balls, and some things he honestly couldn't recognize.

'What do you say?' Paul said.

'Sure,' Joanna said. 'Let's go buy some toys.'

WHEN THEY ENTERED THE HOTEL LOBBY, THEY NEEDED THE doorman to help them make it into the elevator. They'd gone a little overboard – *they'd* been like kids in a toy store.

There seemed to be so much more to buy than when *they* were children. It was pretty much G.I. Joes, Barbies, and Slinkys back then. Now there were vast new categories to contemplate, numerous subcategories too. Things that talked and walked and beeped and flashed and zapped and pirouetted and sang.

All of them seemed to have Joelle's name on them.

The doorman managed to get them into the elevator without a major mishap.

When they opened the door to their hotel room, Galina wasn't there.

'She's in the bathroom,' Joanna said.

Paul opened the bathroom door, stuffed giraffe in hand, but Galina wasn't in there either.

When Paul turned around with his hands up, Joanna turned an ugly shade of white.

It wasn't just Galina that was missing.

It was their daughter.

She was gone too.

*   *   *

38

'NO, MR BREIDBART, I DIDN'T TALK TO YOUR NURSE.' THE concierge retained his air of helpful solicitude, but up against Paul's full-blown panic, it seemed woefully inadequate.

'They're not in the room,' Paul said. *Do you understand me?*

'Yes, sir. I understand.'

Paul had come down to the lobby – after checking the rooftop pool, the restaurant, the hair salon, the game room. Joanna had remained up in the room in case Galina called.

'Perhaps she went shopping,' the concierge offered.

'Did you see them leave the hotel?'

'No. I was busy with several guests.'

'Well, did *anyone* see them leave the hotel?'

'I don't know, Mr Breidbart. Why don't we ask?'

The concierge led him over to the front desk, where he interrupted the registration clerk, who was in the middle of checking in a guest. He spoke to him in Spanish, gesturing to Paul. Paul heard him mention Galina's name, then *niña,* that word again. The registration clerk looked at Paul, then back to the concierge, and shook his head.

'He didn't see them,' the concierge said. 'Come with me.'

They walked outside the hotel where the doorman who'd just helped them into the elevator was flirting with a striking woman in a midriff-baring tank top.

The doorman immediately straightened up, deserting the woman in midsentence. After the concierge had explained the problem, he looked over at Paul and slowly nodded.

'*Sí,*' the doorman said. Apparently, he *had* seen Galina and Joelle leave the hotel. '*Hace una hora . . .*'

An hour ago. Which would have been just after he and Joanna had left the hotel.

'Ahh, mystery solved,' the concierge said, smiling stupidly. 'She is taking your baby for a walk.'

His baby had been napping.

Why would Galina take a sleeping baby for a walk?

39

Paul felt dizzy; the ground seemed to be tipping. The concierge was still talking to him, but Paul wasn't processing the words. There was a steady hum in the air.

'She's taken my baby,' Paul said.

The doorman and concierge were looking at him oddly.

'Did you hear what I said? *She's taken my baby.*'

'Yes,' the concierge finally responded. 'For a walk, Mr Breidbart.'

'I want you to call the police.'

'*Policía?*'

'Yes. Call them.'

'I think you are maybe too excited here . . .'

'Yes, I am excited.' The ground was tipping one way, then the other. The sun had gone cold. 'My baby's been taken. I'm excited about that. Call the police.'

'I don't think . . .'

'*Call the police.*'

'You are accusing your nurse of kidnapping, Mr Breidbart.' It was said as a statement, not a question, and it seemed to Paul that the concierge's voice had somehow changed, gone from warm and helpful to cool and unhelpful.

'My baby was napping. The nurse told us to go get some fresh air. Then she left the hotel two minutes later and she's not back.'

'The baby woke up perhaps.'

'Perhaps you're right. All the same, I want you to call the police.'

'Maybe we wait a little and see if she returns, no?'

'No.'

'She has been used as a nurse many times here, Mr Breidbart.' Yes, the concierge's tone had definitely undergone a transformation.

Paul was accusing a Colombian woman of a crime.

A sweet-looking Colombian woman with laugh lines and patient gray eyes who was taking care of a *Colombian baby.* A baby that he, an American, was spiriting out of the country because there evidently weren't enough American babies to go around.

'I don't care how many times she's been used. She took my baby without permission. She didn't tell us. I need to talk to the police.'

The concierge might not have agreed with him and might not have even liked him, but he was still a concierge.

'If that's what you want, sir,' he said stiffly.

He walked back into the lobby and up to his desk, where he lifted the phone with painful resignation and dialed out. Paul waited silently as the concierge said a few Spanish words into the receiver. He hung up the phone with undue force. The click echoed through the sterile lobby, causing several people to look up with alarmed and puzzled expressions.

THE POLICEMEN HAD THICK BLACK LEATHER BOOTS AND GUNS THAT looked like Uzis strapped to their hips.

Paul didn't notice any black nightsticks.

The concierge spoke to them in Spanish while Paul patiently listened. In the interim between the concierge's call and the policemen's arrival, Paul had called Joanna again.

No news.

One of the policemen spoke decent English. Even if he hadn't, his meaning would have been all too evident.

'Why you think your nurse *stole your baby?*' he said. He didn't look like he wanted an answer.

Paul explained as best he could. Joelle was napping, the nurse had suggested that they leave, then she'd left herself. She had neither asked permission nor left a note. They didn't know where she was.

'He says this woman is good.' The *he* the policeman was referring to was the concierge, who was standing off to the side with a semi-scowl on his face. In the game of good cop, bad cop, it would've been hard to choose who was who.

'Perhaps you didn't understand me,' Paul said, and saw the policeman flinch. He remembered those bloodied heads sticking out of the ground, and for a moment he wondered whether he would already have been slugged on the head and hauled off to jail for making false accusations if he hadn't been an American.

He was in the middle of explaining the rightfulness of his position, of laying out all the reasons for his full-fledged panic, of carefully explaining why his nurse wouldn't simply have gotten up and *left* with their baby unless she had something bad in mind, when Galina walked into the lobby with Joelle.

EIGHT

Hours after Paul had apologized to the police, the concierge, and Galina – in that order – then apologized to Galina *again,* just to make sure she understood how sorry he was, he lay on the bed with Joanna and wondered aloud if paranoia wasn't part of the strange new province of parenthood.

'We're in a foreign country, Paul,' Joanna said, and Paul couldn't help thinking she was right figuratively as well. 'We came into our room and our baby was gone. She didn't tell us she was taking her. *No.'*

In point of fact, Galina *had* told them that she was taking Joelle. She'd left a note tucked under the cream-colored ashtray in the bathroom – when they got back upstairs, Galina had gone in and retrieved it. Perhaps if they hadn't been so quick to panic, they would've seen it. And known that Joelle had woken up from her nap just two seconds after Paul had closed the door. And that her forehead had felt just a little hot to Galina – not dangerously feverish, no, but a little hot, and that Galina wasn't the type to take chances. And they would've known that among the things they *hadn't* brought with them from New York was a thermometer. For which

Galina had taken Joelle in search of a pharmacy. To purchase with her own money.

As it turned out, Joelle had a 101-degree temperature. Nothing to worry about with a baby, Galina reassured them, but something that had definitely needed to be checked out.

Galina forgave them, yet he noted an unmistakable glimmer of hurt in those soft gray eyes. Even anger. Something that said even saintly patience has its limits.

THE NEXT DAY PABLO TOOK THEM TO THE U.S. EMBASSY.

When they entered the outer gate, where they were forced to walk through not one, but two metal detectors, they passed a familiar face coming the opposite way.

The bird-watcher. The somnolent man who'd patiently sat for eighteen hours on the plane with them.

'Hello,' he greeted them. He was already wearing the uniform of the bush. A safari shirt with large pleated pockets, khaki knee-length shorts, and thick brown hiking boots.

'Hello,' Paul said.

'Ahh,' he said, repositioning his glasses and staring down at Joelle as if she were a new species of Colombian finch. 'Yours?'

'Yes,' Joanna said. 'Her name's Joelle.'

'Well, congrats,' he said.

'Thanks,' Paul said. It was nice to run into someone from back home – even if it was someone he'd known for eighteen hours. 'We need to get a little paperwork done so we can take her home. How about you?'

'How about me what?'

'The embassy?'

'Oh, if you want to go into the jungle, you have to sign a release. They don't want your next of kin complaining they were negligent and didn't warn you. I think what they really don't want is anybody suing them.'

44

'Well, good luck,' Paul said.

'Yeah. You too.'

When they entered the spacious anteroom, they passed under a portrait of a smiling George Bush. It didn't really sound like an embassy, though, more like a nursery at feeding time. The room was crammed with couples holding, rocking, shushing, and changing a varied array of agitated Colombian babies. If running into the ornithologist was a welcome reminder of home, this was more like an actual homecoming. All the new parents were, of course, American. Joanna and Paul managed to find two seats next to a thirty-something couple from Texas. Paul *assumed* that they were from Texas because the man was wearing a T-shirt that said *God Bless Texas*. When the man said *howdy*, it was more or less confirmed. His wife was holding a baby boy with a noticeable harelip. Paul immediately chided himself, ashamed that his first impression of the boy hadn't been whether he was big or small or shy or friendly, no – he couldn't help zeroing in on the boy's physical imperfection.

He was kind of disappointed in himself. But as he looked around the room, he thought it was possible that he wasn't the only one doing some comparison shopping. Every parent seemed to be mentally taking notes. Perhaps it was the nature of being handed a ready-made kid.

They were called into a fluorescent-lit room where a dour-looking Colombian woman asked them for Joelle's birth certificate. Which didn't, of course, say *Joelle* on it. Paul hadn't really known what the birth certificate said, since it was entirely in Spanish. Among the Spanish words was apparently the baby's name – the one given to her by her birth mother.

'Marti,' the woman said as she scribbled something down.

The biological mother was a complete unknown to them. María Consuelo had offered them information about her, which they'd promptly and politely declined. It was a kind of denial mechanism, they knew, a sophomoric one at that. It went something like this: If they didn't know about the mother, she wouldn't really exist. And if she didn't really exist, it would be easier to believe that Joelle was all theirs.

The woman asked them a few questions. Her manner was polite but aloof. Paul, on the lookout for any antipathy from the natives, was unable to read anything particularly malicious in her line of questioning. Still, he was relieved when the interrogation was over.

'YOUR BABY'S COMPLETELY HEALTHY,' THE DOCTOR SAID.

Their second stop of the day.

Adopted babies needed to undergo a medical exam before they were allowed to leave the country. Pablo had driven them to a pediatrician near the hotel.

Dr Dalliego was middle-aged, balding, and coolly efficient. He weighed, poked, and prodded Joelle with machinelike detachment as Paul and Joanna stood by with mute anxiety. Was it possible the physician would find something wrong with her? Her modest fever had disappeared this morning as quickly as it had come, but was there something that the orphanage had missed? Something that would necessitate returning her and leaving Colombia empty-handed and brokenhearted?

Occasionally, the nurse would interrupt the doctor with a telephone call, and he'd hand Joelle back to Joanna while he patiently listened to some other baby's mother or father pour out their fears. He'd calmly utter a few words of Spanish into the receiver, nod in a kind of affirmation of his wisdom, return the phone to the nurse.

Then back to the baby at hand.

After a while Paul grew tired of looking for clues in the doctor's expression. He decided he'd simply wait for the final verdict.

Which was apparently first-rate. *Your baby's completely healthy,* Dr Dalliego said. *She's fine.*

Which was more than you could say for her father.

Paul finally allowed himself to exhale.

NINE

They were back in the hotel room.

Galina had left for the day. Joelle was asleep in her crib. Slats of amber light were slanting in through the window.

He'd remember this exact moment for a long time. Just about forever. He'd remember the way it looked – how the rays of light crisscrossed the bedspread and seemed to cleave Joanna's naked leg in two. He'd take a photo of this moment and paste it into the album of very bad things.

Joanna was lying half in and half out of the bedsheets, staring straight up at the ceiling. She looked kind of morose.

Once upon a time Paul had resisted asking Joanna why she looked unhappy, because he always knew what the answer would be, and it always involved him. He was hoping things were different now – that the two of them were positively *suffused* with happiness – so he went ahead and asked.

'What's wrong?'

'You're going to think I'm crazy,' she said.

'No, I'm not.'

'Yes, you are. You don't know what I'm thinking. It's ridiculous.'

'Yes, I do. You're thinking I'm going to think you're crazy.'

'Besides that.'

'What, Joanna?'

'It's nuts.'

'Okay, it's nuts. Tell me.'

'She smells different.'

'What? *Who?*'

'Joelle. She smells different.'

'Different than what?'

'Different than . . . before.'

Paul didn't know quite how to answer that.

'So?'

'So?'

'So she smells different. I'm not –'

'Don't you understand what I'm saying?'

'No.'

Joanna rolled onto her side and faced him. 'I don't think it's *her.*'

'What?'

'I don't think it's her,' clearly enunciating each word this time so he'd know exactly what it was she was saying. Which was clearly and patently, well . . . nuts.

'Joanna – of course it's her. We took her to the doctor today. You were with her the whole day. Are you . . . ?'

'Crazy?'

'I wasn't going to say that,' Paul said. Of course, that's exactly what he was going to say. 'I just . . . I mean, it's just so . . . She's Joelle.'

'How do you know?'

'What do you mean how do I know?'

'It's a simple question. How do you *know* it's Joelle?'

'Because I've been with her two days. Because . . . it *looks* like her.'

'She's one month old. How many other babies have you seen here that look exactly like her?'

'None.'

'Fine. Well, I have.'

'Joanna, because she *smells* different? Don't you think it's kind of . . . paranoid?'

'You mean like when we thought Galina kidnapped her?'

'Yes.'

'Maybe we weren't being paranoid. Maybe Galina *did* kidnap her.'

'Do you hear what you're saying? Do you? It's ridiculous.'

'You didn't think it was ridiculous yesterday.'

'Yes, I didn't think it was ridiculous yesterday. That was before Galina came *back* with her. She had a fever, so Galina went to get her a thermometer. Remember?'

'Joelle didn't have a fever when we went for a walk, did she?'

'How do we know that?'

'Because I'm her mother. I held her before we left. She was fine.'

'Babies get fevers, honey.'

Joanna sat up. She took Paul's hands in hers – her palms felt cold and clammy.

'Look. Joelle had a beauty mark on her left leg. Right here.' She reached over and touched his leg, just below the knee. It nearly made him jump. 'I saw it. I felt it. When you fell asleep the first night, I went to her crib and just . . . well, looked at her. I couldn't believe we *had* her. I woke up and thought I was dreaming maybe. I had to see her again. To know she was real. You understand?'

Paul nodded.

'Okay. When the doctor examined her today, I didn't *see* it. I told myself *maybe you're wrong, maybe you didn't really see a beauty mark before*. It was dark in the room. Maybe it was a speck of dirt, a smudge. Only . . . all day today I was thinking that she smelled different than she did before.'

'Honey . . .'

'Listen to me. Please.' She squeezed his hands, as if she were trying to physically press her belief into him, as if it were something that could be caught, like a disease. Only he didn't want her disease.

49

He wanted her to stop this, to go back to being the ecstatic new mother who woke up in the middle of the night just so she could gaze at her daughter. 'Joelle had this . . . I don't know, musky smell. She had it when we picked her up at the orphanage, and she had it here. She stopped having it when Galina brought her back.'

'Okay. Why didn't you say anything then?'

'Because I knew you'd think I was crazy. Just like you're thinking now. I told *myself* I was crazy. But I didn't see the beauty mark today. So maybe I'm not.'

'Why would she switch babies, Joanna? Why? For what earthly reason?' Paul was trying to make her see how silly this all was. Belief was immune to logic; it operated by its own laws. And this scared him, if only because there was a tiny part of him that was, well . . . starting to listen to her. The fact was, Joelle *had* smelled a little musky. Now that Joanna had mentioned it, okay, yes, she had.

'I don't know why she'd switch babies, Paul. Maybe because of our fight.'

'What fight? You mean about putting her to sleep?'

Joanna nodded.

'That's ridiculous.'

'Okay, it's ridiculous. I'm ridiculous. I just think that two days from now we're going to be leaving this country with the wrong baby. Then it'll be too late.'

'What do you want me to do, Joanna? Even if I believed you. What would I tell the police? *What?* That I know we apologized to them for insisting our daughter had been kidnapped, but guess what, now we think she was *switched*?'

'We can go back to Santa Regina,' Joanna said. 'We can have them check her out for us.'

'And what do you think María would say about that? How stable would she think we are? How much would she want us to have one of her babies? Nothing's final yet, Joanna. They can still take Joelle back.'

'This baby's not Joelle.'

'I happen to disagree with you. Okay? I happen to think she is. Because the alternative makes no sense. None. Listen to yourself. You're basing this on a *smell,* for chrissakes. On something you *think* you saw in the middle of the night.'

'Let me ask you something, okay?' Joanna said.

No, he wanted to say – it's not okay.

'Let's say there's a one percent chance I'm right.'

'What?'

'That's fair, isn't it? One percent?'

'Look, I –'

'I'm asking you a simple question. You want to attack me with logic, fine, I understand. So I'm asking you a logical question. You love percentages, don't you? You're an actuary – pretend it's one of your insurance charts. Is there a one percent chance I'm right?'

'You want me to put a percentage on something I think is totally ridiculous?'

'Yes, I want you to put a percentage on something you think is totally ridiculous.'

'Okay, fine – there's a one percent chance she's not Joelle. And a ninety-nine percent chance she is.'

'Okay. Are you willing to leave the country with even the *chance* she's not ours?'

For a moment he was going to say Joelle wasn't theirs anyway – because in the usual God-given sense, she wasn't. But he couldn't say it. It wasn't true anymore. From the second he'd clasped her to his chest, she'd become theirs.

She was their daughter.

So now what?

TEN

It seemed an eternity before Galina opened her door.

Maybe because Paul was no clearer about what he was going to say to her than he was before, and so was standing there frantically trying to come up with something. In addition to hoping she wouldn't be home, that no one would actually answer Pablo's knock.

Pablo had driven the three of them to Galina's house in the Chapinero district, a working-class area of dun-colored apartment buildings and modest homes. When they'd slid into the backseat, Joanna hadn't taken their daughter from Paul's arms as she normally had in the two days they'd been with her.

She was making a statement.

This isn't my daughter. You hold her.

Well, Paul thought, they'd see.

'Hello, Galina,' Paul said when the door finally opened.

She seemed surprised to see them, but not in a way Paul construed as alarmed. In fact, she smiled, then leaned over and whispered a sweet hello to her very favorite baby. Paul felt like turning to Joanna and saying *see, satisfied now?* Joanna didn't look any different than she had during the ride over, which was nervous and unhappy.

Galina invited them in.

The door opened onto a small living room. It had a brown leather couch and two worn but comfortable-looking chairs facing a television. A lumbering yellow dog barely shifted from its sprawled position on the floor. Galina had been watching a soap opera; at least Paul assumed that's what it was. A perfect-looking young woman was kissing a perfect-looking young man.

'Please sit,' Galina said, gesturing to the couch. *Do you see this,* Paul kept up his running, albeit silent commentary to Joanna, *she's inviting us in. She's asking us to sit on her couch.*

Galina brought out cookies and four cups of industrial-strength Colombian coffee in what must have been her fine china. She turned down the TV.

They made small talk.

'How did the baby sleep last night?' Galina asked.

'Fine,' Paul answered. 'She woke up once around two, I think, and then went right back.'

'You're lucky. She's a good sleeper.'

'Yes,' Paul said. Joanna remained conspicuously silent.

'You have a lovely house, Galina,' Paul said, continuing to search for anything to talk about except the actual reason for their visit.

'Thank you.'

'What's your dog's name?' he asked.

'Oca,' Galina said. At the sound of his name the dog lifted his head and sniffed the air.

'Did Pablo take you to the doctor yesterday?' Galina asked.

'Yes.'

'And what did he say?'

'Everything's fine.'

'Wonderful,' Galina said. She smiled; her laugh lines fairly cackled.

Then Joanna spoke.

'Her fever was gone.'

'That's good,' Galina said.

53

'I wonder what it *was*?' Joanna added.

'Who knows?' Galina lifted her hands up in the universal gesture of the human limitation to understanding the mysteries of the universe.

Which is what Joanna was trying to do, of course. Understand, at least, one mystery.

Paul knew that he was expected to take over.

If he sat back and said nothing, Joanna would accuse him of non-support, of aiding and abetting the enemy. Except the enemy was treating them to coffee and cookies and the general hospitality of her home. The enemy had run to a *farmacia* to buy Joelle a thermometer when she was sick. Still, he was counted on to do certain things. Support her, for example. Something he hadn't done when she'd insisted Joelle, the *real* Joelle in her mind, had been put to sleep the wrong way. Something he was firmly and unquestioningly expected to do now.

'Uh, Galina . . . we were wondering about something,' he started.

'Yes?'

'This is going to sound a little silly, okay?'

'Okay.' Galina repeated his American slang with evident amusement.

'My wife . . . both of us, really, have noticed this difference. About Joelle.'

'Difference. What do you mean difference?'

'Well, I said this is going to sound silly, but the fact is, she kind of smells different. Than she did before.'

'*Smells?*' She looked over at Pablo, as if for confirmation she'd heard him correctly. Apparently, she had. Pablo looked as confused as she did.

'She had this kind of musky smell,' Paul blundered on, 'and now she doesn't. It seemed to change after, uh . . . when we thought she was . . . when you went to get her the thermometer.'

'Yes?'

'We were just wondering about it,' Paul said. 'That's all.'

'All right.'

Evidently, Galina still had no idea what he was talking about.

'We were hoping maybe you can account for it?'

'Account for what?'

'Why she seems to be . . . different.'

Galina put her cup of coffee back down on its china saucer. The sound seemed to echo unnaturally. Maybe because the room had suddenly turned uncomfortably quiet, the only sound a vague murmur emanating from the lowered TV. If the five of them were on that soap opera, Paul thought, there'd be a dissonant organ chord now to signify the portent of something dramatic. In this case, Galina's growing realization that she was being accused, albeit clumsily, of something she still didn't understand.

'What are you saying?' she asked now. 'Are you suggesting . . . *what?*'

'Nothing, Galina,' Paul said, a little too quickly. 'We were just curious, that's all.'

'About *what?*'

'About why she smells different.'

'I don't understand. What are you asking me?'

We're asking you if you stole our baby, Galina. If you switched her.

'Nothing.'

'Then why are you here?'

Paul felt like asking Joanna that himself.

'We wanted to know . . . ,' and here Paul suddenly went blank.

'She had a beauty mark,' Joanna said.

'What?' Galina turned to look at Joanna.

'She had a beauty mark when we got her. It's not there now.'

'Beauty mark?'

'My daughter had a beauty mark on her left leg. And she used to smell like . . . well, like her. The beauty mark's gone. She smells different. *I want to know if it's the same baby.*'

Okay, Paul thought, Xena, warrior princess, was in full battle mode. The cat had been let out of the bag. Only it wasn't a cat as much as a Tasmanian devil, something large, carnivorous, and re-pulsive-looking. Probably the way the two of them looked to Galina right at this moment. After all, her back had physically stiffened – one of those clichés that evidently rang true. Her gentle gray eyes had turned hard as glass.

Paul found himself trying to look anywhere but at her, searching for a hole he might be able to hide in.

There was a box of cigars sitting on her mantel.

It had a photograph of a man in a white panama hat.

Paul wondered if Galina smoked cigars. A pair of brown slippers nestled like cats on her front welcome mat. The dog, who'd roused itself from its semicomatose state, had picked up one in his mouth, then dropped it by Pablo's feet, where it landed with an uncomfort-able thud.

He forced himself to turn back to Galina. She still hadn't said anything – Joanna's accusation had turned her mute. She looked more or less horrified.

Later, much later, Paul would wonder if there's such a thing as pe-ripheral hearing. Something that impinges on the ear but only an-nounces itself later on.

He was trying not to stare at Galina's pained expression. He was wondering whether he should apologize to her. He didn't notice the muffled sound emanating from the inner recesses of the house.

Galina did. Which accounted for her expression.

Joanna had noticed it too.

Because she reached out and dug her fingernails into his arm. He almost cried out. Which would've made it two people crying in the house instead of just one.

Him and the baby.

There was a baby crying in the house.

He'd finally heard it.

He'd finally processed it. Because when he looked down at Joelle, she was sleeping. Which meant that there was a baby crying in the house, yes, only it wasn't this baby.

'Who's that?' That's the first thing he said. Stupid, okay, but then, he was obviously a little slow on the uptake today.

Galina didn't answer him.

'Whose baby is that?' he said, even though he was starting to have a good idea whose baby it might be.

'Pablo. Can you go see who it is?'

Pablo didn't move.

'Galina?'

She hadn't changed expression. Or maybe she had. The hardness in her eyes was still there, and there was something else now, a scary sense of focus and fortitude.

'Galina, is that our daughter? Is that *Joelle*?'

It took Paul a while to realize that Pablo *still* hadn't moved. That Galina still wasn't answering him.

Paul stood up with the baby in his arms – the question was, *whose* baby? He felt faint. 'Okay, I'm going to see who it is.' Announcing his plan out loud as if seeking approval.

He reached out to give Joelle to Galina and then, of course, stopped himself. Galina wasn't exactly his nurse anymore; it was possible this baby wasn't Joelle. He felt as if he were teetering on the edge of a deep and dangerous abyss – physically and emotionally hovering right over the edge. The room itself seemed to be swaying.

Then things flew into motion.

Joanna stood up and said *I'll go look,* and immediately began walking toward the sound of the crying baby. Pablo roused himself from his chair.

Paul offered up the baby in his arms so he could go join his wife, but it seemed to take an enormous effort to lift her.

'Sit down, Paul,' Pablo said gently.

He was offering to look himself. He was telling Paul to sit down and take care of the baby. Pablo was being Pablo.

Paul gratefully reclaimed his seat as Pablo followed Joanna into the hall. The baby was crying louder, screeching even. And Paul finally and completely acknowledged what Joanna had feared was true.

He *recognized* that crying.

He remembered it from the first day in the hotel room when their daughter had wailed endlessly for food. Until Galina had shown up and made everything all right again.

Galina was still stiffly seated in her chair – only she appeared to be physically closer to him than she'd been before. How was that possible?

For a minute or so nothing happened.

The baby continued to cry from somewhere in the house; Galina continued to stare at him with an odd and unsettling calm.

Then Pablo reappeared, walking back into the living room while supporting Joanna with one strong arm. She was leaning against him, her head laid back on his shoulder as if she were very close to fainting. Where was the baby?

Joanna clearly looked distraught, while Pablo appeared helpful. There was undoubtedly a causal connection between those two things, but Paul wasn't sure what it was.

Something was wrong.

Look closer.

Her head on his shoulder. It took Paul a few seconds – seconds in which the world changed from A to Z – to understand that the reason it was lying back on Pablo's shoulder like that was that Pablo had his wife's dark luxuriant hair wrapped tightly in his fist.

Pablo was pulling Joanna into the room by her hair.

Her mouth was open in a half-muted scream.

He threw Joanna down onto the couch, flung her backward as if she were a piece of luggage he'd thrown into the car at El Dorado Airport.

'*Sit,*' he said. The way one barks commands at a dog. A stupid, stubborn dog, a dog who should know better.

Paul felt rooted to the couch, a spectator to a horrifying drama that had suddenly and inexplicably become real. He was waiting for the intermission, when he could stretch his legs, shake the cobwebs out of his brain, and thank the cast for their stunningly convincing performance. The play continued.

Galina stood up.

She methodically began closing the wooden shutters on each side of the room as she talked to Pablo in a steady stream of Spanish. As if he and Joanna weren't even in the room. She seemed to be chastising him – Paul's Spanish was beginning to come back like a long-repressed memory, and it seemed like he could understand every fifth word or so. *You. Called. Not here.* For one regrettably stupid moment Paul wondered if she was yelling at Pablo for throwing Joanna down on the couch like that.

For not getting their baby.

For *turning* on them.

But that was like hoping you're asleep and dreaming when you're completely and terrifyingly awake.

Paul handed the baby to Joanna – the baby he'd thought was his daughter and that he now knew wasn't – and stood up to protest Pablo's treatment of his wife, to reason this out, to get Joelle and have Pablo take them back to the hotel this instant.

'I told you to sit down, Paul,' Pablo said.

Somehow he delivered this statement over Paul's prone body. This was an enormous surprise to Paul. That he wasn't standing. He was lying down on a wooden floor smelling of wet fur and shoe polish. *How had that happened?* He heard Joanna's sharp intake of breath.

'I'm okay, honey,' he said. Oddly enough, he didn't hear the words. His tongue was strangely obstinate; it had decided to lie down on the job. Just like the rest of his body, which felt absurdly heavy. There was a strange metallic taste in his mouth.

He tried to lift himself up from the floor. No go. He felt vibrations traveling through the floorboards, some kind of rebalancing of

59

weight from one place to another. He heard heavy shuffling and sensed a quickening in the air itself.

They looked like marines.

Five men in mottled green uniforms who'd suddenly flowed into the room like a brackish river breaching its banks. Young faces with stolid expressions of dumb determination. Each of them carried a rifle.

'Please,' Paul said.

The room was eerily dark; Galina had closed all the shutters but one. It felt like the moment before everyone yells *surprise*.

The surprise is for us, Paul thought.

Then he passed out.

ELEVEN

Blackness.

But not completely. There were endless visions and dreams flickering through the blackness. Like being in a movie theater for a very long time.

He was eleven years old and suddenly afraid of the dark. He hadn't been afraid before, but he was *now*. Maybe because it was dark at the top of the stairs where his mother had recently taken up residence. Not just dark – a thick, suffocating blackness like a wool blanket pulled up over his head. *Your mother's resting,* his father told him. *She's sleeping. Don't disturb her.*

He crept up the stairs, where it smelled unpleasantly medicinal. He listened outside the door and heard the distinct sounds of a TV game show: a buzzer, a voice, phony audience laughter.

His mom wasn't sleeping, after all. It would be okay to open the door and crawl into her arms. But the darkness inside the room was even gloomier than the darkness outside in the hall. Only the soft glow coming from the portable TV with sadly bent rabbit ears made seeing possible at all.

It took him a while before he could make out the monster lying on the bed.

Last Halloween he'd gone trick-or-treating as a skeleton – all black, except for the white bones where his arms and legs were supposed to be.

It looked like that.

In the dream this skeleton lifted up a bony arm and waved for him to come closer.

Eventually, he woke up. Movie over.

'MORNING,' THE BOY SAID.

Just as he'd said it every morning since they'd taught it to him. Not on purpose. When Paul had finally opened his eyes after losing consciousness on Galina's floor, the boy was there listening when he asked Joanna what time it was. Was it *morning*? The boy repeated it several times as if trying it out. Now he used it to greet them.

This morning, which was either the third or fourth morning they'd been here, the boy waited for some kind of verbal acknowledgment.

'Good morning,' Joanna said.

Then the boy placed their breakfast – corn cakes and sausage – on the floor and left.

They were in a house somewhere in Colombia.

It was impossible to know *where* in Colombia, since they weren't allowed out. The windows were boarded over. They could hear little from outside – the distant rumble of passing cars, occasional disembodied melodies trickling through from God knows where, a parrot squawking. All they knew was that it wasn't *Galina's* house.

They'd been transported somewhere else.

A claustrophobic room with a filthy mattress on the floor and two plastic chairs. There was a bucket in the corner.

That's it.

That first morning, Joanna had woken before Paul. When she couldn't rouse him – apparently, she attempted everything but jumping up and down on him – she'd tried opening the door.

Locked tight. She managed to pry open a shutter, only to see solid wood staring back.

When Paul finally and groggily woke up, he was greeted with the sight of Joanna rocking herself back and forth in the middle of the floor. 'Oh God,' she was murmuring, 'oh God . . .'

He'd tried to comfort her, of course, even as he attempted to make sense of what had happened, to fight through a stultifying haze that seemed to have wrapped itself around his head. She seemed oddly distant, even with his arms enclosing her, as if she were obstinately holding a piece of herself back. He thought he knew why.

'I'm sorry, Joanna,' he said. 'For not believing you.'

'Yes. Okay. Great.'

'It seemed ridiculous. Switching babies. I couldn't imagine . . .'

'Where is she, Paul?' she cut him off. 'What do they want?'

It was a hard question to answer.

The first day they saw no one but the boy. He was dressed in mottled green camouflage like the others. He carried a rifle that seemed far too big for him. He might've been all of fourteen. Except for his *good morning*s, he remained mute.

The next afternoon they were finally visited by someone higher up the food chain. A man in his mid-thirties, a face Paul thought he recognized from Galina's house, just before he'd found himself staring at the ceiling.

'Look, we're not *political*,' Paul said when the man entered the room and locked the door behind him. 'I work in insurance.' This reminded him of something else. 'We aren't rich.'

The man turned and looked at him. 'You think we're *bandidos*?' His English was passable. He had what looked like a Kalashnikov looped around his shoulder, but he seemed neither violent nor unsympathetic.

'Where's my baby?' Joanna said. 'I want my baby back. Please.'

'I think I ask the questions here,' he said, not particularly rudely. Just as an unequivocal statement of fact.

'You've been captured by FARC,' he said, 'the Revolutionary Armed Forces of Colombia,' spelling it out for them in case they weren't up on their acronyms. 'We are the legitimate voice of the Colombian people.' Paul thought it sounded like a speech he'd made hundreds of times before. 'You are our political prisoners. *Comprende?*'

Paul said, 'We can't help you. I told you, we're not political. We have no *money . . .*'

He was interrupted by a rifle butt to his midsection. Delivered with enough force and precision to bring him straight to his knees.

'*Paul!*' Joanna recoiled, the obvious reaction when your husband is physically assaulted right in front of your eyes.

'When I ask a question, answer me,' the man said. 'You must remember this.'

Paul attempted to get up, for Joanna's sake, if not his own. He felt her fear as if it were a physical entity, cold and dense and implacable. But he couldn't straighten up; his stomach was on fire. His eyes were tearing.

'You are political prisoners of the Revolutionary Armed Forces of Colombia. *Comprende?*'

'Yes,' Paul said, still on his knees, still gasping from the vicious blow to his solar plexus.

'You won't try to escape. *Comprende?*'

'Yes.' Paul gave it one more try, gathered himself in an effort to scale what seemed like a sheer wall of pain, and finally managed to make it to a barely standing position.

'You step away from the door when we come in the room. You step away from the door when we leave. You stay away from the windows. Yes?'

'Yes, we understand.'

'How are you feeling?' He was addressing Joanna.

'I'm nauseous.' Her voice shaky if even-toned, as if she were desperately trying to maintain some semblance of composure, but pretty much failing. 'I feel like throwing up.'

He nodded as if he'd expected this. *'Escopolamina,'* he said.

'What?' Joanna asked, breaking the don't-ask-questions rule, this time apparently without consequences.

'A street drug. They use it to rob the *turistas* here.' He shook his head and uttered a dismissive sigh, as if that kind of thing – robberies and such – was beneath him. 'We were late – she was frightened, huh.'

Galina, Paul thought. He was referring to Galina.

'She put something into our coffee,' Joanna stated flatly.

The man shrugged. 'You'll feel better tomorrow. Pretty much.'

He turned and walked to the door, then hesitated there as if waiting for someone to open it. He turned and stared at them with an expression of clear expectance.

What?

'Oh,' Paul said. He took Joanna's hand and led her to the opposite wall.

'Good,' he said, as if addressing children who'd cleaned their room just like they'd been told to.

He walked out, locked the door behind him.

THEY SPENT MOST OF THEIR TIME ALONE REMINISCING.

They took turns remembering all the things they liked about New York. Even things that, oddly, they hadn't liked before – holiday crowds, for instance. The swarm of visitors that executes a stranglehold on the city from Thanksgiving to Christmas, creating bottlenecks from Times Square to Houston Street. Paul had always found the human traffic jams annoying and suffocating, only now he remembered them as joyous and even soothing. The inescapable smell of garbage waiting to be picked up was an aroma to be missed and cherished. The obstacle course of construction cranes, pothole barriers, and squat Con Ed vans every New York taxi was forced to navigate on its way from one side of the city to the other was a loop-de-loop of urban excitement.

It was all a matter of perspective. And right now their perspective was skewed through a rat hole in Colombia.

They remembered places outside the city too. They retraced every single one of their vacations.

The rough-hewn cabin in Yosemite, where they'd gone when they were just dating but already moon-eyed. The Sea Crest Motel in Montauk that opened onto the whitest sand they'd ever seen. The ridiculously expensive but extravagantly lovely George V in Paris – honeymoon heaven.

They tried to reconstruct every great meal they'd ever eaten – Prudhommes to Pinks. Eclectic appetizers, bountiful entrées, sugary-sweet desserts.

They recounted their first meeting – two tired business travelers sharing the same gate. They theorized what the odds were of running into each other like that, of falling in love, of getting married.

They did all of this as a way to pass the time.

They talked about the past so they could avoid thinking about the future. There was an air of complete and utter unreality about this. Was this *really* happening to them – it couldn't be, could it? *Kidnapped?* Someone was going to yell *stop* and it was all going to end. It had to. It must.

Better to keep talking about the past.

ON WHAT MUST HAVE BEEN THEIR FOURTH DAY OF CAPTIVITY – IT was hard to keep count – Joanna said, 'Why do you think they told us not to go near the windows?'

Paul, who'd gradually descended into listlessness, barely managed a shrug.

'Because we must be where people could see us,' Joanna answered her own question. 'We must still be in Bogotá.'

'Okay.'

'We might be right on a street somewhere.'

Paul didn't like where this conversation was heading. Joanna had that *look,* the I'm-ready-to-tackle-something look. The one he'd seen when she was going up against an entrenched superior, a human resources transgressor, the very look she got when she'd decided that hell or high water, she was going to have a baby.

'There's just wood on the windows,' she said. 'We can pry it off.'

'With what?'

'I don't know. Our hands.'

'I don't think we ought to do that.'

'Really? What *ought* we to do, then? Sit around and do nothing?'

Yes, Paul thought. So far, they hadn't been told anything – why they were there, what was in store for them. The only thing that had actually been communicated to them was *not* to go near the windows. They'd been told *that.*

'Stay by the door and listen,' Joanna said. 'If you hear them coming, I'll stop.'

This was where he was supposed to volunteer for wood-prying duty. Or say *no* – it's too dangerous, forget it, let's just sit tight.

Joanna didn't appear ready to be talked out of it.

Okay, he'd give it a try. The wood looked pretty well nailed in. One good shake with no results would probably be enough to dissuade her, send her back to the mattress, where they could continue to reminisce about old times.

Paul said, 'I'll do it.'

Joanna took up sentry duty by the door. Paul moved the shutters back, revealing two solid planks of wood. He thought he could hear faint sounds of traffic out there.

He was able to grip one plank by its bottom. He pulled.

There was some give there.

You could see the wood wobble before snapping back into place. Joanna could *certainly* see it.

'I *told* you,' she whispered.

Paul gave it another strong pull. This time the wood gave even more. He'd opened it a good half inch.

Yes, there was definitely traffic out there. Fairly steady too – they had to be close to a major thoroughfare. Somewhere people were going about their perfectly ordinary lives, shopping, eating, heading to work, all within earshot of two kidnapped Americans.

Paul resumed with renewed vigor, gulping in sudden streams of sweet-smelling air. He developed a steady rhythm, pull, rest, pull, rest. Slowly, bit by bit, the wood yawned open; he could see a red slate tile – a courtyard?

Joanna crouched by the door, a bundle of nervous energy urging him on with her eyes.

Suddenly, the wood snapped – broke right in half. It sounded like a gunshot, *louder,* and Paul stood there with half a plank of wood in his hands, waiting for the door to burst open with armed guards.

Joanna stiffened – put her ear to the door. Paul held his breath and waited.

After what seemed an eternity, Joanna shook her head. Nothing.

Paul allowed himself to breathe again.

He took his first actual look out the window.

Yes, it was the courtyard, all right. There was an adobe wall around it, holding several lopsided pots of cacti. A lone wooden table sat in the center of the garden with no chairs around it. And there was something else. A way *in;* a simple wooden gate led to the outside. Paul stared at it. There was a girl in a school uniform staring back.

Paul barely managed to stop himself from yelling *help!*

They were stuck in the room; the window was maybe two by two, and that was with *all* the wood removed. It was anybody's guess if they'd be able to worm their way out.

Paul spoke to Joanna without turning away. He was afraid if he stopped looking at the girl, she'd disappear, like a mirage or a really good dream.

'There's someone out there.'

Joanna immediately abandoned her guard duty, ran to the window.

For a moment the three of them simply stared at each other, as if seeing who would blink first. The girl looked to be eleven or twelve years old, clutching schoolbooks that appeared too heavy for her, and staring wide-eyed at what must have been two desperate-looking Americans staring back.

'*Hola,*' Joanna said to the girl – somewhere between a whisper and normal conversation.

The girl didn't answer.

'*Hola!*' Joanna tried again. She stuck her hand through the window and waved, like a desperate wallflower hoping to be picked at the dance.

She remained on the sidelines. The girl continued to stare at them without offering the slightest response.

It was agonizing. They were staring possible rescue in the face, only that face was decidedly and maddeningly blank.

Paul racked his brain, trying to remember the Spanish word for *help,* but came up empty. Maybe *help* was universal. Maybe the girl took English at school. Maybe . . .

'*Help!*'

He didn't recognize his own voice. It sounded high-pitched and desperate. 'Help,' he said again. 'Please . . . help us . . .'

The girl cocked her head, took a step back.

'We're prisoners,' Paul continued, pushing both hands out the window, wrists together as if they were tied, in a kind of primitive pantomime.

It looked like a glimmer of understanding passed across the girl's face. Then she turned to her left, as if someone had called out to her. She looked back at them, smiled sweetly, walked off.

'*No!*' Paul shouted.

He'd forgotten where he was.

In a locked room. Under armed guard.

It was just a matter of time.

He heard them seconds later. The sound of boots running on tile, of a key being jammed into the door lock, of nervous, angry jabbering.

He desperately tried to put the plank of wood back in the window, to shove it into place and hope they wouldn't notice. Like a child trying to glue a smashed vase back together before his parents make it through the front door. It was useless.

The first man through was the one who'd laid out the rules for them. It obviously didn't escape his attention that they'd broken at least two of them. *Thou shalt not go near the windows. Thou shalt not attempt escape.* For a moment he simply stopped and stared at Paul, who was standing there holding the piece of shattered wood in his hand like a shield. It didn't provide much protection. The man made it over to Paul in three quick strides and smashed him across the face with the rifle butt. Paul's head snapped back and hit the wall. He tasted blood. The piece of wood clattered to the floor.

Paul could see Joanna's ashen face staring back at him. The man swung his rifle again, clipping Paul under the chin. He bit his tongue, tasted bits of broken tooth. He retreated against the wall, hiding his face behind both hands.

'Put them down,' the man said.

This was real power, Paul realized. There wasn't a need to force Paul's hands away; he was going to make Paul do it himself.

'*No,*' Joanna said. 'It's my fault. I *told* him to do it. Leave him alone. *Please.*'

'Put your hands down,' the man repeated.

'I said it's *my* fault.' Joanna tried to insinuate her body between Paul and his attacker. 'Hit me. *Me.*'

The man sighed, shook his head, gathered the neck of Joanna's dress in his fist, lifting her up off the ground.

'If you don't move your hands, I beat her. If you put them there again, I beat her worse.'

Paul dropped his hands.

TWELVE

Sometimes they were given newspapers.

They were allowed this small luxury by the powers-that-be. An *infinitesimal* luxury, since neither of them spoke Spanish. But things were coming back to Paul – dribs and drabs, words and phrases, sometimes entire sentences.

Anyway, it gave them something to do. Paul discovered you needed things to do to keep your mind off the unspoken question of the hour. *What was going to happen to them?*

The boy dropped off whichever newspapers their guards had discarded – mostly of the tabloid variety.

The back pages were filled with the local scores. After a while Paul understood that the front pages were too. It was as if Colombia were one big soccer match, both combatants going goal for goal, playing to the death. Guarding the left goal were their captors, FARC, and guarding the right one, the USDF, with the government ineffectually attempting to referee.

Kidnappings, bombings, and executions were how they kept score.

There was invariably a kidnapping story on the front page. A file picture of the snatched state senator, missing radio personality, or waylaid businessman. (The Breidbarts were conspicuously absent from the gallery of the gone.) There was generally an accompanying photo of the weeping wife, teary children, or somber family spokesperson.

The Spanish word for kidnapping was *secuestro*.

Bombings were only a little less frequent. For example: A ten-year-old boy named Orlando Ropero who liked soccer and *ventello* music was asked to deliver a bicycle by a teenager in the town of Fortul. He was given the equivalent of thirty-five cents as an inducement. When the bicycle and bicyclist, an excited and gratified Orlando, reached an intersection where two soldiers were stationed, he simply exploded. *Remote control,* said the papers.

Responsibility was placed at the doorstep directly to Paul's left. FARC. He decided to keep this particular article to himself.

Then there were the obligatory retaliatory bombings from the right: the paramilitary units of the United Self-Defense Forces, *self-defense* apparently consisting of killing as many people as possible with no particular regard for innocence. The generalissimo of this august organization for law and order was currently residing in a U.S. prison for drug smuggling.

Paul had read about Manuel Riojas in the States, of course.

Who *was* he exactly? Drug kingpin, legitimate politician, USDF commander, songwriter. He was one of those, two of those, or possibly all four. Certainly a songwriter. He'd reputedly written a number one hit for the Colombian songbird Evi, which had gotten some play in the States. A love song titled 'I Sing Only for You.' A title that took on ironic implications when she was discovered lying half dead on the floor of her penthouse apartment with her vocal cords surgically removed. Apparently, the lovers had experienced a falling-out. Evi had declined to press charges – *I don't remember,* she'd scrawled on a pad when she was asked to explain who'd done that to her.

Murder and torture were said to be Riojas' other vocations.

He was one of those people whose names were always followed

by the word *alleged*. It was *alleged*, for example, that he had his own zoo on one of his many haciendas, used to *allegedly* feed his rivals to the tigers. That he *allegedly* enjoyed dropping people from a Blackhawk helicopter into a pool of writhing piranhas. That he offered human sacrifices in bloody and bizarre rites of Santeria – that was *alleged* too. He was clearly the stuff of tabloids; the tabloids took full and voracious advantage.

Paul and Joanna passed the newspapers back and forth till the ink stained their hands and their eyes grew blurry.

ONE NIGHT JOANNA WOKE PAUL AND ASKED HIM TO LOOK IN ON the baby.

It took Paul a moment to understand that she was deluded.

That they weren't in the hotel room sleeping next to Joelle, but in a locked room with no air.

His face stung where the man had repeatedly smashed him with the rifle butt, a beating that had lasted at least five minutes and felt much longer. He'd lost at least one tooth; his lip was split open and still covered in dried blood. Afterward, they'd had to watch contritely from the center of the floor as two guards came in and hammered a new piece of wood back into place, muttering at them the whole time.

'Shhh,' Paul whispered to Joanna. 'You're sleeping.'

She opened her eyes.

'I thought I heard . . .' She began to cry. Soft, muffled sobs that seemed even more nakedly pitiable with no other sounds around to cloak them.

Paul put his arms around her. 'Please, Joanna. We'll get out of this. They're not going to kill us – they had their chance when they caught us at the window. We're going to get out of here. We're going to get Joelle back. I promise.'

He wondered if promising Joanna anything was a good idea. But

73

hope was the one commodity that hadn't been taken away from them. Not yet.

Then she did a strange thing. She stopped crying and disentangled herself from his arms. She put a finger to his lips.

'Listen,' she whispered.

'What? I don't hear anything,' he said. Only the sound of their breathing. Soft, regular, and strangely in sync.

'Listen,' she said again.

Then he heard it.

'It's the TV,' he said.

'Maybe it's real.'

'Probably not. No.'

'Listen, Paul. Listen. It's *her.*'

A baby crying.

Just like in Galina's house, only different than Galina's house.

'I know,' Joanna said. 'I just *know.*'

In Galina's house the sound of a baby crying had frightened them.

Here it had exactly the opposite effect.

She wrapped herself around him in the dark. She put her head on his chest, and both of them lay there and listened to the sound as if it were a beautiful rhapsody. As if it were their song.

IN THE MORNING THE MAN CAME BACK.

This time he wasn't alone.

Someone of evident importance was with him. Paul could tell from the way his attacker deferred to him. His role had changed; he was there to interpret now.

This became clear when the new man looked at Paul and Joanna and said something in Spanish.

'He asked you to sit down,' their original captor said.

Paul knew what the man had asked them to do. But he was still smarting from his previous beating. He thought it better to think

74

things over before committing to even the simplest action. The man had asked them to sit, fine – maybe it was better to make *sure* he wanted them to sit. Joanna had remained stationary for another reason, he knew. Sheer willfulness, courage in the face of fire.

The man motioned them to the two plastic chairs. Once upon a time those chairs must've sat in the courtyard, that heavenly vista they'd fleetingly glimpsed before it disappeared again behind newly nailed oak. Dirt was ingrained in the white plastic, the kind that accumulates after too many winters spent outdoors.

They sat.

The man in charge spoke to them in soft, measured tones. He focused mostly on Paul, maintaining eye contact between puffs of a thick pungent cigar sending blue plumes of smoke drifting gently up to the ceiling. Paul recognized the brand: the box on Galina's mantelpiece. He had a scraggly beard; his skin was pocked from childhood acne. He spoke entirely in Spanish, at a pace leisurely enough to allow his lieutenant – that's how Paul thought of him now – to translate his words into English.

'This is what you are going to do for us,' the man said.

And they finally learned why they were there.

THIRTEEN

There were three boxes of condoms on the table.

A French brand. *Cheval,* the boxes said, over the picture of a white stallion with fiery eyes and windswept mane.

An Indian woman wearing incongruous-looking bifocals was bent over the table, carefully stretching out the condoms one at a time. She was wearing black latex gloves and no top. Just a gray sports bra with a black Nike swoosh on it.

At the other end of the table, another woman wearing black latex gloves and sports bra was methodically chopping up blocks of white powder with a gleaming surgical scalpel. The lieutenant was leaning against the door, eyes fixed on the half-naked women like a man in love.

Paul was sitting against the wall, waiting.

They'd made him give himself two enemas spaced an hour apart. As he waited for the second one to take effect, he stared at the thirty-two bulging condoms already gathered in the middle of the table and tried not to feel sick.

He was reminded of one of those inane reality shows that had so recently swept the country. *Fear Factor* – wasn't that the one? Raw pig brains, bloody offal, cow intestines, laid out on a table before three or four greedy contestants. *Go ahead* – the smarmy host intoned every week – *whoever gets the most down wins.*

And didn't they dive in with unabashed gusto? Didn't they chow down to the last morsel, their eyes firmly on the prize? It helped Paul to think of them. They were his newfound role models. If they could do it, so could he.

After all, he wasn't striving for mere money here. The grand prize on this show was two lives.

His wife's and his daughter's.

Thirty-two condoms became thirty-three. The woman at the end of the table had just added to the pile.

He felt the familiar rumblings in his gut. He asked Arias – that was the lieutenant's name – if he could go to the bathroom.

Arias nodded and beckoned him forward. The women kept working without interruption, assembly line workers who hadn't yet heard the lunch whistle.

Arias opened the door and pushed him out. There was a bathroom just down the hall. Arias watched him as he went in and swung the door shut behind him.

The door didn't make it to the closed position.

Of course not. Arias' booted foot stopped it, just as it had stopped it the first time Paul ran to the bathroom.

The door swung back the other way as Paul sat down on the dirt-streaked toilet seat and tried not to notice Arias watching him. That was kind of hard. He closed his eyes and thought of his bathroom back home, where a dog-eared copy of *The Sporting News Baseball Stats* sat just to the right of the toilet. Not because he particularly liked baseball – he didn't. He liked *stats*. He visualized page 77 – Derek Jeter. Batting average, home runs, RBIs, stolen bases. Numbers *always* told a story, didn't they? It comforted him to think of numbers now. Numbers imposed order on the universe – you could lean on them, take comfort in them. They always added up.

For the second time in an hour, it felt as if every bit of his insides had come out of him. Then, with Arias still watching, he stood up and cleaned himself.

Back to the table. Where three more condoms had been added to the pile.

'*Sí,*' Arias said, staring at Paul and stopping the women in mid-motion. 'Start swallowing.'

THIS IS WHAT THE FARC COMMANDER HAD TOLD THEM.

'We are a revolutionary army. We are involved in a long struggle against oppression. We are in need of financing this struggle, so we must do whatever we can.'

Whatever we can turned out to be exporting pure Colombian cocaine to the eastern seaboard of the United States.

That's how he began, as if he were seeking some kind of approval from them. Explaining the distasteful nature of the drug trade as a kind of necessary evil. A means to an end.

When he paused, Paul nodded, even nervously smiled, bestowing a kind of absolution on him. Perhaps that's all he wanted, Paul thought, someone to take the message back to the world.

Yes, we smuggle drugs, but only to further the cause.

Of course, that was stupid. They weren't going to kidnap them to relay their apologies. Of course, Paul hoped otherwise. Up to the minute the man told Paul he'd be swallowing thirty-six condoms stuffed with two million dollars' worth of cocaine and bringing it to a house in Jersey City.

He would do that if he wanted to see his wife and new daughter alive again.

Then and only then did Paul understand the full enormity of their predicament.

Yet there were still things Paul didn't understand.

The man asked him who knew they were here in Colombia – not *everyone,* just the people who kept tabs on them, who'd be expecting them to return on a certain date. Paul told him. Starting with his boss – Ron Samuels, head actuary of the firm he'd called home for the past eleven years. His in-laws, of course, Matt and Barbara, who resided in Minnesota and were due to fly in bearing gifts for their first grandchild. Finally, John and Lisa, their next-door neighbors and best friends.

Paul was ordered to write them letters, pretty much the *same* letter, three times.

Things are taking a little longer than expected down here and it will be a few more weeks before we can return with our adopted daughter – that was the general theme. They made him add a part about there being no need to call, since they'd be running from place to place with little time to chat.

Paul thought, *they don't want anyone to know.* Not yet.

They'd forgotten something, hadn't they?

'Pablo checked you out of L'Esplanade,' Arias said. 'The reservation clerk thinks you changed hotels. That's all.'

So they hadn't.

No one would know they were missing.

Not for weeks.

They gave him three sheets of paper and a blue ballpoint pen that someone had virtually chewed the end off of. Paul wrote the letters with Arias hovering over his shoulder, evidently looking for any hidden messages, disguised cries for help.

When Paul finished, Arias read them out loud.

Later that afternoon, as Paul and Joanna sat on the mattress with their backs against the wall, Paul said, 'I think I know why they switched her.'

'What?'

He'd been thinking this through; he thought he understood now. 'Why they switched babies. Why they didn't just wait and take all three of us together.'

'Okay. Why?'

'Remember when Galina came back with the thermometer? You

79

said we hadn't been paranoid, that we were in a foreign country. *Paranoia* is a foreign country, Joanna.'

'I don't understand.'

'Galina took Joelle that day so we would come back and find her gone. So we'd call the police. There was no note – remember, *she* went into the bathroom and found it.'

'Why would they want us to call the police?'

'Because they wanted the police standing there when Galina walked back in.'

'That doesn't make any sense.'

'Sure it does. You're in the country of *paranoia* now, remember? Think like a citizen. They wanted us to cry wolf. They wanted to make us look crazy.'

'Why?'

'Because crazy people have no credibility. Crazy foreigners have even less.'

'I still don't –'

'First we called the police and insisted our baby was kidnapped. Only she wasn't kidnapped. Then we noticed we had the wrong daughter – so she *was*. Only, if we called the police a second time, we would have looked more deranged than before. They *wanted* us to know they'd taken her.'

Joanna seemed to contemplate this notion. 'Okay. What if we *hadn't* noticed? I did – you didn't.'

Paul shrugged. 'If we'd never noticed, they would've called and told us. *We've got your baby – come and get her or else.* Either way, we couldn't have gone to the police without looking like lunatics. Maybe it was a kind of insurance policy: if one of us got away, if they botched the kidnapping, if I'd refused to drink that coffee and never passed out. Who knows? Maybe they were always going to make that call. We were *early*, he said, remember? Galina was yelling at Pablo about something – maybe it was *that*, bringing us there before she was ready.'

'Okay,' Joanna said. 'Why us?'

'Why *not* us? They must pick people they feel no one will bother at customs. The last time I looked, I didn't *look* like a drug smuggler.'

Joanna said, 'You're not a drug smuggler.'

'Not yet.'

She turned to look at him as if to gauge his expression for degree of seriousness. 'You're going to do it?' she asked. It sounded more like a statement.

Paul looked back at his wife. Her face had changed, he thought. Four days of mostly not eating or sleeping had sharpened her cheekbones and dug craters under her eyes. Yet even now when she was hollow-eyed and terrified, he saw something etched there on her face, as if the last few days had removed everything extraneous and left the only thing that really mattered. He'd like to think it was *love*.

'Yes,' he said.

'They'll arrest you. You can spend twenty years in jail for smuggling drugs. You're not a criminal – they'll see right through you.'

Yes, he thought, everything she was saying was true.

'What other options do I have?'

Joanna had no answer. Or maybe she did. She leaned her head against his chest, somewhere in the vicinity of his heart.

Thump, thump, thump.

'What if they're lying? What if they're lying about letting us go?'

Paul had been waiting for that question, of course. He gave the only answer he could.

'What if they're not?'

FOURTEEN

He would have eighteen hours.

Three-quarters of one day. One thousand eighty minutes.

That's it.

In those eighteen hours, he would have to swallow thirty-six condoms filled with two million dollars' worth of pure, undiluted cocaine, take a plane to Kennedy Airport, and get to a house in Jersey City, where he'd be expected to deposit them onto a dirty Newark *Star-Ledger*.

If he made it to the house one minute after the eighteen hours allotted him, Joanna and Joelle would be killed.

If he made it to the house and only thirty-*five* condoms came out of him, Joanna and Joelle would be killed.

If he didn't get the condoms out in time and one of them dissolved inside his stomach, *he'd* be killed.

His heart would go into cardiac arrest, his body into toxic shock.

He'd begin salivating from the mouth and shaking uncontrollably. He'd be dead before anyone knew what was wrong with him.

This was carefully and painstakingly laid out for him by Arias. To get his attention, to have him maintain focus.

A kind of pep talk.

Of course, if he made it to the house in eighteen hours with all thirty-six condoms still inside him, a call would be placed to Arias.

Joanna and Joelle would be set free to join Paul in New York.

They had Arias' word on it, as a FARC revolutionary in good standing.

THE NIGHT BEFORE THEY HAD BROUGHT HIM TO THE CUTTING house where mestiza women in sports bras worked tirelessly on Colombia's number one export, they heard someone singing that plaintive lullaby just outside the door.

Joanna, who'd been trying to grab some sleep on the ripped and dirty mattress, immediately woke and lurched to a standing position. The lullaby continued, seeped through the door like the irresistible aroma of a longed-for food.

The door opened.

Joanna put her knuckles to her mouth in an effort to stifle a sob, but she was only half successful.

'Please,' she said. *'Please.'*

Galina. Standing there with Joelle nestled against her chest.

'Please . . . Galina . . .'

Galina entered the room as someone locked the door behind her.

She met Joanna in the middle of the room, gently placing Joelle into her already reaching arms. Paul believed that gentleness like that couldn't be faked. That Galina was someone who loved children even as she kidnapped their parents, a dichotomy he found hard to reconcile.

There was no such dichotomy with Joanna. She folded her daughter against her chest and silently wept.

Paul stood next to her with his arm around her shoulders, the circle made whole once again. He couldn't help looking outside the circle. At Galina. He wanted her to look *back* – he thought that might be hard for her to do. He was wrong.

She met his gaze with perfect equanimity.

She even smiled, as if she'd just taken Joelle for another walk around the block and was ready to resume her duties as übernurse.

'See,' Joanna said to Paul. She'd rolled up the left leg of Joelle's blue stretchie and was pointing at an amber beauty mark just below the knee. Right where she'd said it was.

'Joelle,' she whispered, and kissed her daughter's face. 'Can she stay with us tonight?' she asked Galina. 'Please?'

Galina nodded.

'Thank you,' Joanna said.

And Paul thought how quickly captives become so grateful for any kindness from their captors. *Please* and *thank you* to the people who've snatched you from the world and locked you away in an airless room.

Galina reached into the pocket of her loose black shift. She brought out a baby bottle already filled with thick yellowish formula, and two diapers.

Paul took the bottle from her; he couldn't help remembering that the last time he'd accepted liquid refreshments from her, they'd been laced with *escopolamina*.

Galina turned to leave.

Paul wouldn't let her go without some acknowledgment of what she'd done to them. Some declaration of responsibility, even if it was defiant or angry or unpleasant.

'How many people have you done this to, Galina?' he said.

Galina turned back. 'It isn't your country,' she said slowly. 'You don't understand.'

Before Paul could answer her, before he could tell her that *understanding* and *kidnapping* didn't belong in the same universe, much less the same sentence, she turned around and knocked twice on the door.

The boy opened it and let her out.

JOANNA UNDRESSED JOELLE.

She looked over every inch of her body for any bruises, scratches, or suspicious discolorations. Any evidence at all that they'd hurt her daughter. Apparently not. Paul could sense the joy Joanna was experiencing just to be touching Joelle again, feeling her heartbeat, stroking her hair.

'It's going to fall out, you know,' Joanna said softly.

'What?'

'Her hair. It comes in like this when they're born, then they lose it.' Joelle's hair was ink black and soft as angora.

'When does it grow back?' Paul asked, even as he wondered if they would be around to see that. He sensed that Joanna might be asking herself the same thing.

'Six months, I think,' she answered. 'Around that.'

There was something surreal about their conversation. As if they were having it back home in their apartment, two new parents just like any other new parents, wondering aloud at the miracle that's their daughter. As if the future stretched limitlessly ahead of them – preschool and kindergarten and grade school. Graduations, confirmations, and birthday celebrations. Girlfriends and boyfriends. Diaries and dance lessons.

Paul understood. They'd have this one night before he left. They'd treat it as normally as possible.

PAUL AND JOANNA SENSED THAT IT WAS MORNING WITHOUT actually knowing it. Their watches had been taken, the windows were boarded up tight. But their bodies had grown attuned to the different times of day, like blind people whose other senses compensate for lost sight. The morning *felt* different than the night.

This morning felt different than other mornings.

In a little while Paul would be leaving Joanna behind. He'd be leaving the country and leaving her *here*.

She'd fallen asleep with Joelle in her arms, and sometime later he'd fallen asleep with Joanna in his. When he opened his eyes, it took him several minutes to realize that Joanna was also awake – he could tell by her breathing, neither one evidently ready to face the other.

Not yet.

Then Joanna said, 'Good morning.'

'Back to you.'

His arms were numb from holding her all night, but he didn't dare move them. It might be the last time for a while. It might be the last time, period.

'At least they brought us Joelle,' she whispered. 'Maybe they're not so bad. They didn't have to do that.'

'They weren't being kind, Joanna,' he whispered back.

'No? Then why'd they do it?'

'To remind me, I think.'

'Of what?'

'What's at stake. What I'll lose if I don't get the drugs there – if I fuck up. I think they wanted to make her real again for me. That's all.'

Joanna pressed her back against him, as if trying to burrow right up inside of him.

'Paul,' she said slowly, 'if you get there and decide to tell someone, *do* it. I'll understand. Maybe they can be negotiated with. Maybe you can give them something in return.'

'Remember the pictures we saw on the airport wall – the deputy mayor of Medellín? They found his head two blocks from the car bomb. I think that's pretty much how they negotiate. I'm going to deliver the drugs and then they're going to make that call and they're going to let you go. You and Joelle.'

They lay there silently for a while.

Then she said:

'Sometimes I think we've been pretty unlucky. Sometimes I think just the opposite. We couldn't have a baby – that was tough, the toughest thing I've ever gone through. Before this. I mean who has to go through *this*? We're a newspaper story now, aren't we? But then, I've loved you. All this time I have. And I think you've loved

86

me too – despite everything, I do. And that's lucky, isn't it? So who knows.'

It was her good-bye to him.

Just in case.

He was trying to think of *his* good-bye. He was trying to string together the right words to convey the ravenous ache that was gnawing at his insides. He was trying to articulate hope. He was trying to compose himself; to say good-bye without breaking down. There was a shuffle outside the door.

Then it swung open and Arias was there.

FIFTEEN

Retardo.

One of the eight million Spanish words he still didn't know. Sometimes Spanish words sounded like English words. The trick was to consider their context.

The context here was the huge black departure board in El Dorado Airport. And the words and symbols that preceded it.

Flt#345 a JFK. Nueva York.

That gave him some useful and solid clues.

Only Paul was attempting to ignore those clues. He was being willfully ignorant, a detective on the take who has no intention of putting two and two together.

He'd swallowed the thirty-six condoms two hours ago in a house outside Bogotá.

He'd been driven to the airport by Pablo, the very man who'd greeted him here just over a week ago.

He'd made it through security and customs.

The flight was *retardo.*

Okay, boys and girls, his Spanish teacher, Mr Schulman, used to say. *Any guesses?*

There was another clue here – one that was practically impossible to ignore. His gate companions. They were groaning, muttering, shaking their heads at each other with that same-old, same-old look of resignation.

Paul got up from his chair. He walked over to the check-in desk. He could feel the condoms sitting inside him with every step. It felt as if he'd swallowed a basketball. A lethal jump shot from Kobe, ready to drop through the net and kill off a possible rally in its tracks.

'Excuse me,' Paul said to the winsome-looking Colombian woman behind the airline counter.

'Yes, sir?' she said. She had that *look* – the one you saw at return counters on the day after Christmas. Defensive fortifications being readied for the coming onslaught.

'Is everything okay with the flight?'

He knew that everything wasn't okay with the flight, of course.

If everything was okay with the flight, the word *retardo* wouldn't be up there on the departure board. His fellow travelers wouldn't be uttering collective groans of frustration. But until the woman confirmed this, he'd stay dumb. He'd stick to the timetable in his head – the one that had him arriving in JFK approximately four and a half hours from now, and arriving at that house in Jersey City two hours later.

'The flight's delayed, sir.'

Suddenly, the only thing that felt heavier than his stomach was his heart. It sank like a stone.

There was still one more question to ask.

'How *long*?'

'We don't know. We'll make an announcement when we know more, sir.'

Paul felt like making an announcement himself. I'm carrying thirty-six condoms filled with cocaine inside my stomach, and if I don't get them out of me soon, they'll dissolve and kill me.

Then Arias will kill my wife and daughter.

A Colombian policeman was standing between gates. He was

smoking and watching the legs and asses of every passing female – an equal opportunity leerer.

If you decide to tell someone, do it, Joanna had said. *I'll understand.*

What an easy thing to do. To talk. To tell.

He would unburden himself to the policeman, who'd stop scoping out the passing women and bring Paul to the nearest hospital, where they'd flush the drugs from his stomach. They'd take a report from him, including a full description of the kidnappers. They'd arrest Pablo and Galina.

How easy was that?

Only this was a Latin American country with an inflationary economy. Where everything was nominally expensive, but in actuality, cheap. Life, for instance. Life was cheap here. Joanna's was *dirt* cheap. If he opened his mouth, he was pretty sure he'd be closing hers forever.

The policeman threw the glowing butt of his cigarette onto the floor, where he ground it out with an impressive black boot.

And then walked away.

Paul sat.

Every fifteen minutes or so he got up and approached the check-in desk, where the Colombian woman he'd already talked to scattered for cover. She always seemed to find something to do, check the flight manifest or align the tickets into a neat little pile. He was getting on her nerves, an annoying suitor who refused to take no for an answer.

'We don't know anything yet,' she answered the second time he inquired when the plane would leave. He noticed she'd pretty much dropped the *sir*.

'I have to get to New York for an important meeting. I can't be late. Do you understand?'

Yes, she understood. But she didn't know anything, so if he would please take a seat again and wait for an announcement?

Fifteen minutes after waiting for an announcement that didn't come, he was back again. Then fifteen minutes after that.

'*Look,*' she said, 'I've already told you. We don't have a report yet.'

'Well, is the plane here? You can tell me if the plane's here, can't you?'

'If you'll just have a seat, I'll make an announcement when they tell us something.'

He didn't want a seat. He wanted answers. 'Who's *they?*'

'Excuse me?'

'Who's this mysterious *they?* The *they* that's going to tell you something?'

'Please sit down.'

'I'm just asking you a question. I'm trying to find out how long I'm going to be sitting here. I'd like a clue, a guess, *something*. Is that too much to ask?'

Paul realized that his voice was louder than normal. He sensed this because several tired passengers in the waiting room had looked up from their crossword puzzles and newspapers and magazines to stare at him. They looked half alarmed and half supportive. Maybe because he was only doing what they themselves wished they were – venting a growing anger – even if he was doing it in a way that offended decorum. They'd keep their distance and silently root him on. He remembered another passenger who'd once upon a time harangued a different airline employee for information. Long ago and far away.

The woman behind this counter – *Rosa,* her name tag said – offered no such support.

'I *told* you. When they *tell* me something, I'll make an announcement. Now, I have to ask you to –'

'Fine, I'll sit down. If you tell me who *they* are.'

She decided to simply ignore him. She went back to her busywork as if he'd already turned around and gone back to his seat.

Paul felt something rise up his esophagus. For just a moment, he thought that a condom must have burst inside his gut, that in one moment he'd be down on the floor, drowning in his own vomit. But it wasn't cocaine. It was *rage* – all the poison he'd built up over the last five days of captivity. Rage at Galina and Pablo and Arias and the man with the cigar – it all focused on this woman who was refusing to tell him if he'd get out of Colombia in time to save his wife and daughter.

'I asked you a fucking question,' Paul said. Or shouted. *'I'd like a fucking answer.'*

Everyone pretty much lost the supportive look. Their faces registered pure alarm. Rosa's included. She stepped back, as if he'd physically assaulted her.

'There is no reason to use that language,' she said sharply. 'You're being abusive, and I'll call the authorities if you don't . . .' Paul lost track of what she was saying. Mostly because he could see several people in blue uniforms hurrying to the scene of the commotion. He wasn't sure if they were airline employees or a Colombian SWAT team.

If the police arrest me, I won't make the flight. This is what immediately went through his brain. *The flight might be delayed and it might be taking off God knows when, but if they arrest me, I won't be on it.*

'I'm sorry,' Paul said. 'Forgive me. I'm just under pressure because of this meeting. I'm sorry. Really.'

The blue uniforms were airline people. Three men and one woman who'd surrounded the counter in an impressive display of support. Airline people tended to stick together these days, now that they were operating on the front lines.

'Is there a problem here?' one of the men addressed Rosa.

She hesitated, then shook her head. 'No, it's all right,' she said. 'Mr Breidbart's going back to his seat.'

Mr Breidbart went back to his seat.

The plane was already one hour late.

He had seventeen hours left.

SIXTEEN

They were showing a comedy with Reese Witherspoon. Paul knew it was a comedy because several passengers were laughing.

He was watching the movie too. He had no idea what it was about.

Something was wrong with his stomach – other than the obvious. When he touched it, it felt tight as a bongo drum. He could play 'Wipe Out' on it. He was increasingly nauseous.

I will not throw up, he told himself.

If he threw up the condoms, he'd have to swallow them again; it had been hard enough to get them down the first time. Each swallow had triggered a reflexive urge to vomit. How had he managed it exactly? By using various and only half-successful stratagems.

First he'd pictured Joanna and Joelle sitting in that room – focused on the end benefit. That worked only for a while. So he'd changed tack, imagined each condom as a kind of local delicacy – a strange-tasting delicacy, even a repulsive one, but one that as a politically correct visitor he felt honor-bound to try.

When that didn't work either, when he gagged and almost brought everything back up, he'd thought of them as individual doses of *medicine*. Something prescribed to save his life – his life and theirs.

Somehow he'd managed to get all thirty-six down.

The hard part was keeping them there.

The plane had taken off two hours behind schedule. In order to avoid an unexpected turbulence over the Caribbean, the pilot had climbed to thirty thousand feet. This would add time to the flight, the pilot explained, but *better late than bumpy,* he added in that neutral midwestern twang every pilot in the world seemed to speak with. He was amending the flight path with their comfort in mind.

Paul's comfort was in negative integers.

Negative numbers had always fascinated him. They were the dark side of the moon, the antimatter of the numerical universe that he called home. He was traveling through this universe now.

'Are you all right?' the man next to him asked. Evidently, he wasn't watching the Reese Witherspoon movie. He was watching Paul. Paul looked weird.

'Just a little nauseous,' Paul answered.

The man seemed to pull back. Somehow he'd increased the physical distance between them without actually moving. Paul understood – *nausea* was the last word you wanted to hear during a long flight. Next to *bomb,* of course.

One of his industry's standard jokes: *Did you hear about the actuary who brought a fake bomb onto a plane? He wanted to decrease the chances there'd be another bomb on the plane.*

Ha, ha.

'You want me to call the flight attendant?' the man asked warily.

'No. I'll be fine.' Paul could feel individual beads of sweat on his forehead. His stomach was rumbling like thunder before a deluge.

'Well, okay,' the man said. He didn't look like it was okay.

Paul tried to lose himself in the movie again. Reese was a lawyer or something. She kept saying cute things and smiled a lot.

He was going to throw up.

Paul stood and made his way to the business-class lavatory. Only it was occupied and someone else was waiting to use it. A mother holding her four-year-old boy by the hand. The boy was shuffling his feet and periodically grabbing at the crotch of his pants.

'He has to go,' the mother said apologetically.

Paul peered through the half-opened curtain leading to first class. No one was waiting at that lavatory. He went through the curtain toward the front of the plane.

'Excuse me, sir.'

A flight attendant had materialized out of nowhere. He was slim, young, but very determined-looking. Right now he was determined that Paul, a business-class passenger, not make it into the first-class lavatory.

'We like you to use the lavatory in your section,' he said.

'So would I. Only it's occupied. So –'

'If you'll just wait until the lavatory is available,' the man interrupted.

'I can't wait. I'm not feeling well.'

The first-class passengers were all looking at him. Paul could feel their eyes boring into his back. In the hierarchy of planedom, they were Brahmins and he was an Untouchable. This might have embarrassed him in his previous life. But in this life he was a drug smuggler about to upchuck his illicit cargo into the aisle, so he didn't care. He needed to get to that bathroom.

The flight attendant, whose name was Roland, was looking him over as if trying to ascertain if he was telling the truth. Was he really sick, or was he attempting to con his way into the glories of the first-class lavatory?

Paul didn't wait for him to decide. He moved forward, physically brushing past a defeated-looking Roland. He entered the bathroom and shut the door.

His nausea had reached a pretty much unendurable level.

He looked at himself in the mirror. His face was pasty and wet.

He closed his eyes.

He pictured Joanna shut in that airless room. Sitting on that filthy mattress. Alone. He wondered if she was praying for him, revisiting the faith of her youth, when she'd dutifully gone to confession every Sunday and renounced her girlish sins. He hoped so.

I will not throw up. He said this not just to himself, but to God. Okay, they weren't exactly on a first-name basis, but he was willing to give it a shot. He was ready to let bygones be bygones and become friends.

Don't let me throw up.

Rephrased now as an actual prayer, a plea from someone in need of a little godly intervention.

He took deep breaths. He splashed cold water onto his face. He clenched his hands into fists. He purposely avoided looking at the toilet, which seemed like a visual invitation to upchuck the drugs.

It worked.

He felt his nausea subsiding. He was still queasy, but he could actually imagine making it back to his seat without vomiting. Maybe there was something to this religious stuff, after all. Maybe even a jaded God had been moved to pity.

Someone knocked on the door.

'What's going on in there?'

Roland. Still sounding kind of indignant.

'I'm coming out,' Paul said.

'Fine.'

A minute later Paul opened the door and maneuvered past Roland, who smelled strongly of lavender. He made it back to his seat, where the man next to him eyed him suspiciously.

'Everything okay?' he asked.

Paul nodded. He turned onto his side and closed his eyes. He couldn't sleep, but he'd pretend to.

He had two hours left till customs.

THERE WAS A DOG AT THE BOTTOM OF THE ESCALATOR.

A German shepherd with a thick black harness around it.

Paul couldn't see who had hold of that harness, because the ceiling sloped to the angle of the escalator and restricted his vision.

It could be a blind person, he thought. A beggar with one of those white cups in his hand and a sign that said *I am blind. Please help me.*

Or it could be the other kind of person who would be holding a harnessed dog in an international airport. Waiting for a flight from Colombia.

He thought about turning around and heading back up against the flow. The escalator was packed – he'd never make it.

The escalator seemed to be moving at SLP speed, the slowest setting on your typical VCR. The person holding the dog was filling in by small increments, as if he were being drawn by a sketch artist in Washington Square Park.

First the shoes.

Black, sturdy, thick soles. Not necessarily a blind person's shoes, but not necessarily not.

Now the legs.

Thin and short and covered in dark blue.

Denim? Or the polyester weave favored by certain government agencies? It was hard to tell. The man's belt buckle rose into view, something substantial that seemed to serve some greater purpose than merely holding up his pants. The kind of buckle that made a statement.

The shirt began to materialize.

Paul was praying it would be a T-shirt.

Something that said *I Love New York.*

Or *My son-in-law went to Florida but all I got was THIS.* Really praying – like back in the first-class lavatory.

It was white and buttoned. There was some kind of badge on it.

A policeman. A customs man.

When Paul entered the last stage of the slowest escalator on earth, he saw he was right *and* wrong. It was a customs agent, all right, but

97

a woman. She had dyed-blond hair tied into a tight ponytail, ostensibly to keep it from getting into her diligently steely eyes.

It didn't really matter what sex she was. He was focusing on the dog.

A sniff dog – isn't that what they called them?

The officer and dog were set up just to the left of the escalator. Paul tried to edge closer to the right railing. The dog was sitting on his hind legs with his quivering black nose pointed straight into the air.

He was wondering. He believed these dogs were capable of sniffing out drugs inside gas tanks, plastic dolls, even concrete canisters. What about *people*? Through layers of intestines and fat and condoms and skin?

Seriously sweating skin. Skin that had broken out in a veritable rash of sweat that threatened to turn him into a walking dishrag.

He stepped off the escalator. He could sense the customs woman staring straight at him. He could only *sense* this, because he was trying not to look at her. He was trying instead to look bored, blasé, nonchalant – to look this way in a direction that wouldn't bring his gaze in the vicinity of hers.

She must've been wondering what might cause a passenger from Colombia to be sweating bullets. No, more like an actual fusillade.

Paul could actually hear the dog sniffing; it sounded like someone with a bad cold. His chest tightened into a single painful knot. There were three supposed warning signs of a heart attack – excessive sweating, chest pain, and numbness – and he currently had all three. Only his numbness was more of the mental variety. He was so scared he couldn't think.

And then he did a very strange thing.

He petted the dog.

The shepherd had begun emitting a series of nervous whines, and Paul was convinced that in one second the officer would be asking him to step out of the line and accompany her to a special room where she'd X-ray him and then arrest him for drug smuggling.

He was facing his fear head-on. The way his father had once advised him to do when a seven-year-old Paul had confided his terror of roller coasters in the middle of Hershey Park. His father put him on the cloud-scraping Evil Twister, where Paul had promptly thrown up all over him.

Maybe blatant hubris would actually work this time.

The dog went stock-still and stared up at him with an eerily focused expression. His ears flattened – his educated nose quivered.

It was the customs woman who actually *barked* at him.

'Sir!'

Everything stopped. Other passengers turned around to stare at him – a teen with backpack, a family of four lugging loot from Disneyland, an elderly couple attempting to catch up with the rest of their tour group. Another customs officer began walking over from further down the terminal.

'Sir!' the customs woman repeated.

'Yes?' Paul felt as if he'd left his own body. As if he were looking down on this ridiculous if horrifying confrontation, which could only end with Paul Breidbart being led away in handcuffs. And disgrace.

'Sir. Please refrain from petting the dog, sir.'

'What?'

'She's not a pet, sir. She's a working animal.'

'Yes, of course. Sorry.' He took his hand away – it was clearly shaking.

Paul turned and walked toward the sign that said *Baggage This Way*. He silently counted his steps, thinking if he made it to ten, he would have gotten away with it.

He made it to eleven.

Twelve.

Thirteen.

The dog hadn't smelled the cocaine. He was okay.

SEVENTEEN

He took a cab.

The driver was Indian and spoke only broken English. Still, he had no trouble conveying his joy at getting a fare that would make his day. All the way to New Jersey would be double rate.

He took the Grand Central Parkway to the Triborough Bridge, while Paul looked at his watch approximately every ten minutes. Like a distance runner in the New York City marathon – so much real estate traversed in so much time.

So far, he was more or less on pace.

You're doing fine, the cheerleader in his head kept urging him on. *You're doing fine.*

He was attempting to focus on the finish line. FARC's contacts in Jersey City would soon be clapping him on the back for a job well done and placing that call to Colombia. He'd be waiting by the gate the next day for Joanna and Joelle to disembark at Kennedy Airport to begin their new lives together.

Just an hour away.

Then the taxi slowed, crawled, stopped.

They were in a sudden bumper-to-bumper logjam, with no discernible movement up ahead.

Paul needed to get to a bathroom.

This feeling had been intensifying since he walked off the plane. At first just a slighter sense of fullness than he'd felt all day – exactly what you'd expect with thirty-six stuffed condoms sitting inside you. But then a growing and unmistakable need to void, every bit as ferocious as the need to vomit.

For the second time in a space of hours, Paul tried to will his body to listen up and desist. A simple case of mind over matter. His body, however, refused to pay attention; it was having none of it now. It had its own agenda, and it was demanding to be heard.

They hadn't moved an inch in five minutes.

The taxi driver was shaking his head and channel surfing through a sea of foreign-sounding radio stations. The resultant cacophony was harsh and physically grating. It was seriously hindering Paul's ability to concentrate on not going to the bathroom in the backseat of the taxi.

'Could you not do that?' he said.

'Eh?'

'The radio. Could you just pick one station?'

The taxi driver turned around as if he'd just been asked an astounding question. He peered at Paul through heavy-lidded eyes sunk into charcoal caverns of despair.

'What you say?'

'It's annoying,' Paul said. His stomach was beginning to seriously scream at him.

Find a bathroom. Any bathroom.

'*My* radio,' the taxi driver said.

'Yes, but –'

'*My* radio,' he repeated for emphasis. 'I play what I like. Okay.'

Okay. There was a boundary between taxi driver and passenger, and Paul had evidently crossed it.

His stomach was one unending cramp. Something was in there that desperately wanted to get out.

Hold it in.

The taxi driver honked his horn. He obviously meant it as a kind of protest, as opposed to something that might actually accomplish anything. It wasn't as if the cars directly in front of him could do something about it – they were as trapped as he was. He honked his horn again anyway – leaning on it this time, a long wail of frustration and anger.

The taxi driver seemed to enjoy letting off steam in this way. He smiled as if he'd told himself a good joke.

Until someone got out of the car in front of them – a Lincoln with a license plate that said *BGCHEZE*.

The man who walked over to the cabdriver's window seemed constrained by his own clothing, tight maroon sweatpants with a simple T-shirt that appeared more like a straitjacket.

He made a motion with his hand – *roll down the window.*

The taxi driver was in no mood to comply. He'd lost his smile, he was muttering in Indian.

'Roll down your fucking window,' the man said, now that his hand motions had gotten him nowhere.

The taxi driver now made a hand motion of his own. A wave of dismissal – *go away and leave me alone.*

The man didn't react well to this.

'Who you fucking waving at, huh? You like to blow your fucking horn at people? Open your window. I got something for you, you fuck!'

The taxi driver was not going to do that. No. He waved his hand at the man again and turned his head, banishing him from his presence.

'Hey, you fucking towel-head! You understand fucking English? You don't, do you? You don't understand a fucking word I'm saying. Here, I'll make it easy for you. *Roll. Down. Your. Goddamn. Window.*' He pounded the window on each word with a hand that appeared to be the size of Lower Manhattan.

The taxi driver had locked the doors. Paul realized this when the

102

man began pulling on the door handle and it didn't open. This only seemed to make him angrier.

He began kicking the driver's door.

Paul couldn't tell whether the man had noticed that there was a passenger in the backseat. Even if he had, Paul didn't think it would've deterred him.

'Open the fucking door, you pussy!' he was screaming at a now seriously alarmed-looking taxi driver. The taxi driver in fact seemed to be looking around for help – first left, then right, then finally, in-exorably, behind him.

'Maybe he'll just stop,' Paul said, staring into twin eyes of pure panic.

'He's goddamn crazy,' the taxi driver said.

Paul had to agree with him there. Two thoughts were racing through his brain. One: He was not going to be able to hold it in. Two: If the crazy man made it into his car, he was going to kill the taxi driver and Paul would not make it to Jersey City in time. Even if he *could* hold it in.

Paul rolled down his window.

'Look, could we just calm down?' he said to the man. His words sounded pained and filled with anguish – even to him.

His tone seemed to momentarily mollify the man. He looked at Paul as if he'd just come across an interesting artifact worthy of his attention.

'Tell him to open his door,' he said.

'Look, I'm sure he didn't mean to blow his horn. He was frus-trated. All this traffic. Can we just forget it?'

The man smiled at him. 'Sure,' he said.

Then he reached into Paul's window and pulled the door lock up. He pulled the door *open* – accomplishing this in a matter of sec-onds. Before Paul could actually react, the man yanked Paul out of the taxi by his arm.

Paul stumbled, almost fell.

'Hey, come on, stop this,' he said.

Somewhere between *stop* and *this,* the man's fist connected with his chin.

Paul fell straight back onto the pavement. *Smack.* That wasn't the worst part. No.

He'd just spent hours fighting to keep the drugs inside of him, battling with his own body over this unwelcome and unnatural intrusion.

In one humiliating moment, he lost.

EIGHTEEN

They found an Exxon station somewhere in the Bronx.

A Middle Eastern man pumping gas pointed to the back of the station when Paul asked for the bathroom.

Paul had made it back into the taxi in the middle of the Triborough Bridge, with the assistance of a middle-aged woman who'd magically materialized from a white minivan. He'd refused the woman's offer to obtain medical assistance. He'd told the taxi driver, who'd remained snugly in his front seat, that he wasn't interested in going to the police. No. Just 1346 Ganet Street in Jersey City.

First he'd needed a bathroom.

The taxi driver closed the plastic partition between driver and passenger as Paul sat half on his hip the entire way.

When he got into the stifling gas station bathroom – which wasn't so much a bathroom as a hole with toilet – he discovered pretty much what he'd expected.

Everything he'd swallowed back in Bogotá had come out. The condoms were still intact.

He dumped them into the filthy sink, washed them off with warm rusty water. He took off his pants and slathered them with the yellowish gunk that came out of the soap dispenser, then soaked them under the faucet. He cleaned himself up as best he could.

He wasn't going to swallow the condoms again. He couldn't. He would get to the house in Jersey City and tell them what happened – that they'd come out just a few miles from delivery.

He carefully placed the drugs in the overnight bag he'd dragged into the bathroom with him. He went back out to the taxi and crawled into the backseat. The driver had aired it out during his bathroom break. Both doors were wide open, both windows rolled down.

At least the driver didn't say anything to him. Paul had taken one on the chin for him.

His gratitude must have outweighed his disgust.

THIRTY MINUTES LATER THEY ENTERED JERSEY CITY.

Paul was looking on the bright side. Yes, there was a bright side. He'd made it *this* far. Consider the percentages.

He was blocks from delivering his cargo. From fulfilling his part of the bargain.

The taxi driver turned into an area festooned with Arabic signs. They passed a yellow mosque complete with gleaming minaret, an open-air market dripping with exotic-looking fruits and vegetables. They crawled past several women covered head-to-toe in black burkas, drifting down the street like shadows.

My name is Paul Breidbart. I have something you've been waiting for.

He pictured Joanna's face as she got off the plane. Still hollow-eyed and fatigued, but flush with gratitude and relief. She would have Joelle pressed to her chest. They would go home, where their best friends, John and Lisa, would've tied bright pink balloons to the doorknob of their apartment.

My name is Paul Breidbart. I've got something for you.

The taxi stopped. The driver was craning his neck, peering out the side window.

'Are we here?' Paul asked.

'Thirteen forty-six Ganet Street?' the driver said.

'Yes. Is this it?'

'This is Ganet Street,' he said.

'Good,' Paul said. They were in the middle of a block. A grocery, a drugstore, and two check-cashing places were situated on one side of the street. The other side looked residential, which must've been the side he was looking for.

Only something was wrong. The taxi driver was shaking his head and sighing.

'Thirteen forty-six?' he asked again.

'Yes.'

'It's not there,' he said.

'What?'

'It's gone.'

'I don't understand.'

'Look,' the taxi driver said. 'It's missing.'

NINETEEN

Morning.

Joanna could smell fried plantain and smoke. And the familiar musky odor of her baby. Her soft head was tucked under Joanna's chin as she guzzled the pale yellow formula provided by Galina.

Paul had left hours ago. Or was it days?

She'd tried to be brave about it. She'd tried to stay strong for Paul – he'd need it. When he left, when he actually departed from the room, it was as if hope had left with him.

This is what it feels like to be utterly alone, she thought.

And yet there was Joelle. So she wasn't.

Galina had come back soon after Paul left, and Joanna had latched onto her baby like she used to clutch her pocketbook in the face of a possible 84th Street mugger.

You will not take this from me.

And Galina hadn't.

'Would you like to feed her with me?' Galina asked.

'Yes.'

So they had. Side by side, like the young moms with their foreign nannies who congregated on the Central Park benches every morning. Only no swings, seesaws, or slides.

There was another difference, of course. This nanny had kidnapped them.

Joanna didn't bother mentioning that particular fact. She was trying to hold on to the moment. *Don't upset the applecart,* her mother used to say to her when she'd complain about something or other. Meaning be happy for what you have. Why? Because it can always get worse.

If you let me hold her and feed her and be with her, I'll say nothing about what you did to us.

This, admittedly, went against every fiber of Joanna's character. She was used to speaking her mind. But she couldn't take the risk of Joelle being snatched from her a second time.

Galina asked Joanna how she'd slept. She commented on how good an eater Joelle was. She demonstrated the proper way to burp her. Talking to Joanna as if they were still back in the Bogotá hotel room.

And Joanna nodded, answered back, even *conversed.*

'Where were you born, Galina?' Joanna asked after Joelle had been fed and gently rocked into a semblance of sleep.

'Frontino,' Galina answered. 'In Antioquia. North,' she added, realizing that Joanna wouldn't know one Colombian province from another. 'On an orchard farm. A long time ago.'

Joanna nodded. 'What was it like?'

Galina shrugged. 'We were poor. Campesinos. I was sent to school by the fathers.'

At the mention of religion Joanna recalled the black jacket and white collar you could glimpse through the confessional partition. The smell of mothballs, incense, and baby powder.

Joanna was intent on keeping the conversation going. Joelle was asleep, and any minute Galina might stand up and say *hand her over.* Besides, it was undeniably pleasant speaking with another human being.

There was another reason. Talking kept her from thinking.

Eighteen hours, they'd told Paul.

109

Galina reached over and gently and playfully caressed the spiky hair on Joelle's head.

It would be hard not to like a woman like this, Joanna thought. There must be two Galinas; this one you'd willingly hand your baby to.

'When did you come to Bogotá?'

'During the riots,' Galina said. 'When Gaitán was killed.' She explained to Joanna, described what Colombia was like in the 1940s. Jorge Gaitán was a man of the people – not lily-white the way the rest of the politicians were. Half Indian. The hope of campesinos like her father. Only he was gunned down by a madman. The country went crazy, dissolved into *La Violencia* that had never really ended.

Joanna listened, nodded, asked questions. She supposed she was not only interested in keeping the conversation flowing but interested in what Galina was saying. Maybe it would give her a clue.

You don't understand, Galina had said to Paul when he'd asked her how she could kidnap them. *It's not your country.*

Okay, Joanna thought, *help me understand.*

She reached for parallels from Hollywood. Colombia was like *West Side Story* – a movie she'd cried at as an eleven-year-old when she saw it on TV; the Jets versus the Sharks, with the bumbling and ineffectual Officer Krupke in the middle. Here it was leftists against rightists, with the government stuck in between.

Only there was no coming together in the end over death.

Just death.

She held Joelle even tighter within a soft rocking rhythm.

My baby, my own . . .

That song from *Dumbo* just flitting into her brain. Dumbo could fly away just using his enormous ears.

If an elephant could fly . . .

She tried to picture Paul on an airplane somewhere over the Atlantic. Or was he there already? How much time *had* passed since Paul departed?

110

She turned to Galina to ask her this question, but Galina was staring down at Joelle, seemingly lost in thought. Or was it memory?

'I had a daughter,' Galina said.

Joanna was about to ask what her name was, what she looked like, where she was. There'd been the undeniable use of past tense.

'What happened to her?' Joanna asked.

Galina stood up. She reached for Joelle.

When Joanna didn't hand her over, Galina said, 'I'll bring her back.'

Joanna had no choice; she handed her daughter to the woman who'd stolen her.

AFTER JOANNA HAD WOKEN THE NEXT MORNING, SHE PRESSED HER ear up against the rough slats that covered one of the windows. She was trying to expand her universe by feet, even inches.

She heard construction sounds – scattered hammering and a muffled rhythmic pounding. She pictured a pile driver, a steam shovel. Two dogs were barking. An airplane passed overhead. Someone bounced a basketball.

Then Galina stepped into the room. There was no baby with her. This time she was bearing something else.

News.

'Your husband,' she said in a flat, emotionless voice. 'He didn't deliver the coca.'

TWENTY

There was a charred, blackened, and still-smoldering hole approximately a third of the way up the left side of Ganet Street.

Paul finally figured out that this used to be 1346.

'It burned down,' a resident in a white skullcap explained to them.

'When?' Paul asked.

'Yesterday.'

Paul felt something in his stomach – pretty much the opposite of what he'd felt before. The torturous sense of fullness had been replaced by an equally torturous sense of nothingness.

Call it a black hole, sucking in every particle of hope.

'The people who lived there?' Paul asked. 'Do you know where they are?'

The man shrugged.

It turned out that no one really knew where they were. No one really knew *who* they were either.

'Freakin' Ricans,' said a white man holding a beer can half submerged in a brown paper bag.

'Foreign people,' said another man, who appeared to be from Eastern Europe and spoke only a halting English.

The foreign people had kept to themselves. They'd been there only six months or so. They didn't mix much. There were two or three of them, depending on whom you asked. Men.

'No one died, though? In the fire?'

Apparently not. The firemen, at least, hadn't discovered any bodies.

By this time the taxi driver was growing impatient. He'd made his double fare, and he was anxious to get back.

'Keep the meter running,' Paul said.

'You okay?' the taxi driver asked him. He must've noticed Paul's ghostly reflection in the rearview mirror.

They crawled up Ganet Street and found a diner. Through the window Paul could see an empty phone booth in the back. He had left his cell phone at home.

They'd given him a number. Just in case.

He'd explain. *I have your drugs here, all thirty-six condoms. I just need someone to give it to.*

Paul told the driver to wait.

'Sure. Give me the money you owe me.'

Paul pulled $165 out of his wallet and handed it through the partition. The guerrillas had returned his cash and traveler's checks largely untouched.

Do you think we're bandidos?

No. Just kidnappers and murderers.

When Paul entered the diner, he heard the unmistakable sound of peeling tires. When he spun around, all he could see was a thin cloud of blue exhaust where the taxi should've been.

He used his phone card. After a minute listening to the series of dull clicks, the phone rang, but no one answered. One ring, two rings, three rings, four. Paul let it ring for approximately five minutes. They were like dog minutes – each minute the emotional equivalent of a week.

He hung up and tried again.

Still no answer.

He felt feverish.

He walked back to 1346. He searched each passing face for signs of recognition, but they moved past like speeding drivers.

He planted himself in front of the burned-out house, where thin, needlelike cinders were still suspended in the thick, humid air.

They must've been expecting him, he thought. Someone would come back for the drugs.

He stood there for a kind of eternity. People walked back and forth, in front of him, behind him. No one stopped to speak with him. No one asked him what was in the overnight bag.

Then someone did come up to him.

A kid, even though he didn't look much like a kid.

When he ambled across the street and sort of shuffled over to Paul, he thought that maybe this kid had been standing across the street for a long time. He looked familiar.

'Pssst,' the kid said.

'Yes?' Paul asked. He felt a first glimmer of hope.

'I know why you're here, chief.' He looked to be the right nationality – Latino anyway.

'You do?'

'Sure, Holmes.' The kid looked left, looked right, then motioned to Paul to follow him. 'Just waiting for the all-clear.'

'I saw the building had burned down. I didn't know what to do,' Paul whispered, half a step behind him. The kid had turned the corner and was headed down a side street guarded by row houses all painted various uninspiring shades of brown.

'Uh-huh,' the kid said.

'I thought I'd wait till you found me.'

'Good thinking, chief.'

Halfway down the block, the kid turned toward an alley between two houses. They ended up in a backyard paved with cracked and spray-painted cement. Two empty windows with no shades stared at them from the back of the house.

'Let's see what you got in the bag for me,' the kid said.

They'd found him. He was going to make it, after all.

It took just two seconds after Paul had opened the bag to realize he was dead wrong.

It was the kid's expression. He'd looked in the bag and seemed, well . . . disappointed.

'What the fuck is *this*?' he said.

'This is . . . ,' Paul started to explain, then stopped.

'*Money*, Holmes,' the kid said. 'You scorin' or not?'

Not. It made perfect sense that the street where some Colombian drug dealers had been waiting for their cocaine might be a street where other drug dealers waited to sell it. He'd stumbled across one of them.

'No,' Paul said. He started to zip up his bag.

The zipper didn't make it to the closed position; the kid grabbed his arm.

'Wait a minute, Holmes.'

It was like showing meat to a dog.

The kid had recovered from the disappointment. He was starting to realize what it was that he *had* seen.

'Where's the fire?'

'I've got to go. I thought you were someone else, okay?'

'What's wrong with *me*?'

'Look, it's not mine. I need to give this to someone.' Paul was tugging at the bag, but it wasn't budging.

'*I'm* someone, chief.'

'Look, this belongs to some dangerous people, understand? They're going to be mad if they don't get this.'

There was someone else who was dangerous here. The kid had lost the easy demeanor of a salesman. His eyes had gone stone-cold; he'd tightened his grip on the bag.

'Tell you what,' the kid said. 'Let go.'

'No,' Paul said, surprising even himself. The old Paul would have spun the numbers, calculated the risks. He would've let go of the bag.

Not today.

If he lost the bag, it was over.

The kid reached into his pocket for something. Paul saw the dull gleam of metal.

'Look, boss, you want to let go of the bag, okay? You don't want me to hurt you any, right?'

'I can't let you have it,' Paul said.

'You ain't letting me have it. I'm taking it from you.'

Paul didn't let go.

He hardly saw the kid's hand move. It didn't seem possible a hand could launch itself into Paul's left cheekbone *and* make it back to the side of his body all in the blink of a swollen eye. Paul felt as if he'd been hit by a high inside fastball – something that had happened twice in Little League, leaving a slight crack still detectable in X-rays of his orbital lobe.

Surprisingly, he didn't go down. He tottered, teetered, wobbled. Then he did something even more surprising.

He swung back.

The kid had loosened his grip – maybe it was hard to wallop someone with one hand and hold something with the other. Paul wrenched the bag clear away from him, then swung it forward in the general direction of the kid's head.

SMACK.

The kid went down. Hard. Hard enough to bang the side of his face on the cracked cement and look up at Paul with a hint of incredulity, if not outright fear.

Paul stared back.

Maybe it was Paul's expression – he had his game face on. A face that said *come on, just try it again. Just try.* Or maybe, and more likely, it was the police cruiser that slowly drifted into view between the two houses.

Whatever it was, the kid got up and ran.

TWENTY-ONE

Miles answered on the third ring.

'Hello?'

'Miles?'

'Yes?'

'This is Paul. Paul Breidbart.'

Paul was back at the diner. He'd tried the number in Colombia again. Six times. No answer. He could think of just one other person to call.

'Paul?' It seemed to take his lawyer a long time to flip through the Rolodex in his mind and actually place him. 'Well, how the hell are you? Are you and, uh . . . Joanna back?'

Paul wondered if he'd needed a real Rolodex to come up with his wife's name. He guessed, probably.

'No. Yes. *I* am.'

'You are? She's *not*?'

'I'm in trouble, Miles.'

'What's the problem? Everything okay with the baby?'

'Can I come see you?'

'Of course. Call the office tomorrow and make an appointment with –'

'I need to see you now,' Paul cut him off.

'*Now?* I was just on my way home.'

'It's an emergency.'

'This can't wait till regular office hours?'

'No. It can't wait for regular office hours.'

'Well . . . okay,' Miles said after a moment's hesitation. 'It *is* an emergency, right, Paul?'

'Yeah. It's an emergency.'

'You'll have to meet me at my house. You got a pen handy?'

'I'll remember.'

He gave him a street address in Brooklyn.

PAUL USED A LOCAL CAR SERVICE WHOSE NUMBER WAS POSTED ON A crowded bulletin board in the diner's stinking vestibule.

Jersey Joe's Limos.

Stuck between *Stanley Franks Psychotherapy* and *Wendy Whoppers Body Work – In Call and Out Call.*

Paul could've used a session with both.

He needed a limo more.

Although Jersey Joe's Limos apparently didn't have limousines. Ten minutes after he'd called, a forest-green Sable pulled up to the diner and honked its horn twice.

The grossly overweight driver offered to put Paul's bag in his trunk. Paul gripped the handle straps tighter and declined.

He wondered how much time he had. Had he been afforded an extension of sorts? When Arias called that house in Jersey City, no one would answer. There'd be no ring because there'd be no phone. Maybe they'd know something was wrong – they'd take that into consideration. They'd restrain themselves.

They were coming off the ramp of the Williamsburg Bridge, and some very strange-looking people were coming into view. At least strangely dressed. It was summer, but the men wore enormous fur hats and long black jackets. The women wore even more.

118

He hadn't connected the address Miles had given him to Williamsburg, bastion of Orthodox Judaism. Clearly, that's where they were.

At every traffic light, sweating, bearded faces stared at him through the windows.

Miles' home was a handsome brownstone neatly festooned with pots of scarlet geraniums.

Paul paid the driver, then lugged his black bag out of the car, like your friendly neighborhood drug dealer.

He walked up the brownstone steps and rang the buzzer.

The door was opened by a stout, smiling woman who would've been pleasant-looking if it weren't for the thick black wig that sat on her head like a helmet.

'Mr Breidbart?' she asked.

'Yes.'

The woman introduced herself as Mrs Goldstein and led him into a wood-paneled study.

'He'll just be a minute,' she said. 'Please sit down.'

Paul chose one of the leather chairs facing a desk buried in an avalanche of paper.

After Mrs Goldstein had left, he wondered about the wig.

Cancer?

A sudden image of his mother came back to him, meticulously placing someone else's hair onto her head before the dresser mirror.

Paul gazed at the crowded bookshelves that lined two sides of the den, where books and pictures fought for space. Most of the photographs were of Miles. Shaking hands, posing with various Latin American kids. There was a picture of Miles and María Consuelo standing together in front of the Santa Regina Orphanage. There were several framed citations haphazardly mounted on the wall. *Latin American Parents Association Man of the Year.* Sitting just below an honorary degree from a law school and a certificate of service from a local hospital.

When a man entered the room and turned around to shut the

door, Paul almost asked him when the man in the pictures would be coming down.

But it *was* the man in the pictures.

In disguise.

Miles was wearing a black felt yarmulke. He was in the process of detaching a small black object resembling a box from his naked forearm, unwrapping a tangle of crisscrossing leather straps. He was wearing a jet-black jacket that fell all the way down to his knees, looking very much like someone who'd wandered out of a *Matrix* movie.

'They're called tefillin,' Miles said after he'd shaken Paul's hand and sat down behind his desk. He'd added the strange black box with trailing straps to the rest of the clutter on his desk, where it lay like some exotic sea creature, an inky octopus maybe, now dead. 'They're kind of indispensable to morning prayer.'

'It's afternoon.'

'Yeah. I'm playing catch-up.'

'You're an Orthodox Jew?' Paul asked.

'Hey – you're *good*.' Miles smiled when he said it.

'You didn't dress like this at the office. I didn't know.'

'Of course not, why would you?' Miles said. 'Anyway, I'm *modern* Orthodox. And I'm kind of unorthodox about my orthodoxy. Wearing nonsectarian attire is a necessary accommodation I make for my career – it might frighten off the clients. Wearing a yarmulke at home is a necessary accommodation I make for my religion – if I didn't, God might get angry. Got it?'

Yes, Paul got it.

He was eager to get off the subject of Judaism and onto the subject of his kidnapped wife and daughter.

'So,' Miles said, 'you're here. Welcome back. What's the problem?'

'The *problem?*' Paul repeated it, maybe because it was such a hopeful word – problems could be faced and surmounted, couldn't they?

120

'Bogotá,' Paul said flatly. 'It wasn't safer than Zurich.'

'What?'

'I'm in trouble,' Paul said. 'Help me.'

PAUL WAS SIPPING A CUP OF GREEN HERBAL TEA GENEROUSLY provided by Mrs Goldstein.

Good for the nerves, Miles said.

Miles' nerves were evidently okay – he'd declined a proffered cup and was instead sitting at the desk with his hands clasped against his forehead.

He'd pretty much reacted the way a concerned lawyer should at the news that his clients had been kidnapped, with one of them still in Colombia and the other forced to smuggle drugs past U.S. Customs. Maybe more so. His face had dropped, become a puddle of concern, anger, and empathy.

He'd come out from behind the desk and clasped Paul around the shoulders.

'My God, Paul. I'm so sorry.'

Paul allowed himself to be comforted, to soak it in like a parched sponge. Up till now, the only person who'd felt sorry for him was him. Miles wanted details.

'Tell me what happened – exactly what happened.'

He told Miles about the afternoon they came back to the hotel and discovered their baby gone. About the next day, when Joanna had matter-of-factly stated that she was certain that the baby sleeping next to them wasn't Joelle. About the trip to Galina's, the cries coming from the back of the house, followed by Pablo's sudden brutality.

The boarded-up room. Arias. The man with the cigar. The burned-out house. Paul continued right up to the moment the taxi stranded him in Jersey City.

Miles listened intently, made a few notes on a yellow legal pad that magically appeared from the clutter on his desk.

121

'Pablo?' Miles asked him. 'This man was your driver?'

'Yes.'

'Uh-huh. And he was contracted through Santa Regina?'

'Yes. Why? Do you think Santa Regina had anything to do with this?'

'Not a chance. I've known María Consuelo for years. The woman's a saint.'

Paul peeked at his watch. 'They said eighteen hours. That's two hours from now.'

'Okay. Let's think about this logically.'

Paul was going to say that was easier said than done. That it wasn't *Miles'* wife and child in the line of fire. That time was running out. He remained quiet.

'Look, I know it looks pretty bleak, but we've still got something they want,' Miles said. He peered at the black bag on Paul's lap. 'In there, huh?'

Paul nodded.

'Maybe we should lock that up in my safe. I have kids running around.'

'Okay.'

Miles walked around to Paul's side of the desk. He unzipped the bag and looked inside.

He whistled. 'I'm no expert on narcotics, but that looks like a lot of stuff.'

'Two million dollars.'

'I'd say that constitutes *a lot.*'

Miles zipped the bag closed, then tentatively picked it up, holding it at arm's length the way dog walkers carry their pets' droppings to the trash can. He opened a liquor cabinet that wasn't; there was a stainless-steel safe inside.

After he'd locked the bag in, he settled back behind the desk. 'If you don't mind me asking, how did you manage to swallow all that?'

Paul was going to say that it's amazing how much you can swallow when your wife's life depends on it. You can swallow thirty-six condoms and your own fear and disgust.

'I don't know. I had to.'

'Yeah, guess you did,' Miles said. 'Okay, where were we?'

'The drugs. The something they want.'

'Right, the drugs. They're not going to do anything to your wife until they know where it is. Doesn't that make sense?'

Paul nodded.

'Of course it does,' Miles continued. 'That's *two million dollars*. Besides, I believe FARC's been known to hold hostages a long time. Years, even.'

Miles offered that particular fact as a palliative. It had the opposite effect; it made Paul sick to his stomach.

Years.

Miles noticed. 'Look, I was just making a point. They may have told you eighteen hours. I don't think they meant it.'

'How do you know?'

'Call it an educated guess.'

Okay, Miles was saying, you have more time. It's like those threatening past-due bills you get in the mail – they're just trying to scare you.

But Paul *did* feel sick to his stomach – in addition to feeling sweaty, filthy, and physically exhausted. He closed his eyes, rubbed his throbbing forehead with a hand that still smelled of gas station soap.

'You okay?' Miles said with evident concern. 'I mean *relatively*? Look, I need you to stay with me. We'll work this out, we'll find a way – but I *need* you, okay?' He looked down at his scribbled-on pad. 'Let's review our options.'

Paul wasn't aware that they had any.

'One – we go to the authorities.' Miles seemed to contemplate this notion for a moment; he shook his head. 'Uh-uh. Your first instincts were probably dead-on. I mean, which authorities exactly would we go to? The NYPD? The State Department? The Colombian government? They haven't been able to free their *own* people. Never mind a foreigner. Plus, if FARC finds out we've got people looking for Joanna and the baby, she becomes a liability to them. Then they might do something to her. And there's something else. You did smuggle drugs into the United States – *a lot* of drugs. Under duress, sure, the worst kind of pressure, but we're still talking narcotics trafficking, a federal offense. Okay, we don't go to the authorities. Agreed?'

Paul said, 'Yes.' He was enormously heartened by Miles' use of the *we* word. It made him feel a little less alone in the universe.

Miles held up a second finger. 'Two. We could do nothing. We could sit and wait for them to contact you.' He shook his head again. 'Not so smart. How do we even know they know *how* to get in touch with you? Odds are, they don't and who says your wife told them? Okay, scrap that. We can't sit on our hands. Now . . .' He held up a third finger, leaned slightly forward. 'Three. We can contact them ourselves. We can tell them we've still got their drugs. All we're looking for is someone to give it to. *We give you the drugs, you let Joanna and the baby go.* No Joanna and baby – no drugs. Drugs equal money, lots of money. They'll want the money.'

Okay, Paul thought, it sounded like an actual plan.

Perfectly logical, simple, even *hopeful.* Except . . .

'How are you going to contact them? They're not answering that number. I've tried.'

'The driver,' Miles said, snapping his finger. 'Pablo. I'll call Santa Regina. María must have his number somewhere.' Miles opened his desk drawer and pulled out a small phone book. 'Let's see . . .' He scanned down one page, then flipped to the next. 'Consuelo . . . Consuelo . . . here we are.'

He picked up his phone, punched in a number.

Some people chat on the telephone as if the person they're speaking to is right next to them in the room. Miles was like that. When he said hello to María, he grinned, smiled, shook his head, as if she were sitting there right in front of him.

Fine, Miles said, *and you?*

Yes, growing up. And how are yours?

That's wonderful – I'd love to see a picture . . .

They continued in this vein for a minute or two, small pleasantries, polite inquiries, general catching up.

'María,' Miles said, 'I wonder if you could give me the number of a taxi driver – Pablo. I'm not sure what his last name is . . . Yes, that's right. I'm thinking of using him for another couple . . . Really? Oh great.'

Miles gave Paul the thumbs-up. He waited, flipping a pencil back and forth between two fingers.

'Ahhh . . .' He scribbled something down. 'Thank you, María . . . Of course. Talk to you soon.' He hung up the phone.

'Okay.' He looked up at Paul. 'We have the number. Now . . .' He looked down at the pad and dialed again.

This time there were no hellos, no pleasantries exchanged, no small talk. That was because there was no talk at all. Miles waited, flipped the pencil, looked at his watch, stared around the room. Then he shrugged his shoulders, hung up the phone, and tried again.

Same result.

'Okay,' Miles said, 'no one's home.' He put the phone down. 'I'll try again later.'

Paul nodded. The question was, how much of *later* did they have?

'Look,' Miles said, 'I've been thinking about this. You probably shouldn't go home. Not yet. They didn't want anyone knowing you're back, correct?'

'Yes.' He'd been lifted up, borne along by Miles' optimism, but now that they'd failed to connect with anyone, he felt his spirits plummeting.

'Let's keep it that way, shall we? At least for the time being. You can stay here. Until we get through to them. That all right with you?'

Paul nodded again, willing to be reduced to childlike obedience.

125

If Miles were recommending he stay here, he'd stay. *Yes, sir.* He was drained, dog-tired, in dire need of a pillow.

Miles made some explanation to his wife – Paul heard him whispering in the next room. Then he led Paul upstairs, past his children's room, where two boys with remote controls in their hands looked up from their Nintendo.

There was a small guest room at the end of the hall.

Miles clicked on the light.

'Make yourself comfortable. If you want to take a shower, the bathroom's down the hall. There's pillows in the closet.'

Paul said, 'Thanks.' He *did* need to take a shower, remembering what had transpired in the middle of the Triborough Bridge. But he didn't have the energy.

Miles turned to leave, took a few steps, then turned back. 'I'll keep trying the number. If we don't get him today, we'll get him tomorrow. We're going to save them, okay? Joanna and the baby, both of them. We'll do everything we can.'

It was as good a good-night prayer as Paul could hope for.

He took off his shoes and socks and lay down on the bed without bothering to get a pillow.

PAUL WOKE UP IN THE MIDDLE OF THE NIGHT. HIS WATCH SAID 3:14.

There was that moment when he wasn't aware where he was, or even what had happened to him. When it was still possible Joanna lay next to him in bed and in the next room lay Joelle, softly sucking on her pacifier.

Then reality intruded. He knew where he was. He knew *why*. Understood that eighteen hours had come and gone and his wife either was or wasn't alive. He shut his eyes and dug his head into the mattress in an effort to get back to sleep.

He couldn't.

He felt suddenly wide-awake, infused with the energy of the seriously panicked. He turned one way, then another. He got a pillow

126

from the closet; lay back and closed his eyes again. No dice. His mind couldn't stop racing.

Hello, Arias, nice to see you. How've you been?

Buenas noches, Pablo.

Galina, good to see you again.

He pictured Joanna too, locked up in that room. His wife, his warrior princess.

After an hour he gave up.

It was dead quiet, the time of the night when it seemed he might be the only one on earth.

Don't be silly. The darkness can't hurt you, his father used to say to him as he lay shivering under the covers.

Hard to believe that was true. After all, Paul had been assured that other things wouldn't hurt him, only to find out differently. Cancer, for instance, which he'd been told was nothing much, even though it had already reduced his mom to the human skeleton he'd discovered lying on her bed, before it killed her just three days past his eleventh birthday. His father was distant, and not home much. His mom was the nurturer in the family. He'd resorted to serious and constant prayer on her behalf. When she succumbed anyway, when the family priest fastened onto his hand as his mom – not his mom, her *body* – was brought down the stairs draped in a white sheet, he'd secretly renounced his belief in a higher deity. He'd embraced the cool logic of numbers. He'd carefully constructed a universe of structure and compliance. Where probabilities and ratios were your friends. Where you could statistically calibrate the odds of bad things happening to you, then take comfort in them.

It wasn't by chance that he'd gravitated to a career whose sole purpose was controlling risk.

In actuary-speak: *reducing the likelihood of undesirable events.*

His risk management skills seemed to be lacking these days.

He rolled out of bed and stood on his bare feet. The wooden floor felt cool and ancient. There was no television in the room, no radio.

He needed a diversion, something to keep his mind off things. Something to read.

He tiptoed down the staircase, but it still protested with creaks and groans. Having no idea where the hall lights were, he had to feel his way along from banister to wall.

He finally made it into Miles' office, where after some fumbling around he discovered the light switch just inside the door.

Click.

He shuffled over to the bookshelves. Okay, light reading was in order here. He seemed to be out of luck. The shelves contained the kind of books you might expect in the office of a lawyer. Law books, a veritable glut of them: thick, leather-bound, and singularly uninviting. There were a few other books there but nothing that looked particularly enticing. A Jewish Bible with a cracked, peeling binding. The *Kabbalah* – whatever that was. A biography of David Ben-Gurion. A wafer-thin volume titled *The Story of Ruth.*

It won by default.

He could use a good story. The story of *anything*. But when he pulled it out, not without some difficulty since it was wedged between *New York Estate Statutes* and *Principles of Trial Law,* a stack of papers fell out.

Paul reached down to scoop them up.

Letters, old ones by the look of them. Sickly yellow to off-white.

Dear Dad, Daddy, Pop, Father, the first letter began.

One of the video-game players from upstairs. Writing from summer camp maybe?

He felt like a voyeur, an intruder into the Goldstein family history. It made him think of his own family – or lack of one.

He felt a sudden and overwhelming sadness, mixed in with something he clearly recognized as jealousy. Miles was lucky. He had a wife who wasn't sitting in Colombia under armed guard. Two children who dutifully wrote him from camp, delighting in using every existing term for *father.*

Paul would've been happy with one.

128

Dear Dad, Daddy, Pop, Father: Remember when you took me to the zoo and you left me there?

Miles had taken his boys to camp and one of them was registering his unhappiness. Reminding his dad of another time he'd been taken somewhere and left behind. Momentarily separated in the crowd of monkey watchers while Miles went off to purchase some cotton candy. Paul was creating his own version of the Goldstein family history – what familyless people do to pass the time.

He might've continued in this inventive mode if it weren't for a sudden sharp sound at the door. One of Miles' boys, standing there in blue pajamas rubbing his half-open eyes against the glare. He looked about fourteen, Paul thought – that gangly, awkward age between childhood and teen. The boy's legs were too long for his body; the faintest fuzz covered his upper lip like a lipstick stain.

'I heard someone on the stairs,' the boy said.

If Paul had felt voyeuristic before, he now felt embarrassed. Caught red-handed reading personal letters between son and father. As if it were perfectly okay, as if he had the right to.

'I pulled the book out, and they fell out,' Paul said lamely.

The boy shrugged.

Paul slipped them back into the book, wedged it back onto the shelf.

'Well,' Paul said, 'back to sleep.'

The boy nodded and turned as Paul shut the light and followed him out. They trudged up the stairs together.

'Did you go to summer camp?' Paul asked him.

'Huh?' The boy was still half asleep.

'Summer camp? When you were younger?' Paul said.

'Uh-huh,' the boy answered sleepily. 'Camp Beth-Shemel in the Catskills. It sucked.'

'Yeah,' Paul said, 'I didn't like sleepaway camp either.' Paul had been sent to camp the summer his mom died.

At the top of the stairs Paul said good night and went back to his room, where it took another two hours before he actually fell asleep.

By the time Paul woke, it was midmorning and Miles was gone.

'He left for work hours ago,' Mrs Goldstein told him. 'He said to please make yourself comfortable. So *please*' – she smiled shyly – 'make yourself comfortable. He'll call you later.'

He'd found Mrs Goldstein in the kitchen after he'd put his shoes and socks on and ventured downstairs. One of Miles' boys was at the table reading a comic book – *Spider-Man Wreaks Vengeance*. This was Miles' other son – he looked about two years younger than his brother.

'Hello, I'm Paul,' he said to the boy.

The boy mumbled hi without looking up.

Mrs Goldstein sighed. 'Tell him your name. When someone introduces themselves, you introduce yourself back.'

The boy looked up and rolled his eyes. 'David,' he said, then immediately dived back into the adventures of a boy who introduced himself by entrapping and hanging you upside down in his sticky web.

Mrs Goldstein was still wearing her wig, but this time Paul noticed a tuft of her own hair peeking out of one side. It seemed thick and dark, and Paul suddenly understood it wasn't cancer, but religion, that dictated she cover her head.

'Would you like some coffee, Mr Breidbart?'

'Paul. Please.'

'Please you want some coffee, or please call you Paul?'

'Please to both.'

'All right. But you have to call me Rachel.' She pronounced it with a guttural *ch*, like Germans do.

'Yes, Rachel. Thank you.'

'Sit down. He doesn't bite.'

130

Paul sat down next to the boy, who didn't seem particularly surprised to have a strange guest sitting at the breakfast table with him.

The humidity seemed to be gone today. Butter-yellow sunlight was streaming in between the geraniums in the window box. If his wife and daughter were back home, the three of them would've strolled into Central Park today and spread out a picnic blanket in Sheep Meadow. They would've luxuriated in the newfound aura of family.

Later, after Paul had taken a shower, after he had dressed in one of Miles' crisply ironed shirts generously provided by his wife, after he had read two newspapers – one of them Jewish, which he dutifully leafed through without understanding one word – after he had basically done *anything* to keep from jumping out of his skin, Miles called.

'Okay,' he said. 'Brace yourself. I got through.'

'What?'

'I called a few more times last night – nothing. Ten times this morning – still nothing. I finally got him this afternoon. Our friend Pablo.'

'And?' Paul felt the vague stirring of hope.

'He was suspicious, of course. To put it mildly. First he denied even knowing you. Even when I told him who I was, that I know everything that happened there. After a while he said okay, he might know you a little, but he had no idea what I was talking about. He *drove* you places, that's it. I told him to relax – no one's going to the police. His memory seemed to come back then. I told him about the house being burned down. I assured him we've still got the drugs. I think it's going to be okay. He's going to get back to me. He's going to tell us how to deliver the bag. The where and when.'

'And Joanna? And my daughter . . . Are they . . . ?'

'They're fine.'

Paul felt the large knot that had lodged somewhere in the pit of his stomach slowly begin to unwind. At least, a little.

'I asked Pablo if he was absolutely sure about that,' Miles contin-

131

ued. 'I laid it out for him so there'd be no mistaking. No Joanna and Joelle – no drugs. I think he got it. It's like litigation. You have to make them think you've got the upper hand, even if you don't. Who knows? Maybe we do. We've got their drugs, right?'

'Okay.'

'*Okay?* What about *that's great, Miles? That's terrific? I'm positively overjoyed at the news?*'

'I'm positively overjoyed at the news.'

'You don't sound overjoyed at the news.'

'I'm worried.'

'Okay, you're worried. Of course you're worried. Who wouldn't be in your shoes? Have some faith, I'll lend you mine if you like – no charge. I told you. We're going to get this done. He's going to call back, we're going to deliver the coke and get out of Dodge.'

'It's something else.'

'*What* something else?'

'What if we give them the drugs?'

'Okay?'

'But they still don't release them?'

It was the obvious question, of course. The same question Joanna had asked him back in that room. The one he'd been avoiding looking at too closely or too often. Something that was easy enough to do when he was dodging U.S. Customs inspectors and drug-dealing kids.

Not now. Not when he was finally about to get two million dollars' worth of drugs into the right hands.

Miles shrugged. 'I don't know how to answer that. I think trusting them's the price of admission. Sorry, that's pretty much the way it is.'

TWENTY-TWO

They took her somewhere else without warning.

The middle of the night? The middle of the day? She didn't know. Only that she'd fallen into one of those bottomless slumbers and was happily in the middle of a sweet dream. The sweetest. She was home with Paul on what seemed like a lazy summer afternoon. A Sunday maybe, where they'd stumble out of bed around ten or so to secure a Sunday *Times* and two iced Starbucks.

The dream had that Sunday feel.

Then the door slammed open – she perceived it as a thunderclap outside their 84th Street apartment. Rainstorm to follow.

What actually followed was someone pulling her up off the mattress and directly out of her dream. Accompanied by the acrid odor of nervous, sweaty men. And the sound of harsh orders delivered in a quasi English they must've picked up from kung fu videos.

'Chop-chop,' one of the men – boys really – said to her. '*Vamos.*'

Then the ski mask came down over her head, only backward, so that the eye holes were somewhere behind her, and all she could see was blackness.

She wondered if this was it. The end. The first steps on her way to a shallow grave in the middle of nowhere in particular. A candidate for one of those gruesome pictures in the newspapers. She tasted her own fear – a sour tang on the back of her tongue.

She'd been thinking a lot of her own death lately. Ever since Galina had summarily informed her of Paul's failure to come through. It had the power and solemnity of a death sentence being read by a hanging judge.

Not that.

Not *only* that. It was the demeanor of her guards. The boy who brought Joanna her daily breakfast no longer acted like a room service waiter hoping for a tip. There was no smiling *good morning*. Someone had gotten the message to him: She was no longer a cash cow, but a sacrificial lamb.

The other guards too. Gruff, sour, pissed off. They spoke to her with barely restrained anger and thinly disguised contempt.

She could smell the menace in the air.

Now this. She was being pulled out the door, along a hallway, then suddenly down some steps – one, two, three – she stumbled and nearly fell. They'd tied her hands together with rope – the harsh fibers dug into her wrists.

'I can't *see*,' she said. She hated the panic in her voice – the helpless-victimness of it.

She was a veteran of H.R. departments. She was used to victims parading before her desk, please-don't-hurt-me kind of girls – they were almost *always* girls, sobbingly relating one abuse or another. She would nod, smile, and comfort, but there was always a small part of her that wanted to say *why didn't you stand up for yourself? Why?*

Now she was like them, reduced to naked pleading. Her wrists were already burning and she was still inside the house. She could smell the odor of burned grease, butter, pineapple. They had to be walking through the kitchen. Not walking – stumbling, tripping, flailing.

No one had answered her. Or maybe they had. When she said *I can't see,* whoever was pulling her forward had tugged sharply on the rope. She banged her shoulder into the wall.

This was their answer. *Shut up.*

She knew she was outside from the sudden sharp smell of pine, the sweet scent of hibiscus, and the familiar if nauseating smell of gasoline. The air *felt* different – that too. It had the texture of night, already swollen with morning dew. It felt painfully sweet to be outside again. To breathe the cool air and feel a soft breeze against her throat. Only she was being taken away – from what she knew to what she didn't.

From Joelle.

A car door opened.

But it *wasn't* a door. She was pitched forward into a trunk. No gentle hands to break her fall. Her cheek met the car trunk floor flush. She cried out from the sudden pain in her jaw.

'*Silencio,*' one of them said.

The car trunk shut. Panic bound her tighter than the rope around her wrists. There was only so much air in a car trunk. She would run out of it sooner rather than later. It didn't help that she was breathing too rapidly, her chest heaving, as if she'd just come back from a good morning run.

Slow down, she told herself. *Stop it.*

The car started with a loud rumble – she heard two car doors open and close. Then she was moving. Gently at first, like a boat drifting away from a dock. The car turned right, then left in a slow circle, before quickly picking up speed.

They seemed to be going more or less straight.

A highway?

To where? From where?

At least she wouldn't be dead of suffocation when they arrived; as soon as the car accelerated, streams of chilled air rushed in against her face. They'd removed something from the underside of the trunk so she'd be able to breathe.

This heartened her a little. If they were concerned enough to keep her alive for the trip, maybe they wouldn't kill her when they got there. Maybe.

Stay strong.

They traveled for at least an hour, possibly two. The worst part was her cramped position – her bound arms pinned underneath her body. They quickly went numb. Her shoulders were a different story – every time they hit a bump, a stabbing pain shot from her shoulders down the middle of her chest. The car needed new shocks almost as much as the highway needed new paving. A few times it felt as if they were falling into a hole.

The men had turned on the car radio. It sounded like some kind of ball game – a soccer match maybe.

Whatever it was, it had engaged the men's attention. They were laughing, muttering, cursing. There were three of them, she thought – three distinct voices.

As long as she was surrounded by blackness, she could imagine somebody else was there with her.

Joelle.

She'd thought about having a child for five years, was consumed with it, yet when it finally happened, when she'd finally walked into the Santa Regina Orphanage and was handed this extraordinary little girl, she'd been humbled by the power of baby love. Umbilical cords were severed. This connection, she was certain, was for life.

I'll bring her back, Galina had promised.

What was a kidnapper's promise worth? Especially now that Joanna was being driven somewhere else? She felt tears running down her cheeks, only to be blotted up by the ski mask. The wool tasted like dust.

Stop it.

After a while she must've drifted off.

She was suddenly aware that the car had stopped moving. No rushing air. No stomach-turning bumps in the road. The car radio was off.

She heard a rooster crowing loud and clear.

The car trunk opened. A gray light filtered in through the wool fibers. She was pulled out by her legs. Her chin banged against the lip of the trunk. She could smell her own blood.

She was stood up. The man who did so took the opportunity to run his hands up over her breasts. *Bueno,* he said in a singsong way, and laughed.

A sudden chill gripped her. Of all the various ends she'd contemplated, of all the numerous indignities and violations she'd envisioned in her darker moments, she hadn't thought about this one.

But why not?

The man stopped pawing her, began leading her somewhere. She could make out vague shapes through the wool. She was being taken into a house.

In through a door – a big step up which no one warned her about, causing her to trip and smack her knee against solid stone. She was yanked back up onto her feet again and pulled down what must've been a hallway. She could barely sense two walls on either side of her.

It smelled of *farm,* she thought.

Sheep, cows, chickens. Unvarnished wood beams. Baking bread.

Suddenly, they stopped and the ski mask was pulled off her head.

She was in a small room – not unlike the room she'd just left. The windows were boarded up just like that one. There was a dirty mattress on the floor – an identical twin to the one she'd just spent eight nights sleeping on. But there was a major difference.

People.

Two of them. Other women.

When the guards left, they came up and touched her as if they weren't quite sure she was real.

'Hola,' one of them said – a woman of about forty or forty-five.

'I'm American,' Joanna said. 'Do you speak English?'

'Not really. But then, neither do you,' said the other woman. And she smiled.

*   *   *

THEIR NAMES WERE MARUJA AND BEATRIZ.

Maruja was a journalist – or had been one, till she'd been pulled out of her car just across the busy Plaza de Bolívar. Beatriz was a government official who'd recommended stronger action against the guerrillas. She'd paid for this by being stolen off the street in broad daylight and having to witness her bodyguard being shot dead before her eyes.

A morose-looking man the guards called *el doctor* appeared to be in charge. He appeared just minutes after Joanna was placed in the room. He told them they weren't allowed to speak to each other. *No talking.* He wagged his finger at them, like an exasperated mother superior at a convent school for girls.

The other guards were more lenient, Maruja said. Or at least more distracted. At night they mostly listened to soccer matches and soap operas on a small TV in the hall and didn't pay much attention to them.

Joanna had lost Paul, then Joelle. Now she was surrounded by people going through the same thing she was. They had husbands and children and parents. They understood.

The three of them whispered and signed. Maruja and Beatriz related their respective stories. They passed pictures of their children and spouses. Of their houses too, one in the fashionable La Calera section of Bogotá, the other nestled in the hills above the city.

When they asked Joanna if she had children, she told them yes. One. No picture, though, just the one she kept in her head. She told them what had happened to her and Paul. Maruja and Beatriz sighed, shook their heads in empathy.

The three of them slept on the one mattress, head to feet to head. Maruja, an unreformed smoker back in the real world, snored; Beatriz elbowed her in the ribs to make her stop. Apparently, sisterly affection only went so far.

They had to be in the mountains, Joanna thought. It grew icy cold that night – they breathed vapor and huddled against each other's bodies for warmth. In the morning Joanna saw tiny droplets of frost on the wooden slats covering the windows.

By the second day it felt a little like an endless pajama party. They braided each other's hair. One of the guards had procured Maruja a bottle of cheap nail polish – Purple Passion. They took turns doing each other's nails, pedicures too.

The man who'd felt Joanna's breasts kept his distance. Joanna's fear of rape faded, pushed aside by other fears. Death, of course. And another gnawing fear which was a kind of death too: Would she ever get out of there?

Maruja and Beatriz had the gray pallor of the confined and dying. Joanna wondered how long it would be before her own skin turned the same shade.

Occasionally, the guards let them watch TV with them, Beatriz confided. Maruja and Beatriz looked forward to the news shows. Sometimes their husbands would be on, offering messages of hope.

We are negotiating. We are in discussions. Stay brave.

Joanna knew there'd be no such comfort for her. Paul had left and vanished into the ether, as quickly and completely as her former life.

Her third morning, there was a knock at the door. That itself was unusual, since the guards tended to simply barge in on a whim. The three of them might be sleeping, whispering, even partially undressed and sponging themselves from a tepid bucket of water; a *whore's bath* – wasn't that the expression?

This morning they were sitting in the center of the room fully clothed, passing the time constructing lists of their favorite cities. Beatriz had picked Rome, Rio, and Las Vegas. Maruja, San Francisco, Buenos Aires, and Acapulco. It was Joanna's turn. All she could come up with was New York. The city she lived in, the one she was aching to return to.

The door opened and Galina walked in.

It was a measure of Joanna's desperation that the sight of her kidnapper gave her a rush of – what? Pleasure? Relief? Simple familiarity?

Maybe it was because Galina appeared different than the last time

Joanna had seen her, when she'd solemnly informed her about Paul's failure to come through. She seemed more like the *other* Galina now – the one you wouldn't mind hanging out with on a sunny bench in the park.

She motioned for Joanna to come closer – she had something to tell her.

'We've heard from your husband,' she whispered, and squeezed Joanna's hand. 'It's going to be all right.'

And Joanna's heart, spirit – whatever that thing is that allows people to occasionally walk on air – surged. Not just because of the news. No.

Galina hadn't come to the mountains alone. One of the guards – a shy boy who looked all of thirteen – entered behind her.

He was holding Joelle.

TWENTY-THREE

They'd traveled over the Williamsburg Bridge, then through the Lincoln Tunnel, headed to a place somewhere outside Jersey City. It was five o'clock. They were on a mostly empty road flanked by fields of swaying cattails. *High as an elephant's eye.* The lyrics were from Joanna's favorite musical, *Oklahoma!* They'd attended the revival on their last anniversary, Paul told Miles.

The word *last* stuck in his throat.

It was three days and eighteen hours since he'd left his wife and child.

The swamp was throbbing with the steady hum of insects. Still, you could hear the Major League scores clear enough. Miles was listening with rapt attention.

'Baseball,' Miles said, 'is the hardest sport to handicap. Brutal.'

'You mean bet on?'

'Yeah, bet on. You've got to give runs, two, three, depending on the pitcher. The worst team in the world wins sixty times a year. Go figure. It's a sucker's bet.'

'You bet on sports?'

'Well, sure. Penny-ante. You know, twenty, thirty dollars – just to keep things interesting. It's my little rebellion against prescribed living. Orthodoxy has little rules for everything. It can drive you nuts.'

Paul guessed that going to work without his yarmulke was another one of Miles' little rebellions against prescribed living. 'Did you ever think about *not* being Orthodox?'

'Sure. But then what would I be? It's sort of like asking a black person if he ever thought about not being black. You can think about it all you like, but it's kind of who you are.'

'So? Are there rules about betting on baseball games?'

'Yeah – you have to stay away from the Padres.' Miles turned up the radio for the National League scores.

Paul felt like mentioning that he and his coworkers had spent more lunch hours than he cared to remember establishing risk ratios for specific pitches thrown to specific batters in specific parks. A bunch of regular Bill Jameses. He could've told Miles, for example, that throwing a down-and-in fastball to Barry Bonds in 3-Com Park had a risk-to-reward ratio of three to one. Every two times you got Barry, he'd launch one into the stratosphere.

He didn't, though.

Paul understood Miles was talking about sports so they wouldn't have to talk about something else. What they were doing. Meeting drug dealers in a swamp outside Jersey City. If they talked about it, they would be forced to acknowledge that they were hopelessly out of their element.

'Thank you,' Paul said.

'For what?'

'For doing this with me, I guess.'

Miles remained silent for a minute. 'I sent you to Bogotá. I told you you'd be safe. That makes me kind of responsible, doesn't it?'

'Great. Can I hire you to sue yourself?'

'Sorry. I don't do suits.'

'How long have you been a lawyer?' Paul asked after turning up the AC.

'How long?' Miles repeated, as if he'd never been asked that particular question before. 'Too long. Not long enough. Depends on the day.'

'Why did you want to be a lawyer?'

'I didn't. I wanted to be Sandy Koufax. God didn't cooperate. My fastball was more like a change. If you can't be Sandy, you get to be a doctor or lawyer. Indian chief wasn't available – it should be, we're a *tribe*, aren't we? I went for lawyer. Maybe not the kind of lawyer they expected.'

'They?'

'You know, all the wise men of the tribe. Everyone goes real estate, tax, or corporate. I went legal aid. Juvenile division.'

'What was that like?'

'Crazy. I had a caseload of about a hundred fifty. I'd get about ten minutes with each kid and a quick glance at their file before saying hi to the judge. That was it. And it's not like I could do any pleading-out there.'

'Why not?'

'You couldn't threaten the prosecutors with a long jury trial because there *are* no juries in juvenile, and kids don't really have any information worth trading. No one wants to deal. The best I could do was get them committed to a Bronx hospital, because it was safer than putting them in a juvenile hall.'

'Hospital?'

'Yeah, a mental hospital. They'd do their time popping meds instead of getting gang-raped. Trust me – it was heaven next to your average juvenile prison. For them it was the safest place on earth. Anyway, when I got to court and began mistaking Julio for Juan, and María for Maggie, I thought I might be in trouble. I told my supervisor he had to lessen my caseload – that I was committing borderline malpractice. He said *keep dreaming*. I left.'

'So you went from juvenile delinquents to Colombian babies.'

'Yeah. I thought I'd get involved at an earlier stage of development. It pays better. What about you?'

'Me?'

'Yeah. Hard to believe you always wanted to be an insurance man. What did you do – fall into it?'

No, not fall, Paul thought. *My mom died,* he wanted to say. *My mom died and I got scared.* He felt like explaining this to Miles, that like Einstein, he was merely trying to impose order and probability on a cold universe.

'More or less,' was all he said.

A dirt road appeared to the passenger side of the car – not so much a road as an indentation in the muck. A trail to nowhere in particular.

Miles slowed, then pulled over.

'They said a dirt road about three miles down,' he said, trying to peer ahead down the mostly hidden path. 'Oh well . . .' He turned the car into the opening, bouncing over a small hump.

Suddenly, cattails were scouring both sides of the Buick, making it feel as if they were traveling through a car wash. Paul, who'd hated roller coasters as a kid, hadn't liked car washes much either. His fervid imagination had attributed a malevolence to those stiff bristles, smothering sponges, and scalding jets of water.

He felt the same kind of vulnerability now. The car was safety. Outside in the swamp, who knew?

He peered through the windshield, which had quickly become a battlefield of slaughtered swamp bugs. Miles turned on the wipers in an effort to clear them – but it was as if they were beating against a monsoon.

When the road ended, they were in a small clearing all by themselves. Miles stopped the car.

'I guess this is it,' Miles said. He tapped the steering wheel, once, twice, peering nervously from side to side. Miles might've felt half responsible for Paul's predicament, but it seemed like he might be having second thoughts about actually accompanying him. 'What's the protocol with drug deals? Half-hour waiting time?' He looked at his watch. 'We're five minutes early.'

Paul said, 'Are you sure this is it?'

144

'No.'

'Great. Just checking.'

Ten minutes went by. Miles commented on the weather, then immediately ran out of small things to say. Paul understood. Making conversation when you're scared shitless was an effort. Paul rubbed his hands together and attempted to swallow his own dry spit.

Paul heard the car first.

'Someone's coming,' he said.

A minute later a blue Mercedes-Benz emerged out of the cattails and came to a lurching stop about twenty feet from them.

Both cars sat there, facing each other.

'Okay,' Miles said after a good minute went by, 'I guess we get out.'

Miles flipped the trunk switch, pushed his door open, and gingerly stepped out of the car. Paul followed.

They met at the back of the car.

'You want to hold it?' Miles said. 'Or me?' The well-traveled black bag was peeking out from under an old tarp.

'I'll take it,' Paul said. 'I'm the one who was supposed to deliver it in the first place.'

He pulled his bag out. No one had gotten out of the other car. It was still sitting there, its engine idling, no discernible movement from inside.

'Did you hear the one about the lawyer and the actuary?' Miles said.

'No.'

'Me either.'

They approached the Mercedes side by side. It reminded Paul of a western – just about every western ever made, where the two lawmen stride toward the gunslingers shoulder-to-shoulder in the movie's final showdown. As a responsible actuary he would be remiss not to mention that legions of western heroes had defied the odds – roughly fifty-fifty – of getting their heads blown off.

The Mercedes' driver's door opened. Two men stepped out of the

145

car. They might've been car salesmen. No mirrored sunglasses, heavy gold chains, or garish tattoos. Instead, they wore well-pressed chinos and golf shirts. One in a powder-blue Izod, the other opting for a striped Polo.

The driver – he was in Polo – nodded at them. 'You guys look a little nervous.'

Okay, Paul thought, give him points for being perceptive.

'Which one's Paul, huh?' he asked. He spoke with a noticeable accent – Colombian, Paul assumed. His voice was high-pitched, almost girlish.

Paul had to restrain himself from raising his hand.

'Me. I'm Paul.' They'd stopped about five feet from each other. The black bag seemed to be growing heavier by the second.

The driver nodded, slapped his neck. 'Fucking mosquitoes. I'm gonna get West Nile.' When he took his hand away, there was a blotch of bright blood on his neck.

He looked at Miles. 'Who are *you,* my friend?'

'His lawyer,' Miles said.

'His lawyer?' He laughed and turned to his companion. 'Fuck me, I don't have a lawyer.' He turned back to them. 'Are we going to have to sign papers or something?'

Miles said, 'No papers. If you could just make sure they give him his wife and daughter back.'

'Hey, don't know what you're talking about. *Not my job,*' he said, affecting a thicker accent for comic effect. No one laughed. 'I'm here to sight the white, okay?'

'Okay,' Miles said.

Paul remained silent. Good thing. He was too scared to speak.

'So, boss?' the driver said. 'You here to give me the bag or ask me to dance?' The other man laughed.

Paul held the bag out at arm's length.

'Open it,' the driver said. 'I like to see what's inside first.'

Paul laid it on the dirt ground and zipped it open. When he bent down, he felt light-headed and nearly tipped over. Something began humming in the swamp, an überhum, the biggest insect in the pond.

The driver stepped forward and gazed down at the bag.

'Huh? Looks like fucking *rubbers* to me.' He had a lazy left eye; he seemed to be looking in two directions at once.

Paul started to explain. 'They're filled with –'

'Shit, I *know* what they're filled with. I'm goofing with you, boss.' He smiled. 'Let's take one out and make sure, okay?'

When Paul hesitated, the man said, 'You do it. No offense, but they were up *your* ass.' He turned to his pal. '*Culero*, eh?'

The insect hum had gotten louder – Paul's ears were ringing. Paul reached into the bag and took out a condom, neatly tied in a knot by one of those women back in Colombia. He held it out in his now seriously sweating palm.

The driver pulled something out of his pocket.

Click. A sinuously shiny blade caught the light. Paul tensed, and Miles took one step back.

'Relax, *muchachos*.' He gripped Paul's hand, almost gently, and pointed the blade straight down. Paul wondered if the man noticed his hand was shaking.

He did.

'Don't worry,' he said to Paul. 'I've only slipped a couple of times.'

He flicked the blade at Paul's palm. When Paul twitched, he laughed and did it again. The other man – the one wearing the Izod with the little green alligator – said something in Spanish. He had a thin, almost whispery voice.

The driver jabbed the end of the blade into the condom, opening up a tiny slit. He was reaching down to scoop up some of the white powder onto his finger when something happened.

It was that hum.

It had grown even louder, *annoyingly* loud, as if it were causing vibrations in the ground itself. You wanted to shout *shut up,* to swat whatever it was with a newspaper, to crunch it under your shoe.

147

It would have been useless, though. Using your shoe.

The two cars plowed out of the cattails at about the same time.

Jeeps, the kind with fat, deeply treaded tires and juiced-up engines. They were belching black smoke and closing fast.

The man looked up and slapped his neck again. And just like last time, his hand came away with smeared blood.

'They shot me,' he said.

He grabbed the bag and ran. The other man too. They vanished into the cattails. Polo and Izod.

Paul felt frozen to the spot. It took something whizzing past his ear and puck-pucking into the ground about a foot from his left shoe to actually get him to move. That, and Miles, who grabbed his right arm and yelled, 'Run.'

He scrambled after Miles into the weeds.

He could hear this behind him: the sound of rumbling engines being shut off, of car doors slamming, of shouts and screams and war whoops. He thought westerns again: the outlaw band riding into town on a Saturday night intent on letting off a little steam, firing their six-shooters into the air. *Jeep Riders in the Sky.*

Only they were shooting semiautomatics, and they were shooting them in their direction.

Paul ran straight through the cattails, dry thin stalks whipping his face and arms. He followed the shape of Miles' disappearing body. The ground wasn't conducive to running for your life – it was wet, thick, and mucky. Ten seconds into the weeds his socks were soaked to the skin.

Behind him the men were still screaming. They were still shooting too – cattail heads were disappearing like airborne dandelion spores.

And something else, something that had become uncomfortably and chillingly clear.

The gunmen were *following* them.

The cattails, Paul gratefully noticed, *were* as high as an elephant's eye. Wonderfully, gloriously high. High enough, Paul thought, to

148

completely swallow them. He could barely make out jittery patches of blue sky overhead. The dealers had chosen an impenetrable place that would be hidden to just about everyone.

They stood a chance.

He remembered something. In the childhood game of rock, paper, scissors – paper, the most fragile substance on earth, always won out over rock. Why?

Because paper can *hide* rock.

Somehow the thought didn't comfort him.

He kept running, panting after Miles as if he were a faithful hound out duck hunting. He tried not to dwell on the fact that they were the ducks. His feet churned up dollops of mud, his blood jack-hammered into his ears.

The men were behind them and gaining.

Paul wasn't certain whom it occurred to first – Miles or him. It seemed like they both stopped running at almost the same moment. They turned and stared at each other and made the same unspoken decision more or less in unison. They dropped straight to the ground.

If they could hear the men chasing them, then the men could hear them.

Lie down and do nothing.

Their pursuers would have to get lucky.

Do the numbers. He imagined it as an actuarial problem that had been dropped on his desk. The square mass of two bodies, divided into the square mileage of this swamp, divided by six or seven people looking for them. What were the odds of being found? Substitute the cattails for hay, and they were the proverbial needles.

They hugged the ground.

It soon became apparent that Izod and Polo had different ideas.

They were still running. Somewhere off to the left – the sound of two small breezes whipping through the weeds.

But behind them a kind of tornado.

Run, Paul thought. *Run, run.*

149

They had the drugs. They were carrying Joanna's fate in their hands. They had to make it out of the swamp.

But the sounds of separate footsteps seemed to converge into one dull roar. Then someone screamed, and suddenly all sound stopped. Even the insects seemed to bow their heads in a moment of silence.

After a minute or so it picked up again, like a skipped record finding its groove.

What happened?

Paul received his answer almost immediately.

'Hey!' someone shouted. '*Hey!* We got your dancing partner here. He looks kind of lonely.'

They'd captured one of them. Izod or Polo. Just *one*. The other one was still out there. He was probably lying low like them – being a needle.

The sound of the gunmen searching wavered in and out, like a faulty shortwave signal. Once Paul glimpsed a red Puma sneaker about ten feet from him – that's it. He shut his eyes and waited for the bullet in his back. When he opened his eyes and peeked, the sneaker was gone.

He went back to the problem that had been dumped on his desk. Risk ratios had to be formulated, tabulated, and segmented for another potentially dangerous activity.

Plane Travel.

Driving a Car.

Construction Jobs.

Lying in a Swamp Being Pursued by Homicidal Gunmen.

'Tell you what,' one of their pursuers screamed. 'Got a deal for you, *bollo*. You come on in now, we won't kill you. How's that?'

Bollo. Pussy. One of the Spanish words eighth graders taught themselves, snickering, between classes.

Okay, Paul wondered, why were they only concentrating on the other drug runner in the weeds? Was it possible they hadn't seen Miles and him in the clearing? Was it?

Miles answered the question for him. 'He must have the bag,' he whispered. 'They want the *drugs.*'

The man with the high-pitched voice and lazy eye. Polo. He'd snatched Paul's bag when the shots rang out.

The gunman shouted for the lazy-eyed man to come in, called him a *bollo,* an *abadesa,* a *culo* – all not-so-nice things, Paul imagined. He repeated his proposition. If he'd only stand up and walk toward them bag in hand, he'd get out of the swamp with his life – honest injun.

Still no answer.

Paul assumed Polo didn't believe a word of it. They'd already put a bullet into his neck – if he wasn't going to die of West Nile, he might expire from that.

'Okay,' the man shouted, 'okay, that's cool. How about some music while you think it over? For your listening pleasure.'

Someone walked back to the Jeeps and turned on a CD player. Or maybe it was the car radio. Latin samba came wailing through the cattails. Screeching trumpets and a good steady beat. *Music, that's nice of them.* Only something seemed wrong with this music. It sounded shrill and off-key.

It took a minute or so for Paul to understand why.

At first Paul thought it might be a trick of the air, an aberration in sound waves caused by the thick cattails and even thicker heat. It wasn't.

It was a man screaming. Izod.

They were torturing their prisoner in time to the music.

To cover up the sound. Or because it made it more fun. Or because they liked samba.

One, two, three . . . scream.

They kept at it for an entire song – the longest song on earth.

'American Pie' might be nineteen and a half minutes. This song was longer.

Finally, it stopped. 'What ya think?' the man shouted. 'Celia Cruz, *mi mami.* A fucking scream, no?'

151

Paul turned to Miles.

'Who are they?'

When the Jeeps had burst through the weeds and the men surged out with guns drawn and firing, he'd thought *the police. Government agents. Narcs.*

Not now.

Miles didn't answer. Maybe because his hands were up over his ears. His eyes were closed as if he didn't wish to see anything either. A long bloody scratch went from one side of his forehead to the other. He'd done Paul a favor, he'd extended himself beyond the call of reasonable duty, and now it was very possible he was going to die because of it.

'Julio.' Another voice now, thin and whispery. *'Juliooooo . . .'*

There was something pitiful about this voice.

'They broke my fingers, Julio. They broke my whole hand. My hand, *Julio . . . You gotta come in! You hear me! I can't . . . Please . . . They want the* llello, *man, that's it. For fuck's sake, come in!'*

The torturer's deal had fallen on deaf ears. They'd changed tack. It was Izod's turn.

'Listen to me . . . They broke my fingers, all my fingers, Julio . . . every one of my fingers . . . Bring in the hooch . . . They're killing me . . . Please, Julio . . . please . . . You hearin' what I'm sayin'?'

Julio remained mute.

They gave it another song.

Another samba, played with the volume cranked down, so the man's screams were louder, in your face, standing out even over the spanking rhythm and blaring horns.

Sometimes he screamed actual words.

Ayudi a mi madre!

Please help me, Mother!

The music stopped again.

Paul heard sniffling, a horrible mewling sound.

'Julioooo . . . my ear. They cut my ear off. It hurts . . . oh, it hurts,

152

Julio . . . oh, it hurts . . . Come in . . . Please come in . . . Please . . .
You GOT to . . . They cut my ear off, Julio . . . You understand . . .'

Julio might've understood – he would've had to be deaf, dumb, or *dead* not to understand. He wasn't coming in.

Paul pushed his head to the ground. It stank like rotting vegetables. If he were an ostrich, he would've stuck his head into the ground and kept it there.

It was hard listening to a man being tortured. Even one you didn't know. He knew him well enough to *see* him. Neatly pressed pants and a powder-blue Izod turned bloodred. There was a black hole where one of his ears used to be.

'No . . . no, please no . . . Don't . . . No, not my balls . . . please, not my balls, no . . . Julio, don't let them cut my balls off . . . Pleeeeease, Julio, no . . . Don't let them do that . . . No –'

A bloodcurdling howl.

It was so loud one of the torturers told him to *shut the fuck up*. The man whose testicles he'd just sliced off.

The man *did* shut up.

For a while there was mostly silence. Just the insects, the slightest breeze rustling through the cattails.

May I have some water?

It was him again.

I'd like some water. Please. Some water . . .

Softly and politely, as if he were in a restaurant talking to a waiter.

As if they might politely answer him back.

Sure, still or sparkling?

Eventually, he stopped speaking. At least actual words. All verifiable human language ceased. He reverted to a guttural, indecipherable whimpering.

His tongue.

They'd cut out his tongue.

Paul couldn't listen anymore.

He needed to stop hearing.

153

The odds of accidental death from being struck by lightning are 1 in 71,601 for an average lifetime.

The odds of dying from being bitten by a nonvenomous insect are 1 in 397,000.

The odds of drowning in a household bathtub are 1 in 10,499.

The odds of . . .

'*Maricón,* see what you made us do. Fuck – your boyfriend bled like a fucking *cerado.* All over my goddamn shoes. We gave you a chance, you cocksucking motherfucker.'

Their prisoner was dead.

Someone went back to the Jeeps. Paul could hear doors being opened, then slammed shut.

'What are they doing?' Paul whispered to Miles. But Miles still had his hands over his ears – his skin had turned the color of skim milk.

They were on the march again – one or two of them, slowly moving through the fields.

Paul smelled it first.

If Joanna were there, she would have sniffed it out minutes sooner, he knew. She'd have lifted her head and said *how odd, do you smell that?*

It was wafting in through the cattails. When Paul lifted his head again in an effort to make sense of it, he heard sounds of splashing.

'They're making a line,' Miles whispered, his first actual conversation in the last half hour. He'd finally taken his hands off his ears – was *all* ears now, but he clearly didn't like what he was hearing.

A line? What did Miles mean? *What* line?

'The wind's blowing that way,' Miles said. First an enigmatic pronouncement about *lines,* now the weather report.

'They're going to burn him out,' Miles said in a weirdly detached voice. 'They're going to make him run right *to* them.'

That smell.

Kerosene.

Okay, Paul finally understood. He got it. Much as he didn't want

154

to, much as he wanted to remain dumb and clueless. They were laying down a line of *kerosene*. They were making this line behind them, behind the wind itself, which was blowing away from them. Paul pictured it – a solid wall of flame. And he pictured something else – that house in Jersey City. What *used* to be a house in Jersey City. The place he was supposed to meet the two guys in the blue Mercedes, Polo and Izod. Only he hadn't met them, because someone had burned down the house – reduced it to a dark primeval hole.

Who?

The same guys who were circling them with kerosene in their hands. That was the logical conclusion – what the empirical evidence would lead you to.

Paul had twice tried to deliver the drugs, and twice he'd been stopped by the same band of arsonists.

Paul turned to Miles once again to ask him something, but the question flew out of his head at the sight of Miles edging backward on elbows and knees. He looked . . . odd. Like a white person trying to dance black. Like he was doing the *worm*. He was doing it double-time; moving at the speed of panic.

Paul saw why.

The odds of dying from smoke or fire are 1 in 13,561.

The first flame had shot up into the air about fifty yards behind and to their right. It looked biblical – like a solid pillar of fire. The line of cattails would light up like briquettes soaked in lighter fluid, then be spurred forward by the wind. If they ran from the fire, they would only wind up facing another kind of fire, the kind produced by semiautomatic weapons. Miles, who'd been known to bet on a baseball game or two, was betting that he could go the other way – that he could go *toward* it. That he could make it out before the entire line lit. That he could race the fire and win.

By the time Paul caught up to him, Miles had turned himself around. They shimmied through the weeds on their bellies just a

155

few feet apart from each other, noses inches above the pungent stink of the swamp, an odor still preferable to its alternative.

Burned flesh, Paul couldn't help noticing, smelled sickly sweet.

The men had miscalculated – tried to get someone to run who was very possibly past running. *The bullet in his neck,* Paul thought. The man in the Polo shirt was dead.

They kept crawling.

Picture those half-fish creatures in the Pleistocene era, slithering out of the water onto dry land on their way to a better future. If they'd only known what awaited them, Paul thought, they might've turned around and gone back.

He felt only half human now. Covered in slime and mud, bleeding from the razor-sharp weeds and furiously biting insects. Breathing was next to impossible – sinewy lines of choking black smoke were already snaking across the ground.

He was traveling blind. His eyes were dripping – half from the smoke and half from the awful knowledge that he'd failed.

He could sense the fire to their left. How far away? Twenty yards? Close enough to feel the heat like a wave – the kind that tumbles you into the surf and just won't let you go. Faint blisters were rising up on his forearms.

Faster. Faster. Faster.

What were the odds they'd make it now? The actuary in him said: Nil. Zippo. *Nada.*

Give up.

He couldn't. Self-preservation vanquished self-pity. If his wife and child were going to make it out of Colombia, he had to make it out of the swamp.

Paul could see the first jagged slivers of fire flickering through the stalks. The cattails were crackling, snapping, literally disintegrating in front of his half-blinded eyes. It felt as if every bit of air were being sucked out of there. The men were screaming over the fire's deafening roar like college students before a pregame bonfire.

Miles collapsed to his right.

He lay there on his belly, wheezing, desperately trying to gulp in air.

'Come on, Miles. A little further.' It took an enormous effort for Paul to get the words out of his mouth. They tumbled out half formed and garbled, as if he were speaking in tongues. They had zero effect. Miles lay there, unmoved and unmoving.

The fire was making a beeline for them. It was almost there.

'I . . . can't . . . ,' Miles whispered between gasps. 'I . . .'

Paul grabbed his shirt collar – hot and steaming, like laundry fresh from the dryer.

He pulled.

It made no sense. It was merely symbolic, since he didn't have the strength to pull Miles from the fire, any more than he had the strength to stand up and take on the murderers who'd started it.

He pulled anyway.

Suddenly, Miles seemed to gather what little energy he had left. He moved. Just a foot or so. Then another foot. And after coughing up some black phlegm, a foot more.

It was too late.

They were in the mouth of the furnace. It was yawning open for them. They weren't going to make it.

Though I walk through the valley of the shadow of death, my . . . My rod and my . . . My rod . . . Where were the words when you really needed them? He was down to crawling on bloodied hands and knees. He was doing what any atheist does in foxholes. He was mumbling the magic words he'd abandoned as a sad and lonely little kid.

Miles was there beside him. The fire lit him up like someone in a flash-frame.

Paul's flesh began to sear – to literally burn off. He took one last lunge, then covered up his face, hoping it wouldn't hurt.

That was all.

TWENTY-FOUR

Nothing had been said to her. But she knew just the same.

Galina might've told her it was going to be all right, but it wasn't all right.

It was monotonous and deadening and endless.

Every moment, at least, that she wasn't holding Joelle in her arms. Those moments, by contrast, were achingly life-affirming.

She got to experience those moments only twice a day – for morning and evening feedings. Galina would bring her to another room in the farm – she was fairly sure it *was* a farm, since she could hear roosters and chickens and the bleating of cows and sheep. She could smell them too – mixed in with the unmistakable odor of freshly turned manure. She'd been born in Minnesota, farm country, and her olfactory senses had been honed on those earthy smells.

When she asked Galina what happened – whether Paul had delivered the drugs like he was supposed to – she shrugged and didn't answer.

No answer was necessary. He had or he hadn't, but Joanna knew that she needn't be packing her bags anytime soon.

It was the routine that saved her – those morning and evening feedings, waited for with a tingling anticipation. It was routine that was murdering her too, bit by bit. The sameness, the torpor, the sense of unyielding and unbroken siege.

Her emotions, raised to the sky by Galina's whispered assertion, were all dressed up with nowhere to go.

She was losing weight too – she'd become familiar with certain bones in her arms and rib cage she hadn't known were there.

One night she heard a furious slapping from somewhere in the house. Followed by someone moaning – a man.

She sensed Beatriz and Maruja awake and listening next to her on the mattress.

'Who's that?' she whispered.

'Rolando,' Maruja whispered back.

'Rolando,' Joanna echoed the name. 'Who's he? Another prisoner?'

'Another journalist who's become the story,' Maruja said.

'Like you?'

'No. Not like me. Bigger. His son . . .' And her voice trailed off as if she'd fallen back asleep.

'His *son*. What about his son?'

'Nothing. Go to sleep.'

'Maruja. What . . . ?'

'He had a son . . . that's all. Shhh . . .'

'What happened to him? Tell me.'

'He became sick.'

'Sick?'

'Cancer. Leukemia, I think. He wanted to see his papa one more time. Before he died.'

'Yes?'

'It was in the newspapers,' she whispered. 'On the television. A big kind of national soap opera. They let Rolando watch. The talk shows. He saw his son on TV speaking to him, pleading with them to let him go.'

Joanna tried to imagine what it must've been like for a father to witness his dying son on TV, but gave up because it was too painful to contemplate.

'People came forward – how do you say . . . *los famosos*. Politicians, actors, *futbolistas*. They volunteered to take Rolando's place. Take *us*, they said, so Rolando can be with his son. He had a few months to live.'

'What happened?'

Maruja shook her head – Joanna's eyes were getting used to the dark, and she could make out the vague outline of Maruja's pointy chin.

'Nothing happened.'

'But the boy . . .'

'He died.'

'Oh.'

'Rolando watched his funeral on TV.'

Joanna wasn't aware she'd begun crying. Not until she felt the wet mattress against her cheek. She'd never been much of a crier. Maybe because she spent most of her workday getting other people to *stop*, even as she secretly resented their public displays of weakness. But now she thought it was both terrible and wonderful to cry. It made her feel *human*. Knowing that she was still capable of being moved by someone else's tragedy, even in the midst of her own.

'Rolando?' Joanna asked. 'How long has he been here?'

'Five years.'

'*Five years?*'

It didn't seem possible. Like hearing about one of those people who've survived for decades in a coma, kept alive in a kind of suspended animation.

'When his son died, Rolando became very angry with them. He doesn't listen. He talks back,' Maruja said, as if she were snitching on another child. Joanna wondered if Rolando's defiance made life difficult for Beatriz and Maruja. Probably. 'He ran away once,' Maruja whispered. 'They caught him, of course.'

160

Ran away. The very sound of it caused Joanna's heart to quicken – what a mysterious and exotic notion.

To run away. Was such a thing possible?

She heard some more slapping, yelling, what sounded like someone being slammed into a wall. Joanna shut her eyes, tried not to picture what was going on in that room. Rolando was *tied to the bed,* Maruja said.

She imagined what running away would be like instead – how it would feel. She pictured the wind at her back, the scent of earth and flowers, the dizzying sense that every footstep was putting distance between her and them. It was such a delightful dream she almost forgot whom she'd be leaving behind.

Joelle.

They had her baby.

The fantasy dissipated – *poof.* She was left with an empty ache in her chest, the hole that's left when hope takes off for parts unknown.

Eventually, the slapping subsided – a door slammed shut.

She had trouble getting back to sleep. Maruja and Beatriz were slumbering away, but she remained obstinately awake. In a few more hours it would be morning and Galina would bring Joelle to her, and together they would feed and change her.

It was something worth holding on to. Even in this place. Sleeping three to a bed, and in the next room a man tied up like a barnyard animal.

She dozed off but was awakened what seemed like minutes later by the crazy rooster who seemed to crow all hours of the day and night.

JOELLE HAD A COUGH.

When Galina placed her in Joanna's arms, her little body shook with each tiny eruption.

'It's just a cold,' Galina said.

But when Joanna tried to feed her, Joelle refused the rubber nip-

161

ple. Joanna waited a few minutes, tried again, Joelle still wouldn't eat. She kept coughing with increasing and violent regularity. Each cough caused her deep black eyes to go wide, as if she were surprised and affronted by it. Joanna pressed her lips to Joelle's forehead – something she'd seen friends do with their own children.

'It's *hot*, Galina.'

Galina slipped a hand under Joelle's T-shirt to feel her chest, then laid her cheek against her forehead.

'She has a fever,' Galina confirmed.

Joanna felt her stomach tighten. *So this is what it's like,* she thought. Being terrified not for yourself, but for your child.

'What do we do?'

They were in the small room Galina always took her to for feedings. Four white walls with the faint impression of a crucifix that must've once hung over the door. They walked her there maskless now, something that had both comforted and terrified her the first time. It had seemed to make an astonishing statement to her: *You're in for the long haul.* There was no need to play hide-and-seek with her anymore.

When Galina put her hand on Joelle's forehead, she pulled it away as if it were singed.

'Wait,' she said, and left the room.

She came back waving something. A magic wand?

No. The thermometer she'd purchased for them in Bogotá. Joanna numbly let Galina remove Joelle's diaper – her thighs were chafed and red. Galina placed her stomach-down on Joanna's lap and told her to hold her still.

She gently eased the thermometer in.

When Joanna saw the mercury climbing, she said, 'Oh.' An involuntary response to naked fear. When Galina took it out and held it up to the light, it was nudging 104.

'*She's sick,*' Joanna said. This wasn't the little fever babies get from time to time. This was for real.

Galina said, 'We need to sponge her down.'

162

'Aspirin?' Joanna said. 'Do you have baby aspirin here?'

Galina looked at her as if she'd asked for a DVD player or a facial. They were obviously somewhere rural – a place where the guards were relaxed enough to watch TV at night and not really bother to stop Maruja, Beatriz, and Joanna from talking to each other. A place as far away from a stocked pharmacy as it was from the USDF patrols looking for them.

Her daughter's fever was sky-high. It didn't matter. They were on their own.

'Please.' Joanna heard the pleading in her own voice, but this time it didn't surprise or disgust her. She would beg on hands and knees for her baby. She'd offer to give her right arm or her left arm, or her life.

'If we sponge her, it'll bring her fever down,' Galina said, but she didn't sound very convincing. The worry lines in her face had taken on an aspect of true fear. Joanna found that far more terrifying than the sight of the soaring thermometer.

Galina left in search of a wet rag.

How strange, Joanna thought. That Galina seemed able to effortlessly change back and forth between kidnapper and nurse, first one, then the other.

She came back carrying a pewter bowl filled with sloshing water. Somewhere she'd found a small hand towel, which she liberally soaked while sneaking worried peeks at a still-screaming Joelle. She wrung it out and began gently sponging her down. Joelle didn't cooperate – she twisted and turned on Joanna's lap as if the touch of the rag were physically painful.

She was screaming in anguished, heartbreaking bursts. Her tiny body quivered.

Joanna grabbed Galina's hand. 'It's not helping. It's making it worse.' The wet rag hung down limply, drops of water softly hitting the rough wooden floor.

Pat, pat, pat.

'Look at her, for God's sakes. *Look at her.*'

163

'It'll bring the fever down,' Galina said. 'Please.' But she didn't attempt to yank her arm away. What would the guards think if they saw Joanna with her hand wrapped around Galina's bony wrist?

Joanna let go.

When Galina finished, she felt Joelle's forehead again. 'A little cooler, yes?'

But when Joanna felt it, it was like touching fire.

Galina diapered Joelle, lifting her off Joanna's lap, rewrapped her in a rough wool blanket. Joelle was still wailing away – her red face clenched like a fist – as Joanna rocked her against her breasts and shuffled back and forth in the small space allotted to them. She sang to her, barely above a whisper.

Hush, little baby, don't say a word,
Mommy's gonna buy you a mockingbird.
If that mockingbird don't sing . . .

Her mother used to sing that to her. She'd play the James Taylor, Carly Simon duet on the living room stereo and dance around the Castro Convertible with Joanna in her arms. It had always made Joanna feel safe and adored.

It wasn't working with Joelle.

She'd stopped screaming, but only because she'd cried herself out. When she opened her mouth, there didn't seem to be enough energy left to emit a human sound.

Galina said, 'I have to take her now.'

'No.'

'They'll get angry if I don't.'

Joanna was too scared to notice, but later she'd turn Galina's words over and over in her mind.

They'll get angry if I don't.

The first tiny admission that in the us-versus-them dynamic of the household – Maruja, Beatriz, and Joanna versus their guards – there might be another *them* too.

Galina and her.

164

Galina would've left Joelle with her, only she couldn't because *they'd* get angry.

In a world devoid of tangible hope, you grasped at verbal straws.

She gave Joelle back to Galina. She was led back to her prison, otherwise known as their room, where Maruja and Beatriz saw the expression on her face and asked what was wrong.

WHEN EVENING FEEDING CAME AROUND, GALINA SHOWED UP AT the door looking ghostly pale. That wasn't the alarming part.

She was Joelle-less – *that* was the alarming part.

'What happened? Where is she?' Joanna asked.

'In her crib. She finally cried herself to sleep. I didn't want to wake her.'

She took Joanna to the feeding room anyway, past two mestizo guards playing cards – one of them a girl with chestnut skin and shimmering black hair that fell to the small of her back. After Galina shut the door, she said, 'She has pneumonia.'

'Pneumonia?' The word resounded like a slap. 'How do you know? You're not a doctor. Why would you say that?'

'Her chest. I can hear it.'

'It could be a virus? Just the flu?'

'No. Her lungs – they're filled with *flúido.*'

Fear gripped Joanna and refused to let go.

'You've got to get her to a hospital, Galina. You *have* to. Now.'

Galina stared at her with an expression that under different circumstances Joanna might've termed tender.

It was the tenderness shown toward the hopelessly brain-addled.

'There *are* no hospitals,' Galina said. 'Not here.'

THAT NIGHT JOANNA COULD HEAR HER DAUGHTER SCREECHING.

It made the guards unhappy. It got on their nerves. In the middle of the night one of them pulled her off the bed, where she'd been

holding Beatriz' hand to keep from running to the door and screaming at them.

'*Vamos,*' he said, shoving her toward the open doorway.

Beatriz got up to protest.

'*Para eso –*'

The guard, who was called Puento and was usually docile and
amiable, shoved Beatriz against the wall.

A crying baby can test a new parent's patience, according to *Mother
& Baby* magazine.

Where was Puento taking her?

After he'd locked the door behind them, another guard walked up
to them carrying Joelle at arm's length. Later Maruja would tell her
that FARC *guerrilleros* were particularly nervous about getting sick,
since there were no doctors around to treat them.

The jittery boy literally dumped Joelle into her arms, then motioned her toward the feeding room. He ushered her in at a safe distance, giving Joanna a small shove in the back with the rifle butt. He
slammed the door behind them.

Joelle was swimming in sweat.

Every breath produced a strangled, raspy gurgle. When Joanna
put her ear to Joelle's chest, it sounded like someone dying of em-
physema.

Where was Galina?

Joanna pounded on the door – once, twice, three times. Eventually, Puento opened it, looking intent on pounding something back.

Joanna asked him to get Galina to come immediately, right now,
this very second.

No response.

She asked for a rag instead, nervously pantomiming the act of
wringing one out. She couldn't tell whether Puento understood her,
and if he did, whether he cared.

She'd say no. He slammed the door in her face.

Minutes later, though, he returned with a piece of filthy cloth. He
threw it in her general direction.

166

She'd neglected to ask for *agua* – fortunately, the rag seemed damp enough without it. Joanna went through the now familiar ritual of unwrapping and undiapering her baby, trying not to notice her nearly blue skin and hummingbird shiver. She wiped her down the way Galina would have.

'It's going to be okay,' she whispered to her daughter. 'We're going to get home and see Daddy. You're going to like New York. There's a merry-go-round, and in the winter we can ice-skate. There's a zoo with polar bears and monkeys and penguins. You'll love the penguins. They walk kind of funny.'

She held her baby the entire night. Most of the time Joelle screamed and moaned and gurgled. Those were the good moments. The terrifying ones were when Joelle slipped into sleep and her breathing seemed to stop altogether.

Once, when Joelle was clearly and demonstrably alive, basically screaming her lungs out, Puento opened the door and looked in with a nearly murderous expression. He raised his ever-present Kalashnikov – that's what Paul said they were called, *Russian-made rifles,* ancient and unreliable – and pointed it straight at Joelle's head.

'I'll make her stop. She's sick. I'll get her to stop. I promise.'

He lowered the rifle and shut the door.

Joanna must've nodded off.

She woke up when someone shook her by the shoulder.

It was Galina.

The first thing Joanna noticed was the utter lack of crying, the absolute and shocking quiet. The second thing she noticed was that there was no Joelle in her arms. Gone. For one heart-stopping moment she thought her daughter hadn't made it through the night. That Galina had come to tell her that Joelle's body had been taken away, buried in some field.

She was about to start screaming when she *saw* her.

She was lying peacefully in Galina's arms.

167

She was breathing better, not normally, no – but absolutely, unequivocally *better*.

'I got her medicine,' Galina said. 'Liquid drops. *Antibióticos*. She's going to make it, I think.'

Galina had traveled over one hundred miles, Joanna would learn later. She'd called a doctor she knew – she'd gotten a *farmacia* to open up and give her the drops.

She's going to make it, I think.

Joanna's new mantra.

Joelle had grown noticeably cooler, her cough had quieted to manageable, she'd mostly stopped shaking.

Galina watched Joanna feed her. Galina seemed oddly transfixed, even mesmerized. Maybe it was lack of sleep, Joanna thought.

No, this was different, as if she were borne away by memory.

Joanna remembered.

I had a daughter.

'Galina?'

It seemed to take a minute for Galina to come out of her reverie and actually answer her.

'Yes?'

'Your daughter. What happened to her?'

Galina turned, cocked her head at an awkward angle, as if she were trying to hear something from the next room. Or maybe it was from somewhere further away.

'She was killed,' Galina said.

'Killed?' Joanna wasn't prepared for that word. Dead, yes, but *killed*? 'I'm so sorry – that's horrible. How, Galina? What happened?'

Galina sighed. She looked away, up at the shadow of the crucifix still visible on the wall. She made the sign of the cross with a slightly trembling hand.

'Riojas,' she whispered. 'Have you heard of Manuel Riojas?'

TWENTY-FIVE

Galina was staring at mother and child.

She was thinking:

Holy Mary, Mother of God.

For just a moment it was like that picture on my bureau. Faded almost to black and white after so many years, but suddenly come to life. Yes.

It was me. And her. My child.

She was back in my arms. She was that young again.

Just a niña. *My* niña.

Was she ever that small?

Was she?

You can remember, can't you?

CLAUDIA.

Clau-di-a.

Her name was like a song. Scream it down the streets of Chapinero around suppertime, or down the stairs of their *apartamento* after school, and it was hard to keep its singsong rhythm out of your voice – even when you were good and mad. Even when you were

169

pretending to be mad, because Claudia hadn't done her homework yet, or she was late to dinner.

It was impossible to *really* be mad at her. She was that kind of child. The gift from God. She always got around to doing her homework eventually, and she always did it well enough to get As.

She might be late for supper too, but when she arrived, out of breath and suitably contrite, she'd barrage them with a dizzying recounting of the day's events.

Turn down the radio and eat, Galina would say.

But the truth was, she enjoyed listening to the radio more than she enjoyed seeing her scrawny daughter eat.

Claudia was one of those oddly *aware* children. Precociously sensitive to the world and to most of its inhabitants. An unrepentant toy-sharer, even after her favorite doll – Manolo the bullfighter – had his leg torn off by the bratty girl down the hall.

She was the kind of child who wore out the word *why.*

Why this, why that, why *them*?

In a country like Colombia, Galina always believed *why* was a word best avoided.

Maybe it was destined, then, that when Claudia got to La Nacional University – with honors, of course – she'd fall in with a certain crowd. That when she started getting answers to those persistently indignant questions – like why do one percent of Colombians control ninety-eight percent of the wealth, why has every program to alleviate poverty and hunger failed miserably, why were the same people saying the same things in the same positions of power, why, why, *why* – she'd align herself with those who might do something about it.

Or, at least, *talk* about doing something.

Simple political clubs at first. Harmless debating societies.

Don't worry, Mama, she'd tell Galina and her father. *We drink coffee and argue over who's going to pay the bill. Then we talk about changing the world.*

Galina did worry.

170

She had a reasonably developed social conscience herself; it had never done her much good. She could still remember the rallies for Gaitán – the half-mestizo leader determined to democratize Colombia – and recall with poignant fondness the feeling that had wafted through the streets like a spring breeze in the dead of winter. *I am not a man, I am a people.* She could remember his riddled body on the front page of her father's newspaper. After that, a kind of fatalism had set in – like hardening of the arteries, it came progressively with age. The young were inoculated against *that* particular disease; it took years of wear and tear before idealism crumbled like so much bric-a-brac.

Claudia began spending more time out of the house.

More late nights, which she'd attribute to one boyfriend or another.

Galina knew better.

Claudia was flush with love, yes. But not for a boy. That nervous agitation and those shining eyes were for a cause. She had a monstrous crush on a conviction.

Now when Galina warned her about becoming involved in *la política,* she was invariably met with stony silence or, worse, an exasperated shake of the head, as if Galina could have no concept of such things. Of what was wrong and needed *fixing.* As if she were an imbecile, blind and deaf to the world.

It was precisely the opposite. It was her very *knowledge* of the world – of how things worked in Colombia, or didn't, because in truth nothing worked in their country, nothing at all – it was *that* painfully accrued understanding that made her so frightened for her daughter.

When did Claudia first make contact with *them?*

Maybe when she told Galina she was going on a holiday excursion with girlfriends. *To Cartagena,* she said. When she returned ten days later, there wasn't a tan line to be seen. If anything, she looked paler. *The weather was awful,* she explained. Galina was sorely tempted to check the papers to confirm this. She didn't.

171

Cartagena was north. But so, she knew, was FARC.

These little trips became more and more routine.

To a university seminar, she'd explain.

To visit a friend.

A camping trip.

One lie after another.

What was Galina to do? Claudia was of age. Claudia was in love. What were Galina's options, other than to wait it out, hope it would pass like most first loves do. She was being handed a tissue of lies, and she was using it to dry her tears.

Claudia began dressing down. All kids did to some extent, but Claudia wasn't making a fashion statement. More a statement of *solidarity.* She began going days without makeup, without so much as peeking into a mirror.

She didn't know that it only made her more beautiful.

Had Galina mentioned how lovely Claudia was? How perfectly exquisite? Almost *feline.* Sinuous, graceful. Her eyes, of course. Oval, deep amber, and her skin what Galina's *madre* used to call café au lait. She must've inherited her looks from someone other than Galina. Maybe from her paternal grandmother, the chanteuse, a *ventello* singer of some renown who'd reportedly left broken hearts from Bogotá to Cali.

One day Claudia went away and didn't come back.

Another holiday excursion, a seaside jaunt with friends. But when Galina called these friends, frantic, panicked, two days after Claudia's supposed return had come and gone with no Claudia, they professed total ignorance.

What holiday trip?

Odd. She didn't feel surprise. Just confirmation. That, and simple, unrelenting terror. She sat by the telephone, trying to will it to ring. Trying to keep herself from picking it up and dialing the *policía.* She *knew* where Galina was; bringing the *policía* into it would've been worse than doing nothing.

Eventually, Claudia *did* call.

Galina ranted, raved, screamed. The way you admonish a child. How could Claudia not call, how *could* she?

Claudia wasn't the little girl late for dinner anymore.

I'm with them, because to not be with them is to be with the others, she said.

She spoke assuredly. Logically. Even passionately. It's possible there was a part of Galina, the long-buried part of her that once cheered beside her father for Gaitán, that might've even *empathized* with her.

In the end she said what mothers say. What they're allowed to say. Even to revolutionary daughters who've gone to the hills.

You'll be killed, Claudia. They'll call me to pick up your body. Please. Come back. Please, I'm begging you.

But Claudia dismissed her pleas – the way, as a little girl, she had scoffed at wearing rubber boots in the rain.

Then I can't feel the puddles, Mama.

Claudia, above all, was a girl who wanted to feel the puddles.

Her father was devastated. He threatened to go to the *policía,* to haul her back home. *You should've known,* he accused Galina, *you should've known what she was up to.* Galina knew he was speaking out of frustration and wounded love; he knew that going to the *policía* was dangerous, and going after Claudia useless, since he wouldn't begin to know where to look.

So they sat in their private cocoon of pain. Waiting for a spring that might or might not come.

Occasionally, friends would pass on messages. It's better if she doesn't call you, a certain young man explained, a fellow traveler from the university who sported a four-inch goatee and wore a black beret in the fashion of Che. She's all right, he told them. She's committed.

Galina was committed too. To seeing her daughter's face again. She needed to touch her; when Claudia was a child, she'd settle like a nesting bird in the billows of her dress. *I'm a kangaroo,* Galina would whisper, *and you're in my pocket.*

Now her pocket was empty.

One day they received another message from the young man.

Be at such and such a bar at eight tonight.

When Galina asked why, he said *just be there*.

She didn't ask again.

They dressed as if going to church. Wasn't this, after all, what they'd been praying for? They arrived hours early. The bar was uncomfortably dark and seedy, patronized mostly by prostitutes and transvestites.

They waited an hour, two hours, three. In truth, Galina would've waited days.

Then she felt a tap on her shoulder, no, *more* than a tap, a warm hand alighting on her shoulder like a butterfly. She knew that touch. Mothers do. It had *her* blood coursing through it.

How did Claudia look? Ragged, thin, sick?

If that had been the case, maybe they would've been able to talk her back – the way you talk someone down off a ledge. Maybe they could've simply lifted her off her feet and carried her back home.

Claudia didn't look ragged. Or thin. Certainly not sick.

She looked *happy*.

What's your greatest wish for your children?

The wish you end each nightly prayer with?

The one you whisper to yourself when they tell you to blow out the candles for another birthday you'd rather not be celebrating?

I wish, you murmur, *for my child to be happy.*

Only that.

Claudia looked radiantly, unmistakably happy.

Was *beaming* too strong a word?

If she'd been in the throes of first love before, now she was clearly in the midst of a full-fledged affair. One look at her, and Galina knew they'd be leaving without her.

Claudia kissed Galina, then her father.

The three of them held hands, just like when Claudia was four and she'd coerce them into another game of dog and cat. Claudia was always the cat. And the cat was always captured.

Galina asked her how she was.

But she already knew the answer.

'Good, Mama,' Claudia said.

'Why didn't you *tell* us?' Galina asked, then began doing what she'd promised herself she wouldn't. Crying, crumbling, falling to pieces.

'Shhh . . . ,' Claudia whispered, daughter-suddenly-turned-mother. 'Stop, Mama. I'm *fine*. I'm wonderful. I *couldn't* tell you. You know that.'

No. All Galina knew was that Claudia was her heart. And that from now on life would consist of hurried meetings in transvestite bars and furtive messages from friends.

Claudia told them little of anything specific. Where she was. Whom she was with. She mostly asked about home. How was her cat, Tulo? And her friends, Tani and Celine?

For their entire time together, Galina refused to let go of her hand. She must've thought, in some primitive part of her brain, that if she never let go, Claudia would be forced to stay with them. That as long as they were touching, they couldn't be apart.

She was wrong, of course. Hours flew by, the opposite of all those days waiting to hear from her when she'd felt stuck in time.

Claudia announced she had to leave.

Galina had one last, enormous plea left in her. She'd been practicing it as Claudia asked about home, about relatives and schoolmates, as Galina sat and held her hand like a lifeline.

'I want you to listen to me, Claudia. To sit and hear everything I have to say. Yes?'

Claudia nodded.

'I understand how you feel,' she began.

She did understand. It didn't matter.

'You think I'm too old. That I can't possibly feel what you feel. But I do. There was a time, when I was very young, that I was just

175

like you. But what I know, I know. FARC, the USDF – it doesn't matter. Both sides are guilty. Both sides are blameless. In the end they are each other. Just as innocent. Just as murderous. And everyone dies. Everyone. I'm asking you as your one and only mother in the world. Please. Don't go back to them.'

She might've been speaking Chinese.

Or not speaking at all.

Claudia couldn't hear her, and even if she could, she was incapable of understanding a word.

She patted Galina's hand, smiled, the way you do to those already claimed by senility. She stood up, embraced her father while Galina remained frozen to her chair. Then Claudia reached down, put her head in the hollow of her neck.

'I love you, Mama,' she said.

That's all.

On the way home, they sat in complete, numbing silence. They'd dressed as if going to church, but they returned from a funeral.

There were just a few messages from her after that.

From time to time the boy from the university called with news. Every time Galina opened the paper, she held her breath . . .

THE DOOR CREAKED OPEN.

Galina stopped talking.

Tomás – one of the guards – nodded at her, motioned for her to get up.

Joelle was out of danger now. Joanna would have to give her back, return to her room.

'What happened to her?' Joanna asked Galina, transferring Joelle to her, suddenly desperate to know the ending. 'You didn't finish the story.'

Galina simply shook her head, pressed Joelle to her chest. Then she headed to the door.

TWENTY-SIX

He didn't know he was alive and kicking until he realized that's what he was doing. *Kicking.* Moving his legs back and forth in an effort to put out the fire that was crawling up his skin.

He must've passed out from the smoke. He remembered the wall of flame bearing down on them like an act of God. Maybe it wasn't an act of God – because he seemed to remember he'd *prayed* to God just before everything went black and here he was *alive.*

So maybe he and God had made up. Maybe God said enough with numbers and equations and risk ratios and let's try blind faith for a change, okay?

He wasn't actually on fire. Not literally. His pants, what was left of them, were smoking. And the skin poking out from their tattered remnants appeared baby pink – the telltale sign of first-degree burn.

Somehow they'd made it past the line of kerosene.

Everything to his left was a charred, smoking black. The wind had taken the fire in a single direction. Meaning Miles was right. They'd headed *toward* the fire and won.

Or he had. Miles was missing in action.

What about *them*?

Paul tentatively raised his head and peeked.

It looked volcanic. Picture one of those Discovery Channel specials where islands of lush vegetation are reduced to boiling stews of smoke and fire. Here and there scattered bursts of flame still shot high into the air.

Overall it was lunar-empty.

They were gone.

With this ecstatic realization came an equally horrific one. They were gone; so were the *drugs*. They were interred in the black soot. His one and only chance of saving Joanna had vanished. *When God shuts a door, he opens a window,* his long-dead mother used to say. But going along with his newfound doctrine of faith, it was entirely possible the reverse was also true. That when God opened a window, he shut a door.

Paul was alive; Joanna and Joelle were dead.

Soon enough.

He collapsed back onto the still-steaming earth, as if shot.

Someone said hello.

A creature with a completely black face, save for the eyes, moon white like those of a minstrel singer, his whole person surrounded in rising wisps of smoke.

An *angel*? Come to earth to tell Paul he was wrong, sorry, he hadn't survived the fire, after all? Given Joanna and Joelle's probable fate, would the news be that unwelcome?

It wasn't an angel.

It was Miles.

THEY FOUND MILES' CAR PRETTY MUCH WHERE THEY'D LEFT IT. Both doors were yanked open and the windshield was smashed.

That wasn't what upset Miles.

Not that they'd trashed his car, but that they'd actually *seen* it, taken note of it, jotted down his license number or maybe his registration, which was stuck somewhere in the glove compartment. Now that the euphoria of actually surviving had worn off, Miles seemed to understand that it might not be for long. He retreated to somewhere inside himself.

That made two of them.

Paul had apologized to Miles on the way to the car – *sorry for almost killing you*. Miles reiterated that he was the one who'd sent Paul and Joanna to Colombia. Only this time he hadn't sounded very convincing.

Then they'd both shut up.

The spiderweb cracks in the windshield made driving an exercise in guessing. There either were or weren't cars in front of them, lights were either green or red, road signs were anybody's guess. On the way out of the swamp they passed four fire engines screaming down the highway.

Paul tried to navigate with his head out the window.

Somewhere between Jersey City and the Lincoln Tunnel, Paul said, 'Who were they?'

Miles didn't immediately answer.

'They must've burned down the house in Jersey City,' Paul added. 'It had to be them.'

Miles nodded. 'That makes sense.'

'So?'

Miles seemed lost in thought. Either that or he was still feeling too depressed to talk. They'd entered the white fluorescent glow of the Lincoln Tunnel – always a kind of sci-fi experience.

After a while Miles said, 'I don't know who they are. I can *guess*. The other side.'

'What other side? The Colombian government?'

'The Colombian government's not going to be shooting people over here.'

'Okay. Then who are we talking about?'

'The other side in the war. Those right-wing paramilitary nuts. Manuel Riojas.' He didn't appear to be very happy about this suggestion.

'*Riojas?* I thought he's in jail. They extradited him. To Florida.'

179

'Sure. *He's* in jail. They're not.'

'*They?* Who's they?'

'His people. His gang. His foot soldiers. You know how many Colombians there are in New York City?'

Miles tried to clean his hands by wiping them on the seat divider, but it only succeeded in making it black.

'They followed FARC's drug contacts?' Paul said, trying to work it out as he spoke. 'That's what you're saying? Found that house in Jersey City and burned it down? Then tailed them here?'

'Maybe. Why not? They're on different sides, but they pay for things the same way. Drugs mean money. Money means guns.'

Okay, Paul thought. He wondered if sometimes money just meant money.

'Consider it a two-for-one. They get to kill a few of FARC's friends, and score some drugs at the same time. Just my theory.'

Given what Paul had read about Manuel Riojas, it was a theory you'd rather not spend too much time thinking about.

'What now?'

'I can bullshit you and say I've got a great idea. Would you believe me?'

MILES INSISTED THEY STOP AT HIS OFFICE IN THE CITY.

'I might have a hard time explaining to my wife why we look like we've just returned from Baghdad. There's a shower there. And some clothes.'

Miles' office was in a brownstone on the East Side. Three months ago Paul and Joanna had walked in there and been told they'd have a daughter in two months.

Miles parked the car in a single-car garage beneath the building.

When they exited the car, Paul could smell that peculiar odor of garages everywhere – mildew, dust, and motor oil. Joanna, he noted with a pang, would have been able to discern a few other things as well.

180

They entered the house through a side door, opening onto a hallway with gray cement walls covered in a sheen of condensation. A single naked bulb supplied what little light there was.

They took the stairs up to the first floor, which contained a modest waiting room filled with out-of-date magazines. Paul remembered sitting there with Joanna, flipping through a strategically placed issue of *Time*. *Infertility – the New Scourge* was the cover story.

'Bathroom's upstairs,' Miles said. 'Want to go first?'

'Thanks,' Paul said. 'I have nothing to wear.'

'I'll lend you some jeans.'

When he turned on the shower, the water at his feet turned black. The skin on his legs and arms felt scrubbed raw, and he wondered if he needed medical attention.

When he got out of the shower, he examined himself in the bathroom mirror. His face seemed okay – a little pinker than usual, certainly more despondent-looking. There was nothing a doctor could do about that.

Miles had left blue jeans and a white button-down shirt just outside the bathroom on a chair. They were about two sizes too small. He waddled out to the hallway where Miles was patiently waiting his turn.

He wordlessly passed Paul on his way to the bathroom.

When Miles came out, he was back to more or less normal skin color.

'Let's go to my office,' he said without any particular enthusiasm.

Being in the very place where Miles conducted his business, where he pulled strings and conjured up babies, didn't seem to do anything to improve his disposition. He sat behind his desk and looked strangely lost there – as if he'd forgotten what it was he did for a living.

Paul only had to look above the desk to remind himself.

He who saves one child saves the world.

Okay, Miles. There's another child who desperately needs saving now. And her *mother.* Her too.

He scanned the rest of the room while Miles sat there silent and brooding. In between an honorary degree from Baruch Law School and a citation from the board of a Bronx hospital was a poster he hadn't seen before. *The All-Nazi Baseball Team,* it said, a diamond grid with each player's name affixed by position. *Joseph Goebbels* was on the pitcher's mound. *Always threw curves* was the scouting report on him. *Hermann Göring* was behind the plate – *great defense,* it said. *Joseph Mengele* was in right – *lethal arm. Albert Speer* at third – *surprising power.* The ball girls were *Eva Braun* and *Leni Riefenstahl.* The manager? *Hitler,* of course: *a great motivator.* Not great enough: The poster reminded everyone that the team *Lost World Championship in 1945.*

Ha, ha.

Paul wondered if Jews other than Miles found that particularly funny.

'I don't suppose you have the kind of money to make it up to them?' Miles finally said. He was looking down at his hands where his fingernails were still black, even after the shower.

'Two *million?*' Paul said. It might just as well have been two billion.

'Okay.' Miles shrugged. 'Just asking.'

Paul had come to a decision of sorts. It wasn't an easy one, but it was clearly the *only* one. It didn't matter that he'd smuggled drugs into the country. Not anymore. The drugs were gone, the cupboard bare. His family was hanging by a string.

'I'm going to the authorities,' he said.

'The *authorities?*' Miles repeated, as if it were a strange and foreign concept. 'Okay. Which authorities are we talking about?'

'The police, the government, whoever has a chance of doing anything. The State Department, the Colombians. Every authority there is – all of them. I'm going to tell them everything – throw myself on the mercy of the court. Isn't that the expression?'

182

'The mercy of the court? Oh yeah, that's an expression. Absolutely. That's pretty much all it is. I don't think mercy is allowed through the metal detectors. You might want to reconsider.'

'*Reconsider?* What do you suggest I do? Tell Pablo I lost two million dollars' worth of drugs, but if he doesn't mind, I'd like my wife and daughter back anyway? I've got to do something. It's the only thing left.'

'Maybe not,' Miles said.

'What are you talking about?'

Miles stood up, stared at the four walls, began pacing back and forth behind his desk, slowly, bit by bit, seeming to regain that can-do aura right before Paul's grateful eyes, until he stopped, looked up, and snapped his fingers.

'Plan B,' Miles said.

TWENTY-SEVEN

His name was Moshe Skolnick.

He was a Russian businessman, Miles said.

What kind of business? Paul asked.

'I have no idea,' Miles answered. 'But he's awfully good at it.'

Whatever the nature of his business, Moshe did a lot of it with Colombians. 'He's got contacts there,' Miles said. 'He flies to Bogotá at least three times a year.'

Plan B, going to Moshe, was preferable to Plan C, going to the authorities, Miles said, because Paul needed someone who knew the right people. Or, more accurately, the wrong people.

'Someone who's got credibility with both sides.'

Paul had agreed to give it one more shot. If Paul was fueled by sheer unadulterated panic, Miles seemed fueled by sheer stubbornness, as if giving up would be a personal affront. Once upon a time Miles had promised them a baby and he'd only half delivered. He seemed determined to finish the job.

They were driving to Little Odessa.

'How do you know him?' Paul asked.

'That's the thing about being in my line of work. You meet all sorts of people you wouldn't ordinarily meet.'

'He was a client?'

'More like a client of a client.'

'Not a friend?'

'You don't really want him as a friend. You don't want him as your enemy either. He owes me a favor.'

First Miles dropped Paul off at his apartment.

He needed his own clothes; Miles' pants felt like they were cutting off his circulation. He needed his own surroundings and his own life. Lying low didn't much matter anymore. He and Miles had decided that if he ran into his friends John or Lisa, he'd blame Joanna's absence on a visa screwup, something Paul had come back to work out from this end. With any luck he'd avoid seeing them.

He took the stairs to lessen the odds. He made it to his apartment without running into anyone he knew.

When he shut his door, very gently because he didn't want John or Lisa to hear, he saw a crib sitting in his living room. It had pink wooden slats and frilly bedding decorated with teddy bears. An oversize red bow was stapled to it, looking like an enormous hothouse flower. It was conspicuously empty.

He walked over and picked up the card Scotch-taped to the headboard.

Congratulations on our new grandchild! Figured you'd need this when you got home. Matt and Barbara.

Joanna's parents, making their first down payment on grandparenthood.

He felt a stab of pain somewhere under his heart. If heartache was a misnomer, if emotions resided somewhere in your brain and not lower down, why did it physically hurt *there*?

They should've been home by now. The three of them.

Friends would've come calling, toting bakery cakes, bottles of champagne, tiny pink baby clothes. Joanna's parents would've settled into the guest room for a solid week or so. The apartment would've been pulsing with life.

185

Its current emptiness seemed to accuse him of something. He knew what too.

All he had to do was look at the clock sitting on the living room TV, the time and date prominently displayed in numbers the color of blood.

Miles would be back in fifteen minutes to pick him up. He dressed in chinos and a T-shirt, threw his cellular phone into his pocket, and headed for the door.

His answering machine was pulsing green.

Oh well.

He hit the play button.

Hello, Mr Breidbart. I'm calling on behalf of Home Equity Plus. We're offering a special rate on refinancing good for this month only . . .

Hey, it's Ralph. When you get back, give me a call, would you? I couldn't find your charts on McKenzie. By the way, congrats on the baby. Cigars to follow.

Hiya! It's Mom, honey. Got your letter, but we don't know when you're coming back. The hotel said you checked into another one. Call us, please! Love ya! How do you like the crib?

Hello, Mr and Mrs Breidbart. This is María. I'm calling to check up and see how everything is.

María Consuelo, making that follow-up call she'd promised them.

This call was followed by two more follow-up calls from María. Then a *spectacular one-time-only offer* from a carpet company. Followed by an automated solicitation from an assemblyman up for re-election. Then another message from María.

By this fourth one she clearly sounded annoyed. She'd called them four times, *four*, and there was still no word. She'd appreciate it if they would do her the honor of calling back and letting her know how things were.

Hi, María. As a matter of fact, things aren't going so well. The baby you gave us was kidnapped by your nurse and driver. I smuggled drugs into the country to try to get them out, but we were attacked and al-

186

most burned to death. So, all in all, things could be looking better. Thanks for asking.

LITTLE ODESSA SEEMED LIKE ITS NAME. LIKE ANOTHER COUNTRY. The evening had turned gray and misty, and a strong wind was whipping in from the ocean. You could see flecks of white foam out there and little whirlwinds of sand dancing across the beach.

Half the store signs were in Russian. The street fronting the beach was crowded with nightclubs, most of them named after Russian cities.

The Kiev. The St. Petersburg. Moscow Central.

Lack of shut-eye was catching up to Paul. He'd nodded off going over the Williamsburg Bridge – only the combination of metal grating and worn shocks revived him, bouncing him awake to a scene of stark black and white. The little bit of sleep had been painfully sweet – once his eyes were open, the dread quickly returned.

Moshe worked at a sprawling warehouse.

Miles pulled into the back lot. Two men were leaning against the only other car – a maroon Buick – smoking cigarettes and jabbering in Russian.

When they got out, Miles waved at them, but they didn't wave back.

'Friendly guys,' Miles said. 'They love me.'

The parking lot faced a half-open loading door. They ducked underneath. The inside was astonishingly huge – the size of your average Home Depot. It might've contained just as much merchandise.

There were rows of washers, dryers, refrigerators, TVs, stereos, computers, and furniture. There were bicycles, basketballs, golf clubs, clothing, and tires. There were video games, books, lawn furniture, and gas grills.

A group of men were milling around the home appliance section. One of them turned and waved.

'That's Moshe,' Miles said.

187

Paul thought he was slickly dressed for a warehouse. He was wearing what looked like a thousand-dollar suit, complete with blue silk tie and nicely buffed shoes that came to a distinct point. He had a goatee and thick eyebrows, which seemed to give him a look of perpetual amusement.

He walked forward and grabbed Miles in a bear hug, bestowing a kiss on both cheeks.

'Heyyyy . . . Miles . . . my favorite lawyer.' He had a smoker's voice, husky and low, layered with a thick Russian accent.

After Moshe had put Miles back down – in his enthusiasm he'd actually lifted him a good inch or so off the ground – he turned to Paul and smiled.

'Paul?'

Paul nodded. 'Hello,' he said. 'Nice to meet you.'

Moshe shook his head. 'Not so nice, I think. Miles tell me your . . . situation. Catastrophe. My sympathies. Your wife and child, huh? Those guerrilla –' He uttered what must have been a Russian curse. 'You know what we do to guerrillas in Russia, huh? Remember that theater in Moscow – those Chechen bastards? Boom – boom – gassed them to fucking hell.'

As Paul remembered it, the Russian authorities had also gassed about two hundred innocent hostages to hell as well. He thought it better not to mention this to Moshe.

Instead, he asked Moshe if he could help.

Moshe put a large arm around Paul. 'Look, I know those bastards. Some of them. We see what we can do, okay? Sometimes things can be negotiated. They are about as Marxist as we were – everyone's a businessman, okay? Listen – they won't kill them. Not likely. I make some calls.'

'Thank you. Really.'

'Don't thank me yet. I haven't done shit.' He smiled. 'We see.'

He looked through the half-open loading door and shook his head.

'Hey, Miles, my fucking genius lawyer, how many times I tell you not to park there? You're blocking the door.'

Miles said, 'Oh, sorry. I'll move it.'

'Give your keys to one of my guys. He move it for you, okay? We go to the office and talk.'

'One of your guys dented my fender last time they moved it for me. I'll do it,' Miles said.

A man walked by, groaning under the weight of an enormous crate on his left shoulder. It looked in imminent danger of tipping over and smashing to bits. The man had *CCCP* tattooed on his arm – the letters of the old Soviet sports federation.

'Go ahead,' Miles said to Paul. 'I'll be back in a minute.'

'Park it on Rostow, okay, *meshugener*,' Moshe said. 'You park it on Ocean, they gonna ticket you.'

Miles said *okay*. He slipped back under the loading door.

'Paul.' Moshe motioned him to follow. They went through a side door and into a hallway where the walls were paneled in cheap imitation wood. Moshe's office was down the hall – *El Presidente*, it said on the mottled glass. Paul assumed that was a joke.

'We wait for Miles, okay?' The office had a waiting room with two couches. He pointed to one of them. 'Please.'

Paul sat down as Moshe slipped into the inner office.

RING.

Ring.

He'd fallen asleep. Apparently, his cell phone had jolted him awake.

How long had he been out?

His phone had stopped ringing – he remembered its ring like an echo. He fished it out of his pants pocket, flipped it open, and checked the number. An area code he didn't recognize.

Where was Miles?

The inner door opened and Moshe was standing there smiling.

189

He looked down at his watch – a shimmering kaleidoscope of gold and diamonds.

'What the fuck,' he said. 'We get started.' He walked back into his office.

But Paul's cell phone rang again.

'Mr Breidbart?'

It was María Consuelo.

'Yes, hello.'

'I have been calling you for three days. Do you know that?'

'Yes, María. We've been –'

'I always make a follow-up call to the new parents. I told you and Mrs Breidbart this, yes?'

'Yes, you did. We were . . . staying at a relative's.'

'I was getting worried. We need to make sure our new families are settling in. How is everything? Is the baby fine?'

'Yes, she's fine.'

Moshe was just visible through the half-open door of his office. He was pointing at his watch.

'Just a minute,' Paul said to him. But Moshe couldn't hear him; he cocked his head and cupped his left ear like a comedian searching for laughs.

'What?' María said.

'No, not you. I was talking to someone else. The baby's fine. I really have to run. I certainly will –'

'Can I talk to *Mrs* Breidbart, please?'

For a moment Paul couldn't bring himself to answer. 'No,' he said. 'She's not here.'

'Oh? She is well?'

'Yes, she's well. She's just not with me. Not at the moment.'

'Can she call me? I'd like to speak with her.'

'Yes. She'll call you.'

'All right. You're sure everything is good?'

'Yes, everything's okay. Couldn't be better.'

'All right, then.'

Paul was going to hang up, was just about to, but he suddenly couldn't resist asking a question of his own.

'María?'

'Yes?'

'I'm just curious. How long have you been using Pablo? How well do you know him?'

'Pablo?'

'Yes. The driver you gave us. Have you been using him a long time?'

'I gave you a driver? No.'

'No? What do you mean, no? I'm talking about *Pablo*. You hired him to take care of us in Bogotá.'

'No. I didn't hire him.'

'Okay, someone from your staff. Someone took care of it for you.'

'Accommodations and transportation are not supplied by us. The contract clearly stipulates this, yes?'

'So who . . . ?'

'Who? Your lawyer. Mr Goldstein, yes?'

Your lawyer, Mr Goldstein.

'Miles,' Paul said.

'Yes, certainly. It's his responsibility to provide accommodations and . . .'

'Transportation.'

'Yes.'

Moshe was still waiting for him in the office. He was still smiling.

'Mr Goldstein called you two days ago, María,' Paul said, keeping his voice low. 'Remember – he asked you for Pablo's number.'

'Called me, no. Mr Goldstein didn't call me.'

'He didn't call you. He didn't call you and ask you for that number? Two days ago – Wednesday night?'

'No.'

A vision came back to Paul. Miles on the telephone – smiling,

191

nodding, laughing, *emoting* for someone who wasn't actually there in front of him. But someone *was* there in front of him.

Paul.

'Okay. Thank you.'

'Was there a problem with your driver?'

'No problem.'

'Please have Mrs Briedbart call me.'

'Yes. Good-bye.'

He was operating by rote – the way you can steer your car left or right, stop at lights, and accelerate on highways, even when your mind is somewhere far away. Paul's mind was far, far away, stuck in a place between terror and helplessness.

'Coming?' Moshe was suddenly standing right in front of him.

He was still smiling, but Paul understood that it was like Galina's smile when she'd opened her front door and welcomed them into her home.

'Is there a bathroom?' Paul asked. 'I need to use the bathroom.'

It's amazing how the survival instinct takes over.

How you can be frozen to the spot, your body positively numb with fear, and you can still move your mouth and ask for the bathroom – ask for *anything* that will prevent you from walking into that office. Because you know with absolute certainty that if you walk in, you won't be walking out.

Moshe seemed to contemplate this request for a moment.

'Back there,' he said, pointing with his thumb. 'Out the door to the left.'

Paul stood up. His legs felt like they had back in María's office, like soft jelly. He was trying not to let Moshe know that he was in on the big secret, that he understood he was the only actor in this charade who hadn't been given his lines.

'Down the hall,' Moshe said, but Paul noticed that he'd stopped smiling.

'Okay. Be right back.' He turned to go.

Moshe put his hand on his shoulder. Paul could feel sharp fingernails digging into his flesh.

'Hurry,' he said. His teeth were yellow and misshapen, something that hadn't been evident from a distance. Now that Paul was close enough to smell him, he could see the physical legacy of what must've been an impoverished Russian childhood.

'Sure. I just need to use the bathroom. Then I'll come right back.' It sounded like bad exposition – he was giving too much information.

'Good,' Moshe said, seemingly unawares. 'We got lots to do, huh?'

'Yes. Lots to do.'

Paul walked through the door, resisting the overpowering urge to run. It's what you do in the face of mortal danger, isn't it? It's wired into your system – this need to churn your legs and take off like a bat out of hell.

He could hear Moshe stepping out into the hall behind him, evidently making sure Paul was going where he said he was.

The bathroom was about ten yards down the hall. *Hombres,* the door said – perhaps it came with the El Presidente model in the Spaghetti Western Collection.

He didn't have a plan when he said he needed to go to the bathroom. He didn't have a plan now.

Just a goal. To make it out of there alive.

He could sense Moshe still there in the hall. Watching him.

He went through the bathroom door.

It had a sink, a dirty urinal, and two narrow stalls.

What now?

His *phone.*

He could call the police. He'd tell them he'd been threatened, that he was trapped, in physical danger.

He went into the first stall and locked the door. He sat down on the toilet seat.

Paul pulled out his phone and dialed 911 – a number that was now and forever associated with the date of the same number.

Nothing. That grating three-note announcement heralding that he'd done something wrong. That his party has moved or changed numbers.

He checked the number in the display window: 811.

Okay, nerves. He dialed again – wondering if his cell phone was on vibrate and ringing, since it seemed to be shaking in his hand. Even as he asked himself this, he knew perfectly well it wasn't his phone that was shaking.

This time he got through.

'Emergency. How can we help you?' A female voice that sounded vaguely automated.

'I'm in danger,' Paul whispered. 'Please send the police.'

'What's the problem, sir?'

Hadn't he just told her what the problem was?

'These men . . . they're trying to kill me.'

'Is this a break-in, sir?'

'No. I'm somewhere . . . in an office. Not an office . . . a warehouse.'

'Have you been attacked, sir?'

'No. Yes. They're about to attack me.'

'Where are you located?'

'Uh . . . in Little Odessa.'

'Little Odessa. That's in Brooklyn, sir?'

'Yes, Brooklyn.'

'What's the exact address, sir?'

'I don't . . . Somewhere by the . . .' There were footsteps coming down the hall. Paul stopped talking.

'Give me your name, sir.'

The footsteps stopped just outside the door. The door opened. Two men walked in, one of them whistling 'Night Fever.' The faucet turned on, one of the men began washing his hands.

'Sir? Your name, sir?'

194

Someone coughed up phlegm, spit it into the sink. The men began talking. They spoke in a haphazard mixture of Russian and English, switching from one to the other seemingly at random.

The man washing his hands said something in Russian, then asked if someone named Wenzel made the vig?

The whistler stopped. 'What?'

'Wenzel. He pay vig or not?'

'Oh, sure thing.'

'Fucking GNP of Slovakia, right?'

The other man answered in Russian, and they both laughed.

Then some back-and-forth, mostly in English – *you see Yuri around, tell that motherfucker he eat me* – interrupted by the sound of one of the men urinating.

'Sir . . . are you still . . . ?'

Paul clicked the phone off. He suddenly realized that he'd been holding his breath ever since the men walked in. When he let it out, it sounded like the whoosh of a just-turned-on air conditioner.

Both men turned around and faced the stall. That embarrassing moment when you realize someone's there, has been there the whole time you've been speaking.

Paul could just make out their feet underneath the stall door. Those hybrid sneaker-shoes, felt with garish nylon racing stripes.

One of the men said something in Russian.

When Paul didn't answer, he switched languages.

'You whacking off in there, Sammy?'

'No.'

Silence. They didn't recognize the voice.

'Okay,' one of the men said. 'Just checking – we're with whack-off patrol.' They laughed, then turned and walked out.

Paul was about to press send again, but he could hear them through the closing door. Someone was out there speaking to them – Moshe?

He'd be asking them if Paul was in there.

Yes, they'd say. There was someone whacking off in the stall.

Okay, that gave him maybe five minutes. Less, before Moshe himself walked in or sent one of his men back. To do what?

Pull Paul out of the stall and finish him off.

The emergency operator had asked him for the address, but he didn't know it. They should hold seminars on this: If you're going to be killed somewhere, *note address.* Note *name* too; he'd forgotten the name on the warehouse roof.

He stood up and pushed the stall door open. There was one small window. He lifted it open. Almost. Halfway up it stuck tight. It looked like it hadn't been opened in years, at least not from inside – dead spiders were littered between the window and rusty screen.

And one not-dead spider. Black, fat, and stubbornly sticking to its fly-littered web. *Spiders* – stuck alphabetically between *retroviruses* and *ticks* on Paul's long list of things to be frightened of.

Paul flushed the urinal to cover the noise, then gave the window a monumental push. It flew open.

First things first. The spider.

He attempted to crush it against the screen with a wad of rolled-up toilet tissue, but the screen was so rusted it fell off.

Good. *Double* good – the spider disappeared with it.

Paul stepped onto the sink and, using it for leverage, began to push himself through the window. He was facing the back lot. Miles was long gone. Only that maroon Buick remained; the man with *CCCP* tattooed on his arm was leaning against the driver's side door, smoking a cigarette.

If the man turned just a little to his right, to scratch his arm or spit or just stretch his neck, he'd have a perfect view of a terrified man squeezing himself through a window.

It didn't matter. Going back wasn't an option.

It was a tight fit. The window was about the size of the window in the Bogotá house, the one he'd put his arms through in an effort to make that bewildered schoolgirl understand they were crying out for help. He was still crying *help,* but if the smoker saw him, he wouldn't get it.

196

Keep worming.

The window frame seemed to be scraping off layers of skin; he thought he might be bleeding. He remembered a startling scene from Animal Planet, an enormous python actually coming out of its skin. If only *he* could do that – leave his burned and battered self behind for something fresh and new.

The smoker threw his cigarette to the ground and watched it for a moment, seemingly hypnotized by the little wisp of smoke undulating in front of him.

Paul was down to his lower half, but there was nothing to hold on to. His upper thighs were taking the entire weight of his body. It felt as if he were literally going to break in half.

He felt a tickle on the small of his back. He twisted his head back.

The spider.

Black, hairy, and back. It was taking a constitutional across his naked skin where his shirt had ridden up.

He pushed and strained with renewed vigor, keeping one jittery eye on the spider.

He should've been looking the other way.

When he finally turned around to check on the man with the *CCCP* tattoo, he was staring right at him.

He'd straightened up off the car; he'd begun to amble over as if he were trying to get a better look. What an odd sight – *a grown man crawling out of a window.*

Or not crawling. Paul was pretty much stuck. He could feel the individual prickly hairs on each of the spider's eight legs.

'The fuck you doing?' The man had stopped about ten feet from him. A Russian bear. He had serpentine stretch marks on his arm where his muscles bulged enough to give the tattooed letters an odd lilt. He looked like a poster child for steroid use.

'There's a spider on me,' Paul said. It was the first thing that flashed into his mind, probably because other than the giant standing in front of him, it *was* the first thing on his mind.

'Spider?'

197

'Yes. I panicked,' Paul said.

'Huh?'

'I jumped through the window.'

'Spider?' He began laughing. Real, gut-wrenching, roll-in-the-aisle laughter, like a laugh track on the WB. Any minute, tears were going to start copiously flowing down his cheeks.

'Scared of *spider*?' he said. 'Ha, ha, ha.'

Okay, at least he believed him.

'Can you get me out of here?' Paul asked.

The Russian sluggishly stepped forward and grabbed Paul by his arms.

Paul could feel the enormous strength in the man's muscles – like something inhuman, even mechanical. When he pulled, Paul thought either he was going to come flying through the window or his arms were going to come flying out of their sockets. Fifty-fifty.

Suddenly, he was on the ground, arms intact.

That might not have been a good thing.

The man had walked over to his left, where he made a show of picking up a large chunk of cement, which had broken off the base of a parking meter that for some reason was lying there in the yard. He weighed it in his hands, then looked at Paul with an odd smile.

Paul stepped back.

The man lifted the ragged chunk up over his head and began advancing toward Paul.

'Wait . . .'

But he didn't wait.

The Russian brought the cement block down with full force. About six inches from Paul's right shoe.

He smiled, lifted it up, admired the ugly starburst of brown blood. Some of the spider's legs were detached but still twitching.

'No more,' he said.

Before Paul could move, there was a sudden sound from inside the bathroom. Moshe's face was staring at them from the open window.

No one said anything.

Moshe looked confused. Paul had evidently just crawled out his bathroom window – how else could he have gotten outside the warehouse? – but he must've been wondering whether Paul actually *knew*. He had to be undecided as to which Moshe he should be playing here. The concerned friend of a friend, out to help Paul save his wife and daughter?

Or the man who'd been asked to murder him?

'He was scared of spider,' Paul's benefactor said, still looking amused by the whole thing.

Moshe didn't share his amusement. He looked at Paul and said, '*What* spider?'

'On my back,' Paul said. 'I was standing at the sink and the spider landed on me. I have a kind of phobia. I panicked.'

'Phobia?' He evidently wasn't familiar with the term. He was probably very familiar with lying. He was staring straight into Paul's eyes – the way the gamblers on *Celebrity Poker* lock onto their competitors' faces in order to know whether they're bluffing. It felt *physical,* like an actual pat-down.

Moshe said something in Russian, out of the corner of his mouth. *What?*

Paul decided not to wait to weigh its nuances.

The man with the tattoo on his arm could've easily moved, flattened Paul with one lazy punch, or simply knocked the cement block out of his hands. The one he'd discarded in the dirt but Paul had picked up. It must've been a complete and utter shock that someone scared of spiders was capable of committing a physical assault. The man didn't actually move until the cement block made contact with the top of his head. He went down with a sickening thud.

Paul ran.

'*Paul!*' Moshe shouted behind him.

He'd never make it out of the yard. He'd gotten rid of the steroid user, sure, but in a minute there'd be others. Lots and lots of others.

He heard shouting, the sound of the loading door sliding open.

He didn't have enough of a lead. It was hopeless.

Sometimes you get lucky.

As any good actuary could tell you, sometimes the odds are just that. Odds. Numbers. They don't matter. You can be absolutely certain that if you live long enough, one day they'll rise up and bite you in the ass.

Or kiss you on the mouth.

His path to the open gate took him right past the parked Buick. Even in a full-out sprint – okay, not much by Carl Lewis standards, but okay by your average weekend warrior's – he was able to glance inside.

The keys were dangling from the ignition.

He stopped short, pulled the front door open, and slid in. He turned the key and put the pedal to the metal.

He whooshed out of the gate. Just as three men came running after him.

But their cars weren't in the lot.

They were parked on Ocean or Rostow so they wouldn't block the loading door.

TWENTY-EIGHT

In the early-morning light Miles' Brooklyn brownstone looked darker, even forbidding.

The black tower of fairy tales.

Paul had spent the night in his car, parked in a deserted lot underneath the Verrazano Bridge. He'd ruled out going back to his apartment – he was afraid someone might be there waiting for him. He'd woken to a street bum rapping on his window, staring at what must've been a mirror image of himself.

Paul peeked in the rearview mirror to check. Yes – a worthy candidate for bumhood. His skin was pasty. His eyes were rheumy and bloodshot. His head hurt.

He kept asking himself *why?*

It felt like he'd entered the bizarro world of the Superman comics he used to read as a kid. Where everything was upside down, inside out. Where people who looked like your friends, weren't. Where you didn't have a clue.

A piece of his rational brain kept asking if he could've been mistaken. About everything. If he might've misunderstood what María said on the phone. If he'd put two and two together and come up with five.

Maybe Miles *had* hired Pablo. Maybe Miles' Wednesday night call had simply slipped her mind.

And Moshe? Maybe what he'd whispered to the steroid user had been an innocent crack. Something about the spider – about actuaries with silly phobias.

And those men running after him? Why *not*, if he'd just clobbered one of their coworkers over the head.

Maybe.

Only he couldn't forget the way Moshe looked at him through the office door – that smile dripping with chilling insincerity. The way Moshe watched him walk down the hall to the bathroom, as if sighting his prey.

And something else. *Miles had gone to move his car but never came back.*

Things were beginning to stir in the neighborhood.

People were trickling out of their houses – young, old, even ancient. Unlike Miles, these were people who didn't dare offend God, even if he did scare off a client or two. The men wore long corkscrew sideburns falling down to their shoulders like Victorian ringlets. They all wore black skullcaps. They must be headed to worship, Paul guessed, suddenly realizing it was Saturday.

Eighteen hours and four days. Dread seized him and refused to let go.

Miles' house remained conspicuously quiet.

Paul waited twenty minutes – eight o'clock, a reasonable hour to be awake and functioning.

He got out of the car and walked up to the brownstone steps.

He thought he saw a flash of movement through the living room window, slight and insubstantial, like the shadow of a butterfly.

When he knocked on the door, he only had to wait ten seconds before Rachel opened it.

She was dressed in her Saturday best, wig firmly in place under a black wide-brimmed hat, evidently ready to join the throng making its way to prayer. She peered at him quizzically, giving a phantom glance at her watchless wrist.

Yes, it was kind of early for visitors.

'Hello,' Paul said as normally as he could muster. 'Is Miles here?'

It was an obvious question, Rachel's face seemed to say. Where else would Miles be at eight on a Saturday morning but in his home?

'He's not feeling well. I was about to take the children to shul, Mr Breidbart. Was he expecting you?'

Good question, Paul thought.

When Miles asked Rachel *who's there?* from behind the door and groggily walked into view without waiting for a response, Paul decided the answer was no.

He wasn't expecting him.

Miles looked surprised, even shocked. It wouldn't be amiss to trot out an overused cliché and say he looked as if he'd seen a ghost. He *didn't* look like he was feeling well, but the sight of Paul had evidently made him feel worse.

Miles recovered. Maybe his lawyerly instincts took over, reverting to the kind of expression he'd be expected to maintain if one of his clients had just confessed to murder on the stand. Of course Miles didn't practice trial law – he'd gone into foreign adoptions. And a few other things you maybe didn't need a license for.

'Paul,' he said, a quasi smile plastered to his face. 'I said I'm always available, but this is ridiculous, no?'

Okay, Paul thought, give him credit for grace under fire.

Something was bothering Paul – besides the obvious.

Think.

Miles brought him to Little Odessa to have him killed. Paul had assaulted someone, hijacked a car, and escaped. Moshe would've called Miles with that piece of news.

So why was he so shocked at seeing Paul in the flesh and still standing?

'I ran into a little trouble,' Paul said.

Rachel was standing between them like a referee who doesn't

understand the bout's begun. 'You should go upstairs and rest,' she said to Miles with just enough wifely edge to make her point. Business was business, but this was his day off.

'Trouble?' Miles responded, ignoring his wife. 'By the way, sorry I was called away yesterday. Did Moshe tell you?'

More to the point, Paul thought, did Moshe tell *you*? And if not, why? For the fiftieth time that morning, Paul asked himself if it was possible he'd gotten it wrong. He would've given anything for that to be the case.

Rachel cleared her throat.

'It's okay, honey,' Miles said. 'I promise that after I talk to Paul here, I'll take a nice long rest.'

Miles looked like he could use it. He appeared feverish and tired, as if he hadn't slept in days.

That made two of them.

Rachel clearly wasn't happy about Paul's intrusion, but she silently acquiesced. She called her sons.

They slipped through the front door and trooped down the brownstone steps behind their mother with no great enthusiasm.

It was just the two of them now.

Miles said, 'Come in.'

He led Paul into the familiar clutter of his office. 'So what did Moshe say? Can he help you?'

Paul still desperately wanted to believe Miles.

He wanted to apologize for braining that man with a cement block and for stealing a car.

He wanted to cling to the image of a Miles who'd braved death with him in the Jersey City swamps.

He couldn't shake Miles' initial expression at the door. His surprise at Paul's *aliveness*. Miles had known what awaited Paul in that warehouse. If Paul was wrong about everything else, he was right about that.

'What's the matter?' Miles asked, still the friendly lawyer out to help. 'You said you ran into trouble. What happened?'

'María called me,' Paul said, letting that simple statement hang there for a moment.

'María?' was all Miles said.

Paul noticed that the telephone Miles had used to call María Consuelo – or *not* call her – was lying off its hook. Then he remembered something.

Religious Jews weren't allowed to take calls from sundown Friday to sundown Saturday.

Orthodox rules.

Miles thought Paul was dead and buried, because Moshe hadn't been able to call and tell him otherwise.

'That night you picked up the phone and called María?' Paul said. 'You *didn't* call her. You just pretended to.'

Paul made sure to speak slowly so Miles would be able to grasp the full import of what he was saying – and because it was hard to actually get the words front and center. 'If María hadn't called and told me, I would've walked into that office with your friend. I'm pretty sure I wasn't going to walk out.'

Everything seemed to drain out of Miles' face. Paul remembered a Thanksgiving Day balloon he'd seen punctured on TV when he was a kid – the huge smiling visage of a cartoon sheriff running into a streetlamp and deflating into something wrinkled and insubstantial.

'You're an insurance actuary,' Miles said, 'right?'

'Yes.'

'Okay. What are the odds of you making it out of here alive?'

He was pointing a gun at Paul's head.

It had suddenly materialized from behind the desk; he must've pulled it out of a drawer.

'Let me give you the facts,' Miles said. 'It's how you guys work, right? Facts – then figures. This is an Agram 2000. Croatian made, machine action. It used to belong to an honest-to-God KGB assassin – at least that's what Moshe told me. They liked the Agram because it's small enough to stick in your pocket and highly accurate up to twenty feet. More facts. We're alone – my wife and sons are praying to a just and benevolent God. Also, that funny thing on the end of the barrel? A silencer. No one will hear me shoot you. Okay, now, what would you say the odds are?'

'Poor,' Paul said. And getting poorer by the second, he thought. Miles was having trouble keeping his hand steady – the one gripping the Agram 2000.

'Why?' Paul asked.

For a moment it appeared that Miles hadn't heard him; he seemed to be listening to something else. He stood up, walked to the window, peeked out through the curtain – all the while managing to keep the gun trained on Paul.

'You see anyone out there?' he asked.

'Anyone? What do you mean?'

'What do I mean? I mean, did you see anyone out there? Anyone not wearing a yarmulke, for example? Never mind. Doesn't matter.'

He came back behind the desk, sat down.

'Why?' Paul asked again.

'Why? You sound like a child asking one of the four questions. Why do you think?'

'Money.'

'Money. Well, sure, money's *part* of it. You ever bet on anything, Paul?'

'What?'

'You ever bet on anything? Guess not. Stupid question. It's probably against the *actuarial* code. Remember the 1990 no-huddle Buffalo Bills?'

Paul was having trouble remembering anything except the gun pointed at his head.

'My first colossal blunder. You know you can bet straight up if you've got the guts. If you just *know*. None of those annoying points to deal with. Only you've got to lay three to win one. That's okay. I was sure. I *knew*. My religion prescribes one ritual bath a year. That was mine.'

'You lost.'

'Oh yeah. Sure you didn't see anyone out there, Paul? Someone driving by the house maybe?'

'No.'

'Good.'

'You said you bet thirty dollars here and there,' Paul said. 'Just to keep things interesting.'

'I fibbed. It's *more* interesting when you bet thirty thousand. I'll tell you how I got started. One day I was sitting and waiting by the phone. You know what for?'

'No.'

'Neither did I. Something. When it rang and I picked it up, the person on the other end said Mr Goldstein, *this* is your lucky day. It was a touting service. A Delphic oracle of the ESPN generation. They toss you the first pick for free, just to show what excellent prognosticators they are. They were excellent – *that* day. I won. I even won again. That's the problem. You start feeling kind of omnipotent. You forget that's reserved for the man upstairs. I began practicing a personal form of downside economics. I bet more than I actually *had*.'

Someone started up a car outside. Miles jerked his head toward the window, gripped the gun with knuckles turned suddenly white.

'It's just a car,' Paul said.

'Sure. It's just a car. Everyone *walks* on Shabbat.' He kept one eye on Paul, and the other on the window, at least until he heard the sound of the car engine slowly drifting down the street.

'Are you expecting someone?'

'Yes. I'm expecting someone. I'm just not sure when I'm expecting them. Sometime soon, I think.'

Miles closed his eyes, wiped his forehead.

'My bookie wasn't very understanding, Paul. About not having the money. What were the odds he'd say *no problem* and wipe the slate clean? Come on, Paul . . . numbers?'

'I don't know.' Paul was continuing to answer him, back and

forth and back, as if they were in that car in New Jersey, just shooting the breeze. As if the pet weapon of the Russian KGB weren't trained on his head. Maybe something brilliant would occur to him.

'You don't know? Come on. You've *met* him. Moshe, the Russian businessman. By the way, he doesn't really do a lot of business with Colombians. He doesn't have to. He does perfectly fine taking bets from me.'

Paul remembered the conversation he'd overheard in the bathroom. Had Wenzel *made the vig*? one of the men asked. *Fucking GNP of Slovakia.* And they'd both laughed.

'By the way, you know what the Russians call the Colombians?' Paul shook his head.

'Amateurs.' He smiled, wiped his forehead again. 'Moshe called me his favorite Jewish lawyer back at the warehouse? Because other Jewish lawyers *take* his money. I'm the exception. I'm the gift that keeps on giving. See, I owed Moshe what I didn't have. What were the odds I could wiggle out of that one?'

Paul was calculating other odds – trying to gauge the distance to the office door, wondering how long it would take him to make it to the front door of the house if he made it out of the office.

'You're still here,' Paul said.

'Yeah. I'm still here. You can have smarts and you can have luck. I needed both. I opened my arms and waited for manna from heaven. And I was delivered.'

'How?'

'*How?* That's what I've been trying to tell you.' The gun was still drifting – every so often Miles would notice with a slightly sheepish grin and attempt to re-aim it.

'You don't want to shoot me,' Paul said.

'I don't? That's odd. That's really odd. You see my neck's back in the noose again. Not from you – you're just *inconvenient*. It's those assholes with Uzis and kerosene I'm worried about. They looked through my car – they know I'm here. They're smelling blood. They're starting to put it together. I can *tell*. They're closing in.'

'Put *what* together?'

'Maybe they *are* amateurs next to the Russians, but not by much. In the pantheon of assassins, let's call them lower Division 1. I'm cooked.'

Miles looked cooked. His face was in full flop sweat. Paul couldn't help wondering if his trigger finger was sweating as well, if it might unintentionally slip.

'I don't understand,' Paul said.

'I know you don't.'

'The men in the swamp. You said they were Manuel Riojas' men. What does he have against you?'

'What are the odds poor little Paul's ever going to figure *that* one out? Let's just say no good deed goes unpunished.'

'What good deed?'

'Okay. No bad deed goes unpunished.'

'I don't –'

'He who saves one child saves his ass.'

It was as if Miles were speaking in fragments, Paul following a step behind, collecting each piece and desperately trying to glue them together.

'Joanna!' Paul nearly shouted it. Miles had lied about calling María. It suddenly occurred to him that he might have lied about something else. 'You said she's fine. Is she?'

It seemed to take Miles a second to refocus, to concentrate on the question being asked of him and actually answer it. 'Sure,' he said. 'Under the circumstances. Sorry about your wife and kid. Not my fault – sort of. It wasn't supposed to happen like this. Can't help you there. Wish I could.'

'Miles . . .'

'Uh-uh.' Miles waved his gun at him. 'My turn. I've got one more question for you. Last one, honest. It's not even an actuarial question. Ready – pencils out?'

Paul was preparing to launch himself at the door. Or across the desk. *Pick one.* He had nothing to lose.

'Know what's the worst sin in Orthodox Judaism – other than marrying a shiksa, of course?'

'No,' Paul said.

'Sure you do.'

Paul made it only halfway across the desk when the bullet exploded out of the barrel. It entered the cranial cavity, which governs memory and social skills, exiting below the neck and embedding itself into the cover of *New York State Adoption Statutes*. He'd gone *toward* Miles because he thought it might give him the element of surprise.

He was wrong about that.

Miles had surprised him first.

The worst sin in Orthodox Judaism?

It wasn't murder.

No.

I promise that after I talk to Paul here, I'll take a nice long rest, he'd told his wife.

He'd kept his word.

TWENTY-NINE

Joanna was granted one of those rare afternoon feedings where she was allowed to linger with her baby, rock her into sleep, and simply stare at her.

When she came back to her room, Maruja and Beatriz were gone.

There had been talk lately. Something in the wind. A possible prisoner exchange or straight cash ransom. The last time Maruja saw her husband on TV, he'd hinted at imminent release.

Joanna had caught Maruja praying with the rosary beads that had been given to her by one of the guerrillas – Tomás, sad-eyed and secretly religious, who'd fashioned them from cork and presented them to her after she'd asked him for a Bible.

The man they called *el doctor,* who periodically visited them like a dutiful concierge making the rounds, told Maruja and Beatriz that they might be taking a little trip soon and winked at them.

Joanna had felt like two people. One of these people was overjoyed for Maruja and Beatriz; they'd become like sisters and she felt their pain at being separated so long from children and family.

The other Joanna felt devastated, jealous, and abandoned.

Now Maruja and Beatriz were gone.

The room reeked of loneliness, of people who've packed up and left. It was freshly tidied – the mattress fluffed and turned, the floor swept. The meager clothing Maruja and Beatriz had accumulated over time – castoffs from the *kids,* as Beatriz called their guards, most of whom *were* kids – was conspicuously missing. Beatriz had fashioned a makeshift dresser from two milk crates – when Joanna looked inside, there was only the sweatshirt with the logo of the Colombian national soccer team that Maruja had graciously handed down to her.

Joanna sat in the corner and cried.

After an hour or so she knocked on the door and asked to see *el doctor.* It was opened by Tomás, looking even more melancholy than usual, who didn't respond one way or another. But a few hours later the doctor knocked on the door and walked in.

'Yes?' he said, flashing that magnanimous smile that Joanna found incongruous from the person imprisoning her.

'Where are Maruja and Beatriz?' Joanna asked him.

'Ah. Good news,' he said. *'Released.'* As if he'd been pulling for them all along.

'Oh,' she said. 'That's wonderful.'

'Yes.' His smile grew even wider. 'Next. You.'

Joanna allowed herself to believe him – for a moment she did.

'And my *baby.*'

'Yes, of course. Babies belong with their mothers.'

'What about Rolando?' she asked.

The doctor ignored her. Instead, he gazed at the surrounding sparseness. 'You have more room now, yes?'

Joanna nodded.

'Good.'

THE FIRST NIGHT A.B. – AFTER BEATRIZ – JOANNA HAD TROUBLE sleeping. The mattress, which had always felt crowded if snugly warm, now felt uncomfortably roomy and ice-cold. There was a strange, slightly nauseating smell in the air. She woke up thirsting for company. Somehow this translated into something more tangible.

She knocked on the door and asked for water.

The female guard with long black hair opened the door. She was watching the TV, where a somber news anchor was reading from a sheet of paper.

When she went to get Joanna water, she made a point of turning the TV off.

The water, which was tepid and acidic, did nothing to help Joanna sleep. She lay with eyes wide-open, staring up at the ceiling. Beatriz had drawn a multitude of stars on the plaster ceiling with a felt pen. A way to break down their prison walls and create a pathetic illusion of freedom.

Joanna dug her head into the mattress and selfishly wished Beatriz were back beside her.

That smell. *What was it?*

It seemed stronger now. She decided it had to be the mattress itself. They'd turned it over in a clumsy stab at neatness, but the side she was sleeping on – or attempting to – had been against the dirty floor forever. It was the *absence* of smell too, she thought – the familiar scent of departed friends.

She stood up, turned the mattress back over, then lay down again.

She didn't notice it right away.

The room was too dark. It took her eyes getting used to the blackness and the fact that the smell, instead of improving, grew exponentially worse.

It took Joanna turning first left, then right, even reversing her position on the bed. It took her placing her head facedown into the foam and nearly gagging.

She lurched to a sitting position and stared at the place on the mattress where her head had been seconds before.

It was like a Rorschach blot. Staring at an amorphous mix of color and shadow and finally finding the haunting image within.

A large, uneven stain.

She thought she knew what it was. A stain the approximate size of a human head.

She closed her eyes and pressed a finger into the middle of rusty brown. It felt damp, like cellar earth. When she looked at the tip of her finger, it was stained brown. Blood.

She staggered to a standing position. She lurched around the room as if drunk, chased by a growing panic.

She banged furiously on the door.

Tomás again. She wanted to say their names out loud – to state them clearly and unmistakably. But she saw something dangling out of the crook of his pants pocket.

The rosary made of cork. The one he'd given Maruja, the one she'd sworn to always keep with her as an eternal symbol of faith, hope, and dogged survival.

Joanna waited till he shut the door, till she slumped onto the floor and buried her face in her hands.

Then she screamed bloody murder.

They knew she knew.

About Maruja and Beatriz.

She probably told them herself, every time she jumped when one of them entered the room or came within two feet of her. She couldn't help wondering *which one* pulled the trigger, drew the knife. Was it Tomás, who seemed to mope about even more than usual these days? Or Puento, who'd pointed a rifle at Joelle when she was in the screaming throes of pneumonia? Or both?

She had to reassure herself each time that they hadn't come for *her*.

She was absolutely certain they knew she knew when *el doctor* came in and apologized for having to chain her to the wall.

He seemed genuinely remorseful about it but explained that it was for her own good.

'If USDF patrols begin shooting,' he said, 'you'll be safer like this, no?'

No. Joanna asked just once for him to not do it. Please.

He shrugged and sighed. It was out of his hands, he explained. It was just for nighttime – that's all.

They chained one end to a piece of a long-defunct radiator. The other went around her left leg.

It wasn't physically uncomfortable – the pain was psychic. It put a punctuation mark on her existence. She was now literally under lock and key.

One of them would come in to unlock her in the morning. Joanna wouldn't start breathing normally again until this ritual was actually accomplished. Then she'd know she was alive for at least one more morning. She could let herself look forward to feeding time. This living from hour to hour was taking its toll. She was generally jumpy, weepy, and exhausted. There were times she found herself unable to stop shaking.

When she told Galina that she was pretty positive Maruja and Beatriz had been murdered, Galina shook her head and said *no, they were released.*

'They weren't released,' Joanna said. 'Tomás has Maruja's rosary beads. She never would've left them behind. The girl turned off the news that night when she saw me looking. There was blood in the bed. I know.'

Galina wouldn't listen. She went deaf.

It was maddening. It was sickening.

It was clear that talking to Galina about certain things was like talking to a wall. Joanna knew what *that* was like, because she talked to her wall in lieu of talking to Maruja and Beatriz. She'd decided it was slightly more rational than talking to herself.

Sometimes the wall became someone she knew. Paul. From time to time she tried to imagine where he was – in a prison for drug smuggling? Dead? When she felt suffocated with fear, she'd place him right there beside her and fill him in on her day.

Sometimes Paul answered back.

What's wrong?

They killed my friends.

Maybe you're wrong about that.

No. There was blood on the mattress. I discovered it the day they left.

Maybe one of your friends cut herself.

No. It was a lot of blood. And Maruja left something behind.

Still.

You have to believe me. Sometimes I feel like I'm going crazy, but I'm not going crazy.

Okay. I believe you.

I'm scared now. Every day I'm scared.

Stay strong. You're Xena, my warrior princess, remember? Besides, I'm coming for you.

When? I want to be home, Paul.

Soon, honey.

When?

Soon.

SHE ASKED TOMÁS FOR THE ROSARY BEADS.

'Maruja gave them back to you when you released her, I guess,' Joanna said.

Tomás didn't answer her. But when Joanna asked for them, he handed them over.

She'd been watching the way the door locked. A key turn from outside slid a small bolt into the lock. That's it. The wooden jamb looked ancient and wormy.

Joanna ripped off one cork bead from the rosary. The cork was barely malleable, like half-hardened clay.

When Galina took her out of the room for the next morning feeding, she pushed the small piece of cork into the lock hole, grinding it in with her thumb.

216

That night she watched as one of the girls left the room, closed the door behind her, and dutifully turned the lock. Joanna listened for the telltale click. She didn't hear it.

A growing excitement took hold of her. A warm glow, like a shot of aged brandy when you're really, really cold.

Beatriz had drawn stars to get out of prison, only Beatriz had been murdered in her bed.

This was better.

Only she was still chained to the wall. And she couldn't leave without her baby.

There was the question of what to do next. She didn't wake up one morning with an escape plan. She hadn't talked strategy with the wall. She took this first step and said *if it works, we'll take another.*

Then something presented itself, something that took care of two major obstacles at once.

Joelle got sick again.

Just a bad cold this time – enough to make her sniffly, irritable, and slightly feverish.

Joanna asked Galina if Joelle could stay with her. Not just for an hour or two, but all night, like the time Joelle had pneumonia and she'd walked her back and forth for hours on end.

Galina said yes.

Then Joanna asked her something else. Could they unchain her? What if Joelle needed to be rocked? Joanna might need to walk her around the room. It would be immeasurably helpful if she wasn't chained to the radiator.

Galina seemed less accommodating there.

Joanna pleaded her case, and finally, Galina said she'd talk to the guard.

It was Tomás. Maybe he liked her more now that she'd gotten religion. Maybe he was making amends for murdering her friends. He said fine. No chain tonight.

217

When he closed the door behind him and turned the lock, Joanna held her breath.

No click.

So here it was. She'd taken one step, then another and another, and suddenly, she'd reached a door. It was tantalizingly open.

For a moment Joanna wondered if she could actually walk through it.

The bloodstain on the mattress both prodded and held her back. If she failed, they'd kill her for trying. If she stayed, they'd kill her eventually.

Courage.

She waited for hours – till her internal clock placed the time at somewhere around two in the morning. She was reasonably sure there wouldn't be anyone outside the door – when she'd needed that rag in the middle of the night, she had to bang on the door for five minutes before Puento answered.

She tiptoed to the door and put her ear up against the wood. Nothing.

She turned the knob.

It didn't move. For just a moment she said *okay – I was wrong. The cork didn't work. The door's still locked. I'm stuck.*

Then she gave it a bit more pressure.

The knob turned.

The door edged open.

It was like the door in a haunted-house movie – the door you shouldn't open but do. The door that has something evil waiting for you on the other side.

There was nothing there.

Empty hall.

Since they'd removed her mask for walks to the feeding room, she'd learned enough to know where things were. To her right was the kitchen, the feeding room, the place they kept Rolando – if he was still actually there.

To the left – freedom.

Joelle was sleeping fitfully in her arms. She had visions of her waking up and screaming – the best alarm system a FARC guard could ask for. She'd have to move very slowly and very carefully. She'd have to inch along.

When she stepped out into the hall, it felt as if she were moving through something physical – a force field of science fiction. She stopped and breathed. Then she turned left and padded down the hall, one small shuffle at a time, till she came to what had to be the outside door – the one they'd brought her through blindfolded and terrified.

She was *still* terrified.

She pushed it open.

THIRTY

Trajectory.

Atoms have it. Electrons and neutrinos. Lives too.

The trajectory of the bullet that killed Miles, that left him slumped and oddly peaceful-looking with the Agram 2000 still glued to his hand, went through his neck and directly into one of the dusty legal tomes that took up most of his bookcase. *New York State Adoption Statutes.* The bullet's force sent several other books flying, scattering pages like confetti.

Paul ignored it at first. Trajectory.

Instead, he assumed a helter-skelter trajectory of his own. Nearly flying off a suddenly blood-splattered desk, then staggering around the room like a boxer on his last legs, unsure whether to go down or keep fighting.

He remained upright.

Clues, his brain nagged him.

Miles was his last link to what happened in Colombia.

Clues.

Miles had been right about the silencer. No one would've heard the gun go off – it sounded like the small pop you make by pulling a finger out of your cheek. Like a cartoon sound effect.

There was plenty of blood, though. The room stank of it.

Paul came around the side of the desk where Miles still sat – his *body*. He tried to ignore it – this lifeless lump of flesh that used to have a name and a voice and a family.

Know what's the worst sin in Orthodox Judaism?

Paul opened the desk drawer. Papers, staples, pencils, two half-empty packs of gum. Wrigley's spearmint. A calculator, ticket stubs, paper clips, envelopes. He had no idea what he was looking for.

Clues.

The question was, what *was* a clue? How did you divine clues from ordinary office things, the stuff of daily life?

They're starting to put it together. I can tell.

He looked through some of the papers in the desk drawer. A W-2 tax form. A solicitation for subscription renewal from a legal journal. A coupon from Toys 'R' Us – circled in red ink. *Chatty Cathy.* A New York Giants schedule from 1999.

A phone book.

The one Miles had looked through when he'd pantomimed calling María – when he'd snapped his fingers and said *the driver. Pablo. María must have his number somewhere.*

María's number was in there, of course.

Pablo's would be also.

Paul didn't know his last name – he'd just been Pablo the driver, Pablo the hired help.

Then Pablo the kidnapper.

He had to search through A, B, C, D, E, F, G, H, I, J, and K before he found it. *Pablo Loraizo.*

Odd, the last name seemed familiar.

He ripped out the page and stuck it into his pocket.

He was searching for clues, but he was clueless. About what to do. Call the police? Find the local shul and inform Rachel and kids that their husband and father had just blown his brains out?

Leave.

Leaving sounded good. When the police came to talk to him,

he'd tell them they'd chatted, then Paul had left. *Suicide?* What suicide? Or he'd tell them everything – that Miles had sent him to Colombia to be kidnapped and his wife and daughter held for ransom. *What* ransom? Two million dollars' worth of uncut cocaine he'd dutifully smuggled through customs. Maybe he'd leave that part out.

He felt light-headed, like in Galina's house when he'd stood up to confront Pablo and ended up lying down instead. His thinking was all over the place, scattershot. Unlike the bullet that flew through Miles' head.

He took notice of it now – its trajectory.

It had made a mess. Book pages were scattered all across the floor. No, they weren't book pages. On closer look they were handwritten.

Letters.

Okay, Paul remembered.

The night he couldn't sleep and wandered down here to find something to read. He'd ended up reading that letter from summer camp – *Dear Dad: Remember when you took me to the zoo and you left me there?* Feeding his loneliness by gorging on someone else's family.

He was stepping over the sheets of paper to make his way out of the room when he noticed something else.

He read, bent down, stood there transfixed, hands on knees.

A bullet's trajectory is governed by physics, he thought.

By the forces of propulsion, drag, and gravity. And the position of the shooting hand itself. This is important. Which way the hand's pointing.

Maybe just before Miles decided to put a bullet into his brain, he'd reflected on the odds of *poor Paul ever figuring this out* and decided to better them.

He said *I'm pointing here.*

This way.

THIRTY-ONE

He was back in the comfy surroundings of home – he'd been unable to think of anywhere else to go.

Except it wasn't comfy. There were too many reminders.

He pushed the crib across the apartment and halfway into the closet so he wouldn't have to look at it, pink teddy bears grinning up at him on their ride across the room, as if amused by his childish attempt to hide the hopelessness of his situation.

Lisa must've heard it rolling across the floor, because a second later Paul heard a knock at the door. When he tiptoed over to squint through the eyehole, Lisa, Joanna's best friend, was squinting back, her puzzled expression causing her mouth to twist nearly sideways, an endearing affectation Paul had always found vaguely sexy. Not today. Either Paul and Joanna were back – suddenly and unannounced – or someone was burglarizing their apartment.

Paul *felt* a little like a burglar, an intruder into his own life.

Paul waited her out.

He had the visa story all ready to go, but he was in no mood to use it. Not yet.

After Lisa had knocked once more, then shrugged and left, Paul picked up the stack of letters he'd taken from Miles' office. If you sniffed them closely, you could still smell his blood.

He closed the blinds and turned off the phone. It would take Rachel a while to locate him. He couldn't remember whether she knew his last name, probably not. It didn't matter – at some point she'd look through Miles' phone book, with the police over her shoulder, and collect all the *Pauls*. They'd winnow it down to him. Eventually, they'd call.

I went to talk to Miles about my adoption problems. When I left the house, he was alive. Was he depressed? A little – he mentioned something about gambling debts. I'm so sorry to hear about this.

The letters weren't dated.

But he was able to organize them chronologically by color. From parched yellow to off-white.

The most recent was the letter he'd read that night, the letter Miles' son had written from summer camp. It was the other letters he was interested in. The other letters that had come tumbling out of *The Story of Ruth*. These letters were different. These letters weren't written by a child.

They were written *about* a child.

Dear Mr Goldstein, the first one began.

I have a child in desperate need of adoption.

Most people wrote to Miles wanting to adopt a child. Needing, asking for, even *begging,* for a child. This letter was different – it was offering one up.

Consider this a special request, this letter continued. *This has to happen immediately. There's no time to follow the usual paperwork. That's why I'm writing to you directly. That's why I need your help. I have to hear from you now. Today. Tomorrow. I beg you to answer me as soon as humanly possible.*

Paul went on to the second letter, then the third.

He read them slowly, carefully, sometimes going back to reread something before pushing forward through time. All the letters, of course, were written *to* Miles. He didn't have the letters Miles wrote

224

back. It was like eavesdropping on one-half of a phone conversation. You had to supply the responses yourself. You had to fill in the blanks.

The letters went on to explain who this child was. A three-year-old girl. The letter writer insisted the child needed to leave Colombia now. It explained why. Her father was after her. The girl was in terrible danger. And finally and most tellingly, the letters explained how this was all going to take place.

After he'd read the last letter, he reread them all. And he remembered how Miles had spoken in fragments and how he – Paul – had followed behind trying to collect the fragments and glue them together.

What are the odds poor little Paul's going to put this together?

Bad, Miles, he thought now, *awful,* but it's just possible the odds were getting better.

The full name of the little girl's father never appeared. Just an initial. *R.* Somewhere between letters, his name must've been whispered in Miles' ear, then never mentioned again.

But the letter *writer* was there at the bottom of every page. That's what Paul had noticed exiting the room, blood in his nostrils – what had made him stop and look and read. The signature at the bottom of the page.

A lovely lilt to the letters, especially the *G.*

For Galina.

THIRTY-TWO

At first he thought the sound at his door was a dream.

Maybe because that's what he was doing. Dreaming, at least half dreaming.

About his wife and daughter.

About the little girl.

And that sampler that sat over Miles' desk.

He who saves one child saves the world.

Who was this little girl? Galina's granddaughter.

She'd clearly stated that in her second letter to Miles. And she'd written about the girl's father. *That* too.

Once I thought my own daughter was safe from him, she'd scrawled. *I was wrong.*

She'd begged Miles for help. Her granddaughter needed to get out of the country.

Her father is looking for her. He won't stop till he finds her. As you know, R has the power and means to do so.

She needed to be adopted by someone in America. This needed to happen fast.

As the letters continued, she told him a little more about the girl.

She's seen things no child should ever have to see, she'd written. *No one should have to see. She has nightmares.*

By the fourth letter it became obvious that Miles had said okay. That he'd help. More than help. He'd evidently made an offer of stunning generosity and selflessness. He'd agreed to adopt Galina's granddaughter himself.

Are you sure? she'd written him. *As overjoyed as I am, you must understand this is not a sometime thing. It's a forever thing. You won't simply be her parent. You'll be her protector. Her guardian. Her only hope.*

Yes, Miles must've written, he was sure.

But he'd wanted something in return.

What?

It was hard to say.

It was obvious Galina's joy had more or less vanished. Her letters had taken on the sober tone of a business negotiation.

Understand what you ask might not be possible, Galina wrote. *I don't know them. I don't speak for them. I can only ask them.*

Them.

Paul was like a two-year-old, beginning to understand that meaningless words stand for meaningful things.

Them said yes.

They must've, because Galina's last letter was a heartrending plea for her granddaughter's future.

I ask a few things of you, she wrote. *To comfort her when she wakes up frightened in the middle of the night. Please read to her — she likes stories about trains and clowns and rabbits. Teach her what she needs to know in her new country. Protect her. From time to time, I ask you to please let me know how she's doing. Not every week, not every month. Now and then. This is my last letter to you. The less contact we have after this, the safer it'll be. I ask just one more thing. It's the most important thing. For you and your wife to love her.*

There was someone at the door.

He was suddenly wide-awake, staring at the bedroom ceiling.

He heard it again.

227

A soft scratching. It sounded like a cat asking to be let in.

He didn't have a cat.

He continued to lie there on his bed; he wondered which door it was. The closed door of his bedroom, the apartment door itself? This was important. If it was the apartment door, he still had a chance. If it was the bedroom door, he was dead.

He concentrated; tried to fine-tune his hearing. Blood was pulsing into his eardrums; his breathing was tight and shallow and noisy.

The scratching sound seemed faint and muffled.

Okay, he thought, the *apartment* door.

He slid off the bed and resisted the temptation to crawl underneath it. The front door was locked. He was still master of his domain. He could keep them out – he could protect himself.

He was dressed only in boxer shorts. When he glanced at the full-length mirror against the wall, he looked comically vulnerable. He stood stock-still, craned his neck to listen.

Scratch, scratch.

It's those assholes with Uzis and kerosene I'm worried about.

The men from the swamp, he thought.

Or.

It's the man with *CCCP* tattooed on his arm.

He was at the front door. The one Lisa had squinted through, which, if memory served him correctly, was locked tight.

Even double-bolted.

He gingerly opened his bedroom door. He stepped out. He stared at the front door as if seeing it for the first time. Really *looking* at it. It appeared solid enough – in need of a paint job, sure, but strong as steel. This analogy comforted him.

He could swear he'd double-bolted it but couldn't remember whether the oblong knob was supposed to be vertical or horizontal.

He suddenly realized he hadn't heard a sound since he'd walked out of the bedroom. He realized this because he heard it now.

This much closer, it seemed raw and amplified. *The fog comes on little cat feet* – a poem he remembered from childhood. But this wasn't a cat, and this wasn't childhood.

A weapon.

His eyes zigzagged around the apartment, jittery, in circles, like a fly caught between windowpanes.

The metal paperweight from Sharper Image. Maybe.

The polished African walking stick Joanna's parents had brought back from Kenya. Possibly.

A dull glass egg sitting in the middle of the dining room table. No.

The dining room table.

Knives.

He stared at his kitchen, trying to remember where Joanna kept the steak knives.

He resisted the overwhelming urge to run there.

Walk. Tiptoe. Float like Muhammad Ali. They didn't know he was here. They were guessing. They might get tired of trying to jimmy the lock. They might give up.

Not if they knew he was in here.

He *drifted* to the kitchen, visualizing himself as light and noiseless, even though he felt heavier than lead, aware that the sounds at the door were growing louder and more insistent.

They were trying to fit something into the lock – that's what it sounded like. Frustration was setting in. They were trying to *force* it in, like date rape – first polite and consensual, then insistent and brutal. The lock was screaming *no*. The intruder didn't give a shit.

Paul opened a kitchen drawer. It squeaked.

The scratching stopped dead.

Silence.

You have to do something about these drawers, Paul. If Joanna had said that to him once, she'd said it a thousand times. And a thousand times Paul had told her to *hire one of those guys in the back of the Pennysaver.*

The handymen had remained unsummoned. The drawers continued to complain every time they were opened.

The people behind the door knew he was in here.

More bad news.

The open drawer contained Joanna's phone book, some pencils, paper clips, a take-out menu from Hunan Flower.

No knives.

The scratching came back. Harder.

The second drawer down, he hit pay dirt. It contained the entire Ginzu Knife Collection, for which they'd sent $49.95 in five easy monthly installments. Those remarkable knives you saw cutting through tissue paper in thirty-minute infomercials. Forged by actual samurai masters in Yokohama. He wrapped his fingers around a cool plastic handle and pulled one out.

He turned and faced the door.

Maybe ten feet from it. From *them*. It seemed inconceivable and ridiculous that a mere *door* could save him. He could almost smell their need. He was sure Joanna could've.

Call 911.

This time he could actually tell them his address.

He could summon a patrol car. Scare them away.

Make them think they were coming any minute.

The phone was on the other side of the apartment. It seemed as vast and impassable as the Sahara.

Wait. He didn't have to call. He just had to *pretend* to.

'Yes, is this the police?' he suddenly shouted. 'Yes, I'm at 341 West 84th Street, apartment 9G. Someone's trying to break in . . . Yes, that's right . . . You'll be here in two minutes? Thank God.'

Oddly enough, his fake phone call didn't cause the man or men to stop. No.

Maybe he should've asked himself *why*?

Maybe if it wasn't five in the morning, and if he wasn't scared out of his mind, and if he was just a little brighter about these things, he would've.

Then he would have understood that the only reason a fake phone call to the police wouldn't deter someone from breaking into your apartment is if they *knew* it was a fake phone call.

And the only way they could know that is if they knew you didn't have a phone.

If, say, they'd taken the precaution of disconnecting it.

THIRTY-THREE

He felt his sheer strength at first.

The overwhelming, undeniable *there*ness of it.

The knotty muscle. As if the *door* weren't made of steel, but the man who'd burst through it was. *CCCP,* he thought.

One moment Paul was standing ten feet from the door with the Ginzu in his hand. The next, an amorphous black shape was hurtling straight at him.

He lunged at the black apparition with his knife, but the man deflected his arm with almost comical ease.

The knife went skittering off somewhere on the floor.

Before the man could kill him, Paul kept going.

Momentum carried him past the man's swatting arm and back into the kitchen, where he attempted to ransack the second drawer without slowing down. But he cut himself on one of the other Ginzus – perhaps the apple-corer they'd received free because they'd acted *now*. His hand came up bloody and, more important, *empty*.

The man was right behind him. He could hear him breathing hard, as if the exertion of kicking in the door had tuckered him out.

Only momentarily. Not enough to make him stop.

232

Paul zigzagged into the bedroom like a broken-field runner. He slammed the door shut.

No.

The man had made it to the other side of the door just before Paul could actually close it.

He was pushing back.

Adrenaline was a kind of drug, Paul thought. He could feel every single muscle crackling with energy. He felt powerful, relentless, even indomitable.

He didn't stand a chance.

Adrenaline could only do so much. The person on the other side of the door wasn't human. He was a freakish force of nature. The door was moving backward.

One inch.

Two inches.

Paul's hand was slipping in his own blood.

'Fuck!' Paul shouted. *'Fuck!'* Grunting, trying to summon a last reserve of strength.

He could bellow all he wanted. He could push and scratch and fight and pray. He was going to lose.

It ended with a bang *and* a whimper. The door slammed into the wall with a loud crack. Paul went backward; no – he flew, soared, catapulted. He careened off the bed. He grabbed for the phone – dead.

The man came for him.

Paul put his hands up to defend himself. He screamed. Nothing came out.

The man had put one hand around his mouth, the other against his windpipe.

He felt like a rag doll whose head was about to be smashed.

But the man didn't smash Paul's head.

He spoke to him.

Whispered even.

'Breathe,' he said. 'Nice and easy. That's it.'

There was no Russian accent. No Colombian accent either. That was the first surprise.

There was another.

LATER, AFTER PAUL HAD STOPPED SHAKING, THEY TALKED ABOUT old times.

Not really *old* times. Fairly recent in memory, just far enough away from now to be ancient history.

The delay in Kennedy.

The layover in Washington, D.C. Eight excruciating hours sitting on the tarmac with nothing to do.

Only it hadn't seemed excruciating for the man. No. He'd sat there with utter calm staring at the seat back in front of him.

He was used to waiting, he'd said. *Remember?* he asked Paul.

He was a bird-watcher.

THIRTY-FOUR

Jungle gym.
The Jungle Book.
In the jungle, the mighty jungle, the lion sleeps tonight.
Jungle boogie.

Joanna was reciting the entire known canon of jungle references. She was being her own google.com. Some of these jungle references were clearly sanitized, the jungle made friendly. Something to dance to, sing to, for four-year-olds to innocently clamber over.

There were other, scarier references.

The concrete jungle.
It's a jungle out there.

She would just as soon not think of those.

The real jungle, the humid infestation of invisible buzzing, shrieking things and rotting, tangled vegetation, was scary enough.

For one thing it was dark.

Darker than dark.

A suffocating canopy of branches blotted out whatever moonlight there was. It was like stumbling around a closet – the kind children are convinced harbors hideous monsters.

There were definitely things going bump in the night. She could hear them directly above her head. Rustling branches, sudden growls. *Monkeys?* Or something worse?

Jaguars, ocelots, boa constrictors?

Joelle had woken up soon after they'd made it down a small clearing and into the thick trees. She'd begun wailing for food – or because she was cold or just plain sick. Joanna didn't know. She was still learning the foreign language of infancy – something Galina seemed to have down pat. It didn't matter. She had no baby formula with her, and she couldn't do anything about the surrounding chill the baby blanket was doing little to counter.

'We're going home,' she whispered to her daughter, though it was solely for her own benefit. Speaking out loud helped pierce the darkness, let her know that *she,* at least, was present and accounted for. Of course it might've been doing the same for any animals in the vicinity. Human or otherwise.

Occasionally, invisible flying things smacked her in the face. She nearly swallowed an enormous moth – just managing to spit it out, then bending over and retching when she realized what had been fluttering around her mouth.

She had no idea where she was going.

She'd decided she'd maintain a straight line from the house. Even if she didn't know where she was headed, she'd know where she was headed *from*. There was a problem, though – as with all thought-out, rational plans of attack. The enemy had a vote.

The jungle wasn't cooperating. There were innumerable obstacles in her way – massive tree trunks, several of which she almost walked into, sudden steep drops, a black stream complete with invisible waterfall that sounded, for one instant of comfort, like TV static.

She kept making detours till she felt like *it* in blindman's buff. She'd been spun around too many times to know which way was which. She desperately needed someone to tell her if she was getting warmer.

Right now she was getting colder. And hungrier. And more frightened.

236

The simple rocking motion of putting one foot before the other lulled Joelle back to sleep. Joanna was tempted to join her. In the morning she'd at least be able to see – survey her surroundings and make an educated guess where she was.

She was worried someone would peek in the room – Tomás or Puento. That they'd send out searchers who knew the jungle and, more important, knew how to *track* someone in it. She had to keep moving.

She stumbled into a large clearing.

It was as if someone had flicked on the room lights. She could suddenly see her legs, Joelle's sleeping face, the *sky*. She hadn't seen the sky since . . . well, she couldn't remember. She was momentarily stunned at the tapestry of glittering stars – so many of them that it seemed artificial, like an enormous disco ball. She stood there and caught her breath.

Odd. Here she was in the middle of a jungle, but if she didn't know any better, she would've sworn she was standing before a *field*. Something cultivated, regular, attended to. There was a dank but distinct odor in the air. What?

She stepped forward till she stood on its very edge.

Of course.

Coca. She'd stumbled across an illegal cocaine field, the kind they grew deep in the jungle to shield from government patrols.

Joanna felt a surge of – what? *Hope?*

She was trespassing on dangerous ground. But at least it was ground trod by humans.

If she waited till morning, someone might come – the farmer who tended it. But what if it wasn't a campesino looking for a little supplemental income? What if it was one of – *them*? Maybe they grew their *own* fields – maybe this was one of them. She felt caught between competing and equally compelling inclinations. She would do anything not to go back into the jungle. If she stayed, if she lay down and curled up till morning, she might end up having waited for the wrong people.

237

Go or stay?

Then it was decided for her.

The field itself was an indistinct blanket of mostly black. Even as her eyes grew accustomed to her moonlit surroundings, it stayed that way. Black.

It had an odor with an almost physical dimension – wet, pasty, and bitter.

Then she understood. The field looked black because that's what it was.

Black as ash.

It'd been burned to the ground. She could see it now – a tangle of five-foot coca plants reduced to shattered, twisted stumps.

A government patrol had discovered and torched it. Or the USDF. Or the farmer who grew it. Maybe they practiced a kind of slash-and-burn agriculture.

Anyway, it was abandoned. No one would be coming in the morning.

She had to keep moving.

Which way?

It seemed like you should be able to tell from the stars. *How?* Paul knew this kind of stuff – she'd bought him a telescope for his thirty-fifth birthday that proved virtually useless on the roof of their apartment building. The bright lights of New York City didn't just blind starry-eyed newcomers – they did a pretty good job on amateur astronomers. Still, more than once Paul had tried to point out one constellation or another to her. She wished she'd paid more attention.

Okay, which direction?

She swung her arm in an arc and decided she'd stop it when it felt right. Like throwing darts blindfolded.

When her arm stopped moving, it was pointing left.

She kissed Joelle on the top of her head and moved back into the jungle.

*   *   *

238

MORNING WAS COMING FAST.

The light had changed from deep black to charcoal gray. She stopped having to worry that each footstep might land her in quicksand, or into a hole, or on top of some animal's head.

That was the good part.

The bad part was that she could see some of the screeching, growling, slithering things that she'd only *heard* up to now. Imagination might be scarier than reality, she decided, but not by much.

What looked like a kind of baboon swung past her by inches, emitting a threatening screech that almost shattered her eardrums. It landed in the crook of a tree branch four feet above her head and shook a vine in her direction. It displayed its teeth – they looked large and frighteningly sharp.

Joanna turned to her right and stumbled through the underbrush, hoping the monkey wouldn't come after them.

It didn't.

Later, she saw a tree branch suddenly move right in front of her. Literally get up and begin detaching itself from the trunk of an enormous tree dripping lacy veils of green moss.

Of course it wasn't a tree branch. It was a *snake* – clearly enormous and clearly alerted to her presence. It was as thick as her arm, with dead yellow eyes and a black flickering tongue. Scared stiff and trying not to scream, she watched it uncoil for what seemed like minutes.

It slid off into a thick patch of ferns.

With the growing light came the heat. It covered them like a wet towel and left her drenched in sweat. The insects seemed attracted to perspiration; clouds of white gnats descended on her from all directions. She tried swatting them away, but they were as oblivious as New York City pigeons – short of actual gunfire, they weren't budging.

Then there were the mosquitoes – or their very large cousins. She was a movable feast for them – her bitten arms were covered in red bumps, as if she'd broken out in hives.

Joelle had started crying again and didn't seem in any mood to stop.

Even to someone unschooled in the lingo of infants, it was obvious that while Joelle might be hot and uncomfortable, it was all about hunger now. For the first time, Joanna wondered if she'd done the right thing. She should've planned – stockpiled baby formula. She was guilty of criminal lack of foresight.

Nothing seemed to calm Joelle down; soon Joanna needed calming as well. Fear lodged somewhere in the pit of her stomach and physically constricted her, as if her legs were bound by rubber bands. She was living through one of those dreams of being chased, where you can't, for the life of you, *move*.

They were as lost as lost can be.

The jungle had swallowed them whole – eaten them alive. They weren't going to get out.

She kept walking anyway – something inside her ordering her to lift one leg, then the other. Sheer stubbornness maybe.

Walking songs – front and center.

I'm walking, yes indeed, I'm talking, yes indeed . . .

These boots are made for walking . . .

Walk like a man . . .

She decided she'd keep walking till she couldn't. That was fair. Go as long as she could and then drop. Fight the good fight.

It was early morning – save for the brief respite by the abandoned coca field, she'd been walking six straight hours.

Then she smelled it.

She stopped dead, closed her eyes, crossed her fingers.

Sniff.

She smelled it again.

Sausage.

Was that possible?

Hot, sizzling, aromatic *sausage*?

Maybe it was some kind of plant? An animal? A jungle smell she was simply unfamiliar with?

240

She sniffed the air again, taking her time. No. It was clear as day. Someone was cooking breakfast.

Her heart leaped, soared, did pirouettes. She stopped rocking Joelle and brought her up under her chin.

'We made it. We're going home. We're free.'

She couldn't see anyone – the same panorama of trees, vines, stumps, and ferns. A massive dew-laden spiderweb refracted the sun into sparkling carats of fire.

She followed the smell.

Left, then right, then straight ahead.

Nose, don't fail me now.

The jungle seemed to thin – not all at once, but slowly, inexorably. The air lost its heaviness, her lungs eased, the insects drifted off.

The smell intensified, tickling her taste buds, reeling her in.

Now she could see patches of empty space through the trees.

She quickened her pace – if she'd been wearing sneakers instead of half-inch heels, she would've broken into a run.

Even Joelle seemed to sense a change in the air. Her crying lessened, then stopped altogether. She emitted a series of gurgles and hoarse sniffles.

Joanna skirted vegetation that had clearly been *stepped* on. Someone had walked here, snapping stems, grinding broad green fronds into the dirt. She thought she could make out an actual footprint.

The smell was intoxicating. She was nearly drunk on it. She lurched past a massive banyan tree and was suddenly staring into thin air.

A lone figure was standing there, backlit by a sun the color of marmalade.

The figure was saying something to her.

Joanna dropped to the ground, Joelle nestled in her arms. She hung her head, rocked back and forth, began weeping.

'No,' she whispered to herself, to Joelle, to the person standing in the clearing, maybe to God. *'No . . .'*

The clearing sloped uphill to a ridge where a modest farmhouse stood.

It had a smoking chimney, lime-green shutters, and a dilapidated back pen holding roosters, goats, and cows.

It was the first time she'd seen it from the outside.

'Quick,' Galina said, 'back to the room before they see you.'

THIRTY-FIVE

Galina snuck her back into the house. Not without being detected. The Indian girl with long black hair came out of the bathroom and nearly bumped into them. Galina had an explanation.

She fainted, Galina told her in Spanish, *she needed some air.*

The girl nodded, seemingly disinterested.

Once Galina ushered Joanna back into the room, once she closed the door and sat down, she said, 'It was stupid. You don't *know* the jungle.' She took Joelle from her exhausted arms, changed and fed her. 'You would've died out there.'

'I'm going to die anyway,' Joanna answered. It was the first time she'd uttered that thought out loud. It seemed to give it an awful legitimacy.

Galina shook her head. 'You shouldn't say that.'

'Why not? It's true. They'll kill me like they killed Maruja and Beatriz. You don't want to talk about it. They killed them in here – in this room. I can show you their blood.'

'Her cold's worse,' she said, referring to Joelle, continuing to avoid any mention of the two ghosts still hovering in the room.

'Yes, her cold's worse. And her mother's still chained to a wall. And we won't talk about two murdered women.' Joanna's own voice seemed alien to her now – flat, emotionless. It's *hope,* she thought – she'd lost it out there in the jungle.

'I'm going to put her to sleep,' Galina said.

'Yes. Wonderful idea. While you're at it, put me to sleep.'

Galina winced and rubbed her left arm.

Nurse. Kidnapper. Friend. Jailer.

'I don't understand you,' Joanna said.

'What?'

'I don't understand. You. Why you're here. Why you're with these people. Killers. Murderers. You were a mother.'

Galina had turned to leave, but now she stopped, looked back at her. It was that *word,* Joanna thought.

Mother.

'You never finished your story,' Joanna said. 'Tell me. I need a good story tonight. I do. I need to understand why.'

THIRTY-SIX

I need a good story tonight.'
Just the way Claudia used to say it to me because she didn't want to go to sleep yet.
A story, Mama, she'd beg. A story.
Well, okay.
A story.

AFTER GALINA AND HER HUSBAND HAD LEFT THE BAR THAT NIGHT, they didn't speak to Claudia again.

Sometimes the boy from La Nacional would call them.

There was a firefight with helicopter-borne Special Forces in the mountains. A new initiative by a just-sworn-in president who'd promised to get tough with the *guerrilleros.* The boy said Claudia was there – army officers reported a beautiful young girl in camou-flage fatigues. *Don't worry,* the boy said, *she wasn't hurt.*

These government forays were infrequent and entirely for show. Getting tough on the *guerrilleros,* everyone knew, was simple pos-turing. There might be two tough factions in Colombia, but the government wasn't one of them.

There was FARC, the Revolutionary Armed Forces of Colombia, on the left.

And on the right, the United Self-Defense Forces.

All names in these kinds of conflicts were exercises in irony. *Self-Defense* – as if they'd been punched in the nose and were simply defending themselves from a playground bully. Maybe that's what some of them believed they were doing.

Just not the man who ran it.

If you wanted to understand what happened to Claudia, you had to understand him too. If you saw Claudia tripping down the alleyways of Chapinero as a sensitive and easily bruised eight-year-old, you had to see *him* growing up in Medellín and doing a generous share of the bruising. They were counterparts. If Claudia was the light, he was the dark.

They were due to collide.

How do you explain a Manuel Riojas?

Bogeymen aren't usually born, they just are. They lurk in the swamp of human fear and misery. They don't have beginnings, just ends. But even then, they never go quietly, not before they leave behind desolate swaths of scorched earth.

Real bogeymen *do* have beginnings. They have birthdays and confirmations and school graduations. They live in neighborhoods, not swamps. Manuel Riojas grew up in the grimy Jesús de Navarona neighborhood of Medellín.

Galina had visited relatives there once. She remembered how a steady gray rain washed the garbage downhill. It was possible she'd driven by Riojas himself – later she'd wonder about that. If he might've been carjacking by then. If he might've picked their car – pointed a pistol through the window and ended everything before it began.

It's said he grew up on the stories.

The legends of Colombia's *bandidos*. Desquite and Tirofijo and Sangrenegra. *Revenge, Sureshot,* and *Blackblood*. Galina came to believe that countries where much of the population is poor and oppressed are doomed to worship the wrong people. People who steal from the rich, even if they never actually give anything back to the poor. It doesn't matter – they *are* poor. Or were. They might be vicious, murderous, clearly psychotic. They're victimizing the victimizers. That's enough to make them folk heroes. Enough to make children who grow up in uncertain circumstances daydream of becoming them.

Riojas' criminal beginnings were murky. It's said he went back and had police files altered, court records erased, various acquaintances from his early life eliminated. It's known he was arrested at least once by the time he was fourteen – possibly for petty theft. It's believed he bartered fake lottery tickets, hijacked cigarettes, stole cars, before moving on to something infinitely more lucrative. The particular scourge of their godforsaken country: drugs. Specifically, coca. He started as a runner, a small dealer. He was apparently a favorite of the local *contrabandista,* who made the fatal mistake of trusting him, promoting him through the ranks. Somehow the severed head of this *contrabandista* ended up stuck on a pole on a mountain road outside Medellín. Somehow Riojas ended up in charge of the Medellín cocaine trade. This was generally acknowledged to be the first exhibition of Riojas' particular business ethos. He didn't compete with rivals. He murdered them. He did it in ways meant to discourage others. Children were murdered in front of their parents. Mothers were raped in front of their husbands. Enemies were tortured and mutilated, their freshly slaughtered corpses placed on public display. More fodder for the newspapers.

Property wasn't excluded. Warehouses, factories, competing cocaine fields, were torched and obliterated.

The stories grew; the legend took form and substance.

He rose to nearly unimaginable heights.

That's necessary for a bogeyman. To tower over the cringing. And they *did* cringe. Not just rival gangs, the Ochoas, the Escobars, who soon disappeared in a series of vicious and prolonged bloodbaths. But the *familias* who pulled the strings. They bowed down too. Riojas ate the heart of his enemies, then became them. He was elected state senator. They say he'd promised this to his mother. Respectability. They say he'd pledged this to the idols he kept in a secret chapel on one of his haciendas. *Santeria,* they whispered, the bastard religion practiced throughout much of the country outside Bogotá.

But rulers demand more than obedience. They demand armies. The one belonging to the government was toothless. It didn't take any particular intelligence to realize that the only army worth fighting lived in the mountains north of Bogotá and called themselves FARC. They spouted Marxist mumbo jumbo about toppling the *elite,* talked about the *people* as if the people actually mattered. Under different circumstances, Riojas might've sympathized with them, even *joined* them. After all, he came from the same impoverished background. Now he was another successful *capitalista* trying to protect his investments. They were the enemy.

He armed his own militia. He gave his most trusted executioners titles. *Captain. General. Major.* That made them more or less an army. He demanded money from the five *familias* to fund it.

Now they could have a real war.

Riojas could conduct it the way war was supposed to be conducted. When the USDF wanted to keep campesino villages from harboring FARC guerrillas – not that they had, not that they'd even thought about it, just that they *might* – they'd pick twenty campesinos at random. You, you, and you. They'd make them dig their own graves, then force their fathers or brothers or uncles to execute them. Whoever refused, joined them in the pit. This was the kind of muscular teaching a simple campesino could understand.

Claudia was captured by the USDF two years after she walked out of that bar.

The boy from the university called and told them.

After Galina had dropped the phone to the floor and stared at it as if it were something alien, after she had reluctantly picked it up and found her voice, she asked the boy if her daughter was dead. Only it wasn't *her* voice – it sounded like someone years older.

No, he said. She'd been captured alive.

He didn't add that it wouldn't be for long.

He didn't have to.

For one entire year Galina assumed Claudia was dead.

She thought of having a proper funeral but was always dissuaded at the last moment. Sometimes it was something she found as she cleaned the house. She cleaned all the time now. Ceaselessly, relentlessly, *religiously*. She'd trudge back from caring for someone else's daughter or son and immediately grab a mop, a sponge, a dustpan, desperately clinging to routine as a way to stave off thoughts of suicide. One day while vacuuming under Claudia's desk, she found a birthday card an eight-year-old Claudia had drawn for her in school. A stick-figure mommy holding a stick-figure baby in her arms. *Te adoro,* the baby whispered.

Galina said *not yet.* The funeral would wait.

Sometimes memory would be triggered by something completely ordinary. Stuffing a bedsheet into the washer and suddenly remembering Claudia's first period, how Galina had stood flustered and embarrassed before Claudia's soiled bed one morning before middle school. Even as her daughter remained oddly composed, even comforting. *I know what it is, Mama – it means I can have grandbabies for you.*

Galina pushed the funeral off again.

Everything that follows, Galina would find out later.

Claudia was captured in the town of Chiappa. They'd sent her there for supplies, and someone spotted her. Stories about her had been circulating for months. The beautiful university girl with the revolutionary fever. Someone was sitting and waiting for her. He followed her from town, called in reinforcements. When Claudia got back to the ravine where her fellow soldiers in the war against capitalism were holed up and waiting, a USDF brigade was already circling in for the kill.

249

When she opened the flap of their makeshift tent, just a few shirts strung together to keep out the rain, bullets rained down on them instead.

Three of the *guerrilleros* were killed. Two made it back through the jungle, one of them dragging a shot-up right leg that was later amputated.

Why wasn't Claudia killed like the others?

Maybe because they were told not to.

Because Riojas had heard the stories and was curious to see her in the flesh. More than curious. *Desirous.*

He left a state dinner in Bogotá that night. Someone whispered into his ear, and he flew by helicopter to a hacienda in the north. When he entered the room where Claudia was on her knees, both hands tied tightly behind her back, he was still wearing his tuxedo.

He took his time. *Examining* her, the way you appraise horseflesh or hunting dogs. Apparently, he had plenty of both.

He must've liked what he saw.

You can imagine what happened during the next two days. You can close your eyes and say a prayer and peek. Riojas personally took charge of her *interrogation.* She came very close to dying. She prayed for it, hoped to God that the next time he beat her into unconsciousness she wouldn't wake up. Despite having joined the army of the godless, Claudia still *believed.* Somewhere inside herself she retained her Catholic core. She spoke to it now.

She'd heard the stories: prisoners pushed out of helicopters, fed to the tigers. It would happen to her.

But two days turned into three.

Then four.

An entire week passed.

No one came to take her off in a helicopter, or for a trip to the tiger cage. Yes, there *were* tigers. She squinted out her window through nearly beaten-shut eyes and saw them pacing back and forth like sentries. In the afternoon someone threw a live pony into the cage and the tigers ripped its throat out.

Then something odd happened.

One day Riojas came in and didn't beat her. He asked her something instead.

To open her legs for him. Politely requested it. Claudia said no, shut her eyes, waited for a fresh onslaught of pain.

Riojas left the room.

The next time he came in, he was bearing gifts.

French lingerie.

Riojas asked her to try it on for him. Claudia said no.

Again he didn't touch her.

By the third time, Claudia began to understand something.

She wasn't experienced with men; she'd had a casual boyfriend or two.

She could tell when someone was in love.

It had happened before – boys in primary school, then university, who'd begin acting stupid around her, wholly outside the realm of normal behavior.

It became increasingly clear that Riojas wasn't going to kill her.

He was going to court her.

Why?

Maybe because Claudia was Claudia.

Because he coveted what he couldn't destroy. *Love is strange* – isn't that what the songs say?

At some point Claudia began to understand that this adoration might save her. Maybe not forever. Just for a while. Somewhere she stopped wanting to die and began wanting to live.

When he asked her a fourth time to dress in French lingerie, to turn around and please kneel on the bed for him, she said yes. She understood it wouldn't do to *always* deny him. Eventually, he'd tire of that. Then he'd tire of her.

There's something truly pathetic about a captor falling in love with his prisoner. Claudia needed to *use* that to her advantage. She needed to hold something back. To sometimes give in, but always deny the one thing he wanted more than anything else. Reciprocity.

Her heart – as the poets say.

She began to dine with him, at an actual dinner *table*. Set with gleaming silver, translucent china. Dressed up in whichever five-hundred-dollar dress he'd picked out for her. Sometimes she'd wear something else, deliberately ignoring his wishes. He'd throw tantrums that subsided only after most of their dinner had ended up on the floor.

He delighted in telling her what he'd done to other women. Women who'd crossed him. That singer – Evi, the pop star who'd thought she could carry on with a musician while seeing *him*.

I went up to her apartment with my personal doctor. I held her down while he cut out her vocal cords, then I sat there and watched as he sewed her up. She no longer sings very well.

He was trying to evoke fear and obedience. Claudia would act bored. She was convinced if she did the opposite of what he expected, she could survive another day.

He loosened the leash a little.

She was allowed outside – always accompanied by one of his goons. She listened. She observed. She memorized things.

Where were they? She smelled salt in the air. Not all the time, just on the days when the wind blew hard from the north. They had to be on the coast. Even so, they were hopelessly isolated. There wasn't a single roof in any direction. Just lush palms, overgrown ferns, tumbling birds-of-paradise. Wild parrots serenaded her on her walks around the hacienda.

Then she observed something else.

Something horrible.

Riojas had always used protection with her. Lately, he'd become careless. He was usually drunk or coked up.

She missed a period. Then another.

One morning she woke completely consumed with nausea and spent half an hour on the floor of the marble bathroom, staring at her warped reflection in the gold-leaf fixtures.

She decided she would kill herself.

She came to this decision calmly and rationally.

There were knives in the kitchen.

There were two swords mounted above the fireplace in the den. She would put one of them right through her, through his *monstrosity,* before anyone could stop her.

Riojas was away. She cleansed her face, meticulously applied the French makeup Riojas had brought for her, dressed in a charcoal pantsuit she thought suitable for a funeral.

The armed guards he kept stationed around the house were fortuitously absent from the den.

The swords appeared to be ceremonial. Japanese, she guessed – delicately curved steel fixed to bright hand-painted hilts. They were hung on nails, crossed at midblade.

She was reaching for one of them when she felt it. Or maybe she just imagined she had.

Like a *kick in the gut.*

She'd touched the instrument of her own death, and something had moved in the pit of her stomach. She sank to the floor.

She understood. She knew what it was.

More than that. She knew she couldn't bring herself to kill it.

It was half her.

It means I can have grandbabies for you, she'd once whispered to her mother, Galina. Maybe she remembered saying it that morning. Maybe it gave that tiny movement in her belly a face, a place in the world.

She hovered between despair and worse.

She'd made a decision to live, but it was a decision impossible to live *with*. So she made another kind of decision.

When Riojas returned from Bogotá, Claudia feigned happiness, guiding his hand onto her stomach as if helping him claim new territory. Another piece of the world ready to be affixed with his monogram – those cartoonish-looking *R*s prominently displayed on every one of his handkerchiefs, napkins, undershorts – anything capable of bearing thread.

He began pampering her. Within limits, of course. She wasn't his wife. He had one of those back in Bogotá, in addition to three obscenely rotund children. He couldn't squire her around town. But he showed what might be termed *deference*. The leash grew looser. A captured rebel, even one showered with mink coats and five-hundred-dollar shoes, might run. But a girl carrying his child?

He stopped talking about the women who'd crossed him.

Except for the day she told him.

He asked for sex and she turned him down, pregnancy being a convenient excuse, one to be added to all the others.

Of course, he said, he understood. But before leaving her room he turned and spoke to her.

If you ever try to leave with my baby, I'll hunt you down and kill you. Both of you. However long it takes, no matter where you've gone. Do you understand?

She nodded, forced herself to smile, as if that were a sentiment worthy of admiration. A macho declaration of love.

Good, he said.

She began venturing further. Past the tiger cages. Down a twisting dirt path into the jungle. She *had* smelled salt air. The hacienda's property ended on a bluff overlooking the Caribbean, where a small fishing village sat directly below the cliff. Skiffs sat half beached on the sand, spidery nets drying in the sun.

A bodyguard still came with her, but the distance between them seemed to increase in proportion to her swollen stomach. He'd often leave her alone with a book, let her nap undisturbed on one of the hammocks overlooking the water.

She befriended the zookeeper; in addition to the tigers, there were ostriches, llamas, chimpanzees. His name was Benito, and unlike the other men in Riojas' employ, he seemed to lack the psychotic gene. He'd been trained in zoology. He let her know that feeding live horses to the tigers wasn't his idea. Feeding two-legged things to them wasn't either.

A job was a job.

He let her watch as he fed them freshly cut hunks of sheep and cattle, venturing into the cage dangling the day's lunch from a long hooked pole.

Claudia waited for Riojas to make one of his numerous trips.

She slipped out of bed at 3 a.m. She opened her top drawer, removed a change of clothes, wrapped them around the kitchen knife she'd slipped into the waistband of her pants.

She'd unlocked one bay window in the den before retiring. She opened it wide enough to slip out – no mean feat considering her swollen stomach. She stepped out onto the blue grass.

She'd rehearsed this at least a dozen times.

She could've walked the route in her sleep.

She waddled past the tiger cage to the zookeeper's shack.

She removed the keys from the bent nail. She pushed the sleeve of her shift back to the elbow, pulled out the knife, and placed it against her skin.

She used the extra clothes she'd taken from her drawer to soak up the blood. She walked back out to the tiger cages and pushed the bloody clothes through the bars.

Claudia carefully placed the keys into the cage-door lock and left them dangling there.

She turned to the path that led to the sea.

She was buying time.

In the morning they'd discover she was missing. They'd find the keys to the tiger cage still sitting in the lock. As if someone had let themselves in and locked the door behind them to ensure that there would be no way out. In case they lost their courage and changed their mind. They'd discover her bloody clothes. Shredded to pieces.

Riojas would be called in Bogotá. He'd think back to their last night together. He'd replay everything. Her smiles and laughter and demure assurances, and he'd see only lies. Had she killed herself? Had she *really*?

Eventually, he'd know the truth. They wouldn't find any ground-up bones. They'd understand the charade she'd perpetrated, and Riojas would start to make good on his promise.

If you ever try to leave with my baby, I'll hunt you down and kill you. Both of you. However long it takes, no matter where you've gone. Do you understand?

Maybe Claudia heard those words as she walked through the jungle that night and down to the sea. As she sat and crouched in one of the slowly rocking fishing skiffs and waited for the fishermen to appear like ghosts out of the early-morning light . . .

THE SOUND OF A CRYING BABY. IT STARTLED JOANNA BACK TO reality. Back from that hacienda and the tiger cage and the jungle.

Joelle had woken up.

It was her cold. Galina reached over and wiped Joelle's nose, cleared the crust from her eyes with a tissue. Joanna gave her the bottle, urged the nipple into her mouth, gently rocked her. Soon Joelle's eyes grew sleepy, fluttered, closed into two tiny slits.

Galina was hugging herself as if she were suddenly freezing.

'What happened, Galina?' Joanna asked. 'What happened to Claudia?'

GALINA SPENT THE EMPTY DAYS DUTIFULLY FEEDING AND BATHING and powdering other people's daughters.

She ritually and repeatedly cleaned house.

She discovered bits and pieces of Claudia and arranged them in a kind of shrine. Old birthday cards. Photographs. Letters. Half-burned incense candles. Little items of mostly cheap jewelry. She did what people are supposed to do at shrines. She prayed for a miracle.

Sometimes they actually happen.

Sometimes you wake up and dress yourself in the same dowdy shift as the day before. You sit down at the kitchen table and listlessly eat a breakfast of stale corn cakes and fruit, because you're supposed to eat, even if you have no appetite. You vacuum a carpet you've already vacuumed enough times to wear smooth. You dust every piece of furniture in the house. You rewash the dishes and scrub the floor. Then you sit back down at the kitchen table because it's time to eat lunch.

And sometimes you hear a soft knock at the front door. You wearily stand up to answer it, not *immediately,* because you hope they'll go away and leave you alone. But they don't, so eventually you have to get up, shuffle over to the door, ask who it is.

And you hear a murmur from the other side. Something with an *M.* A voice you can't quite place that seems to touch some distant part of you. And you ask again. *Who is it?*

And now the *M* comes with other letters attached to it. It's no longer an orphan. You suddenly understand that the person on the other side of the door isn't telling you their name. They're stating *yours.* Only it's a name only one person in the world can use.

Your heart stops beating as if there's some kind of electrical short in your wiring. You turn the lock with trembling fingers. You fling open the door and the person whispers it again.

Mama . . . Mama . . . Mama.

And she falls into your arms.

THEY FOUND HER A HIDING PLACE.

Colombia was a big country.

Riojas was bigger.

Aunt Salma wasn't an aunt by blood, but by affection, a spinster who'd been semi-adopted by the family long ago and was from then on always present at holidays, confirmations, and funerals. Back in Fortul, where Galina was born.

They drove Claudia there the next day.

Claudia assured them Riojas didn't know her last name. All FARC converts changed their surnames to save their families from retribution.

Galina knew that would protect her only so much.

257

Claudia was striking and pregnant. Riojas would be beating the provinces to find her.

It was a measure of Galina's manic joy that she hadn't noticed. Not immediately. Certainly not at the door, where she'd gazed teary-eyed at her; not even at the kitchen table, where they'd clung to each other like shipwreck survivors.

But when they finally separated and she checked her daughter for damage, she saw the kind she hadn't expected.

'You're pregnant.'

Two years ago Claudia might've had an answer for that – a comment on her mother's diminishing powers of observation. She simply nodded.

'Whose is it?'

Claudia told her. She was never going to speak about it again – just this one time. She held both of Galina's hands. She spoke slowly, softly, calmly. It was good she kept Galina's hands prisoner. Galina felt like using those hands. To hit something. To cover her ears. To wrap around her mouth to prevent herself from screaming. It was impossible for a mother to sit there and listen to this. It was beyond endurance.

The subject of abortion never came up.

It's possible the pregnancy was too far advanced by then. Maybe it didn't matter. It wasn't how either of them had been raised.

Aunt Salma lived near a dairy farm outside the city, where it was possible Claudia might live in relative privacy and anonymity. At least for a while. At least until the baby was born.

They told Salma just enough to understand the gravity of Claudia's situation. They constructed a story for anyone who couldn't be avoided. An unfortunate love affair. An unplanned pregnancy. A girl who wanted to be left alone with the result of her bad choices.

Galina and her husband visited every two weeks, making sure to leave late at night, to stop several times along the way to check for any suspicious cars that might be following them. Any more than two weeks might be risky. Any less would be unbearable.

With the help of a local mestiza midwife, Claudia gave birth to a baby girl.

Galina had wondered how she'd feel. If she'd ever be able to embrace the baby as her actual *grandchild*. When the infant emerged headfirst, Galina saw Claudia in every facet of her features. She felt transported through time. To a hospital bed in Bogotá, the smell of blood and alcohol and talcum, a screaming baby who even then seemed to grab for something just out of reach.

She was named for Claudia's paternal grandmother. Sofía, the *ventello* singer. She was swaddled, baptized, showered with affection from the small circle of people allowed to know of her existence.

For a time, brief and fleeting, Galina allowed herself to relax and luxuriate in the peculiar pleasures of being an *abuela*. When she visited Fortul, baby toys in hand, she was like anyone else visiting their grandchild. She pretended that Claudia lived in Fortul because her husband worked for one of the refineries there. That Claudia never made the return trip because the baby wasn't ready to travel. That they always stayed inside because the weather was nasty or because Sofía was sensitive to the sun.

Then it became impossible to pretend.

Salma returned from the market one day looking nearly anemic. She told Claudia that people were asking questions. Someone was showing a *picture* around. Claudia remembered her first days of captivity when Riojas had interrogated her, when he'd posed her naked in various positions intended for maximum humiliation. Even with her eyes swollen shut, she could see bursting flashbulbs shooting out of the black like Roman candles.

They had to move them.

Another family resource was contacted and imposed upon. And it *was* an imposition. Whoever hid them was keenly aware they were putting themselves in the line of fire. A kind of ad hoc system developed. Claudia and Sofía were *shuttled*. Back and forth and back between whichever relatives and friends were momentarily able to swallow their fear and provide them with a temporary home.

It wasn't easy for Claudia to be passed around like an unwanted relative. But that's what she was. A burden, an albatross. Albatrosses meant death; so might Claudia. She'd spend a few weeks to several months at each house or apartment before leaving. Usually in the middle of the night. She became adept at packing quickly, bringing just enough from one place to another to make each new stop seem remotely like home.

Slowly, pressure eased. Stories of *paramilitares* inquiring after a beautiful girl with a small baby became more sporadic, then stopped altogether. Claudia's stays lengthened, routine replaced fear. Sofía grew from infant to toddler – in an instant, it seemed to Galina, who only saw her in carefully parceled-out increments. Claudia seemed to grow as well, regaining pieces of herself that had been taken away from her in that hacienda. She began venturing outside, baby in tow, disguised in sunglasses and an enormous straw hat.

Galina accompanied her on some of these walks. She let herself imagine that life might reach some kind of normalcy. It had been *four years*. If one read the papers correctly, Riojas had more than enough to keep him occupied. They were threatening to extradite him to the United States for narcotics trafficking. Maybe he'd forgotten about Claudia. About *them*. Maybe he no longer cared.

When the three of them strolled hand in hand – lifting a begging Sofía over the curb by both arms – it was easy to imagine this was true.

Later Galina would understand that's what he'd wanted them to think. So they'd begin to believe it was over. Become a little more carefree, even care*less*. So they'd stop peeking around corners.

She never knew how it happened.

Not *exactly* how it happened. She would never know that. She would have to *imagine* it, which was worse than knowing. Because the imagination can conjure up every nightmare never dreamed.

Someone spotted Claudia. That much she knew.

Galina received a panicked call from her daughter. Or rather, her answering machine did. For the rest of her life she would admonish herself for going shopping that day. For opening the refrigerator and somehow seeing the necessity for food. She would have hours and days

260

and weeks and years to imagine what was being done to her daughter while she performed the mundane tasks of daily living. To ponder a single question. If she'd been home to take Claudia's call, would she have been able to *save* her?

When Galina *did* get home, when she casually pressed the button on her answering machine and heard her daughter's clearly terrified voice, she knew it was already too late.

She buried her panic, did what you're supposed to do when someone calls you. Call *back*. Claudia's uncle – the one she'd been staying with for the last month and a half – answered the phone. He didn't know where she was, he said. Her or the baby. They must've gone for a walk.

Someone saw me at the market. That's what Claudia had whispered into the phone.

She hadn't waited for her uncle to return home. Out of self-preservation, out of the desire to protect *him,* she'd gathered up Sofía and run. Later they'd notice some of her things were missing. Not everything; some of Sofía's clothes and a small picture of the three of them – grandmother, mother, and baby – she'd managed to tote from one hiding place to another.

Claudia had been spotted in the market, and in a near panic she'd called the one person she trusted most in the world.

Galina wasn't there. She was out shopping.

Claudia had decided she needed to leave *then.*

After that, who knows?

After that, you're left with the clinical police reports and a few eye-witnesses who may or may not have seen anything.

Mostly, you're left with the body.

She was found on the edge of a barrio.

No one was aware it *was* a she at first. It was an amalgam of flesh and bone, a jigsaw puzzle that took two police pathologists a solid week to piece together before proclaiming it was *her.* They knew this much. What had been done to her had taken time and patience. There were traces of rope found around her neck. What *once* was her neck. There were acid burns everywhere. *Every inch of her skin.* That's what the police report said. It was supposed to be kept confidential to spare the family, but it was leaked to a newspaper, which printed it as a small item on the weather page. She'd been burned and mutilated. The report didn't mention if she was alive and conscious during the ordeal.

It didn't tell Galina *who* did it either.

It was another unsolved homicide. To be added to the thousands of other unsolved murders in Colombia.

Had Riojas been there in person?

Had he gotten another one of those calls in the middle of a dinner, coolly whispered in his wife's ear that he had urgent business to attend to? Had he smiled, rolled up his sleeves, walked in on a bound and terrified Claudia, just like he had four years before? It's impossible to say.

But Galina *saw* him there.

When she pictured it, as she did over and over and over again, dulled by alcohol, pumped full of whatever pills she'd managed to wheedle from yet another doctor, Riojas was always there. Wielding the knife. Spilling the acid. Choking the life out of her daughter.

He was always there.

WHEN GALINA FINISHED, JOANNA COULDN'T THINK OF ANYTHING TO say. She sat in stunned silence.

It wasn't until Galina stood up to leave, till she whispered good-bye and turned to the door, that Joanna realized there was a missing piece of the story.

'Sofía?' Joanna said, hesitant to ask because she was afraid to hear Galina's answer. 'What happened to your granddaughter?'

Galina stopped just before the door. 'Dead,' she said without turning around. 'Like her mother.'

There were other questions – how had their deaths led Galina to FARC? But Joanna didn't ask. If she thought about it hard enough, she could probably fill in the blanks herself.

After Galina left, Joanna lay on the floor and curled her body around her daughter, as if to protect her from fatal harm.

262

THIRTY-SEVEN

From the outside it looked like a taxi garage. *Dial-a-Taxi,* it said in big yellow block letters.

Apparently not.

For one thing there were no taxis inside.

There were no taxi drivers.

There were dark hallways that seemed to lead nowhere. There was a big room with faint oil stains on the floor. Maybe it had been a taxi garage once, but not now.

This was where the bird-watcher took him.

He'd been escorted down his apartment stairway with the bird-watcher's hand on his arm, then bundled into a car with gray-tinted windows and driven outside the city by a faceless chauffeur. Queens, Paul thought – that vast unknown that Manhattanites traversed on their way to the East End, only stopping for gas or the occasional Mets game.

'You don't watch birds,' Paul said to him sometime during the ride.

'No,' the man said. 'I watch other things.'

*   *   *

It took Paul a while to understand that he was being interrogated.

They were asking questions and it seemed as if he was answering them. Yes, there were *two* of them. After a while he noticed that one of the men always stayed out of sight and directly behind him – the two of them switching off like beach-volleyball players rotating between net and serve. He wondered if this was a tactic meant to scare him. One of them hiding behind him, doing God knows what. If so, he felt like telling them they needn't bother – he was scared enough already.

When they got to the garage, the bird-watcher had slipped on a blue vinyl jacket. No, *slipped on* was too casual a description. He cloaked himself in it, like a Masters champion displaying the green jacket.

This jacket had *DEA* prominently displayed in white letters, each half a foot tall. Paul imagined that was so there'd be no mistaking who was bursting through the front door of some walk-up in Spanish Harlem. Apparently, the bird-watcher hadn't felt the need to announce his affiliation when he'd burst into Paul's Upper West Side co-op.

'Know what this spells, Paul?' the bird-watcher asked him.

'Yes,' Paul said. 'Drug Enforcement Agency.'

'Wrong.'

'D . . . E . . .'

'Wrong.'

'I thought DEA is –'

'Wrong. This jacket spells *Paul is fucked.*'

Yes, Paul thought, okay. 'Do I get to call a – ?'

'You know *why* it spells that, Paul?' the bird-watcher interrupted him. 'Can you guess?'

'No. Yes.'

'*No. Yes.* Which is it?'

'Excuse me. Can I call a lawyer?'

'Sure you can call a lawyer. How about *Miles Goldstein*? He's a lawyer, isn't he?'

Paul didn't answer. The bird-watcher had shed his glasses, and with them any suggestion he was involved in the gentle and scholarly pursuit of ornithology.

I watch other things.

'Paul, I asked you a question. Perhaps you're not familiar with the dynamics of DEA interrogation. That's okay. I'll explain. We ask. You answer. It's pretty simple. So what do you say – we clear on this?'

Paul nodded.

'Great. Terrific. So what did I ask you before? Hey, Tom, you remember what I asked Paul?' He was addressing the man lurking behind him. Paul turned to peek, but immediately felt the man's arm on his shoulder forcefully turning him back.

'You asked him if Miles Goldstein was a lawyer,' Tom said.

'Yes,' Paul answered. 'He's a lawyer.'

'Wrong,' the bird-watcher said.

'He's an adoption –'

'Wrong.'

'We went to him because –'

'Wrong. Miles Goldstein is *not* a lawyer.'

Paul shrugged, stuttered – he felt like the dumb and picked-on student unable to divine the right answer.

'Miles Goldstein *was* a lawyer. Was. His brains are splattered all over his home office. But you know that, Paul. Do we have to review the dynamics of DEA interrogation again?'

'No.'

'No? Okay, Miles Goldstein was a lawyer. What else was Miles Goldstein? Besides a cocksucking Jew bastard. You think Jews have infiltrated the corridors of power, Paul? Do you think they've co-opted our foreign policy? Hijacked the banks, corrupted our corporations, polluted our bloodline? You think that, Paul?'

'No.'

265

'No? It's okay, Paul – we're just shooting the shit. You can tell me – some of your best friends are Jews, yada yada yada . . . but come on, you mean to tell me you don't curse the Yids every time you open the paper? You think Osama picked *Jew York* because he hates the Yankees?'

'I don't know.'

'Well, sure, you don't *know*. But you can *guess*. You can have a sneaking suspicion. Come on, Paul: Jews – yea or nay?'

'Nay,' Paul said, surrendering to peer pressure. He wanted the bird-watcher to smile at him, pat him on the back, hail-fellow-well-met. He wanted to get out of this garage and save his wife.

The blow to the back of his neck drove his face straight into the table. He came up sputtering blood.

'Paul. *Paul* . . .' The bird-watcher slowly shook his head, but the image became increasingly blurred – Paul's eyes were tearing up. 'I'm surprised at you. *Tom* is a Jew. You offended him deeply. Why would you want to go and insult Tom like that?'

Paul tried to tell him he didn't mean it, he was just trying to be liked. He was in too much pain to speak. Initial numbness had given way to a searing and excruciating agony. Thick drops of blood were leaking onto the table.

'Try to avoid offending us from here on, Paul. Just a word of advice, okay? One friend to another. Me, I'm the calm type, but Tom's been up on more brutality charges than the LAPD. Now, where we? What *else* was Miles Goldstein?'

He got Paul a tissue, then waited patiently until Paul cleared enough blood from his throat to answer.

'I don't know,' Paul whispered. 'He was a kind of drug dealer, I think.'

'Ya *think?*' The bird-watcher smiled, but it wasn't the kind of smile Paul had been seeking. No.

'Yeah, Miles Goldstein was a drug dealer. You're right. Absolutely. Who did the dirty work for him? Who were his couriers?'

Me.

Paul said, 'Really. I want to call my lawyer.'

'Really. You really, really want to?'

'Yes.'

'No.'

'You haven't . . . I'm supposed to get a call. You haven't read me my rights.'

'There's a reason for that, Paul.'

'What reason?'

'You don't have any.'

'What?'

'See, we could read your rights to you, but you don't have any rights. Where've you been? It's Giuliani time.'

'I'm not a terrorist,' Paul said.

'No, Paul, you're not a terrorist. You're a mule. You're a *culero*. You're an up-the-ass FedEx package. We know what you are. But Goldstein was playing ball with those crafty little left-handers in *Che* Stadium. You know, FARC is a federally designated *terrorist group*. Yeah – they're on the list – the one with Osama and Hezbollah. That's why we supply Colombia with Special Ops nuts and really cool hardware. So if Goldstein was in business with terrorists and you were in business with Goldstein, well, that makes you . . . let me see, what does that make him, Tom?'

'That makes him subject to the newly drafted laws of national security. Or, as we like to say, rat-fucked by Ridge.'

'Yeah,' the bird-watcher said, 'that's about the size of it. No, Paul, you don't get a call. You don't get a lawyer. You don't get three hots and a smoke. You don't get *out* of here. Not unless we say so. And speaking of your fucked situation in life, I'd love to know how Miles and you walked into his office in Williamsburg and only *you* walked out.'

THEY PUT HIM IN A CELL, WHICH REALLY WASN'T ONE.

It didn't have a toilet or a sink. Unlike the room in Colombia, it didn't have a bed. It was just empty space surrounded by bare wall and what looked like a newly installed metal door.

If he wanted to lie down and sleep – and he did, desperately – he would have to lie directly on the concrete floor.

He tried, lay on his back and stared up at a single caged bulb, which didn't appear to be shutting off anytime soon. It was enclosed in metal so he couldn't reach up and break it, use it as a weapon, even against himself. No suicides on their watch.

Before throwing him in here they'd badgered him with questions – the majority of which he'd tried to answer. Mostly, he'd tried to explain what had happened. The kidnapping in Bogotá, the awful position in which he'd found himself, forced to choose between his wife and daughter and breaking six different federal drug statutes.

He couldn't tell whether they believed him or whether they thought he was making it all up.

They asked him a lot of questions about Miles. Interrupted by an occasional change of pace: What school did Paul go to? What does an actuary make? Which company did Joanna work for?

Every time he mentioned his wife's name, he felt a dull ache in the center of his chest. Everything he'd done, he'd done for them. Jo and Jo. He was no closer to freeing them. They were receding into the distance. It was as if he were pulling them up the side of a mountain, really putting his shoulder to it, only the rope kept slipping through his hands, dropping them further and further away.

AFTER A FEW HOURS IN HIS CELL THE BIRD-WATCHER CAME FOR him again.

Tom was missing in action.

'You know what really aggravates me, Paul?' the bird-watcher said. He was inhaling deeply on a Winston, holding in the smoke till the little vein in his forehead throbbed, then letting it out in a blue wispy stream.

'No,' Paul said.

'That was a rhetorical question, Paul. I appreciate you finally grasping the nuances of DEA interrogation, but I wasn't actually seeking an answer. What really aggravates me, what sticks in my craw, is that I worked this asshole for a year and a half, and now he's dead. A really bad case of coitus interruptus. I've got blue balls the size of grapefruits. Know what that feels like?'

Paul kept quiet this time.

'It doesn't feel good, Paul. It hurts. All I've got to show for it is lots of free miles on American – and I've got to put those back into an agency pool. You believe it? All those boring trips to Bogotá watching *Bruce Almighty* and sitting next to shitbags like you, and I get a trip to San Juan next Christmas – if I'm lucky. And I don't *feel* lucky. I mean, a year and a half and I end up with *you*? The last round-tripper on the Goldstein Express.'

Paul had been the last of many, the bird-watcher explained. It had taken him a long time to figure it out. He'd patiently followed the money trail. From Goldstein to Colombia and back. This close to wrapping it up, *this* close, and then . . .

'So what happened in his house, Paul? Monetary disagreement? Contractual dispute?'

'I told you,' Paul said. 'He shot himself.'

'Maybe. Only I'm inclined not to believe you. You've got the bad luck to be the one left holding the bag. Sucks, doesn't it? I need my pound of flesh, and you're it. *He shot himself?* Maybe. Maybe not. Maybe I don't give a shit.'

'I keep telling you, they *kidnapped* us. Miles set us up with a driver. And a nurse . . . *Galina*. She switched babies, and when we went to confront her . . .'

Paul stopped here. The whole thing sounded implausible, even to him. The bird-watcher seemed to be in no mood for any story providing Paul with even a shred of innocence. He was busy lighting another cigarette and staring off into space.

There was another reason Paul stopped speaking.

269

A few things were penknifed into the table. Some dirty epithets, a couple of crude drawings, and a heart cleft in two.

Paul was looking at the letter carved into the larger half of the jagged heart.

It was the letter *R*.

It reminded him of something.

The letters from Galina. And the granddaughter she was determined to protect at all costs.

Her father is looking for her. He won't stop till he finds her. As you know, R has the power and means to do so.

R.

And Paul finally understood.

THIRTY-EIGHT

They called it a *fault tree*. The moribund boys in the loss adjuster department called it that.

When tragedy struck, something was lost, a building burned to the ground, a plane felled from the sky, a bridge collapsing into a river – you needed to apportion blame.

So you worked backward.

You created a fault tree.

You started with the *twigs* – all the little facts you knew, everything. Then you tried to ascertain which ones led back to the *branches*. To the *trunk* itself. If you were lucky, if you did your homework and took your time, you made it all the way back to the *roots*.

There was nothing much to do in his cell but clear wood, attempt to untangle the branches, and put it all back together.

That's what he did.

He cut and pruned and sawed and snapped, and in the end he made a tree.

It began with a Colombian baby nurse.

She helped American couples flooding her country in search of instant families. A good woman really, someone who knew what it's

271

like to desperately want a family, because she had one once, a *daughter,* at least, who might've looked much like Joelle.

The Colombian nurse worked for an American lawyer. Maybe not all the time, a lot of the time. An *adoption* lawyer, sending couples who'd tried everything short of baby-snatching to a country whose first export was cocaine and second was coffee, but third was children. A country with almost as many unwanted kidnappings as unwanted kids.

This lawyer had rejected tax or corporate law and entered the ranks of legal aid, where general disillusionment had eventually led him into foreign adoptions. He put needy babies together with needy families, and he got to pat himself on the back and make a good living at the same time.

Just not good enough.

One day he picked up the phone and a tout whispered in his ear. He was off to the races. Or the hard court, the domed stadium, the baseball diamond, the hockey rink, whichever and wherever men in uniforms played games for the lure of the money, the pleasure of fans, and the deliriousness but mostly agony of the bettors.

With the lawyer it was agony.

He was a respectable man with a dirty habit. And a dangerously ballooning debt. He owed the wrong guys.

Back to the baby nurse in Bogotá.

Her daughter had a daughter with someone.

Let's call him *R.*

Let's imagine he was the wrong kind of person, the guy you wouldn't want your daughter bringing home from a date. Someone dangerous and abusive. Even criminal.

Definitely criminal.

Once I thought my own daughter was safe from him. I was wrong.

Something happened to the nurse's daughter.

She was killed, kidnapped, made to disappear, *something,* because suddenly, it was just the baby nurse and her granddaughter. The daughter was gone, yes, but the little girl – she survived.

272

Only there was a problem.

Her father is looking for her. He won't stop till he finds her. As you know, R has the power and means to do so.

The nurse needed to act. Fast.

She needed to get her granddaughter away from R, and the only way to do that was to get her out of the country.

How?

By going to the one person who could help her. The one person who knew how to get kids out of the country because, after all, that's what he did for a living. She appealed to the adoption lawyer for assistance. One more Colombian child he needed to help *el norte.*

Only this child was different. This child had a price on her head. Oddly enough, there was price dancing around the *lawyer's* head too. All that money he owed to the wrong guys – the Russians with yellow teeth and CCCP tattoos on their arms.

Sure, he wrote, I'll help. You came to the right guy. No problem. Just one little stipulation.

Money.

Not the usual legal fees. No.

Enough to get him out of hock to the Muscovites and enable him to keep all those professional sports prognosticators in business. Lots and *lots* of money. And then he told her how to get it.

Here's the deal, he told the baby nurse. Here's how.

I send you couples looking to adopt, just like before. Every so often – not every time, not even every *other* time, just now and then – one of these couples will have the bad misfortune to be kidnapped. It's endemic in your country, isn't it? What can a lawyer do about that?

Who's going to kidnap them?

Those Marxists in the hills, the ones who've helped kidnapping surpass soccer as the Colombian national pastime.

And what was FARC going to do with these kidnapped couples? Easy. Everyone knew that FARC made their money the old-fashioned way – they *earned* it. *How* they earned it was through the sale and smuggling of pure, uncut Colombian cocaine.

Mules were their method of choice, but they fit a prototype that must have been summarized in every U.S. Customs training film. Colombian, poor, and disreputable. For every two mules who got through, one was snagged, vacuum-cleaned, and exported back home.

What if these mules could be middle-class, American, and thoroughly respectable? What then? What if the unfortunate husbands could be sent through customs packing millions of dollars of cocaine in order to rescue their wives and babies?

The baby nurse simply had to take this idea, this piece of pure brilliance, to FARC. Oh yes, and assist here and there in the kidnappings. There was *that*.

Everyone would get their heart's fondest wish. The nurse would get her granddaughter to safety. FARC would get a foolproof, sure-fire pipeline to New York. And the adoption lawyer? He'd get the money to keep the Russians off his back and bet the over-unders *and* the points.

He who saves one child saves his ass.

And for a time it worked. A *long* time, if you judged by the age of the letters.

Something happened.

Paul. The actuary's actuary, who always figured the odds, but never considered the odds of his nurse leaving the hotel with one baby and returning with another. *The last round-tripper on the Goldstein Express.*

Suitably duped, doped, and dumped in front of a burned-out safe house. And then almost slow-roasted to a crisp in the New Jersey swamps.

How did that happen?

Remember what the lawyer told him before extinguishing his own life?

It's those assholes with Uzis and kerosene I'm worried about.

They're starting to put it together. They're closing in.

And earlier, after they'd driven back from the swamp, when Paul asked him who their near murderers were?

Those right-wing paramilitary nuts. Manuel Riojas, he said. *He's in jail. They're not.*

And remember what the nurse wrote in that letter?

He won't stop looking till he finds her. R has the power and means to do so.

They seemed to be talking about two different people.

Unless, of course, they weren't.

Miles was scared enough to put a gun to his head and blow his brains out.

Galina was scared enough to send her granddaughter off to another country and to never see her again.

One scared of R. One scared of Riojas.

Think of this *R* carved not into the desk of a defunct taxi garage, but right into the trunk of the fault tree. And then you understand.

R is for Riojas.

He had the power and means to find her, and slowly and surely, that's what he did. Those men in the swamp weren't looking for drugs or money – not *simply* drugs and money. They were looking for someone's daughter. They were putting it together. They were closing in.

There it was in all its awful glory, the fault tree.

But when Paul looked at it, he thought he just might be able to use it to find shelter from the storm. Shelter for *all* of them – Joanna and Joelle and himself.

Just one question.

The girl the lawyer promised to adopt as his very own. Galina's granddaughter.

Where was she?

THIRTY-NINE

The bird-watcher bit.

Paul was offering a look at a rare bird. At least the elusive progeny of one. He was offering to lead him to the nest.

'That's an interesting story,' the bird-watcher said. 'How would you catalog it? Fiction or nonfiction? Maybe *science fiction*.' Paul could tell he was more interested than he was letting on. For one thing he slipped the cigarette he was just about to light back into its crumpled pack. He straightened up and peered at Paul as if he were finally worth looking at.

'On the other hand, I'll admit you've created a willing suspension of disbelief, Paul,' he said. 'Of course Manuel Riojas isn't my case. He's case-*closed*. He's sitting in a federal prison on twenty-four-hour butt-bandit alert. So I ask you, why should I give a shit?'

'Because Riojas might be in prison, but his men aren't.' He was echoing a certain lawyer, now deceased. 'They killed two men in New Jersey.'

'Colombian shitbags like themselves. So I ask again, why should I care?'

'Because if he's still sending men to kill people, he's still smuggling drugs. His men are. Isn't your job to stop it?' He was practicing a dangerous kind of role reversal – lecturing his jailer on the right and proper path. Any minute he expected his head to be driven back into the table. Only Tom was still absent, and his back was clear.

'Well, that's a matter of debate, Paul. What my job is. It's usually what the U.S. government says it is. Right now it says my case is Miles Goldstein, which means my case, what's left of it, is you. Not Manuel Riojas. I'll admit he's a lot sexier than you are. But that doesn't mean I can turn cowboy and go riding off in a posse of one. Think what that would do to internal structure – if we all decided to do what we wanted. Think of the *paperwork* involved.'

'Riojas is still awaiting trial. His daughter would be valuable to you.'

'Maybe. If there *is* a daughter. Which, let's face it, Paul, is kind of debatable. I'll admit it, though – I'm intrigued. I am. Riojas' *bandidos* aren't my area of investigation, but if you're telling the truth, they interfered with my money trail. They gummed up the works – which, one could interpret, has placed them into my area of investigation. So maybe I have quasi license to widen the net. Maybe. I'm still not sure how this impacts on your general welfare.'

'I can help you.'

'So you say. How?'

'I was the last person to see Miles alive.'

'Congratulations. Who cares?'

'Rachel. His wife seems like a very decent person. I don't believe she knows.'

'Knows what?'

'What he did. The deal he struck with Galina. The drugs, the kidnappings. The *girl*.'

'Okay, then. If she *doesn't* know . . . ?'

'She knows *something*. She probably doesn't know what it means. She'll talk to me. She'll want to know what Miles said before he killed himself.'

'While we're on the subject, what *did* Miles say before he killed himself?'

'Whatever I say he did. Whatever will get her to lead me in the right direction. To the girl. To whatever money Miles managed to stow away.'

'Paul, you have the perfidious heart of a DEA agent. Who would've *thunk*? Let's review. You want me to let you loose to probe and pry the poor widow. And in return for your government's generosity?'

'No charges. And you help me get my wife and child back.' There. This was his chance, this was his last best hope.

'Sorry. I think you're forgetting your current status as a stateless person. Let's say, however, that charges will be *reviewed*. Let's say that any said help provided by said defendant being held under the Patriot Act will be taken into utmost consideration. That any possible help within the normal channels to extricate defendant's wife and baby will be extended.'

It was the best Paul could get.

Yes, he said.

SHIVAH.

The Jewish version of a wake.

Various members of the Orthodox community were entering Miles' house in a steady stream of black, like ants bringing crumbs back to the queen. Crumbs of respect, condolences, and coffee cake.

The bird-watcher had rummaged through Paul's closets and brought him back a suitably dark suit. He looked like just another mourner.

The first thing he noticed when he walked through the door was the odor. The smell of too many people packed too tightly together in a too-little room. There was no air-conditioning – perhaps it was considered disrespectful to the dead. There was enough disrespect already. Paul sensed a glowering uneasiness in the room, as palpable and uncomfortable as the heat. *Know what's the worst sin in Ortho-dox Judaism, Paul?*

Yes, Miles, now I do.

Paul felt himself being prodded forward, slowly being sucked into a suffocating sea of black.

He found himself standing in front of three backless wooden chairs, containing the remains of Miles' family. His two sons in black suits and even blacker yarmulkes, sitting rigid and tight-lipped as if they wanted to be anywhere but there. And Rachel, accepting whispered condolences with bowed head, as if they were unwanted flattery.

The older boy listened to Paul's *I'm sorry for your loss* with silent resignation. Despite his father's sins, Paul felt only compassion. Maybe because if you threw out the yarmulkes, it could have been his house when he was eleven years old. Numbly welcoming a parade of strangers who kept asking him if there was anything they could do for him, when all he wanted them to do was to give him his mother back. He knew Miles' sons would spend the next few years wondering if God was an underachiever.

When Rachel saw him, it seemed to take her a long while to place him. She looked up, down, then slowly back up again, squinting at him as if trying to focus.

Then she pretty much fainted.

A GENERAL GASP WENT UP WHEN RACHEL FELL.

Poor thing, Paul heard someone murmur. *It's the stress.*

Both boys jumped from their seats as if ejected, clearly fearful that they were going to be made full orphans today.

Rachel was carried to another room by committee, Paul tentatively following in their wake.

When her eyes fluttered open, when she made it back to a sitting position, she saw Paul standing there.

The bird-watcher had made some calls. The story – there *had* to

279

be a story – was that Paul had left Miles alive. That he'd finished his business with him – this unfortunate visa screwup – shook Miles' hand, and went on his way. That all this had already been related to the police.

Paul, in other words, was in the clear.

Still, the sight of him had proved too much for her.

'The last time I saw my husband, you were standing there,' she said. 'I half expected Miles to come walking out of his office. I'm sorry.' They were sitting more or less alone now.

'I'm the one who should be apologizing,' Paul said. 'I didn't consider what it might do to you – seeing me here. I just wanted to pay my respects.'

'Yes, of course. Thank you for coming.'

He wondered how long it would take her to begin asking questions. Knowing that she might've been the second-to-last person to see her husband alive, but that Paul was the *last*.

Not long.

'You have to understand this came as a complete shock,' Rachel said. Her wig had been knocked slightly off-kilter. It gave her the look of someone who'd been blindsided, not just by life.

'I imagine every wife feels the same way. Every *widow*.' She looked down, as if mentioning that word for the first time had made it real. 'Really . . . he didn't seem depressed, or angry, or desperate. He seemed . . . like *Miles*. Maybe a little more harried the last few days. I assumed it had to do with helping you. He said the Colombian government had screwed up royally this time, that your wife and baby were stuck in Bogotá.'

'Yes, it's a big mess,' Paul said.

'Did you sense anything? Did you see something I didn't?' She'd dropped the *Paul*, opting for more formality. But then, what was more formal than death? 'That day when you talked to him, when we left you alone? Did he seem unhappy, upset about something, *suicidal*?' Her eyes were moist, red-rimmed – she probably hadn't slept much lately. She must've lain in bed staring at the same question until it imprinted itself on her eyelids: What had she missed?

'He mentioned something about gambling debts,' Paul said.

True enough.

'*Gambling?* Betting?' Using a different word didn't seem to make it any more comprehensible to her. 'He'd bet ten dollars. He'd look at the sports pages in the morning and say there goes my allowance. *Ten dollars.* How big a debt could that have been?'

'Gamblers lie, Rachel. It's an illness, like alcoholism. He might've told you it was only ten dollars. It's more likely it was ten thousand.'

'*Ten thousand?* It can't be. I would've known. We weren't in debt. I would've seen it.'

No. You didn't know about Miles' other little business. You didn't see the money going out because you didn't see it coming in.

'Maybe he had more money than you knew about. Who did the finances, wrote the checks? You or him?'

'Miles did.'

'See. If he wanted to hide money from you, he could've.'

Rachel seemed to contemplate this notion for real. A new mourner stepped into the room, reached down to take her hand, and whispered something in her ear.

'Thank you,' Rachel whispered back.

The man nodded solemnly and retreated from the room backward, as if it would have been disrespectful to turn around. Paul remembered: the uncomfortable awkwardness displayed in front of family survivors. What to say to a kid whose mother's died of cancer? What to say to a wife whose husband has just shot himself?

Rachel looked up at him. 'I can't *comprehend* it. I would've understood. It's just money. I would've said okay, we'll get you help, we'll deal with it. He would've had the support of the entire community. It would've been okay.'

No, Paul felt like saying. It wouldn't have been okay. The community might've rallied around a gambler, not a drug smuggler. Or a kidnapper.

281

'To kill himself because he owed some money. It doesn't make sense.'

Again, Paul felt like setting her straight. It wasn't money, it was fear. Not just for himself – for them. In the end a selfish person had committed a selfless act. He must've believed if he wasn't around anymore, his family would be out of harm's way. But Riojas wasn't someone who'd shrink from ordering the murder of a woman and children.

'A lot of people kill themselves over money,' Paul said. 'Themselves or other people. I know. I work in insurance.'

Rachel looked down at her hands. She still wore her wedding ring, Paul noticed. He wondered how long it would be before she took it off and relegated it to the bureau drawer.

'What else did he tell you? He seems to have chosen you to tell all his secrets to,' she said with just a trace of bitterness.

No, Paul thought, not all.

'He talked about his family. How important you were to him.'

'Not important *enough*. I think you're telling me what you think I want to hear. Don't.'

Paul shook his head. 'I got the distinct feeling family was it with him. It made me wonder why you never adopted a child yourselves. Being that it was his life's calling.'

Rachel hesitated before answering. 'I'm not sure a Colombian child would be welcome in this community. We're an insular bunch, Mr Breidbart. That's an understatement. It's not a particularly flattering thing to say. It's true.'

'Miles had a kind of love-hate relationship with his community and religion, didn't he?'

'It's not a religion. It's a way of life.'

'I know. I'm not sure Miles felt entirely comfortable with that way of life.'

'You're not supposed to feel comfortable. You're supposed to please God. It's a hard thing to do.'

Someone peeked in, saw the two of them talking, withdrew.

'Did you ever meet any of them?'

'Meet any of *who?*'

'The babies. The adopted children. Did Miles ever bring any of them home?'

'No.'

Then someone did come into the room. An older woman, who leaned down and said something in Yiddish. Rachel nodded, stood up. Paul reached out to steady her, but she waved him away. Paul got the feeling she was stronger than first impressions might lead one to think – strong enough to weather her husband's suicide and the long, lonely nights sure to follow.

She wouldn't be fainting again anytime soon.

PAUL HUNG AROUND FOR A BIT.

He became increasingly uncomfortable. The heat, sure, but more than that, the sideways glances, the whispered conversations in Yiddish, the islands of mourners that seemed to offer him no harbor.

Then, much to his relief, someone as out of place as him.

An honest-to-goodness black man walked in.

For a moment Paul assumed he was there to clean up. To gather the empty platters, the crumb-filled cake boxes and squashed and lipstick-stained paper cups, and cart them out to the curb.

The black man was wearing a suit – ill-fitting, not very expensive, but nonetheless a *suit*. He was a bona fide mourner.

One thing was painfully obvious. If the Orthodox crowd had considered Paul an interloper, they stared at the black man as if he were an *intruder*.

The black man seemed immune to the reaction he'd caused. He went up to Rachel, sitting again on one of the uncomfortable backless chairs – Paul supposed discomfort was the point – reached down, and shook her hand. He said something to her. She looked slightly dazed, no doubt still digesting everything Paul had just told

283

her. Still, she managed to find the energy to nod and say something in return.

When he moved off into the room, staring down at the last cracker topped with chopped liver, no doubt wondering what it was, Paul walked over and told him.

'*Liver*, huh?' the man said. 'Hate liver.'

'It's *chopped* liver. It tastes different . . . It's pretty good.'

'Still don't think so. Not a liver guy,' he said. 'My name's Julius.'

Paul shook his hand. 'Paul Breidbart.'

'Well, hey, Paul, looks like you and me are the only people here not wearing beanies.'

'Yarmulkes,' Paul said, unable to resist the temptation to correct him.

'Yama-*what*? Whatever.'

'Were you a friend of Miles?'

'Friend? Nuh-uh. We crossed paths, like.'

'Professionally?'

'Huh?'

'Are you a lawyer too?'

Julius seemed to think that was funny. 'Nuh-uh. I was on the other side, you might say.'

'What other side?'

'He was representin' me.' Julius had a long scar that trailed down his right hand and onto his wrist.

'Oh. Miles was your lawyer.'

'Thas right. Juvenile court. Going back some now. I was one *badass* then, okay? I was *into* shit.'

'He helped you.'

'Sure. He helped keep my ass out of juvenile jail.'

'He got you off?'

'Kinda. Why you so curious?'

'I'm just making conversation.'

'That's what you're doing, huh?'

'I don't really know anybody here.'

284

'Really? I'm real tight with them.' Julius smiled.

'Why'd you come?' Paul asked.

'Told you, Miles worked his juju, kept me out of juvenile prison.'

'So he *did* get you off.'

'You want the whole 411, huh? Hey, I was into shit. I shot some-body. He got me *classified*. Antisocial *gangsta*. They stuck me in the loony bin till I turned eighteen and walked.'

'That was *okay*?'

'Okay enough. Not bad. You zoned on lith and drew pictures. No one bothered you too much. I read a lot. Hung out in the library. I got my degree. When I walked, I had somewhere to go. Saved me from the fucking wolves.'

'How long were you there? In the hospital?'

'Long enough. Walked into the zoo at fifteen.'

'*Zoo?* You said it wasn't that bad.'

'Nuh-uh. We called it the zoo 'cause it was across the street from the Bronx Zoo. You could hear the elephants at night, man. Some-times the lions. In the spring they took us there on retard patrol. Got us llama food – half the kids *ate* it. That was fucking hysterical.'

One of the mourners, an old Jewish man with a thick gray beard, was staring at them disapprovingly.

'Back in the 'hood that's known as *disrespectin*',' Julius said.

Paul gently steered Julius to another part of the room, ostensibly in search of edible food.

'You kept in touch with Miles?' Paul asked after a suitable platter had been scoped, located, and raided.

'Kinda. Now and then. After I made good, I called – just so he'd know we all didn't end up dead. He was cool.'

'Yes,' Paul said.

IT WAS TIME TO GO.

Julius had left a few minutes after talking to Paul, announcing his departure at the front door.

Julius is leaving the building, he said. No one seemed particularly unhappy about that.

Paul was wondering what he was going to tell the bird-watcher. A vague progress report hinting at promising leads and imminent results.

He said good-bye to Rachel and the boys. She seemed relieved to see him go.

On the way down the brownstone steps he bumped into someone going up.

He glanced up to say *excuse me,* then stopped himself.

'If you can tell me where the car is parked?'

Moshe was dressed in impressive funereal attire, black silk suit with charcoal tie and a knit wool yarmulke attached to his hair with a bobby pin. He wasn't alone.

The man that Paul clobbered over the head was standing in Paul's face. He had a freshly stained bandage wrapped around his forehead.

Paul could feel his physical menace like a disturbance in the air.

'The car, Paul? Where is it parked, please?'

'Queens,' Paul said.

Paul had abandoned the car in Long Island City before taking the train back into the city.

'Queens,' Moshe repeated. 'Any particular part? Near Corona Ice King, maybe? Best ices in the city, you would not believe it. Which part of Queens are we *speaking* about here?'

'Long Island City. Twenty-fourth Street off Northern Boulevard.' Paul was keeping the man with the CCCP tattoo firmly in view. It was hard not to – he was still in his face.

'Good of you to tell me. Appreciate it.'

A moment of silence. Not that it was *quiet.* The air was humming with possibilities, most of them unpleasant.

'You seem nervous, my friend,' Moshe said. 'Spider land on you again?'

Paul stood still as Moshe moved past him up the steps. Paul managed to stand his ground as the Incredible Hulk followed. When Moshe reached the door, he turned around.

'You should relax a little. I'm in cash business, my friend. No cash, no business. Understand?' He nodded at the door. 'The man I was doing business with is deceased. A shame.' He smiled, turned, then looked back as if he'd forgotten something. 'Maybe you should not relax *too* much. My comrade here is righteous pissed at you.' He laughed out loud and went into the house.

FORTY

Paul found himself walking around in a constant cold sweat.

He could hear his wristwatch ticking.

He dreamed Joanna was dead. He was at her wake, talking to Miles.

One morning he thought he heard her voice behind him on the street. When he turned around, it was a young mother pushing a carriage and talking on her cell phone.

Interrogations were called *debriefings* now. They felt the same. Paul's progress report was derided for what it was – the essay portion in a test he hadn't studied for.

'In other words, Paul, you got *ugatz*,' the bird-watcher said. 'It's back to rat school for you.'

'I need a little time,' Paul said.

There was a problem with needing a little time. There *wasn't* any.

He needed to come up with something if the bird-watcher was going to save his wife. If she was still savable.

Now that he was an unofficial DEA rat, he was allowed to sleep in his own bed. Not sleep. Toss, turn, stare wide-eyed at the ceiling.

Two seconds after he'd entered his apartment, someone was knocking on his door.

Lisa again.

This time he couldn't pretend no one was home.

When he opened the door, she practically fell into his arms.

'Where is she?'

Paul was momentarily confused as to which *she* Lisa was referring to. Neither one, of course, was currently available.

'Where's the baby?' Lisa said, scanning the four corners of the room like an eagle-eyed real estate agent, which, in fact, she was.

'There was a problem,' Paul said, ready to trot out the story he and Miles had concocted for general use.

'Problem? *What* problem? Where's Joanna?'

'Bogotá.'

Lisa pushed her blond hair back with one hand. She was one of those East Side women who'd crossed the park – born to money that had inexplicably dried up, but still looking very trust-fund.

'Joelle's visa wasn't in order.'

'In order? What does that mean?'

'It means it wasn't functional. We couldn't get her out of the country.'

'Oh, Paul. That's *terrible*. So what's going on? What are you doing about it?'

'I'm working it out from this end.' Now that Paul was actually trying out the story, he thought it held up pretty well. He himself was a different matter. He wasn't holding up pretty well. Fatigue seemed to have settled into his bones.

Lisa must've sensed this, because she went to embrace him again, bestowing a comforting hug and lingering there long enough for Paul to lean against her.

She smelled like home.

LATER, WHEN JOHN RETURNED FROM WORK, LISA CALLED A babysitter and they both came in, toting a bottle of cabernet.

It was wonderful to see John.

289

It was terrible to see John.

He was Paul's best friend, the guy with whom he'd spent more time than he cared to remember, sitting in various West Side bars, relating the ups and downs of baby-making. The guy who'd bucked him up and, on more than one occasion, dried him out.

So while it was enormously comforting to see John's face, it was discomforting having to lie to it.

Paul was forced to create details on the spot, to make all of it seem convincing, coherent, and perfectly logical. The trick was to mix in enough truthful stuff – everything he remembered about his daughter – to give it the ring of authenticity. Downing two glasses of wine proved only mildly helpful.

It didn't do anything to alleviate his guilt. Or his fear.

Chatting about Joanna as if she were simply waiting for him back in a Bogotá hotel room felt horrifyingly callous. Joanna might be waiting in a room, but it lacked maid service and you couldn't pick up a phone and order a burger and fries at 2 a.m. She might not be waiting for him at all.

There were hidden pitfalls in the thicket of lies.

'Give me her number, for Christ's sake,' Lisa said. 'I haven't spoken to her for ages. Why hasn't she called me?'

'You know what long distance costs from Colombia?' Paul said. A ten-minute call to New York from L'Esplanade had cost him $62.48.

'Okay, I'll call *her*,' Lisa said. 'Got the number?'

'I have to look it up,' Paul said.

The room went silent as Lisa and John waited for him to do just that. And waited.

'Frankly, I'm exhausted,' Paul said. 'I need to turn in. Promise I'll find it for you later.'

Lisa and John reluctantly stood up. They hugged him, told him that if there was anything they could do for him, he shouldn't hesitate to ask.

*   *   *

290

He couldn't sleep.

He called Rachel Goldstein.

He was still hoping she might lead him out of the rabbit hole.

'Yes?' Rachel said after he'd identified himself.

'I wanted to check and make sure you're okay.'

'Why?'

'Why?'

'I hardly know you. I appreciate your concern, but I'm kind of baffled at it. You're not a relative. You're not a friend.'

'I *felt* like a friend,' he said. It's true. For a while Miles had felt like his only friend on earth.

Rachel didn't bother disputing him.

'How are you holding up?' Paul asked.

'I'm holding *on*. Eighteen years of marriage and I'm finding out there was a husband I didn't know. How would you feel?'

One of her sons must've come into the room. *It's all right,* Paul heard Rachel murmur. *I'm fine.* Then the sound of a door gently closing.

'Who *was* he? That's what I keep asking myself,' Rachel said, her voice sounding unbearably weary. 'How do I even remember him?'

'The way you want to, I guess. What's wrong with that?'

'The way I want to,' Rachel repeated, then said it again. Either because she thought it made sense or because she was ridiculing its stupid sentimentality. 'Okay. I'll give it a try.'

Silence.

'I met one,' she said.

'One what?'

'One child. You asked me today if I had met any of the adopted babies, remember?'

'Yes.'

'I did. Once. Not a baby, though.'

'No?'

'A little girl.'

A little girl.

291

'I think I'll remember Miles like *that*. Why not? Walking through the front door with a little Colombian girl in his arms.'

Okay, Paul thought, *slowly*.

'Do you remember her name?'

'Her *name*? It was over ten years ago.'

'You sure? If you thought about it a little.'

'Why do you care what her name was?'

Good question.

'Before we adopted, we talked to a couple who used your husband. They adopted a daughter. She looked, I don't know, around thirteen. I was wondering if it might've been her.'

Rachel went silent again.

Think, Paul urged her, *think*.

'Something with an *R* maybe? Sorry, I don't remember.'

R, Paul thought, like her father.

'What about her parents? You remember them? Why weren't they there?'

'I have no idea. Maybe they couldn't pick her up till the next day.'

'That's odd. You're required to go to Colombia and bring your baby back with you. That's the way it works.'

'Maybe they ran into problems. The girl, as I recall, had some problems of her own.'

'What kind of problems?'

'Emotional stuff. Something was just a little bit wrong with her.'

'What?'

'I'm not sure. She cried and screamed a lot.'

'She was probably scared. Don't you think that's normal?'

'I have two children who've been scared occasionally. Even terrified. They're terrified now. Finding out your father killed himself will do that to you. This was different. The girl was afraid of the dark, afraid of the light – afraid of everything. Something was, I don't know, *off*. I remember Miles going into her room in the middle of the night trying to calm her down.'

292

'Did he?'

'I don't know. Maybe. In the morning he took her to meet her parents. That was that. She had beautiful eyes – I can still remember them.'

'Well,' Paul said, suddenly anxious, even desperate, to get off the phone. Something had been buzzing around his brain, something someone said. 'You should get some sleep. If there's anything I can do.'

She didn't bother saying good-bye.

FORTY-ONE

He couldn't hear the elephants.

Or the lions.

Certainly not the llamas.

He could hear the industrial-strength air-conditioning. The clink of metal trays being loaded onto a wheeled lunch cart. The intercom system marred by sudden bursts of static. The insistent banging against the meds window – a bathrobe-clad teenager demanding his caps *now*.

He could hear the voice in his head too – the many voices banging around in there.

For instance, there was Julius' voice, the kid from Miles' days in legal aid.

Walked into the zoo at fifteen. We called it the zoo 'cause it was across the street from the Bronx Zoo.

And there was Galina's voice. Hello, Galina.

She's seen things no child should ever have to see. No one should have to see. She has nightmares.

And while we're at it, add Rachel's voice to the mix.

The girl was afraid of the dark, afraid of the light – afraid of everything. Something was, I don't know, off.

And then, finally, the last voice, the one shouting to be heard over all the others. The one in the letter that Paul had first attributed to Miles' son, but now knew better.

Dear Dad, Daddy, Pop, Father: Remember when you took me to the zoo and you left me there?

And suddenly, he was listening to his own voice.

'Yes, from the insurance company,' Paul was saying to the matronly woman behind the admissions desk. The woman who admitted you to Mount Ararat Psychiatric Hospital, the redbrick, barred-window, linoleum-floored institution that stood directly across the street from the Bronx Zoo. *Two* zoos, side by side, human and otherwise.

The woman was staring at Paul's business card as if it were a lotto ticket that had miserably failed her. Paul wondered if Julius had looked into the same face at fifteen.

If *she* had?

'What's her name?' the woman said.

'Name?'

'The name of your client's daughter?'

Paul hesitated just a second.

'Ruth,' Paul said. 'Ruth Goldstein.'

Okay, it was a shot in the dark. Or maybe it was more like *twilight,* just light enough to make out the title of that book crammed full of letters.

The Story of Ruth.

Something with an *R*, Rachel had said.

'Uh-huh,' the woman said, staring into a computer screen that seemed to be having trouble waking up. She slammed the mouse with a beefy hand.

'Damn system,' she said to no one in particular.

It might've been an indictment directed at everything, not just the computers. The system, for instance, that made a mental institution smelling faintly of urine a safer alternative to juvenile prison.

That warehoused children in trouble, kept them ignorant and medicated, until they could be loosed on the world at eighteen.

Damn system. Yes.

The computer finally responded, either to the vicious assault on
the poor mouse or to the woman's tongue-lashing. It sprang to life
with an ear-grating hum. A few, this time *gentler* taps on the mouse
elicited the asked-for information.

'Uh-huh, okay,' the woman said. 'Ruth Goldstein. What *about*
her?'

For a moment Paul didn't answer. A part of him had expected to
be told there was no such person here by that name. That he'd been
misinformed. That the door was *that* way.

'I told you,' Paul said, equilibrium regained. 'My client recently
passed away. It was sudden and unexpected. There's a certain
amount of paperwork that needs to be processed. A reevaluation of
who's paying what. Obviously, we need to ensure that Ruth continues to receive the same good care.'

Paul doubted the word *good* was warranted. But he wasn't here
to offend anyone. He was here on a rescue mission – though oddly
enough, the about-to-be-rescued weren't in Mount Ararat Psychiatric Hospital, but three thousand miles away. He could only cross
his fingers and pray they were still breathing.

'So you want the *Financial* Department. Why didn't you say so?'
the woman asked.

'I'd like to see the girl first.'

'The girl? Well, I'd have to ask a doctor about that. You haven't
been properly vetted, have you?'

Paul thought *vetted* was an appropriate term, given that he was
standing in *the zoo.*

'Well, could you ask, then?' Paul said. 'I assume her father was
pretty much the only one who visited her, but he's gone. Someone's
got to tell the poor girl what's happened.'

When the woman didn't immediately answer, he said, 'He did,
right?'

'Did what?'

'Visit her?'

The woman looked down at the computer, hit the mouse a few times.

'*Miles* Goldstein?'

'Yes.'

'He was on the list. Doesn't say whether he visited her.'

'Well, can you talk to the doctor – explain the situation?'

'Okay. I can only do one thing at a time.'

Paul wondered what that *other* thing was that was conflicting with calling the doctor. Apparently, it was picking up a Styrofoam cup filled with coffee and slowly sipping it.

After she had swallowed some coffee, making a sour face in the process, she picked up the phone with extravagant lethargy and punched a few numbers into the keypad.

'Yeah,' she said. 'Dr Sanji? . . . Yes – I have someone from an insurance company here to see Ruth Goldstein . . . That's right. The father died . . . Yeah. He says . . . Uh-huh. Okay.'

She threw the phone back in its cradle – *there, take that.*

'Dr Sanji will come get you.'

Dr Sanji was a woman.

She was Indian. She looked harried, overworked, and pretty much no-nonsense.

'You say her father passed away?' the doctor said in a singsong Indian accent. They were sitting in the waiting room off the lobby. What did people wait for in a place like this? Paul wondered. For sanity? For the bats to leave the belfry?

'Yes. A few days ago.'

'I see. And you came to inform her of this?'

'Yes. And to make sense of the financial arrangements. We want to make sure the girl's still taken care of, just as her father would've wanted.'

297

Dr Sanji looked down at a folder. 'The mother is deceased as well.'

'Yes.' True enough. Miles had lied about everything else, but not about that. 'She's alone in the world.'

'Well, Mr . . . ?'

'Breidbart.'

'Yes, Mr Breidbart. I will tell you she is no more alone than she was before. Of course *psychically*, she is. Her father wasn't what you would describe as doting. He hardly visited. Birthdays, I think. The odd holiday.'

'How long have you been her doctor?'

'Not long, Mr Breidbart. Two years.'

'So you weren't here when she was admitted.'

'Most definitely not.'

'May I ask you how she's doing?'

'Relative to what?'

'Relative to normalcy.'

'*Normal* is a pejorative term. You'd be better off asking how she is doing relative to *her*. To how she was doing last year, or the year before that. It's like golf – a sport that regretfully I've just taken up. You play against yourself. You improve in increments.'

'Okay. Then how's she doing relative to her?'

'Ahh . . . there we have a problem. We speak in relative terms, but you, I'm afraid, are not a *relative*. You are, as you've clearly stated, merely her late father's insurance agent. As such, you are not privy to the information you are seeking. Sorry.'

'She has *no* one,' Paul said. 'Not anymore.'

'Legally, yes. Even, I suppose, literally. But I am bound by confidentiality laws, much as you are, Mr Breidbart. Until you or someone else is appointed her legal guardian, we have little to talk about. Let's simply say that she is no harm to herself or others. That, like Dilsey in one of your great American novels by Mr Faulkner, she endures.'

'Can I see her?'

Dr Sanji launched into another exquisitely presented argument detailing his rights, or lack thereof, in this matter.

Paul interrupted her.

'Look, I know I don't have a legal right to see her. I'm simply asking to. What's the harm? I'm going to be responsible for seeing that she continues to get care. That the bills are paid. And someone needs to tell her that her father's no longer alive.'

'The person who will tell her about her father's death is assuredly not going to be you. You have neither the necessary legal standing nor the necessary experience dealing with the emotionally handicapped. Secondly, these bills you speak of? It is my understanding that Mr Goldstein did little in the way of subsidizing *anyone*. His daughter's bills, I have been led to believe, are primarily covered by New York State.'

'New York State?'

'Yes, indeed. I can only assume that Mr Goldstein pleaded indigence at the time, something, it's clear from your expression, he may have merely pretended to.'

Okay, Miles had struck a business deal and, like most good businessmen, had striven for maximum profit. He'd wanted to keep his overhead costs low, and the fact that his overhead was the care and feeding of a sick little girl hadn't deterred him. Why pay when New York State will?

When had the whole thing occurred to him? Paul wondered. From the very moment he laid it out in that letter to Galina? Or later, when she was already on her way and he thought back to his halcyon days in juvenile court.

The best I could do was get them committed to a Bronx hospital. For them it was the safest place on earth.

Lies to Galina aside, it's clear he never intended to actually *adopt* her. He'd never once mentioned it to his wife. Had he considered – even for a minute – someone else? One of the many childless couples beating a path to his door? A home instead of a ward? Or, like the schizophrenics Paul could hear bellowing on the other side of the double-hinged door, had he deluded himself into a kind of justification? That the safest place for an emotionally disturbed child with a murderous father looking for her was a room with bars on the windows.

Maybe when he went into her room to calm her down that night, he whispered *stop crying, and tomorrow I'll take you to the zoo.*

'Look,' Paul said. 'I can leave, complain to someone, get a writ, come back. All I want to do is see her. I won't say a word to her. Promise.'

HE BROKE HIS PROMISE.

Not on purpose.

After Dr Sanji had relented, he followed her down one ward and up another. He found himself in a kind of dayroom. Board games were scattered across several small tables like props – no one was playing. A TV in the corner was tuned to a talk show.

There were about twelve or thirteen kids there. It could've been the lunchroom in a local high school, various cliques engaged in vibrant discussion. If you looked closer, it was more like the conversations you hear in sandboxes – two- and three-year-olds talking *at* each other.

When an enchanting-looking girl of about fourteen stepped up to him and asked if it was true that hematite had been detected on Mars, he said *I don't know.*

He realized he'd broken his promise to Dr Sanji when the doctor said hello to her.

'Hello, Ruth, how are you today?'

'Fair to middling,' she said. 'And you? How did you play the back nine yesterday?'

'About as well as I played the front nine,' Dr Sanji said. 'Incompetently. Thank you for asking.'

Galina's granddaughter, Paul thought.

Ruth.

'I asked this man here about the recent discoveries on Mars,' she said. 'Hematite would suggest there was water at one time. Water would suggest there was life. Life on Mars, what a wondrous notion.'

She was dressed quite ordinarily, worn jeans and a T-shirt that exposed an inch or so of adolescent stomach. Her eyes, Paul noted, were still as beautiful as Rachel remembered them – wide, deep brown, and radiating an undeniable intelligence.

He'd expected that most kids on this ward *lived* on Mars.

Ruth apparently studied it – with the avid interest of an astronomer-in-training.

'And would you like that?' Dr Sanji asked her. 'Little green men?'

'I'm afraid little green men would scare the bejesus out of me,' Ruth said.

Okay, Paul thought, there was something odd about the way she spoke. Not just the evident smarts. *Wondrous . . . bejesus.* It was as if she'd learned human discourse from books. As if she'd wandered out of an old-fashioned novel.

'I would much prefer a few one-celled amoebas,' she said, smiling in Paul's direction. 'Say, I've got a knock-knock joke for you. Knock, knock.'

'Who's there?' Paul answered, the straight half of that new comic sensation, Breidbart and Goldstein.

'A,' she said.

'A who?'

'Amoeba.'

'That's very funny,' Paul said.

'The appropriate response would've been laughter,' Ruth said.

'I'm laughing inside,' Paul said, duly chastened. 'Believe me.'

'That's odd. I do the same thing *all the time*. Laugh inside.'

In another place, he thought, he would've found her precociously delightful. But here you were forced to look at things in a different light – the sickly fluorescence of a mental ward.

301

He'd followed his hunch and found the nest, but in it was an odd bird.

'Better to laugh than cry,' Paul said. 'Yes?'

'Oh, I do a fair amount of crying as well. Don't I, Dr Sanji?'

Dr Sanji said, 'Yes. You are one of our better criers, Ruth. For sure.'

'Want to see?' she asked Paul.

'Oh, I don't know,' Paul said. 'Maybe later. We can have a contest.'

'I'll win, hands down. What's the prize?'

'Hmmm . . . ,' Paul said. 'I'll have to think about that one.'

Dr Sanji shot him a look that said *time's up*. He'd broken his promise ten times over. He'd come, he'd seen, it was Ruth, he couldn't help thinking, who'd conquered.

Dr Sanji walked him to the door.

Outside the dayroom Paul said, 'She's quite remarkable.'

Dr Sanji nodded, smiled. 'Yes, quite.'

'She seems, almost . . . normal.'

'You said almost, Mr Breidbart. Why?'

'I'm not sure. I got the feeling, I don't know, that she was playing a part. Like a very good actress. Does she read a lot?'

'Volumes. Like the others *eat*. You're fairly perceptive about our Ruth playing roles. I call her the chameleon. She sometimes *becomes* what she reads. Or whom she's listening to. Sometimes I honestly feel like I'm talking to myself. Ruth, of course, has never been anywhere near New Delhi. She could make you think differently.'

'Why does she do that?' Paul said.

'Why? Are you asking for a diagnosis, Mr Breidbart? I'm afraid you won't get one from me.'

'Because you don't know?'

'Because I'm not at liberty to discuss it. This is old territory, is it not?'

Paul nodded.

'I will ask you this,' Dr Sanji said. 'Why does a chameleon change its skin color to that of its surroundings?' When Paul hesitated, she answered for him. 'Come, Mr Breidbart, it's Biology 101. A chameleon changes skin color to protect itself.'

'From what?'

'Predators.'

FORTY-TWO

A, a car backfiring.

B, a gun firing.

C, a firecracker.

D, none of the above.

Joanna was awakened by a series of loud, rapid bursts. In the moment when her heart took up temporary residence in her throat, she devised a multiple-choice test in an effort to divert fear from running rampant. She picked A, *a car backfiring,* because it was the only choice offering a modicum of comfort and plausibility.

Unfortunately, she was totally *onto* her act of self-deception.

Car? *What* car?

She couldn't help remembering that Maruja always feared that the forces of good – admittedly a relative term in Colombia – would try to rescue her and, in so doing, kill her. That they'd barge in guns blazing and set off a conflagration resulting in her bloody demise. It turned out she would've been better off worrying about the menace closer to home.

Joanna heard the bursts again. Louder, sharper, like the cracks of a bullwhip.

She hugged the wall – her one and only friend, if you didn't count

Galina, that is, who'd smuggled her back into the house after her ill-fated escape attempt. The problem with gaining Galina as a friend was that you had to be kidnapped by her first. And there was her annoying habit of remaining blind, deaf, and dumb to the criminal flaws in her housemates.

The door swung open, slamming against the wall, causing little flecks of plaster to fly into the air.

Something else flew into the room. The guard Puento, propelling himself through the door like a man shot out of a cannon. His rifle was slung down off his hip in ready-fire position.

Okay, Joanna thought, *I'm dead.*

Puento scoped the room with nervous-looking eyes. By the time he located Joanna in the right corner, she'd stopped hugging the wall. She was still firmly attached to it, courtesy of her leg chain. Sitting straight regardless, shoulders back, ready to go with dignity.

She was going somewhere else first.

Puento began unlocking her leg chain, sweat dripping off his glistening forehead and causing him to periodically stop and try to wipe it out of his eyes.

'Qué pasa?' Joanna managed to get out, about the limit of her Spanish vocabulary.

Puento didn't answer. He was engrossed in the intricacies of putting key into lock, one ear evidently trained on the outside commotion. That was her explanation for his nonresponse, and she was sticking to it. The other explanation would be that he didn't want to inform Joanna that he was taking her someplace to kill her.

When he finally managed to release her from her chain, he roughly yanked her to her feet.

He dragged her through the door.

The house was in a kind of pandemonium. Panicked guards were racing down halls, springing out of doors, bumping into each other. One of the girls was attempting to load her gun as she ran – several shell casings falling to the floor, where they rolled around, sounding like roulette balls circling the wheel.

Someone was shouting. *El doctor,* she thought.

The shooting continued. Yes, it was *gunfire.* A backfiring car or a few tossed firecrackers wouldn't be causing the house to undergo a nervous breakdown.

Count her among the nervous.

Not for herself anymore – someone else.

Where was her baby?

She was pulled through the outside door. It was early morning, that murky moment between night and day.

'Please . . . *por favor,*' she said to Puento, 'my baby. Joelle.'

Puento remained nervous and unresponsive. He dragged her behind him without looking back. They were clearly headed back to the jungle.

She felt a creeping panic the further they moved away from the house. She had no idea who was shooting at whom. It was happening someplace she couldn't see.

'My baby,' she tried again. 'Please! I want . . .'

And then she heard it.

The sound she found herself listening for now in the middle of the night, the one she'd grown particularly attuned to, like Pavlov's dogs.

She twisted her head around, even as Puento continued to pull her into the jungle. *There.* Coming out of the house, the stooped figure of Galina. She was carrying a crying Joelle in her arms. Away from the gunfire, to safety.

'Wait,' she said to Puento, who seemed in no mood to listen. 'Stop. Galina has my . . .' She dug her feet into the soil, went limp, turned into dead weight.

Puento looked at her as if he couldn't quite believe what she was doing. He had a *rifle.* With actual bullets. She was his prisoner. Didn't she know what they'd done to her friends?

Puento swung his rifle off his shoulder and pointed it at her head. It wasn't the first time he'd pointed a gun in her direction – there was that night Joelle wouldn't stop crying. He'd been making a point then. Now he looked like he just might go through with it. He was clearly spooked.

They were under attack.

Camouflaged bodies were flying past them into the jungle.

'Up!' Puento shouted at her, putting the gun barrel up against her forehead.

Joanna closed her eyes. *If I don't see it, it's not there.*

She would wait till her baby joined them, until she knew Joelle was safe. It's what mothers do.

Puento screamed at her. The cool muzzle jabbed into her skin.

She heard an explosion, felt blood splattering on her face. When she opened her eyes, it was dripping down her hand. *How odd,* she thought. There was no pain, none whatsoever.

When she looked up at her executioner, he wasn't there. He was lying on the ground next to her.

Galina caught up with them. Somehow she managed to avoid looking at Puento's bloody corpse. Joanna wished she had done the same. Galina gently lifted Joanna up from the ground.

One of the girls materialized like magic from the black edge of jungle. She stopped to make the sign of the cross over the prone body, then stared at Joanna with an expression of palpable hatred.

Murderer, her eyes said.

She must've caught Joanna's act of nonviolent resistance. It had cost Puento his life.

She motioned them into the jungle, jabbing her rifle hard into Joanna's back.

They hid in a grove of giant ferns.

Galina gave Joanna the baby. *Shhh,* Joanna whispered, rocking her gently. She could feel the tiny thudding of Joelle's heart against her own.

She wondered if Galina was thinking back to another jungle, to another mother and child who'd never really made it out alive.

The gunfire eventually sputtered, flamed out.

After twenty minutes of waiting, some of the FARC soldiers

straggled back from what must have been the scene of battle. They looked shocked. For some of the younger ones – the fresh-faced kids from the boonies – it might've been the first time they'd ever fired their weapons in anger.

When they shepherded Joanna and Joelle back to the farmhouse, their mood was black. Joanna was rechained to the wall, Joelle pulled from her arms. She could hear arguing going on through the door of her room.

She fell asleep listening to its surging rhythms, like the sound of angry surf.

WHEN GALINA CAME IN FOR THE MORNING FEEDING, SHE WAS PALE and tired.

'What happened last night?' Joanna asked.

'A USDF patrol,' she said, shaking her head. She seemed to be having a hard time meeting Joanna's eyes.

'How many were killed? Besides Puento?'

'Four,' she said.

'I don't care about Puento. He killed Maruja and Beatriz – I *know* he did – him and Tomás. He got what he deserved.'

'*They* care about Puento,' Galina said, still averting Joanna's eyes.

'What were they arguing about last night?'

'Nothing,' Galina said.

'Nothing? I heard them. *El doctor* – some of the others. What's wrong, Galina? Why can't you look at me?'

'They're angry,' Galina said.

'About Puento?'

Galina shrugged. 'Not just Puento. They think . . . you brought the patrol maybe.'

'What does *that* mean? How could I have possibly brought the patrol?'

'They think they came looking for you.'

'For *me*? That's ridiculous. How would they even know I'm here?'

Joanna found that she was talking faster than normal, that her voice had taken on a slight air of desperation.

'Some of them . . . they're only boys. Almost children. They think maybe you're *unsafe*.'

'What happens when you're unsafe, Galina?'

Galina didn't answer. Instead, she reached down to slick back a stray hair on Joelle's head.

'What happens to you when you're unsafe?'

Joanna noticed Galina's hands were shaking.

'Were Maruja and Beatriz *unsafe*? Is that what they decided?'

'I didn't know about Maruja,' Galina whispered.

It was the first time she'd mentioned either of their names since Joanna discovered the bloody stain on the mattress. The first time she'd acknowledged out loud what had happened to them.

'I didn't know about Beatriz,' Galina continued. 'I'm sorry. It had nothing to do with me. I would never have . . .' Her voice trailed off.

Joanna stood up, using the wall for support. She needed it.

'Are they going to kill me?'

Galina looked up, finally met her eyes. 'I told them you're an American . . . Doing something to an American would bring more trouble.'

'Doing something? Killing. You mean *killing* an American. What did they say when you told them that, Galina? *You're right, Galina? Thank you for reminding us?*'

Galina lifted her hands together – fingertips touching. *Make a steeple,* Joanna's mom used to say. *Make a steeple and pray.*

'Promise me something,' Joanna whispered.

'Yes?'

'You'll find her a good mother.'

JOANNA SPENT MOST OF THE DAY TRYING TO MEASURE HER LIFE. NOT too bad a life, she decided, but nothing exceptional either.

The thing she regretted most of all was not getting to raise her daughter. She thought she would've made a spectacularly good mom. It was *that* life she saw hurtling before her eyes – the one missed. Strolling on a carpet of leaves in Central Park on a fall afternoon, taking a spin on a hundred and one merry-go-rounds. All those mother-daughter chats they'd never have. Things like that.

That would've been lovely, she decided.

Toward the end of the day she noticed a tiny stream of amber light peeking through the boarded-up window. A small piece of wood was missing now, blown off in yesterday's fusillade.

She put her face against it, drinking in the smells.

Nightshade. Peat. Chickenshit.

She put one eye there.

Galina was standing outside with someone. She could only see half of them. But she had the strong sensation she knew the other person. Those brown shoes. The tan cotton pants with a sharp crease down the front.

Yes, she thought. Of course.

What was *he* doing here?

FORTY-THREE

He came home from the mental hospital, locked his door, and fished the piece of folded paper out of the bottom of his sock drawer. The page he'd ripped from Miles' phone book in an office reeking of blood.

He sat and stared at the number written in spidery blue ink.

Think of it as his lottery number.

Lotteries were a joke around the halls of his company – the kind of thing actuaries snickered at over morning coffee. These numbers were a one-in-a-million long shot that might just come in.

Cross your fingers.

He took a deep breath and dialed the long-distance number.

When they'd lost the two million dollars' worth of drugs in the New Jersey swamp, he'd thought he'd lost something more important. The only thing in the world he had left to bargain with. He'd been wrong about that.

He'd discovered he had something even better. When he constructed the fault tree that day, he'd understood that its gnarly branches might save him. All of them.

That he might be able to bargain his family to freedom.

Only he wouldn't be bargaining with FARC. No.

This negotiation would be conducted with a party of two, and *only* two.

There was Galina. And there was someone else.

It had occurred to him only when he remembered back to that awful day it began, when they'd gone to Galina's house and woken up somewhere else.

Before their world turned topsy-turvy, while they were still making perfectly polite conversation over *escopolamina*-laced coffee, Galina's lumbering dog had picked up a slipper sitting on the doormat and dropped it at someone's feet.

Boom.

The sound of one shoe dropping, just before the other one did.

Dogs are creatures of habit.

Does Galina live alone? Paul had asked on the ride to Galina's house. And Pablo had hesitated a long moment before saying yes. Why?

Because she *didn't* live alone.

She had a husband.

'Hola?' Pablo's voice, clear and intimate, as if he were sitting right there.

'Hello, Pablo.'

He obviously recognized his voice. Yes. Otherwise there wouldn't have been the ensuing silence.

Paul took a deep breath. Then asked the question he'd been dreading since he'd picked up the phone – even before that, on the long ride home from the hospital.

'Are my wife and daughter still alive?'

Nothing else mattered but the answer to this question. Everything hinged on it.

'Yes,' Pablo said.

Now it was Paul's turn to be silent. Not entirely. He gave an involuntary half-sob, the kind of sound you utter when you make it out of a vicious undertow and discover you're surprisingly and gloriously alive.

Okay, go.

'I met your granddaughter today,' Paul said.

'*Who?*'

Pablo had answered the way Paul would've expected him to, but there was the slightest quaver in that one word that spoke volumes.

'Your granddaughter.'

'I don't understand what –'

'The little girl you sent to America so her father wouldn't get her. I don't blame you. Riojas wouldn't be my idea of an ideal son-in-law either. Are you following me so far, Pablo? If I'm speaking English words you don't understand, please tell me. I need you to understand everything I'm saying today. Every word. Okay?'

'Yes,' Pablo said. 'I understand.'

'Good. You sent your little girl to America because you wanted her to be safe. You arranged things with a lawyer we both know because you knew he could get her out of the country. And because he was going to adopt her as his own. That was the deal, Pablo. Am I right so far?'

'Yes.'

'You broke all contact with your granddaughter. You did this for her own safety. I understand. It made perfect sense. And you took comfort in knowing that she was being raised in a nice home in Brooklyn. Far away from Manuel Riojas. Under a new name. Ruth. That Miles was keeping his promise. To raise her, protect her, even *love* her. Isn't that what Galina made him swear?'

'Yes.'

'After all, you were keeping your part of the bargain, weren't you? The *two* of you? Whenever he asked you to, whenever he gave you the word, you'd help kidnap some couple for your friends in FARC. Just like you agreed to. You did your part and Miles did his. Right?'

'My granddaughter. Where did you . . . ?'

'What did he send you, Pablo? Pictures? Birthday photos? Once a year, so you could put them in a secret album and look at them now and then? A little letter here and there so you'd know everything's

313

okay? What did he tell you? That Ruth's just a typical American kid, living a typical American life? That she's popular in school, pride of the community, the apple of her father's eye?'

'What are you saying? Is something . . . ?'

'Let me tell you about Ruth. Listen closely. She's not a typical American kid. Not exactly. She's not pulling As in school. She's not on the cheerleading squad. She's not dating the captain of the football team. She won't be going to the senior prom this year. Or *any* year. She isn't doing any of the things Miles told you she was. None of them. That was fiction, that was made up. Do you understand?'

'Where *is* she?'

'Not in a nice house in Brooklyn. Not in a nice boarding school in Connecticut. She's in a hospital.'

Silence.

'What *kind* of hospital. Is she sick?'

'Yes. No. Not in her body – in her mind. I have no idea what she went through back in Colombia. I can guess. I have no idea whether she was sick enough to be put in that hospital, or whether *being* there made her sick enough to stay. I don't know. What I *do* know is that Miles never adopted her. I'm pretty sure he never intended to. The day after he picked her up, he dumped her there. She's spent most of her life looking through bars.'

Crying. Paul could distinctly hear the sound of Pablo sobbing.

'How is she?' Pablo asked.

'How's my *wife*?' Paul replied. 'How's my *daughter*?'

Silence again.

'What do you want?' Pablo said. Okay – he'd weathered the storm, he'd come through the other side, and now he was beginning to catch on.

'What I've always wanted. *Them*. On a plane to New York.'

Long ago Pablo and Galina had brokered a deal.

Now it was time for another one, for Paul to use the bargaining chip of all bargaining chips and implement the plan he'd hit on back in that DEA cell.

'Think of it as a prisoner exchange. FARC does exchanges all the time, don't they? With the Colombian government or the USDF? One of theirs for one of ours? Think of this as another exchange, Pablo. Your granddaughter for my wife and child. Okay, it's a little different this time. FARC won't be making the exchange. You will. You and your wife. My guess is, that won't be so easy. I don't care. You'll find a way to do it. *Fast.*'

There was one last thing.

'There's something I haven't told you. Are you listening? Good. Riojas might be in a federal prison here, but he's still *looking* for her. You don't want him to find her.'

FORTY-FOUR

They were on their way to the zoo.

Paul was riding in the bird-watcher's Jeep, just the two of them.

After Paul had hung up on Pablo, he'd needed to make one more call.

The bird-watcher had given him a number if Paul needed to reach him.

Twenty minutes later he showed up at Paul's apartment – *I was in the neighborhood,* he said.

Paul told him about the Bronx hospital. About Miles' little sentencing trick from his days in juvenile court. About finally standing face-to-face with Manuel Riojas' lost little girl.

The bird-watcher was suitably impressed.

'You want an honorary badge? We give them out to schoolkids who take the official DEA tour in Washington. You can be my real make-believe deputy.'

Paul declined. He was up to the hard part, what he needed the bird-watcher to agree to.

The exchange.

'Whoa, I don't know about that, Paul. You didn't mention anything about a *trade*. Last time I looked, that wasn't part of my job description.'

'My wife's an American citizen. You promised you'd help get them out. Here's their chance. Here's how. Miles must've gotten Riojas' daughter into the country illegally. Isn't that normal U.S. protocol – sending illegals back where they came from?'

'After suitable bureaucratic bullshit, which you cannot *begin* to believe. I imagine you're talking just a little bit faster here. And the girl might – and I reiterate *might* – be valuable to us. Wasn't that the nature of your enticement, Paul? The carrot you so artfully dangled in front of us?'

'She's not going to disappear. You can make whatever arrangements you want after you send her back. Put her someplace you can see her – stick her in another hospital. I don't care.'

He was lying, of course.

He did care.

Spending ten minutes with her in that awful place had made him care. If he could effect the trade, he'd be helping three people.

'I don't know, Paul. You're asking me to go outside normal channels. To put my cowboy hat on. I'd have to think about that one. By the way, did the weeping widow mention anything about illicit money? Assuming Miles didn't blow it all on the Cleveland Cavs? There's nothing the DEA likes better than bags and bags of ill-gotten gains. It's how we keep score.'

'No,' Paul said. 'She didn't have a clue about any of this.'

'Okay, fair enough. You've done a bang-up job, Paul. First-rate. At some point we'll have to do a full body search on his bank accounts. As far as your trade scenario, I'll have to get back to you on that one. I admit I'm kind of leaning toward helping you. I mean, fuck those little Marxists, right? They won't be very happy when Pablo kidnaps their hostages. It puts a smile on my face just thinking about it.'

This was two days ago.

One day later the bird-watcher called him with the good news.

317

He'd done some thinking, run it *up and down the flagpole a few times.*

He'd made a few calls to *overseas assets.*

He'd wangled the necessary papers.

In the end he'd put his Stetson on.

The plan. The girl would be taken to a debriefing house in Glen Cove, Long Island. How much she knew was probably negligible, but it was worth the effort to find out, and worth seeing what Riojas might do when he found out they had her. They'd make sure he knew. Maybe he'd send someone to try and get her. It's possible. They'd keep the girl there long enough to find out. To make sure Paul's wife and daughter got on a plane. To flush Riojas' men out of the weeds. Then, if all went according to plan, they'd reciprocate.

Paul, honorary DEA deputy and faux insurance agent of the late Miles Goldstein, would accompany the bird-watcher to Mount Ararat Hospital.

Plan on.

They were currently zooming over the 138th Street bridge. Well, not zooming, moving in fits and starts, due to construction in the left lane.

Clouds were gathering over the East River. It was late morning, hot and humid.

'Looks like rain,' Paul said.

'Thank you, Uncle Weatherbee,' the bird-watcher said.

Paul realized he still didn't know the bird-watcher's name. When he'd asked him, the bird-watcher said he preferred to remain *an international man of mystery,* then asked Paul if he'd preferred *Austin Powers* 1 or 2.

Yankee Stadium was looming off to the left, its graceful arches bone white against the blackening clouds. *Twins vs. Yanks 7:30 tonight.*

When they got to the end of the bridge, they veered left.

'Not exactly prime real estate, is it?' the bird-watcher said. 'If I put my jacket on and yelled *DEA,* half the neighborhood would start running.'

The bird-watcher pointed out a restaurant – *best chorizo in New York.* He nodded at a kid in retro basketball shorts, nervously bopping up and down on a graffiti-scarred street corner. *Ten to one he's pulling guard duty for a skank house.*

Now they were headed up Hunters Point Boulevard.

'Ever been to the Bronx Zoo?' the bird-watcher asked.

He seemed relaxed and chatty today, as if Paul were his partner riding shotgun on a case, instead of an insurance actuary who'd taken an unfortunate detour.

'When I was a kid.'

For some reason Paul had never visited the zoo as an adult.

He knew the reason.

You go to zoos when you're a kid.

Or when you have kids.

THE HOSPITAL SEEMED MORE OPPRESSIVE TODAY.

It might've been purely physical – the air-conditioning was on the blink, someone said – but Paul thought it had more to do with just being there again. Seeing it a second time let him appreciate the full awfulness of the surroundings, what it must've been like for Julius to stare at these salmon-pink walls for three years.

What it was like for Ruth he could only imagine.

Now she'd be leaving it behind.

He felt as if he were at the end of a marathon. Exhausted, yes, but with an exuberance that felt like hope.

After the bird-watcher had presented his credentials, they were ushered into a wood-paneled office, where the hospital administrator offered them seats. The bird-watcher had called ahead. He'd pulled strings, twisted arms, pulled rank, produced papers, done whatever a high-level DEA agent does to get what he wants. Mostly, he'd played the national security card – which, like AmEx platinum, seemed capable of opening all doors and rebuffing all dissent.

The administrator seemed glad to see them, as if he were in the company of minor celebrities. At least *one* minor celebrity.

'I don't suppose you can tell me any details?' the man asked the bird-watcher in a tone of voice that suggested he was more than capable of keeping national secrets.

The bird-watcher declined.

'Let's just say if it wasn't crucially important, I wouldn't be here,' he said.

The man – *Theodore Hill,* the degree on the wall said – nodded knowingly.

'I assume you have doctors waiting wherever this place is you're taking her,' Theodore said.

'Of course,' the bird-watcher replied.

'Her meds are listed in her file. Lithium mostly. She's not much trouble.'

'Glad to hear it.'

Up to this point, Paul Breidbart, *insurance agent,* had remained silent. But curiosity got the better of him – that, and the assumption that what an insurance agent wasn't privy to, a DEA agent was.

'What happened to her?' Paul asked. 'Back in Colombia?'

The bird-watcher turned to look at him with an expression of mild disapproval. Asking questions wasn't his job today. Before the bird-watcher could interrupt, plead time constraints, or simply stand up, the administrator spilled some details.

'I wasn't here when the girl was admitted. Different administration. Naturally, I looked at her file when you contacted me. According to her adoptive father, she witnessed the torture and murder of her mother. Was apparently *made* to witness it. It went on for several days. Some kind of drug lord's idea of retribution – it's quite a country down there, isn't it? I imagine we're talking about a true sociopath with strong sadistic impulses. As you might assume, being forced to watch something like that would have an unhealthy effect

320

on a three-year-old. She evidently became too much for her father to handle.'

Yes, Miles had given it all of one day, Paul thought.

'Well' – the bird-watcher looked at his watch – 'we have to get this show on the road.'

'Of course,' Theodore said, a man glad to be of service to his country. 'They're bringing her down.'

Paul had one more question.

'Does she know her adoptive father passed away?'

'Yes. According to Dr Sanji – have you met our Dr Sanji?'

Paul nodded.

'She said Ruth weathered the storm quite nicely. He was pretty much a father in name only. On the other hand, he was all she had.'

No, Paul thought. She had a grandfather who'd cried for her. A grandmother who'd entered a pact with the devil in order to save her.

'What's she been told?' the bird-watcher asked. 'About where she's going?'

'Per your instructions, she was told she's going somewhere for treatment. Not permanently, just for a little while.'

The bird-watcher nodded. 'Good.'

IT SEEMED LIKE HER EYES WERE OPENED WIDER TODAY.

Maybe she was taking it all in. The surrounding world. Burned-out buildings and potholed highways, looming bridges with pigeon-covered underpasses, roving bands of restless kids trolling the mostly mean streets. Paul wondered how many times she'd been taken out-side the hospital – if they still conducted *retard patrols* across the street where they fed the llamas and threw peanuts to the elephants.

They'd made it out of the Bronx and were this moment coming off the ramp of the Throgs Neck Bridge. When Paul was a kid, he'd wondered what a *frog's* neck looked like.

Ruth remained mostly silent. Every so often she'd utter some-

321

thing that might've come from the pages of *Little Women* or a 1930s comedy.

'Ezooks,' she exclaimed when they passed a particularly huge man lolling against a stripped car, 'get a load of that gorilla.'

Her first sight of the Throgs Neck Bridge elicited a chorus of *gosh*es and *gee whilliker*ses.

Occasionally, the bird-watcher peered in his rearview mirror in an effort to see whether she was really saying what it *sounded* like she was.

Even with the looming rain, Long Island Sound was dotted with sails today.

'Quite a flotilla,' Ruth said.

The bird-watcher pulled a cigarette from his pocket.

'Think she'll mind?' he asked Paul.

'Why don't you ask her?'

'Darling,' the bird-watcher said, 'would it trouble you greatly if I partook of some nicotine?'

Ruth stared at him.

'A smoke? A cancer stick?' he said.

'Cancer is the second leading killer in the United States,' Ruth answered, sounding like an actuary in good standing.

'You don't say,' the bird-watcher replied. 'Well, I'll certainly keep that in mind.'

The bird-watcher lit up, sucked in a generous amount of cancer-causing nicotine, then blew it out, where it drifted to the backseat, causing Ruth to sputter and cough.

'Whoops,' he said, 'maybe I ought to crack open a window in deference to our friend.'

'I don't particularly like cigarette smoke myself,' Paul said.

'Yeah,' the bird-watcher said, 'me either.'

He opened the driver's side window, letting in pure humidity and the sound of a mufflerless beer truck to their left. It sounded like an entire pack of Hell's Angels.

'Lovely,' the bird-watcher said.

'No, it's not,' Ruth volunteered, obviously unfamiliar with sarcasm. 'It's raucous and revolting.'

'You're right,' the bird-watcher said. 'My bad.' He turned on the CD player. 'This ought to help.'

Latin music.

It sounded vaguely familiar.

Paul closed his eyes. *Was that what was playing in Pablo's car on the way to Santa Regina?* His heart had been beating so fast it hurt. About to meet the daughter it had taken eighteen hours and five years to find. He was already forgetting her face, he realized with a pang. How long had he really had with her – a *blip* in time – and yet they'd forged a connection strong enough to still tug at his emotions, to pull them clear across time and space.

He was a *father,* he guessed. That's all.

They were headed east on the Long Island Expressway. Which was decidedly better than heading west on the LIE, since that side of the highway was staying true to its moniker as the world's longest parking lot.

They were close, he thought. About to close the circle again.

He wasn't absolutely sure when it hit him.

But *hit* was the right word.

A realization that came with the force of a punch to the solar plexus. It *staggered* him.

The music.

It *wasn't* the music playing on Pablo's radio.

He'd heard this music somewhere else.

Suddenly, he was back on his stomach in a field full of cattails and screams. Trying not to listen as a human being was tortured to death just fifty yards from him. Hearing every excruciating whimper as they cut off his body parts one by one.

You could almost hear the sound of knife hitting bone. Even with that music blaring. Even with that pounding rhythm and screeching horns.

Even then.

Celia Cruz. Queen of Samba.

Mi mami, one of the men yelled. *A fucking scream.*

That's what the bird-watcher was playing on his car radio. Only it wasn't a car radio. It was a Jeep radio. A green Jeep.

Two green Jeeps had come flying out of the cattails that day.

Paul's eyes were wide-open. They must have matched Ruth's.

He looked at the bird-watcher sitting beside him. A bulge on the left side of his shirt. *Assume shoulder holster complete with loaded gun.*

The bird-watcher was still contentedly puffing away, considerate enough to exhale through the crack in the window. He was humming along to the late Queen of Samba, keeping one eye on the road.

At some point that eye wandered. He noticed Paul noticing him.

Or maybe it just took him a few minutes to suddenly realize he'd screwed up.

'Shit. That was kind of Homer Simpson of me.'

Paul felt familiar tentacles of fear wrap themselves around his newborn hope. And strangle it.

'Oh well,' he said. 'You were going to know eventually. Although I was kind of hoping it wouldn't be while doing eighty on the LIE. It kind of forces me to multitask. Not that I'm not up to the challenge.' He stubbed his cigarette out with his right hand.

Freeing it for other things.

'Okay. Let's get the lay of the land here. I have a *gub*.'

Paul was frozen to the seat.

'Come on, you saw the Woody Allen movie – *Take the Money and Run*? The bank heist – the note he passes to the teller? *I have a gub. Work* with me, Paul. I'm trying to protect our friend back there from needless anxiety. We can talk pig latin if you'd like. No? Okay, what the heck. We'll talk turkey.'

Paul remained mute. He'd already been deaf and dumb far too long.

'You'd probably like an explanation. Okay. It'll pass the time. Where in the world do I start? Oh yeah. Colombia. I can bore you with my trials and tribulations as a DEA agent in good standing. As *our man in Bogotá*. I can chart for you the moment I went from gung-ho to who-are-we-kidding? The moment when I realized it was all a charade, politics, Vietnam with a different jungle. I *could* bore you with all that claptrap, but it would be like the whining of a child. So let's talk like adults.'

He looked into the rearview mirror.

'You okay back there, sweetheart?'

'I'm marvelously comfortable, thank you.'

'*Marvelously* comfortable. Glad to hear it. Not too much longer to go. I'm so used to kids asking *are we there yet?* He glanced back at Paul. 'Beretta. Bore-tip bullets. In case you're wondering.'

'Where are we going?'

'Metaphorically, to hell in a handbasket. Speaking of *we* as a nation, of course. I understand your concerns are more personal. We'll get to that. Do you know what a DEA agent makes, Paul? No? Let's put it this way – when Bush so generously decided to let the rich get richer and the deficit get larger, he wasn't doing *me* any favors.'

A police car was cruising up to them in the right lane.

The bird-watcher closed the two inches of open window. Cranked the music louder.

'Remember, Paul. I'm an official agent of the U.S. government and you're someone facing federal drug charges, not to mention indictment on several newly minted antiterrorist statutes. Your only ally in this car is a mental case. Sorry, darling. Just calling a spade a spade. To be blunt, Paul, I can shoot you on the spot and get a couple of pats on the back from Nassau's finest. Understand?'

'Yes,' Paul said. The police car was almost parallel with them. A female officer glanced out the window at them. The bird-watcher had placed some kind of badge on the dashboard. The officer smiled, nodded, turned back around.

'Wonderful, well done. Still comfortable back there, darling?'

Ruth didn't answer.

'I'll take that as a yes. Oddly enough, I never actually ran into

325

Mr Riojas in Bogotá,' he said. 'Not until our government decided in its infinite wisdom to have him exported to U.S. federal prison. Sometimes we need to show everyone how swimmingly the war on drugs is going. We need someone's head on a platter. He has a very big head. The fact is, he outlasted his usefulness, like Noriega. Back in the days when all we cared about were the little lefties in the hills, Mr Riojas was *very* useful. He was like one of those Colombian vampire bats – ugly as hell and God forbid one should ever show up in your attic, but boy do they do a number on the mosquito population. They perform a useful function. Until they don't. Someone decided Riojas had become a liability. We paid off who we needed to, and one day I get the call. Mr Riojas is coming home for trial. And who do you think gets picked to escort the notorious fugitive to justice?'

The bird-watcher reached forward, readjusted the radio. 'She's got a voice on her, all right, but frankly, it's hurting my ears. How are yours?'

'Working fine,' Paul said. He'd begun tumbling numbers in his head, numbers he summoned front and center for immediate review.

Accident ratios for a typical SUV.

'Great. Still good back there, sweetheart?' addressing himself to Ruth.

'The road sign said *Commack*,' Ruth said.

'Right you are. Commack. You're my official navigator, okay?'

'I'm not entirely confident I'm up to the task,' Ruth replied.

'Oh, sure you are. Just keep looking at the signs and you'll perform the task quite nicely. *What* a vocabulary,' he said to Paul.

'Where are we going?' Paul said. 'What are you going to do with us?'

In a typical year 31,000 occupants of passenger vehicles are killed in traffic accidents.

'Would it kill you to let me finish the story? Where was I? Oh, right. On a plane home, with public enemy numero uno. By the way, we're talking private jet – plenty of legroom and a shitload of cold Coronas. What we do for the *really* bad guys. It's amazing what you start talking about in the back of a plane when you have nothing else to do. He's not a terrible guy, really. A bit excessive on the violence thing, sure, but pretty much on a par with your typical Special Ops guy. Talk about *sociopath with strong sadistic impulses.* Those guys are *brutal.*'

'Riverhead,' Ruth said. 'One mile.'

'That's it, honey. Right again. You're doing a fabulous job. In case you're interested, Paul, I can get the Beretta out of my shoulder holster and into firing position in exactly 2.6 seconds. No lie. We hold tournaments when we start going wacky on surveillance. I'm the official DEA record-holder.'

Of all vehicular fatalities in any given year, sport-utility vehicles account for over 28 percent.

'I would say Mr Riojas was a bit dejected on the ride home. He could see the handwriting on the prison wall. He was clearly preoccupied with *loose ends.* There was a piece of unfinished business that seemed particularly top of mind. He'd made a *vow,* which he'd yet to fulfill. Vows are kind of sacred to these fellows, especially when they make them to their Santeria gods. Apparently, even drug lords imbibe the opiate of the masses. Regardless, he'd made a vow and damned if he wasn't going to see it through. You can guess what we're talking about, can't you, Paul?'

'Exit 70,' Ruth said.

'One more exit to go, people. Keep up the good work, Ruth.'

Most fatalities involving sport-utility vehicles are due to rollovers, of which SUVs have the highest rate among all vehicles, approximately 36 percent.

'It seems a certain ex-mistress of his had the temerity to leave him flat. Carrying his *child* too. What's a fellow to do? It's not like he didn't tell her what was in store for her if she ever ran away. He'd spelled it out. He swore it on a stack of chicken heads. Still, off she went. It took him three years to find her. When he did, he went,

327

okay, a little overboard. He took his time, used all his formidable skills. I'm not condoning that kind of brutality. But it's kind of like charging a jungle animal with intolerable cruelty. It's their survival instinct, how they get to stay king of the jungle. He related it to me in a most matter-of-fact voice. How he decided things. Who'd watch whom? Who first: mother or daughter? He picked mom. He admitted how surprised and delighted he was at how long she lasted. Only there was a fuckup. One of his executioners apparently had a crisis of conscience and went *vamos* with the kid. So now what? Riojas had only completed half the vow. He's not the kind to give up. He kept *looking* for her. Got to the point where he was pretty sure she'd been smuggled to America. Which didn't really discourage him. You know why he was telling *me* all this, Paul?'

Fifty-eight percent of SUV rollover crashes are caused by extreme turns.

'He sensed a man willing to listen. Not just to a story. To an *offer*. Think of me as Cortés hearing the first stories of Latin American gold. And what was he asking me to do, really? Not spring him – he was astute enough to realize that was out of the question. Simply to fulfill the promise of a doomed and shattered man. By the time we touched down in Miami, I'd agreed.'

Forty percent of SUV rollovers are caused by alcohol consumption.

'I went to work. It was the same work I'd always been doing. I just had a new paymaster. It's amazing what happens when you follow the money. You never know where it'll lead. In this case, to Miles Goldstein. And then you. You were kind enough to be my honorary deputy and help wrap it up for me. My signore salutes you. I've already cashed out. Just one thing left. Or two.'

'They tied her to something,' Ruth said.

'What?' The bird-watcher jerked his head around.

'My mother. They tied her to a pipe in the ceiling. They put me on a chair and ordered me to watch.'

Thirty-two percent of fatal SUV rollovers are caused by speeding.

'Now, sweetheart, we don't need to be talking about that, do we? You're my official navigator, correctomundo?'

'They burned her. She screamed and screamed. He showed me his knife – he made me touch it.' Her eyes were lost in time, Paul thought.

'Okay, I think that's enough of that, don't you? Just tell me when the exit comes, all right, sweetie?'

Twenty-two percent of fatal SUV rollovers are caused by driver inattention – e.g., changing radio stations.

'When she closed her eyes, they'd make her wake up again. They would start all over. I was in the chair. I saw it. They took her skin off.'

'Yes, you remember. I understand. No wonder Daddy dumped you in that bad place. Now, how about giving it a little rest?'

Ten percent of fatal SUV rollovers are caused by driver incompetence – e.g., pushing the wrong pedal.

'You're falling down on the job, Ruth. Here's the exit I'm looking for.'

The bird-watcher shifted into the exit lane, flicked on his right turn signal, began turning off.

'Seat belt on, Ruth?' Paul asked gently.

'Yes.'

Six percent of fatal SUV rollovers are caused by inadvertent action – e.g., lifting the emergency brake while the vehicle's in drive.

'Good,' Paul said.

He pulled the transmission into reverse just as the Jeep went into the apex of its turn.

It took probably less than 2.6 seconds, because the bird-watcher was unable to get his Beretta loaded with snub-nosed bullets out of his shoulder holster. It likely wouldn't have made a difference. The Jeep teetered violently to the left, partially righted itself, then went over.

Paul and Ruth were wearing their seat belts.

The bird-watcher wasn't, as cowboys are wont to do.

Nearly two-thirds of passenger fatalities in SUV rollover crashes are unrestrained.

There was that moment when the Jeep hovered between air and ground, when Paul could see asphalt looming like a dark wave he hadn't seen coming. Then it broke over him.

He heard glass shatter, a scream, the awful sound of shearing metal. He must've blacked out. When he came to, he was upside down and staring into a pool of blood. He was still in his seat, but the seat seemed half detached from the car, held there by a few flimsy screws.

Where was Ruth?

He turned his head around, half afraid he wouldn't be able to, that he'd discover he was paralyzed and dying.

No. His head pivoted around just like God intended it to.

The entire backseat had disappeared.

He looked out the shattered window to his right.

There.

It was a surreal photo, something that belonged on the wall at MOMA. The backseat was sitting upright in the grass perfectly intact, and so was the person sitting on it. Intact, seemingly whole, and demonstrably alive. She looked as if she were simply waiting for a bus.

That accounted for two of them.

Where was the bird-watcher?

The entire windshield was blown out. Gone.

The interior of the upside-down Jeep was beginning to fill with thick, acrid smoke. Something else. The putrid odor of gasoline.

He unclasped the seat belt that was digging into his gut. He used his hands to feel his way through the window and out onto the pavement. He pushed himself out. Every inch of movement left a trail of blood.

His face. Something was wrong with his face. Numbness had given way to searing pain. When he touched his cheek, his hand came away bright red.

He stood up, somehow made it to his feet, both arms out for balance like a tightrope walker.

A body was lying about twenty feet from the totaled Jeep.

Paul stumbled toward it.

The bird-watcher.

He wasn't moving. He was still as death.

And then he wasn't.

He moved. One hand at first. Slowly feeling around as if looking for something. Then the other hand, Paul about five feet from him, caught between moving forward and moving back. The bird-watcher lifted himself up onto his palms – executing a kind of half push-up, gazing around like a man appearing out of a hole.

He saw Paul frozen to the spot.

The bird-watcher *had* been searching for something.

He'd found it.

He stood up – one leg, then the other – smiled through an ugly matting of blood and dirt. He pointed his gun at Paul.

'Remember Rock-'em 'Sock-em Robots, Paul?' Something was off with his speech – he seemed to be missing part of his tongue. 'Had two as a kid. You could knock their blocks off, right off their bodies, but it didn't matter, they kept coming.'

He took a few steps forward, gun still pointing at him.

Ruth began crying. When he gazed back at her, she seemed caught up in a shower of green leaves.

Paul turned back to face his fate – one way or another it was going to end here.

The bird-watcher was still stumbling, unsteady, oddly loose-limbed, but inexorably boring in.

'That was some trick you pulled.' He was having problems with his *t*'s. *Ha was some rick you pulled.* 'Learn that in actuary school?'

No. In actuary school you learned the difference between risk and probability. You learned that not wearing a seat belt during a rollover should kill you. *Should*, but not always. But you learned

331

something else about life and its opposite number, something of a mantra around the halls of an insurance company.

If one thing doesn't get you, the other thing will.

A Dodge Coronado had come hurtling off the LIE onto the exit ramp. Safety rules recommend a slowing down of at least 50 percent while turning into a highway exit. The driver of the Coronado must've missed that class.

When confronted with the smashed and smoking Jeep sitting in the middle of the sharply curving exit road, he was forced to swerve dangerously onto the shoulder, then lurch back onto the road to avoid a weeping willow. That brought him face-to-face with another slightly swerving object.

The bird-watcher had no time to react.

He was sent flying into the air, looking like one of those circus tumblers performing a gravity-defying finale.

He came down with a loud thud.

Then lay still.

FORTY-FIVE

She needed to dream tonight.

She'd noticed the looks from Tomás. The fact she'd received no dinner for the first time she could remember. The frazzled look on Galina's face, and her trembling hands.

She'd kissed Joelle good night in a way that really was good-bye. She'd said her prayers, confessed her sins. She'd made peace with it.

She needed to dream.

If she was lucky, this dream would involve being woken in the middle of the night, not by a gun muzzle, not by the sharp blade of a knife, but by Galina's soft whispers.

It would involve Galina quietly opening the lock that chained her leg to the radiator. Whispering directions into her ear. Then slipping silently out of the room the way people do in dreams.

It would involve standing up and padding softly through the door.

Slowly making her way down the empty hall and then pushing open the door to outside, the way she did once before.

It would certainly involve following those directions whispered into her ear. Walking not into the jungle, but the other way entirely, down past the back pens where chickens were nervously pecking at the ground, then onto the one-lane road.

She would walk down this road as if floating, her feet barely touching the ground. She would walk without looking back. Without fear or rancor.

She would come around a bend, and a car would be waiting there for her. A midnight-blue Peugeot. Its engine would be softly rumbling, and its driver would slip out of the front seat to greet her, making sure to put a finger to his lips.

He would reach into the car and pull out a bundle of blanket and hair. Her baby daughter, whom he'd gently place into her arms.

'Thank you,' she'd whisper to Pablo.

Thank you. Thank you.

TWO YEARS LATER

Sunday in June and the Central Park merry-go-round was full.

Paul and Joanna sat on the bench holding hands.

You could smell cotton candy, roasting peanuts, and candied apples. A catchy calypso number drifted over from the circling horses. Something from a Disney movie, Paul thought. *Under the sea . . . under the sea . . .*

Occasionally, Joanna put her head on his shoulder and left it there, and Paul got the strong sensation that the world was, in fact, perfect.

It seemed light-years away from the events of two years ago.

From Bogotá. And Miles.

From that day on the exit ramp of the Long Island Expressway.

And yet, sometimes it wasn't far away at all. It was right there in the room with him, lurking around his office, riding with him in the car, sleeping in his bed.

Memory is like that, a friend from childhood that you never really lose contact with. Even when you desperately want to. Popping up at moments in your life when you least expect it.

In the middle of a balmy Sunday in June, for example.

He wondered sometimes how much he'd tell his daughter.

337

Would he tell her, for instance, about the spectacular assassination of a certain Colombian ex–drug lord in the bathroom of a Florida courtroom? How Manuel Riojas was going through pretrial motions when he was escorted to the men's room to relieve himself and never came back.

Would he tell her that the assassin apparently gained access with the use of a DEA identity badge? This badge evidently genuine, if clearly defunct, having belonged to a DEA agent who'd been dead for more than two years.

An agent who'd been known to don other uniforms from time to time. The uniform of an ornithologist, for example, resolutely searching the jungles of northern Colombia for the yellow-breasted toucan.

A bird-watcher.

Would he tell her how the bird-watcher's badge came to be in the possession of a hired assassin?

Would he *explain,* refer to that day on the LIE when the DEA agent lay dead in the middle of the exit ramp, and the badge that he'd placed on the dashboard lay right next to him, virtually begging to be picked up for some future if undetermined use.

Would he tell her about that day later on, when he brought that badge to a familiar office in Little Odessa, Brooklyn? When he sat on the other side of a door with *El Presidente* stenciled on it. Talking business with Moshe.

You know what the Russians call the Colombians? Miles asked him the day he shot himself.

What, Miles?

Amateurs.

And maybe Miles was dead right about that. The Russians ran a *very* profitable cash business. Maybe because they were willing to do anything for the right price. Just about anything at all. Break-ins, heists, even assassinations.

Including truly spectacular ones, the kind others wouldn't even touch.

338

As long as you had the cash, of course. Lots of it.

But where could Paul possibly get *that* kind of cash?

Would he tell her? Would he explain where?

Would he go back to that day again? The smoking Jeep, the puddle of blood and oil. *I already cashed out,* the bird-watcher had said to him before he went tumbling into the air and took forever and a day to come down.

And when Paul looked back at Ruth, she was covered in a whirlwind of green leaves. But they *weren't* leaves. Because the bird-watcher *had* cashed out, received his wages from his new paymaster, from Riojas. And years of DEA training had given him the perfect place to stash it.

How many cars had he ripped the floorboards out of over the years? Looking for bags of coke, Baggies of pot, bricks of hashish? Enough of them to realize what a fine place it was for hoarding things you don't want found.

Only he wasn't counting on an *accident.* He wasn't factoring in Paul putting the transmission in reverse while they were doing sixty miles an hour.

The impact ripped the Jeep apart, blew out the sidewalls, sending hundred-dollar bills hurtling into the air, where they settled like snow onto Ruth's head.

Would he tell his daughter how easy it was to stuff the money into his wallet, into his pockets, as they waited for the ambulance to arrive?

Would he *remind* her?

The merry-go-round slowed, stopped spinning, came to a halt. Accompanied by the bittersweet cries of disappointed children.

Two of them came toward the bench.

Joelle, of course. Looking quite the little lady in a pink jumper, her black hair pinned up with tiny pink barrettes, pink being her most very favorite color – at least this week.

And carrying her, dragging her away from the merry-go-round that she just *had* to take another spin on, was her big sister, looking every inch a *real* lady, almost sixteen, those astounding brown eyes widened with what Paul fervently hoped was happiness.

Or, at the very least, peace.

This was the daughter he thought he would have to tell everything to one day. Perhaps not. Maybe whatever he'd done to keep her safe would be better left unspoken and unacknowledged, part of a secret history she'd left behind for good. *Protect her,* Galina had once written to Miles. And finally, at last, someone had.

In the end, adopting her had seemed the obvious thing to do.

When Joanna and Joelle returned from Colombia, Paul had called Galina and Pablo to explain as best he could what happened. That completing his part of the deal was now uncertain, and very much on hold. They were once his kidnappers. Now they were simply distraught grandparents. And two people who'd risked their lives to return his wife and daughter to him. He was eternally grateful.

He told them what their granddaughter was like, sent them pictures, described how unusually sweet she was, that she was blessed with the special gift of endearment.

She was facing a statusless limbo – an intercountry wrangling that was going to leave her back in Mount Ararat Hospital for quite a while. Maybe forever.

Paul visited her, visited her again.

One day he brought Joanna and Joelle along.

It became a weekly routine. So did Paul's calls and letters to Ruth's grandparents in Colombia. This time, of course, the letters detailing her life weren't made up. They were genuine. So were the feelings of regret every time the three of them left Ruth at the door of the hospital. She'd stand there and wave at them until their car disappeared around the corner.

He honestly couldn't remember who brought it up first.

Galina and Pablo? Or was it him?

Call it a tie. Colombia wasn't necessarily any safer for Ruth than it was before. It wasn't safe for anyone these days. Galina and Pablo were feeling their age. Suddenly, it was as if all parties involved knew the right thing to do. Where Ruth belonged.

Galina and Pablo gave their permission.

Paul and Joanna filed for adoption and were granted it one year later.

She wasn't out of the woods. It was entirely possible she might never be. She attended group therapy on a triweekly basis, remained medicated, and occasionally lapsed into periods of heartbreaking desperation.

Most of the time she smiled, even glowed. Paul was convinced that her family nourished her, every bit as much as it nourished him.

He'd gone from no family to a full one in the seeming blink of an eye. He'd abandoned the safety of numbers for the uncertain possibilities of life. Odds are, he thought, it would be a good one.

'Come on, sweeties, let's grab some lunch,' Paul told his daughters.

Joelle and Claudia.

Oh yes. On the day they officially gave Ruth their last name, she'd asked them if she might change her first one as well.

'To what?' Paul asked her.

What was my mother's name?

Joanna told her.

'Claudia,' she said. 'Claudia Breidbart. It'll do.'